Ardent . . .
Aching . . .
Aflame!

She belonged to Zane Falconer now, not by marriage, but because her husband had lost her at a game of cards. Now she wondered what Zane would demand . . . what any man would demand of a woman so utterly dishonored.

Resisting the tide that swelled through her blood, Mercy looked him straight in the face. "Let's be clear, Mr. Falconer. I will not be your mistress."

He came to her, drew her up, and, in spite of her struggles, found her mouth. At first his lips were hard, savage, hurting; then his kiss changed. Sweet, wild flame ran through her.

She almost fell when he drew abruptly away. . . .

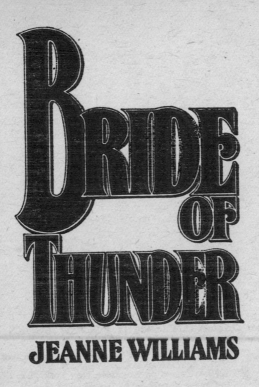

BRIDE OF THUNDER

JEANNE WILLIAMS

P̃ A KANGAROO BOOK
PUBLISHED BY POCKET BOOKS NEW YORK

Distributed in Canada by PaperJacks Ltd., a Licensee
of the trademarks of Simon & Schuster, a division of
Gulf+Western Corporation.

Another *Original* publication of POCKET BOOKS

POCKET BOOKS, a Simon & Schuster division of
GULF & WESTERN CORPORATION
1230 Avenue of the Americas, New York, N.Y. 10020
In Canada distributed by PaperJacks Ltd.,
330 Steelcase Road, Markham, Ontario.

Copyright © 1978 by Jeanne Williams

ISBN: 0-671-81487-7

First Pocket Books printing May, 1978

Trademarks registered in the United States and other countries.

Printed in Canada

**To the most
evolved man I know**

Acknowledgments

Very grateful thanks go to Señora Barbara de Montes, of Mérida and Cancún, for so enthusiastically introducing me to Yucatán and so generously sharing her knowledge on everything from birds to architecture—especially for pointing out private places and knowing it was important for me to sometimes do some solitary brooding. Thanks, also, to David Uicab, who showed me many beautiful things about his country; to Merle Greene Robertson, who revealed fascinating information about Mayan ruins; to Señor Moises Morales for sharing his conclusions about the Mayan decline; and to Señor Alberto Montes Laviada, who smoothed a journey and made it possible to visit his family's henequen hacienda. And I thank the winds that spoke at the cenote of X-toloc and the black vulture that witnessed my intention.

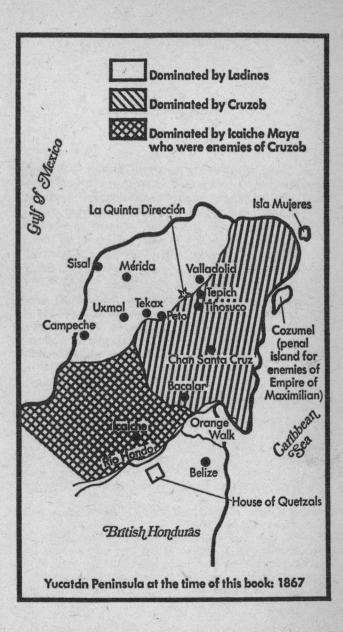

Yucatán Peninsula at the time of this book: 1867

1

Mercy Cameron waited by the softly lit church of Santa Lucia, growing more anxious by the moment. Twilight was changing to night. No unchaperoned woman should be standing about on street corners at that hour, an impropriety edged with danger, for she and her husband had only that day arrived in Mérida after a jolting carriage ride from the little port of Sisal. To make a foreign city and language even stranger, this capital of Yucatán was celebrating the lifting of a fifty-day siege at a place to the south called Tihosuco. An English-speaking merchant who had shared their carriage from the port thirty miles away had tried to explain the tumultuous relief and joy, but all Mercy was sure of was that rebel Mayas had been repulsed and that a war she had never even heard of had been going on in Yucatán since 1848 and still continued, though the government had officially declared it over in 1855, eleven years ago.

Thunderstruck at the news, Philip had deluged the merchant with indignant questions that had put the portly moustachioed Creole very much on his honor as a Yucatecan.

"I marvel," he said stiffly, "at how those who have lost a war are eager to advise men who have at least protected their home."

Philip's eyes flashed and he leaned forward. "By God, sir . . . "

Mercy tugged at his arm. "Philip! Please! Remember, we are guests of the empire."

She invoked that name deliberately. It was their last hope. After the long journey across Texas and Mexico to Vera Cruz, last week they had reached the much-heralded colony of Carlota, named for the empress of Mexico. Since the defeat of the South a year and a half ago, Con-

1

federates had made their way to Mexico, some hoping to fight for Maximilian's empire and, with its triumph, reclaim their home country, others simply wishing to start over on lands offered free or at little cost.

Governors, generals, common soldiers, those who had lost everything in the war or who couldn't accept the grinding humiliation of Reconstruction, adventurers, rascals, and honorable men—all flocked south of the Rio Grande, expecting a promised land of ease, sunshine, and lush, effortlessly grown crops where lost fortunes could be recouped and the Confederacy could live again, even in exile.

But during the eleven-day stage trip from Monterrey to Mexico City, the Camerons heard disturbing rumors. Though the crown of Mexico had been offered to Archduke Maximilian of Austria in 1863, along with the assurance that the Mexicans ardently desired a monarch to save them from revolutions and military coups, it was really the French Army that kept the well-meaning but deluded emperor in power.

When the Civil War ended, United States Secretary of State Seward demanded the withdrawal of European troops from Mexico and that the U.S. begin to supply weapons and ammunition to Juárez, the Indian president of Mexico whose followers had been fighting the Imperialists since French intervention.

Napoleon III had hoped to have his puppet firmly in power before the United States would have time or strength to enforce the Monroe Doctrine. In April of that year, 1866, he had announced a gradual withdrawal of French troops. Carlota, Maximilian's darkly beautiful Belgian princess wife, had gone to France to plead with Napoleon to keep his promises and had arrived the first week in August to find that Austria (and her brother-in-law, Emperor Franz Joseph) had just lost a seven-week war to Prussia, and that the trans-Atlantic cable was now in regular service, meaning she could quickly inform Maximilian of her progress with Napoleon.

She had no good news to send her embattled husband. After delays and evasions, Napoleon told her he could not help, and toward the end of August he wrote Maximilian that he would supply neither another franc nor soldier. Carlota went on to Rome to plead for aid from the pope, was again refused, and on October 18, Maximilian had cables telling of his wife's illness. A few days later he started for Orizaba, apparently to abdicate.

That was the last development the Camerons heard of when they reached Vera Cruz late in October, but they had traveled on to Carlota to find mango trees swaying lacy-green above the almost deserted plaza and most of the thatched bamboo huts empty.

Courtly white-haired General Sterling Price invited them to a meal in his large thatched house and told them how the rush of Confederates into this Cordoba valley had led to a brief boom that collapsed as would-be colonizers could find no way of supporting themselves till crops grew, discovered that hard work would be necessary, encountered yellow fever and typhoid, and were frightened at the way Juáristas had raided an outlying settlement and taken its men captive. The men had been released, but Juárez was undoubtedly winning the war. He wouldn't be sympathetic to foreigners who'd accepted land from an Austrian interloper and sworn allegiance to him. Southerners were returning as quickly as they could to the United States.

"All for nothing!" Philip cried. His thin, well-formed lips twitched as he glanced away from the handsome old general.

Mercy stiffened with dread. She knew what would come later, when they were alone: accusations and stormings that if she hadn't tried to persuade him to stay in Texas, they'd have been snugly settled on a Mexican estate by now and able to ride out a change in governments. As if sensing some undercurrents of Philip's despair, General Price sighed.

"Yucatán is as loyal to the empire as that strife-ridden place can ever be. The empress visited both Campeche and Mérida a year ago, awarded many honors, and aroused wild enthusiasm. There's talk of reestablishing the empire in Yucatán with a view of expanding south."

"Then we'll go to Yucatán!" Philip had vowed, brightening. "I'd rather die than go back to Reconstruction!"

The weary old general looked sorrowful but wished them good fortune. Mercy's urgings that they return to Texas only increased Philip's stubborn determination. They spent their remaining money to travel by steamship across the Gulf of Mexico to the port of Sisal, and then on to Mérida.

Their driver brought them to a small, clean inn, but

3

Philip left immediately to scout the city for "prospects." He had promised to meet Mercy at a nearby church so that they could have a stroll before dusk and find a respectable place to eat.

It was more than dusk. Mercy felt tired, hungry, and forlorn. Philip hadn't been able to settle down after the South's defeat. He'd stayed out later and later, drinking and reliving won battles while trying to forget a lost war. Painfully, Mercy thought back to the year before. Lee had surrendered April 9, and on April 14 Lincoln was assassinated. With him went the chance of generous and healing treatment for the conquered secessionists.

Some Confederate leaders had met in Marshall, Texas, about twenty miles from Mercy's home, before their troops were demobilized. General William Preston of Kentucky was there and so was General Jo Shelby of Missouri, who would later bury his unsurrendered flag in the Rio Grande as he crossed into Mexico. They planned, with other generals, colonels, and leaders assembled there, to send troops to Maximilian in the hope that when his empire was secured, he'd help them free the South from Northern dominion.

But the generals offered this command weren't free yet to leave their posts, and while officers debated, their exhausted men decided the war was over and went home without being formally discharged. Philip had ridden in from Marshall, his blue eyes bright with anger and excitement.

"We've lost the big chance. But Jo Shelby's heading south with five hundred men! That many seasoned troops could make the whole difference to Maximilian. We can help him steady his throne and then he can loan armies to free the South!"

Mercy looked up from plucking the tough old rooster Madge Evans had brought her for nursing the frail new Evans baby through a wracking croup. "More fighting? Oh, Philip, no! It'll take years now for the South to heal and be a good place to live. The sooner we start, the better."

"Under Yankees and traitors?"

"If we work and forget about the Yankees, they'll go away in time." Mercy dried her hands, stretching them out to her husband, but he avoided them with a glance of disgust at the scrawny rooster with its scalded feathers, soggy and odorous.

He was *so* touchy and difficult. Of course, he'd only been home a month. And his knee still pained him from the wound he'd received at Gettysburg, where her father had been killed. Philip had been sent home then to convalesce. She'd often visited her dashing, long-worshipped second cousin, reading to him and, in easing his recovery, finding some surcease from the ache of learning that her father was dead. In normal days it would have been unthinkable to marry at such a time, but no one raised eyebrows when the cousins were married a few days before Philip rejoined his command.

She'd been so thankful when the war ended with him still alive; she had been so overjoyed to look up one day from mixing ointment to see him in the doorway. *Now,* she'd thought, running to him, embracing him, touching his thin face, *they'd put the war, loss, and defeat behind them, start fresh.* Together, they could endure anything. She was so tired of being alone, of trying to fill her father's place with the sick.

Wonderful, wonderful, to have the war over. Wonderful to have a man at home!

But in these few weeks, she was having to secretly admit that it had been easier alone. At least she'd had hope —hope that when Philip came back, things would be better, that he'd take much of the load from her. Instead— the thought burst through in spite of her efforts to deny it—he was another burden, the heaviest of all, for he was the man she'd married, to whom her fate was joined. He seemed absolutely unable and unwilling to settle into everyday life, to make the best of what must be in the South for the next years.

Mercy turned back to her task, concealing hurt at the way he'd evaded her gesture of appeal. "Philip, your knee still pains you when you ride or walk a long time. You're not in any condition to ride hundreds of miles with Jo Shelby, much less fight."

His well-shaped mouth curved downward. "You seem to think I'm in condition to plow!"

"I'd help. And you could take as long as you need and rest when you're tired."

"I'm not a field hand, damn it!" She didn't answer, averting her face to hide tears that would only make him angrier. "I'm not cut out to farm," he growled. "There's no use in trying to make me do it!"

"Well, what is it that you intend?"

5

His eyes narrowed. "Oh, so you're throwing it in my face that we're eating what you grub out of that ugly little garden and what people give you for sitting up with them all night—when they bother to pay at all. That new doctor in town gets cash, jewelry, or something worthwhile for his trouble."

"It's worthwhile if I can help. People give what they can."

"The way they paid your father? If he'd charged the way he should've, he'd have left you pretty well off."

"He did. Remembering the kind of man he was is worth more than lots of money."

Philip groaned. "My God! You're talking about his goodness—honor, wisdom, all that rot?"

Whirling, Mercy trembled. "Talk that way about Father," she said in a shaking voice, "and I'll bar the door to you!"

He stared. This was the first time she'd lost her temper with him. When she met his eyes unflinchingly, he reddened and shrugged. "I'm sorry, honey. Uncle Elkanah was a saint, but it's too bad he didn't look after you a little better."

"We always had enough. And I'm sure he didn't expect to be killed at forty-five."

"It's still a shame"—Philip grinned ruefully, using the charm that could still twist her heart—"especially since you've got a husband who doesn't know how to do anything but soldier."

"You planned once to go into law."

"No money for that now, sugar."

"If it's what you want, we'll manage. I can sell vegetables and . . . "

"You'd give them to people who don't eat right," teased Philip, leaning against the side of the house, which needed painting. He started across the garden toward the pastures and the thickly wooded creek. "Darling, I can't just forget we lost a war, go back to where I was when it started. Even if we had the money, I don't think I could endure the grind of studying, hours in a classroom, when I'm used to wondering if each day will be my last."

Coming to where she stood by a plank work table shaded by a big oak, he closed his arms around her from behind, his hands cupping her breasts.

She didn't know why exactly, but she hated that, to be grasped when she felt exposed and helpless, because her

6

hands were busy with the smelly, wet feathers. Philip's moments of affection were few. If she complained of this unwelcome show, he'd sulk for days and would never turn to her in the night, as he did now only occasionally.

When they'd married, Mercy had been startled at the hurried brutal way he'd breached her, but she had believed his wound and nervousness made him rough. It wasn't much better now. When she wanted simple affection, or when she tried to prolong the kissing and caressing, he ignored her unspoken wishes, either moving away or taking her with neither delight nor tenderness.

Mercy had no woman to consult about this problem. Philip's parents had been dead for years, and his brother's wife, though pleasant, lived three days distant. Mercy hadn't seen her or her brother-in-law since the day she'd married Philip. From what she sensed about Madge Evans and the other married women she'd treated, Mercy concluded their lots were equally disappointing, if not worse, but their husbands weren't young and handsome like Philip; and Mercy, though not vain, knew she was infinitely more desirable than most of the women she'd seen partially unclothed.

When she glimpsed her slim figure in the mirror, firmly rounded breasts and thighs, flawless skin, she wondered what it would be like to have Philip watch her, admire her with his hands, tell her she was pretty.

Her father had never talked directly to her about physical love, but once she'd heard him chiding a man for "rolling on and rolling off." "If you'd pleasure your woman in bed, she'd have fewer headaches, backaches, and doctor bills." he'd growled. "You've got the medicine she needs! Think about her and you'll both be a damned sight happier!"

Mercy came back to the flustering reality of Philip's hands slipping inside her dress. "If I go with Shelby and fight for the emperor, the least he'll do is reward volunteers with magnificent holdings. Native labor's cheap. There are fortunes in coffee, sugar, and cotton." He laughed boyishly, brushing her ear with his lips. "We'd be rich, Mercy! Landed gentry! No truckling to Yankees or scraping to make a start!"

Mercy didn't want to go to Mexico, or farther west or anywhere. It was ridiculous for Philip to act as if he'd lost a great plantation, seen an aristocratic heritage laid to waste. His older brother was ready to share with him the profits—and labor—of several hundred acres of rich black loam, and the huge, old-fashioned farmhouse would accommodate both families.

Or there was Mercy's own small farm. Father, though a doctor, had enjoyed keeping cows, having good horses, and keeping fresh vegetables and fruit on the table. Jeb, a taciturn old steamboat man Father had patched up after a stabbing, tended the cows and garden, but he had gone off to war when her father left to serve as a regimental surgeon. Jeb had died with him, aiding the wounded.

Mercy had kept a garden, but tending the sick made her hours too irregular to take care of the milking She sold the cows, and soon the carriage horses followed, since she couldn't keep them in grain. But the farm had thirty acres of good bottom land and could support them if Philip would try.

Only it seemed he wouldn't.

"What if Maximilian loses?" she asked him.

"He can't lose!" Philip's fingers bit into the tender, secret flesh of her breasts. "He has France behind him!"

"For how long, now that the United States is pressing for the recall of French troops?"

"That won't matter if enough Confederates replace them!"

"I should think you'd have had enough war. I have." Mercy turned toward him. "Please, Philip! Help your brother, or let's do what we can with this place!"

He jerked his hands from her, tearing the worn cloth, and he stormed out of the yard without a word, striding toward the dainty little blaze-faced mare he'd left by the fence.

"Philip!" Mercy cried, running after him. "Don't ride Star back to town. You're too heavy for her, and she doesn't get grain anymore."

But he was swinging up on the bay mare, Elkanah's gift to Mercy on her sixteenth birthday, eight years ago. It was twenty miles to town, and Star had been there and back already today.

"Star can rest in Marshall, dear wife." Hauling on the reins till the soft-mouthed, gently handled animal danced nervously, Philip seemed to enjoy Mercy's distress. "I won't be home tonight. Your preachments would madden any man with an ounce of spirit. I can't support any more of them just now."

8

Spinning the mare, he touched his spurs to her, to Star, always responding sensitively to pressure or a word. In that moment, if Mercy could have shot or roped her husband from the saddle, she would have, and gladly.

I won't let him mistreat her like that, Mercy thought, moving back to the house after a long, bitter time of staring after him in outrage. *He won't ride her again.*

He didn't, but not through any action of her own. A neighbor's wagon had rattled by at dawn and Philip staggered in, smelling of whiskey and tobacco. He fell into bed fully clothed.

"Where's Star?" asked Mercy, wide awake.

Philip opened one blurry eye and grinned foolishly. "Where she'll get lots of grain. Sold her to a man who wants a nice, quiet mare for his ten-year-old daughter."

"You *sold* Star?"

"Well, not exactly." He yawned, burrowing into the pillows. "Cards, my love. Debt of honor."

"You . . . you gambled away my mare?"

"*My* mare, wife What's yours is mine. Anyway, fussy as you were about her, you should be glad. The old nag was wearing out. Now she'll be pampered and fed oats with nothing to do but give some doting child a canter now and then."

His eyes were shut and he was snoring almost before he drawled the last words. Gazing at him for a few minutes, Mercy sprang out of bed barefoot and ran outside to weep against the oak tree. Star was gone! She had been her father's gift, the last link with past, happier days. But if Star had a kind owner who could care for her, it was probably best. A ten-year-old would dote on the pretty mare, groom her lovingly, and bring her oats and apples. And it would have been hard to keep Philip from abusing her.

This was great luck for Star. And yet . . . and yet . . .

Mercy dried her eyes at last, slipped into a dress, and got a pail from the smokehouse. She couldn't bear being close to Philip right now, and there were lots of mayhaws down by the creek where her father had taught her to swim.

She guessed swimming was an unusual accomplishment for a girl, but Elkanah thought everyone should know how to do as many things as possible. She'd never heard him say girls shouldn't do this and that, and ladies didn't say this or that. "We're to do the work of a human

9

being," he'd said, paraphrasing his favorite hero, Marcus Aurelius. "That's a high-enough aim for anyone without hankering to be ladies and gentlemen."

But he had been a very gentle man.

What would he say to her now? What would he say about Philip? Mercy couldn't guess. But remembering him in this place they'd often wandered together made her feel better. She ate a few of the tart, juicy red fruits, washed her swollen eyes in the creek, and dabbled her feet in the sparkling stream. It was late morning when she returned to the house with a pail of mayhaws and a calmer spirit.

Philip sat at the dining room table eating the rooster she'd cooked the night before. The meat was stringy, but it flavored the noodles tastily enough.

"Would you make some coffee?" Philip asked plaintively as she put a few pieces of small wood in the stove and put on the mixture of roasted dandelion roots and ground acorns that she'd used through the war and seemed likely to brew a good deal longer. At least there was honey, brought by old Hughie in return for the syrups she concocted for his catarrh, and milk. Uncle Billy, freed long before the war by a grateful master whose life he'd saved, left a big crock of milk every other day on account of his wife, for Mercy had visited Aunt Hester almost every day of the wasting illness that had sent her to bed for a year before she died.

Even though Mercy had reconciled herself to losing Star to people who could treat her well, she was still not able to sit down peaceably with her husband. She got the water buckets and went to the spring at the bottom of the slope on which the rambling L-shaped frame house had been built among magnolias and loblolly pines when her mother and father moved here from Kentucky right after their marriage. Father never mentioned Kentucky kin, so Mercy dimly supposed that there'd been some family disagreement. She'd wished sometimes for a mother, but, except for that, she'd never needed more family than Elkanah.

Mercy paused before she filled the buckets from the stream that sparkled from a cleft in the rock to flow through halved, hallowed-out logs to the tank where cows and horses had watered. Now even Star was gone.

A slab of oak was fastened between two hickory trees and a stone-and-mortar fireplace with an iron grate was close by, the copper-bottomed wash boiler upside down on it. After scrubbing the white clothes and sheets on the washboard in one of the two large, round tubs by the bench, Mercy rinsed them in the other and then boiled them snowy bright in the boiler before wringing them out and hanging them up to bleach in the sun.

Ever since she was big enough, Mercy had helped Jennie, their housekeeper, with the laundry and other work, but shortly after Elkanah went to war, Jennie's aged mother had broken a hip and Jennie had to move into town to care for the permanently lamed old woman. She'd been troubled about leaving Mercy alone and had suggested she live with them, but Mercy preferred to stay on the farm. She missed Jennie, who'd worked more for love than money, but she was glad when the plump, motherly maiden lady's life had taken a romantic turn. Jennie had caught the eye of a well-to-do cabinetmaker and had married him last spring. Life was so dreary or sad for most people that it was a relief to know that at least someone was happy.

Sighing, Mercy filled the buckets and went back to the house, putting the water on the stand that held the enameled washbasin. The "acorn brew" was bubbling on the stove. Pouring in a little cold water to settle the grounds, Mercy put the pot on the table along with honey and milk. She was leaving to pick fresh mustard greens for dinner when Philip got up and pulled out a chair.

"Come sit with me, honey," he coaxed. "I'm sorry, really sorry, about your horse . . . sorry as hell that I'm not much good for you."

Hope stirred in her. Maybe he had learned a lesson. Besides, he was her husband, and, from long ago, her adored older cousin. It wasn't reasonable to expect him to come home from more than four years of fighting and immediately settle down to a kind of life he'd never dreamed of leading. If they were to have any sort of life together, she must encourage him, be patient.

"If Star can have grain, I should be glad," Mercy said, sitting down. "Maybe someday I can even buy her back. Does the man who bought her live in Marshall?"

"He has a plantation on the way to Jefferson."

"I might know him."

"You don't." Philip didn't meet her eyes. "Stowell's from the North. Just bought Colonel Meritt's old place."

"You played with a Yankee when you say you can't

11

live here because of them?" Mercy asked unbelievingly.

He shoved back the curling fair hair that fell across his forehead. "Well, I'm not proud of it, but it proves I need to get away! Besides, most of my old friends who lived through the war aren't gambling these days. No money."

"We don't have any, either! And now I've got no horse!"

"So you *are* upset! Primed to yell at me every chance you get in spite of that sweetly resigned all-for-the-best act!"

"Of course I'm upset! I loved Star!" Mercy tried to curb her tongue, but she couldn't, and all her hurt, anger, and desperation burst out. "You shouldn't be gambling! You shouldn't be drinking! And you certainly had no right to wager my mare!"

Philip turned red to the roots of his hair. He pushed back from the table, jarring the coffeepot so that the brew sloshed over the clean cloth. He must have remembered that he now had no horse to ride off on, for after a moment he said cajolingly, "Mercy, you must see this is no life for me—for us! Give us a chance, darling!"

"What chance?"

"Everybody's going to Mexico—the governor of Texas, Pendleton Murray, the governors of Louisiana and Missouri, the former governors of Missouri, Texas, and Kentucky, and a whole passel of officers and generals!" He leaned forward eagerly, catching her hands. "Let me go, Mercy! As soon as Maximilian wins, I'll send for you and we'll make our fortune there—a whole new life!"

Mercy shook her head, slowly, painfully. "I couldn't stand it again—waiting, fearing, not knowing if you're sick or wounded or dead." She took a deep breath. "If you're set on going, let's be divorced."

"You're out of your mind! Decent women don't get divorced!"

"Perhaps not, but I will if you go to fight in Mexico."

"Mercy!"

"Can't you understand?" she blazed. "I'm sick of wars, sick to death of waiting for you!"

She was to grow sicker, for, though he gave in, she'd seemed to spend most of the next interminable year waiting—for him to come home, usually drunk, for him to find work, or study law, help his brother, or make something of the farm.

She waited for him to be a husband, not a petulant boy. She wanted him as a lover, as her frustrated but healthy body insisted with mounting urgency that it demanded more than his infrequent, awkward usage.

One night she awoke to a painful nightmare, crying out, writhing at savage hurt as he gripped her by the waist and thrust into her from behind. This wasn't natural! He'd kill her, wreak some terrible damage! But as she screamed and struggled, he convulsed and fell from her, shuddering and spent.

Appalled and bewildered, Mercy bit her lip to keep from whimpering as he got up and washed, then salved her injured tissues. Could that be another acceptable way? No. It hurt too much. Neither she nor Philip ever mentioned it, and the shock wasn't repeated, but the dread that it might be added to her misery.

They had food only because of the garden, a bounty of wild fruit and nuts, plus products exchanged for Mercy's healing skills. Almost daily Philip walked to the main road and got a ride to town in someone's buggy or wagon. As he drank and gambled, the few remaining valuables disappeared—his silver-handled sword, her mother's pearls and garnets, silverware, an antique writing set, and Father's ivory chessmen.

And all the time Philip talked of Mexico. The emperor had issued an invitation to former Confederates to take up land as favored colonists. Hundreds were going. It wouldn't, Philip argued, even be necessary for him to fight. They could sell this piddling, hard-scrabble farm to pay their stage fare to the paradise near Vera Cruz and be rich within a year.

"Let's get away from here!" he pleaded. "I know what I'm doing is disgraceful! I hate myself when I'm sober! But I swear, if you'll come I'll make it all up to you. Please, darling!"

At last, because the life they had was insupportable, Mercy agreed. They sold the farm to Stowell, who was swelling his acres with those of impoverished neighbors, and Mercy watched the furniture she'd lived with all her life sold at auction. All she could take on the stage would be her few clothes, herbs and medicines, and her father's letters and some of his medical books.

She made a farewell round of her patients and took a

gift of apples to Star, who whickered softly, plump and glistening, obviously spoiled by the small girl who watched jealously as her pet's first owner said good-bye. Jennie paid a visit and left a large hamper of delicacies to eat on the journey.

Numbed, scarcely able to believe what was happening, Mercy was like a sleepwalker when they got on the stage and jostled off toward San Antonio. Philip kissed her cheek and squeezed her hand.

"You won't be sorry," he promised. "Bless you, darling, if you'll just love me."

Did she? Now?

2

Frozen by the stark question that forced its way into her consciousness, Mercy's heart constricted and she felt for a moment as if she could not breathe. Of course she loved Philip! He was her husband. Things would be different if he'd been able to finish his education in law and go into practice.

If it hadn't been for the war . . .

What? inquired the suppressed and terrifying part of her. Other men, most men, had gritted their teeth, tempered their pride with patience, and set about the task of redeeming their lives and homeland. Robert E. Lee had refused to seek refuge, saying that he preferred to struggle for the country's restoration and share its fate, that Virginia needed all her sons.

No, men had taken defeat in ways as varied as they'd gone to war. Philip chose to hate the North and pursue any desperate measure that would save him from accepting reality. He saw himself as a cavalier. Mercy fought back tears but could no longer lie to herself.

She saw him as a spoiled boy. And she didn't want a boy, especially not one she had to cajole and humor, one who'd leave her standing on a darkening street in a strange

14

town. If she must have anything at all to do with the male sex, she wanted a *man*.

The street blurred. She blinked rapidly, trying not to remember her father in this public place, for she missed him terribly. He'd been gentle and kind and strong. His letters were among the few precious things she'd brought with her. She was brushing tears away with her sleeve when a carriage, one of the high four-wheelers common to Mérida, drew up and a darkly handsome man smiled and said something in Spanish. Mercy gave him a frosty stare and turned to go to her lodgings.

She couldn't wait any longer. Men could scarcely be blamed for thinking she was for hire. Philip would be angry, but she was angry, too! And now that she'd finally confronted the bitter truth of their relationship, she meant to have a long talk with him, this very night, if he came in sober! They were married. She'd stay with him and do her best if he'd try.

Otherwise . . .

She took a deep breath. Otherwise, she'd leave him! She didn't know how she'd manage. Perhaps she could find work as a nurse-companion here in Mérida till she saved enough for her trip home. But she could not, would not, go on as they were.

Could not. The words drummed in her ears like a marching rhythm so that she didn't really hear the carriage till it stopped.

"Mrs. Cameron?"

An almost Texas-sounding voice, deep and pleasant. Even as she whirled, afraid that Philip had met with some disaster, she was resentfully aware of the strain of male curiosity and speculation in the stranger's tone.

Swinging down from the high little carriage, he closed the distance between them with one long stride, gave her a sweeping glance, which, in spite of its rapidity, did not miss much, and bowed so low that she suspected mockery. Even in the failing light, she could see he had a lean, tanned face, eyes of some shade between gray and black, and a long, rather grim, mouth.

"Forgive my addressing you without an introduction," he said almost brusquely. "The circumstances are most unusual."

"My . . . my husband?"

"You needn't fear for him, Mrs. Cameron. His health

15

is good." The tall man paused, then gave a harsh laugh. "Better than his judgment."

Bewildered, thoroughly alarmed, Mercy swallowed to get command of her voice before she spoke. "I don't understand, sir. My husband sent you to meet me?"

It might have been the shadows, but something like pity seemed to soften his face for a second before he shrugged and slipped his hand beneath her arm. "He sent me. If you'll get into the carriage, I'll explain."

Mercy resisted his lightly insistent grasp. "Indeed, sir, you must explain here and now! How am I to know that you haven't murdered my husband and now plan to . . . to . . ."

"An entrancing prospect, madam." Though he chuckled, there was an undercurrent of sympathy or embarrassment in his tone. Reaching into his coat, he produced a folded piece of paper. "If you like, you may take this back to the light of the church to examine. But perhaps even here you can make out the signature. It's a note from your husband entitling me, Zane Falconer, to your services in settlement for a high loss at cards."

Mercy felt as if the earth had opened up and she was falling into a chasm where no one could hear her cries. She stared blindly at the paper, wanting to say it wasn't true, wanting to scream and call for help.

But to whom could she call, anyway, with her husband *selling* her?

The ugly word brought a purging reality to the melodrama. Assuring herself that it was indeed Philip's signature scrawled at the bottom of a single paragraph, she gave the note back to the stranger.

"You can't fool me, sir. Even though my husband may have been drunk or desperate enough to sign this absurd bond, it can't have validity. Slavery is forbidden in Mexico."

"But debt bondage is not, dear Mrs. Cameron. If a man makes a loan he can't repay, he and his children and their children may become what amounts to slaves, because they're charged for food, clothing, and shelter at a rate that keeps them permanently indebted. I do assure you that I can enforce what's written on that paper."

Numb with shock, Mercy stood silent, motionless. "Get into the carriage," ordered Falconer. He added more gently, "You look weary, Mrs. Cameron, and I believe your husband was to take you to dinner. Let me find you a meal and we'll discuss this reasonably."

"Reasonably!"

"I won't drag you off willy-nilly," he promised roughly. "But you have to be someplace, and presumably you won't want to return to your husband. The next man he lost you to might not care about your objections."

"And you do?" she demanded scornfully.

"My household's harmonious, and I intend to keep it that way." His tone was cool. "Have no fear, Mrs. Cameron. If, after a pleasant dinner discussion of what I require of you, you prefer to take another course, I'll deliver you at whatever address you desire, wish you luck, and trouble you no more."

Whatever address?

Where could she go? Returning to Philip was unthinkable. Making a tremendous effort to hold her head high and check the trembling of her lips, Mercy let Falconer help her into the jaunty little high-wheeled vehicle and climb up beside her.

"Please," she said, "I . . . I don't wish to see Mr. Cameron again, but my things are at an inn a few streets away. Could we collect them now while there's little chance of encountering him?"

"Distress doesn't unbalance you," Falconer said. "I admire that. The name of your inn?"

An hour later the carriage had been dismissed after the driver deposited Mercy's baggage in the entrance hall of a spaciously simple house, and she sat with her host in a courtyard scented with flowers and canopied by trees and vines. A dark young man named Vicente brought plates of chicken and rice and a basket of tortillas, thin corn cakes that Mercy had first found tasteless but was now beginning to relish. There was a small dish of spicy sauce that Falconer advised her to use with caution, plus the most delicious, frothy, hot chocolate she'd ever tasted.

Too hungry to make conversation even if she'd had the slightest notion of what to say in this incredible circumstance, Mercy concentrated on the tasty food. By the time Vicente brought melon and crisp, little honeynut cakes, she was feeling more prepared to face whatever Zane Falconer might propose.

He'd talked easily through the meal, explaining that this house belonged to a friend who was abroad and who insisted that Zane stay here when in Mérida.

17

"Which isn't often," said Falconer with a note of warning. "My place, La Quinta Dirección, is a hundred fifty miles from here, close to Tihosuco, the outpost whose liberation is being so ardently—and, I fear, unjustifiably—celebrated right now."

"But surely the Indians were defeated."

Falconer shook his head. "They abandoned the siege and faded back into territory they've dominated for almost twenty years in spite of countless campaigns and the official end of the War of the Castes. The Cruzob Mayas have their own sacred city, Chan Santa Cruz, where white slaves work for Indian masters and the Talking Cross issues judgments, plans raids, and even, as a sovereign power, makes treaties with the British."

"The Talking Cross? What is that?"

"A cross that first appeared and comforted the Mayas when their rebellion seemed crushed back in 1850. Probably by use of ventriloquism or a sound box, it inspired them to keep fighting, and its guardian, or *tatich,* is what the pope is to Catholics. Of course, the Cruzob are Catholic, but while other Mayas still need priests and rely on the whites, or *ladinos,* for them, the Cruzob have their own priests, or *maestros cantors,* at their own shrine. They aren't dependent on the white world for anything but guns and ammunition, and these they get from the British in Belize. That's a region south of Yucatán that the English crown has claimed from Elizabeth's time, when it was settled by part-time pirates, or extremely casual members of the British Navy, depending on one's view."

"The British supported the Mayan revolt, then?"

"Certainly not," said Zane with a lift of one dark eyebrow. When his face relaxed its stern expression, it was singularly appealing, and Mercy decided he wasn't as old as she'd originally judged. There was no gray in his thick, black hair, and the lines at the corners of his eyes seemed the result of sun-squint rather than age. "Our British neighbors only supplied the weapons they were paid for. Besides, plenty of Yucatecan whites have lived off selling arms to the Cruzob."

Confusing, dismaying, but the overall message was clear even to a newcomer. "Yucatán's not really at peace? There's no chance of Maximilian salvaging his empire here?"

"Yucatán became a part of the empire early in 1864 when the French fleet sailed into Campeche and found troops from Mérida attacking the city. Though neither could whip the Mayas, those two cities have constantly wrangled, especially since Sisal began to rival Campeche's importance as a port." Zane looked somber. "So the French merely took over wanting to make Yucatán the base for a French-Mexican empire. But that's a pipe dream. Maximilian had better abdicate and get out of Mexico while he can. I don't think anyone can unify Yucatán inside the next score of years, much less build an empire from it."

As if reading her mind, Falconer looked across the stone table, his features rendered even craggier by lantern light. "It may have been useless, but I left Mr. Cameron enough money for passage to New Orleans."

Mercy stared, unable to guess the workings of this man's mind. If he had, in effect, paid cash for her, as well as forgiven a gambling debt, would he really let her go? Had he beguiled her to avoid a scene in the street?

Gripped with panic, she was unable to speak for a few minutes. When she did, her voice sounded hoarse. "That was very generous of you."

He smiled. "It would be awkward to have your husband drinking himself into all kinds of stupid embroglios, or, worse, repent his novel method of payment and disturb the hacienda. But don't worry, Mrs. Cameron, if you refuse my offer, I'll bestow you and your belongings wheresoever you will."

Filling the cordial glass, he helped himself to brandy with a deliberation that tautened Mercy's nerves to screaming. "What," she demanded in a tone that shook in spite of herself, "is this offer?"

"I want an English-speaking woman to see that my daughter is properly brought up." At Mercy's surprised glance, Falconer added coldly, "My wife is dead. Jolie, the child, is eight now, and I wish her to grow up under the influence of a . . . lady."

Mercy flushed. "Do you doubt that I am a lady, sir?"

His eyes went over her so slowly that her breath caught painfully. "If I weren't easy about that, madam, be sure you would have met with a very different proposal."

"Indeed?" She flushed.

"Indeed."

The calm flatness of his voice belied his eyes, which had just then a glow of banked embers. With a thrill of danger and awareness of him as a powerful and exciting

19

man, Mercy resolved to have all the facts out before she made a decision that would determine the rest of her life.

"You mean you'd have made me your mistress?" She had never used the word before, but she did it now without quivering.

Their gazes clashed. Mercy found it hard to bear the impact of those strange gray eyes; they overwhelmed her, probing mercilessly to depths that Philip had never touched.

During that silent battle while she labeled him an arrogant freebooter and cynical user of women, she recognized in the core of her being that this was a man. He was a complete person, not a petulant, changeable boy.

"Yes," he agreed, not the least abashed. "Your husband assured me that you were beautiful and refined. It's hard to find such a woman who'll live on the frontier." His laugh was coarse, grating. "You are beautiful, Mrs. Cameron. Since you're undeniably a lady, I could wish that you were plainer."

Resisting the tide that swelled through her blood, Mercy looked him straight in the face. "Let's be clear, Mr. Falconer. I will not be your mistress."

He bowed mockingly. "Let me be equally clear. Even if your marriage is ended by divorce or the death of your regrettable husband, I won't marry you." She gasped at this calm affront as he went on equably. "No need for offense, Mrs. Cameron. I won't marry anyone."

"I share that sentiment," she retorted.

"But you are married."

"I don't consider myself so after my . . . Mr. Cameron's behavior." Mercy drew herself up proudly. "You know my situation. I'm penniless and without friends in a strange country."

He tilted his head and surveyed her with an infuriating smile. "That seems an accurate, though somewhat dramatic, way of putting it," he agreed.

No help, not even in discussing her problem, was going to be volunteered by him. Detestable, cocksure, unchivalrous! He stifled a yawn. Mercy gritted her teeth.

"If you'll loan me enough money to get home, I vow to pay it back with whatever interest you stipulate."

His eyes moved over her in a way that both shamed and aroused her. "An intriguing proposition. What if my interest, payable on the spot, was a night with you?"

Her blood pounded, thick and suffocating in her throat.

He came around, drew her up, and, in spite of her frightened struggles, found her mouth. At first his lips were hard, savage, hurting, and she fought him with all her strength till the irresistible force of his arms held her so close to him that his body muted her hands. His kiss changed; he was not compelling now so much as wooing. Sweet, wild flame ran through her. In spite of all she could do, her body went soft, feeling as if it had no bones. She almost fell when he drew abruptly away.

"Well, Mrs. Cameron?"

Shaken, angrily horrified at the certainty that if he'd gone on holding her like that, worked on her senses and need, he could have taken what he now so tauntingly requested, Mercy turned away so that he couldn't read her face.

"Interest on money is paid with money, sir."

"Sorry." He shrugged and fished out a long, slim cigar. "I only make loans I consider good risks."

Mercy clenched her hands. "You mean the question about . . . interest . . . was just to humiliate me?"

He studied a curl of aromatic smoke. "Let's say I wanted to know how firm your virtuous convictions are."

"If you won't loan me the money, you know I've no choice but to accept the position you offer and pray you have the decency not to further insult a woman in your power."

"Mrs. Cameron!" His eyes glimmered and a corner of his long mouth curved down. "I could have sworn that toward the end you returned my ardor."

"You didn't pay the slightest attention to my feelings! You . . . you're as bad as a Yankee!"

"Your husband, of course, is a model of Southern gallantry."

Mercy glared. Because of what Falconer knew about Philip, she'd never be able to complain much of his behavior—he knew she'd been exposed to worse. Philip had never struck her or been physically cruel apart from his sexual bunglings, but to hand her over for a gambling debt as if she'd been a horse or dog—the way he had lost Star.

Oh, she couldn't bear living with this cool, hatefully courteous man who knew how little her husband had cherished her! Her lip quivered. She bit it savagely, blinking back tears of desolated exhaustion.

A strong hand fitted under her arm and led her into a small, clean room with a dresser, chair, washstand, and hammock hung from pegs in the wall. Her bags were in a corner. "You need a good rest," Zane Falconer told her. "You'll feel better in the morning." When she didn't answer, he said testily, "I admit my thrust about your husband was foul. Pardon me."

"I shouldn't have likened you to a Yankee," she muttered.

He chuckled. "A deadly insult, I'm sure, but quite lost on me, dear lady, because my father and mother were from New Orleans. There's water in the pitcher. If you need anything, pull the bell-rope and Vicente will come." He started for the door but stopped when he saw she was staring helplessly at the hammock. "Know how to get into it?"

She shook her head. "No, and I don't think I could sleep in it, anyway."

"Hammocks are really very comfortable, though there are several beds at La Quinta." He sat in the hammock, well toward the middle, lay back, and lifted his legs at the same time. "Do this and you won't get dumped out."

Even rising from a hammock, he managed to be graceful. "Sleep well," he counseled. "Our two nights on the road won't be so luxurious." At her dismayed look, he gave her a pat on the shoulder, as if he were encouraging an anxious child. "Don't worry about the future. Rest and restore yourself. If, tomorrow, you decide you've no taste for my offer, you may withdraw. I've business to transact and there's a formal dance tomorrow night. But once we start that journey the day after tomorrow, there'll be no turning back."

"I can't see that I have any choice."

"There's always a choice, at least in how one meets a thing." His jaw hardened. "Make no mistake—I won't force you to my bed, won't force you to fulfill Cameron's bond. But if you come with me, I'll have no sulks, indignation, and die-away airs."

"You want a happy slave!"

"Drivel! You're damned lucky to be rid of that worthless drunkard in a way that'll provide for you very handsomely. Further, if you perform your duties as well as you must to be kept on, when my daughter's eighteen I'll pay your passage back to the United States and give you a generous settlement."

"Ten years."

"You won't be much older than I am right now." When that failed to console her, he turned on his heel. "Good night, Mrs. Cameron."

She wanted to hurl accusations and upbraidings after him, but the sane part of her mind insisted that, odious as he was, he'd behaved far better than any other man would have. Philip was the cause of her desperate position, but there was no use in thinking about that or bewailing her current predicament.

She barred the heavy door before undressing, washed at the brass basin, wrapped herself in a cotton spread she found on a chest near the hammock, and cautiously eased into that pecular bed. She had to squirm about considerably and shift her weight several times before, with the help of a pillow, she was reasonably comfortable.

She had not expected to sleep, but she did, almost at once.

3

She slept till awakened by a thunderous knock, then tumbled out of the hammock so swiftly that she fell on the tile floor. Rubbing a bruised knee, dazed by her heavy slumber, she couldn't remember where she was till a deep male voice brought everything back.

"Are you all right, Mrs. Cameron? Mrs. Cameron!"

"I'm fine," she called back before he could break down the door.

"You should buy personal needs today. Let's have breakfast and then I'll escort you around. This afternoon I can attend to my affairs."

Why did his voice send a warm tingling through her, and why was she so eager to see him in daylight? He'd made it clear that, apart from being his child's tutor, his

23

interest could only be dishonorable. If she responded to that, it would be her own fault.

Yet, how could she not respond?

"I'll hurry," she promised and hastily performed her morning toilette, brushing out her thick chestnut hair and coiling it at the nape of her neck. Errant tendrils escaped this severity and softened what Mercy considered too high a forehead, too strong a jaw. The ornate silver-framed mirror above the washstand reflected an almost triangular face with black-fringed gray eyes, the austere forehead and almost straight dark eyebrows contradicted by a cleft in the chin and a rather full mouth.

An unfashionable face. Mercy believed her eyes to be her only good feature. Still, her skin was smooth and glowingly healthy, faintly tanned in spite of her efforts to protect it from the sun. She was small and Philip had complained that her hips were like a boy's, though he'd admired her high, firmly soft breasts.

"You won't thicken with childbearing," he'd predicted, fondling her. "It should ripen you, sweet Mercy, fill you out a bit."

There'd be no child now. How glad she was of that! Thrusting the memory of Philip's husbanding from her with a bitterness so physical that it left a taste of alum on her tongue, she shook out the skirt of her gray gabardine gown in a vain effort to rid it of wrinkles, and stepped into the hall.

The sweet flower smell of the night before was almost befuddling, and she held her breath at the flaming riot of cerise bougainvillaea, trumpet vines, hibiscus, and fantastic orchids of varying shapes and colors.

A table was set under huge trees shielding a splashing fountain. Zane Falconer rose from a cane chair, putting a small notebook in his vest pocket, and she had her first look at him in full daylight.

He looked thinner, harder, and somewhat older. Was that quirk of mockery always lurking at the edge of his mouth? He seemed even taller, broader through the shoulders than she'd judged, narrower through long, taut-muscled horseman's flanks revealed by fawn-colored trousers so excellently fitted that they must have been tailor-made.

Any embarrassment she might have felt in scanning him dimmed in the knowledge that he was appraising her just as closely and, no doubt, more critically. His

24

shirt was snowy-white and faultlessly ironed, his boots glistened, and he was clean-shaven.

"You look a trifle less peaked," he decided, seating her. "You'll need cooler clothing than that most of the year; in fact, I'd advise the native cotton smock for ordinary wear at the hacienda, though you'll want some conventional gowns. Do you have something for the dance?"

Acutely aware of the mended and faded state of the three dresses she'd brought as her best, all of them older than the war, Mercy reddened and shook her head. She had no crinoline left at all. Father had never allowed her to have a corset. Her drawers, chemises, and petticoats were plain and patched. Since her neighbors were in no better circumstances, she'd come to accept shabbiness as normal, but to this well-turned-out man she must seem a scarecrow.

"I'd better not go to the dance," she said. "This is my most presentable dress. Besides, how could we explain my presence?"

"I live on the frontier, Mrs. Cameron, and my friends in Mérida know it. They'll sympathize with my need for a woman to bring up Jolie." At Mercy's dubious look, he grinned and said carelessly, "I can introduce you as a distant kinswoman if you don't mind the relationship."

"Won't anyone know about what happened last night?"

"Oh, it'll be talked of in certain company. The men in our game were all transients passing a few nights in town. If rumor eventually links you to a wagered bride, the gossip will have burned down long before we come to town again. But then there'll be some new scandal."

She shrank at the word. But wasn't that what it was? She dimly remembered that some man in Texas had gambled and lost his wife, who'd been so hurt and angry that she'd left willingly with the winner and later married him.

Mercy writhed inwardly at being in a similarly notorious position. There'd be no reputation-saving marriage, either. Falconer had made that clear. But at least she was a stranger here. There was no one whose opinion could deeply wound her, though she had the ordinary wish for respect. It sounded as if she were going to be buried at the ends of the earth, seeing no one but the members of Falconer's household. She hadn't been to a party in years and longed for at least a glimpse of the dance, but she could never go like this.

25

"I've no money for clothing," she said, "even if it were possible to find something for tonight."

"I expect to provide for your needs," he said calmly. "I think our hostess, a close family friend, might have something you could borrow for the evening. She's never failed me." He tilted his head judiciously. "She's about your height, I should judge, although somewhat plumper."

"It's most improper to speculate about such intimate matters!"

He gave a soft, long whistle. "Is it, now? I do assure you that all men do it, though they may not announce their verdicts."

Vicente brought coffee and poured the steaming brew into cups of soft blue-and-gray glaze. There was hot milk and coarse sugar to add to this, a basket of crusty, hard rolls, and crisp, thin, sweet bread sprinkled with spices and nuts.

Falconer spread orange conserves on a roll and frowned as he looked across the table. "Remember, you have this day to change your mind. You needn't feel obligated for whatever I buy you. One thing you perhaps haven't understood is that there is danger from the Mayas, though they've never raided the hacienda. My workers have never joined the fighting and much prefer not to, but I can't promise that trouble will never come—and if it did, it would be terrible."

There'd been no Indian fights for years in Mercy's part of Texas, but farther west Comanches and Kiowas still took their toll of settlers, and no one mentioned Arizona without a shudder for Apaches.

"Who's ever safe anywhere?" Mercy asked. "If I decide not to go, that won't be the reason."

The bread was tasty and filling. After a second cup of strong coffee, Mercy fetched her reticule and they stepped out into the street.

Mérida wore a different aspect for her now than it had only yesterday. Flat-roofed stone buildings dazzled white against the brilliant blue sky. Church towers rose above these, and down one street Mercy saw the bastions and walls of what Zane told her was the fortress of San Benito.

"It's built on the foundation of the principal pyramid of an ancient Mayan city, T-ho," he explained. "Don Francisco de Montejo the Younger, whose house you'll see on the plaza, struggled to make his way here in 1540

26

and was visited by Indians who told him that more Indians were coming against him than there were hairs on the skin of a deer. Montejo went out hunting them, won a battle and a few submissions, but in June, on the feast of the apostle Barnabas, about two hundred Spaniards watched thousands of Indians gathering. The next day about forty thousand Mayas attacked. Spanish horsemen trampled them down, crossbows and arquebuses made a great slaughter, but the Indians kept coming all that day until the bodies stretched in all directions and kept the Spaniards from following when the Mayas finally ran. That was the last great effort of the Indians to shatter the intruders." He smiled grimly. "Of course, the Mayas came down on Mérida in 1848 and would have taken it, too, except that great clouds of winged ants appeared. These mean rain, and the Mayan fighting men told their leaders they were going home to plant corn. They did. The respite gave the *ladinos* a chance to recover, and that summer and fall they recovered much of the territory the Indians had taken."

They were nearing the plaza, with its vast, looming cathedral. Mercy glanced about the huge square, wondering how it had been during that siege almost twenty years ago, and she felt cold at that and how the Mayas must feel to see this city built on the ruins of their own.

Unreservedly, she wished the Mayas had beaten the Spanish soldiers during that long-ago Feast of Saint Barnabas, just as she wished the eastern Indians had driven the Pilgrims back to England. But once generations had grown up in a place, once it became home to them, too, full of the old and children and babies, it became a lot more complicated.

She wished, for instance, that back in Texas the Comanches could keep their hunting grounds, but how could that be when they slaughtered women and babies on isolated farms? That brought the army to protect the settlers, and it looked as if eventually the Indians would all be forced onto reservations. Mercy felt a sort of vague guilt about it, just as she had never felt comfortable with slavery.

Her father had never owned a slave, openly saying no man should own another; yet he had died defending his homeland. That must be among the strongest instincts, going back to an animal's fighting for its home.

27

What happened when the same region was home to two hostile peoples?

"You mean the Indians would have taken the capital if they hadn't gone home to plant corn?" she demanded, scarcely knowing where her sympathies lay.

"It's a certainty. Hordes of Mayas had taken all the outposts and driven the survivors into Mérida. There were maybe one hundred thousand people in the city, half refugees, and the encamped Mayas were estimated at about twenty thousand. But when those winged ants appeared, the men just said, 'Shickanic'—'I'm going,' put their blankets in their food pouches, tightened their sandal thongs, and headed for their corn patches."

"That's incredible!"

"Not if you know that if the Mayas don't plant and get a harvest, their families starve. When it's time to plant, they plant as they have for centuries. Besides, the ordinary fighters probably thought Mérida could be gone back to later and conquered when there was no corn to plant."

He drew her against an arcade to watch the thronged plaza jammed with carriages, mules, casts, horses, and what amounted to an open-air bazaar. To the east rose the great cathedral, with its towers and bells. Zane glanced at the shops behind the arcade. "I hope we can find what you need, but it's a marvel business is going on at all. As soon as the fiesta of San Cristobal was over, with its nine days of masses, bullfights, and dances, there was the feast of Todos Santos, or the Day of the Dead, and right upon that was the victory parade for Colonel Traconis." He laughed a bit cynically. "I guess you know that he's the commander who was responsible for defending the city of Tihosuco, near my plantation, against a Mayan siege just last year. There'll be another parade the twelfth for his troops, but after all the fireworks and dancing and reading of patriotic poems celebrating the heroes of Tihosuco, that outpost will be abandoned. The Mayas will have their slow victory, exactly as the jungle creeps over and reclaims the pathetically arrogant structures of man."

Mercy's scalp prickled at that prophecy. But today she was in Mérida and wanted to enjoy it, to put away the past and the numb hurt that gripped her when she thought of Philip, and avoid trying to imagine the life she'd have at La Quinta Dirección as Falconer's virtual bond-servant.

At least she had been allowed to choose that or destitution.

Vendors were selling tamales, pumpkin seeds, and sweets along the arcade. Mats displayed jewelry of coral, tortoiseshell, silver, shells, beads, bright scarves, mirrors, belts, and other small goods. Zane steered Mercy past these, the barber shop, *cantina,* and billiard room, evading sellers of lottery tickets and Indian boys eager to polish his boots.

"Here," he said, drawing her into a small, long shop with lengths and bolts of material of every kind, from silk to fine hand-wovens. "Pick out enough for a half-dozen dresses, and if you see anything you judge suitable for Jolie, get that, too. I'll step out to the tobacconist, but I'll be back long before you're through." He spoke in Spanish to the rotund merchant, who murmured understanding and smilingly signaled himself ready to serve Mercy's slightest whim.

With a wistful look, Mercy dismissed the silks, the rich brocades, satins, and velvets. Muslin should be good for this climate. To this she added gray-blue poplin and enough blue challis for herself and Jolie. The merchant displayed a length of satin that shimmered the very shade of a storm sky. Mercy could not resist putting her hand against it, admiring its beauty next to her over-browned hand, but at the urging of the storekeeper, she firmly shook her head.

"No, gracias."

"Sí, por favor," said Falconer, returning from the tobacconist's shop. As the pleased merchant folded up the satin, Zane looked down at Mercy. "Be sure to get plenty of lace and trimmings. I can't stand dowds."

"I'm sure I don't see why my mode of dress should concern you."

"I have eyes."

"If my appearance depresses you, Mr. Falconer, I'll make every effort to spare you."

Those smoky eyes went over her slowly. Her breath seemed trapped in her chest, and she felt as if he were touching her throat, her breasts, and thighs before that cool stare came back to her face. "Let's not play games, Mrs. Cameron. You know you're a damned tempting woman, made all the more so by that style you have of the lady. Apart from my own tastes, we will very occasionally have visitors. I want them to be impressed."

29

Turning back to the merchant, he engaged in brief conversation, produced a small pouch, and paid with silver. "He'll send the material, trimmings, needles, thread, and buttons to the hacienda."

They were in luck. A rich lady with feet the size of Mercy's also had a husband, weary of bills, who'd sent back a pair of quilted gray satin slippers, a pair in bronze kid, and elegant, high-laced shoes of gray kid.

"These are much too fine for every day," Mercy protested, though the delighted shoemaker was already noting down their address.

"Most days you'll probably wear sandals," Zane agreed. "But when those travelers pass through every second or third year, you'll need footwear to match your dresses." He produced a slim gold watch and frowned at the time. "If I'm to find you a dress and tend to my business, I must get you back to the house. I'd advise you to rest this afternoon. We have a long day's journey tomorrow to a friend's hacienda near Uxmal, and we should reach Tekax the next day in time to see something of its fair. The third day will bring us to La Quinta. By then, believe me, you'll have scant trouble sleeping in a hammock —or anywhere else."

As they made their way back to the house, Zane pointed out a brightly painted wooden flamingo perched atop a corner house. "You'll see some such images on the corner house of each street," he said. "Most people can't read, but it's simple to find the street of the bull or the old woman or the elephant."

Mercy smiled at the rather dumpy flamingo. "I like that," she decided. "It's much better than naming streets with numbers."

"Much more confusing." Zane's tone was irritated and his stride lengthened so that she was hard put to keep up.

Did he regret spending so much on her? Mercy winced at the thought and grew angry. He'd insisted on the gorgeous satin and opulent shoes. He'd made it plain that he wasn't doing it for her, but so that her appearance would impress his visitors. If he'd spent more than he should, it certainly wasn't her fault! The almost happy mood of the morning soured. Mercy grew even angrier at the tightness in her throat.

Cry because of this high-handed man who'd appropriated her much as he might have a horse or mule? How could she be so silly? She must become as impervious to his tempers and whims as he was to her feelings.

She swept into the house the instant Vicente opened the door. "Vicente will make you lunch," Zane said. "If I can borrow a gown for you, I'll have it sent so that you can do any altering that's necessary. There must be a few maids around the house. I'll tell Vicente to tell them to help you with the dress and to help you get yourself ready."

"I'll try to do you credit."

His eyebrows jerked up at her cold tone. "Isn't it a woman's fondest desire to outshine other females?"

"No more than it's a man's to be the strongest or most powerful." It was hard to meet his dark gray eyes, but Mercy did, her chin raised high. "Tonight, sir, because of my ambiguous position, I shall be glad to escape attention."

"Forget that," he said and shrugged. "Your situation will seem romantic and dangerous to the ladies and provocative to the men. To top it off, you're a foreigner. You're going to be watched. Don't mope in the shadows or try to hide."

The prospect of a barrage of curiously disapproving or lustful stares gripped Mercy in an icy spasm. "Please . . ." she whispered.

His eyes narrowed. "I thought you Confederates had courage. If you can't face Mérida society, Mrs. Cameron, what will you do if the Cruzob ever attack the hacienda?"

With a short bow and briefer nod, he left her.

Smoldering, Mercy was determined to look as striking as she could that evening, to show Zane Falconer that she was not the spiritless, shrinking creature he seemed to judge her. A hip bath embellished with gilded scrolls and bronze-claw legs had been placed in her room, half full of pleasantly warm water. Arranged beside it were copper vessels holding towels and a bar of perfumed soap.

Mercy touched the water with the soap, rubbed it slightly, and instantly a rich lather appeared. *This must be rainwater,* she thought. Undressing, she brushed out her hair, which shone in spite of feeling dusty and dirty, then knelt by the tub and washed it, rinsing it with water from the other containers. Patting it as dry as possible with the towels, she draped the last one like a turban to leave her neck and shoulders bare.

She washed her face with clean water, then climbed into

the tub and soaked luxuriously before she scrubbed her body with a rough cloth, rinsed off the soapy water, and toweled dry till her flesh glowed. She sighed with the wonderful feeling of being clean from head to foot for the first time since leaving Texas.

Standing naked where the sun reached in through a high grilled window, she stood, legs flexed, head down, and fluffed her hair, tossing it with her hands to speed its drying, reveling in the freedom of no confining garments.

The sun made her skin look like pale honey. As she straightened up, she drew in her breath and let her hands trace from rib cage to hips. Philip thought her skinny, but her breasts and hips surely curved enough. She was glad that all her muscles, including those of her loins and thighs, were firm and strong. Women who swooned had never been that admired in Texas, and the war had put them completely out of fashion.

She brushed her hair now and swayed sensuously with the tugging, her eyes shut, enjoying the delicious cleanliness and fitness of her body. Her father had brought her up to regard bodies as marvelous, complex systems to be used intelligently and respected.

Once when he'd occasioned the wrath of a minister for treating a prostitute, Dr. Elkanah McShane had erupted in a way that brought a crowd flocking, including some avid ladies who later protested that they'd never been so shocked and claimed it a scandal that such a man was bringing up a daughter with no genteel female on the premises.

"Hattie's done this town a sight more good than you have, Parson," Elkanah snapped, his jaw thrusting forward like the bulldog he somewhat resembled. "What you call her vile body has comforted many a man. You bet I'll try to get her well so she can get back to her business, because compassion and common sense is what you never give anyone!"

"A harlot's body would better suffer in this life if it'll lead her to escape the pains of hell!"

"The body is the temple of the spirit," said Elkanah. "And Hattie's helped men escape their hells on this earth. I reckon God will mark that in her favor."

Mercy's eyes stung as she remembered her father. Busy as he was, he'd taught her to ride, paddle a boat, swim, and fish, as well as hearing her lessons and listening to her perplexities. He'd discussed things with her that Mercy

32

now realized he'd have shared with his wife, had she lived—his theories of medicine, lore he'd picked up from old women and a Caddo Indian healer who lived deep in the bayous.

Oh, Father! I can't believe you're dead! I never saw you that way, never saw your grave. Do you mind it, lying up there in Yankee soil?

It was some comfort that he probably didn't mind.

She remembered how he'd written, not long before his death, of marching through a shady Pennsylvania town and how a young woman—*"she reminded me of you, Mercy"*—ran out, waving a Union flag and defying the soldiers to take it.

The commander took off his hat to her, flashing a look back to his men, who all did the same, so gallantly honoring their enemy and her flag that at last she called after them, "I wish I had a rebel flag! I'd wave it, too!" A woman like that might put flowers on Father's grave.

Mercy no longer cried when she remembered him, but the high exultation faded and she felt suddenly tired. She decided to lie down in the hammock for a little while. She dozed off at once, then awoke with startled awareness.

Zane stood beside her. He tossed a sparkling bundle of green cloth onto the nearby chest and swept her from the hammock. "You need a lesson," he said huskily.

Branded by his hands, Mercy fought vainly as his mouth took hers, ruthlessly plundered, forcing her clenched jaw to relax, opening her lips. The sound of a crashing torrent roared in her ears. She felt as if she were drowning, caught in the force of cresting waves powered from unfathomable depths.

Then she was on her feet. Though Zane supported her till her dizziness passed, he had put distance between them. She sensed withdrawal of the essence of himself that had reached, tested, and dominated her in that kiss.

Trembling, shaken to her center, she stood before him, feeling so utterly vulnerable in spirit that there seemed little use in trying to hide her body. Picking up one of the towels, he draped it roughly around her.

"Do you understand?" His voice grated as if he were battling to control it, and the pupils of his eyes had swelled to almost hide the irises.

She reached for anger but could not find it. What she'd felt in his arms was too elemental, too deep and primal a thing. But he watched her with the eyes of an accuser, and she resisted the urge to stretch out her hands.

"Understand?" she echoed.

"What the sight of you like that does to a man . . . or, perhaps," he added with a pitiless laugh and a long step forward, "you *do* know."

She retreated, the ache in her heart spreading through her. How could they blend like that, fire with fire, and then he speak this way, watch her with contemptuous hatred?

"I . . . I don't understand at all."

"I mean you must bar doors when you're unclothed. What if Vicente had come in, or someone from the street? At La Quinta you must never let the workers find you like that. If you do and their hunger overcomes wisdom, you won't get a sympathetic hearing from me."

Mercy drew herself up. That fierce, overwhelming sweetness, then, had only stirred in her. For him, it had been lust, the kind to vent on a whore. "Thanks for your . . . impressive warning," she said. "It hadn't occurred to me that men might come bursting through a woman's closed door."

"I knocked. When you didn't answer, I supposed you were in another part of the house." He turned and went to stand by the window, its light casting hollows under his high cheekbones. "Forgive me if I hammer at this, Mrs. Cameron, but for a married woman you seem to be singularly unaware of a few raw facts. For your safety and general peace, I want to be sure you're aware of your possible effect."

She couldn't help laughing at that. "You sound as if I were some kind of explosive or poison."

"Aren't you?"

Her laughter died at the corrosive bitterness of his voice. "Never mind," he resumed in a more normal tone. "What you may not realize is that the mere sight of a woman can arouse a man as much as I excited you just then, and his instinct, on which life depends, is to seize and enjoy. Try to remember that."

"How can I forget after such a . . . lesson?" What a fool she was, responding as she had to what was sheer randy behavior to him, the mechanical, rutting drive of a healthy male! "I'll keep my clothes on or the door barred. Do you advise a veil?"

He half-smiled. Tension seemed to drain out of his

long, muscular frame. "You've a winsome mouth, but that's not what will get you in trouble." He jerked his head toward the gleam of dark green satin on the chest. "I fetched a dress from Doña Elena before finishing my business because it may not fit exactly. You may want to make some alterations before the dance."

Mercy couldn't pick up the gown without loosing the towel. Grinning as he recognized her predicament, Falconer held up the deeply shimmering cloth for her inspection.

Cut with simple elegance, the dress would expose most of the shoulders, and the bodice laced across an insert of red so dark it was almost black. This same red trimmed the neck and made long, close-fitting undersleeves. It was a dress with medieval flavor that looked black and somber till it caught the light with changing jewel flashes of green and crimson. Mercy burned to try it on even as she gave her employer a rueful glance.

"You don't intend to let me be inconspicuous!"

"There's no way you can do that, so make a conquest of it, Mrs. Cameron."

"I don't like to be called that anymore." Mercy said it almost without thinking.

He stopped on his way to the door. "Yes, I can see that, but what's the alternative? Your maiden name?"

For a moment it was tempting . . . go back to being Mercy McShane, pretending Philip and their marriage had never been. But it couldn't be. There was no return. Zane Falconer's tone was gentler, as if he guessed some of her confused pain.

"There's an easy way to show respect without stiffness. You can be Doña Mercy, or Mercedes, if you like the Spanish regality. People may think it odd that I don't give you a last name, but no one will be rude enough to ask why."

"Wonderful!" Mercy said with relief.

"And I would prefer Zane to being mistered or *señor*ed," he added. "I know that years should elapse before we reach that stage, but under all the circumstances it seems foolish to be so formal. Once we reach La Quinta Dirección, no one will care what we do."

That sounded ominously true. But the prospect of maintaining a formal address with the only person who'd speak her language daunted Mercy. "Very well, Mr. Falconer," she said hesitantly, "after we start our journey, I'll call you Zane—that is, I'll try."

He shook his head. "Are you as naïve as you seem?"

She stared in surprise. For a moment he turned back before, frowning, he hurried out and shut the door behind him.

Mercy barred it, dropped the towel, and picked up the dress.

4

Arms somewhat hampered by the tight undersleeves of what she thought of as the dark jewel gown, Mercy finally secured most of her hair in a French knot, though there was nothing she could do about the tendrils' wilful escape.

The deeply curved bodice showed the swell of her breasts; she wished she had a suitable piece of jewelry to draw eyes to her throat instead. Even a piece of black velvet ribbon tied in a bow would serve the purpose. She was searching through the assortment of trimmings the cloth merchant had sent when there was a loud knock on the door, repeated just as she hurried to open it.

"I wanted to be sure you heard me." Zane's business must have gone well, for a smile lit his eyes and his usually grim expression had softened, making him seem younger and less formidable. He surveyed her for a moment, then lightly touched the coiled mass of hair. "I'd rather see that down, but there's no good in inciting all the men." His gaze traced the ruching framing her shoulders. "Do you have a necklace?"

She flushed, more conscious of the sexual tension between them now than this afternoon, when she'd been naked. "I was just hunting for something. I . . . I'm so *bare!*"

"This might help." He brought out a plaited silver chain with what looked like a broken-off bit of a shiny, black forked twig. "It's not what most women would call jewelry, since it's rough and a bit barbaric, but black coral *is* precious. It's only found at depths few divers attempt. Fit it to hang above the charming depths of your bodice."

Was that a compliment or an insult? With Zane, there was no telling. But Mercy preferred the strange black rarity to any concoction of diamonds or gold, even if such had been forthcoming.

"Thank you," she said. "It's just right with the dress, I think."

"The clasp is tricky. Let me fasten it for you."

His hands brushed the back of her neck. Warm and tingling shocks spread through her. Did she imagine that his hard fingers were unsteady? He stepped around, surveyed the effect, and gave a satisfied nod.

"Exactly. Are you ready?"

A carriage waited for them in the street, and as the little carriage moved off, Mercy wished they were walking, the better to savor the pleasantly cool air and admire the lanterns hanging from balconies and arches.

The square was thronged even more than it had been that morning, and people, nearly all women, were entering the illuminated cathedral. Zane spoke to the driver, sprang down, and beckoned to Mercy.

"You should look inside," he said invitingly. "Even if you're Catholic, I doubt you ever saw the likes of this in Texas."

A vague fear of papacy and foreign domination flavored the religious atmosphere of most of Mercy's neighbors, who were mainly Presbyterian or Episcopalian, though she had always rather wistfully thought it would be comforting to have Mary for a mediator. But her father's rationalist upbringing made her ashamed of that weakness.

Zane brought her up the steps, stopping to speak to an old woman who smiled and handed Mercy her shawl. "Your head must be covered," Zane explained, and he led her through the doorway.

The long way to the altar blazed with double rows of candles taller than the tallest man while lamps glowed from floor to ceiling along the sides. Music seemed to vibrate from the brilliance. The high altar, raised on a platform, with a towering Christ behind it, was a glory of silver, lamps, and flowers. Women in white with white shawls over their heads knelt so close together that there seemed no room for one more in the great hall, with its vaulted cross-ribbing.

Awesome, magnificent, very, very foreign.

Mercy looked up at Zane, who dropped some coins in a box and took her outside, where the withered lady waited for her shawl.

"*Gracias*," Mercy told her, helping the woman place it back over her head. Zane murmured something, seemed at a loss, and then produced from his pocket a small packet that he persuaded their benefactor to take.

"There go your black coral earrings," he told Mercy as they climbed into the carriage. "I couldn't offer her money."

"I'm glad she has them," Mercy said. She felt a bit depressed from her glimpse at an important part of this world she could not enter, and it must have come through in her voice.

"Don't mourn for them," he said coldly. "If baubles are that important, I'll find you another pair."

"It's not the earrings," Mercy retorted. "The cathedral —all those women—made me realize how out of place I am."

Zane shot her a surprised stare, frowned, then gestured at a house where men and women were crowding into a hall through which could be glimpsed tables and benches packed tight with Indians, mestizos, and whites bent over squares of paper. Above a buzzing hum of voices rose a screeching singsong.

"I doubt the lottery would make you feel comfortable, either," Zane remarked. "Will it make your seizure of homesickness better or worse to remind you that my hacienda will not be the least like Mérida? There's a chapel and store and we hold fiestas, but it's a poor country cousin compared to this."

When Mercy didn't answer, he said stiffly, "You have till morning to change your mind, but where will you find a home? In the defeated South, to which your husband will probably drift back? Mexico City, with the empire crumbling?"

"You . . . you're cruel!"

"So is life."

The carriage halted in front of an elaborate portal. Zane paid the driver and lifted Mercy down. They entered with a flurry of guests arriving on foot and moved with them up a flight of steps leading to the second story.

All the furniture in the large room had been moved to the walls and several rows of chairs ran the length of two sides of the room. The orchestra was seated on a platform at the far end.

A diminutive, ripely plump lady in orchid silk embraced the woman in front of Mercy, exchanged a few laughing comments, and then turned, her beautiful dark eyes widening before she smiled, and took Mercy's hands.

"Welcome," she said in heavily accented English, kissing Mercy on the cheek. "You are Zane's kinswoman, come to help him with the small Jolie. How brave you are!" She twinkled at Zane with arched eyebrows. "And how fortunate you are, no?"

He introduced them while Doña Elena looked with approving wistfulness at the gown Mercy wore. "That becomes you well, Doña Mercy. I hope you will keep it, for never on this earth shall I squeeze into it again. Perhaps in heaven I can beg a paradisiacal figure from the good God."

"Nonsense, Doña Elena!" laughed a deep voice behind them. "Every year finds you lovelier, and since I've known you most of my life, that makes you preeminently beautiful."

"Eric, you wicked flatterer!" Doña Elena seemed a trifle flustered as a man so big that he almost made Zane seem of average size bowed over her hand. "I'm glad you stayed for my dance. I was afraid you might need to start back to Belize. With the *indios bravos* repulsed at Tihosuco, they may press to the south."

"Oh, they're always trying to get guns and recapture those of their number who're weary of the wars of the Talking Cross," said the stranger carelessly. "Hundreds of former Cruzob have settled in British territory and are trying to grow their corn in peace. Some even work at my hacienda. But our biggest headaches are with the Pacificos or Icaiche Mayas, who've been driven from their old homes by the Cruzob for not joining them."

"I thought the Pacificos were supposed to harass the Cruzob and keep them off us," protested Doña Elena.

"That was certainly the devout hope," shrugged the huge man. "But they find it healthier to raid Belize."

He reminded Mercy of an archetypal Viking. His fair hair gleamed silver with a sheen of gold, his strong, hawklike face was tanned, and his eyes were the color of ice

39

reflecting a winter sky. When they touched Mercy, she felt seared, as if by freezing iron.

"Doña Mercy, allow me to present Señor Kensington, my nephew by marriage," said their hostess. "Zane, perhaps you know Eric? Eric, meet Zane Falconer. Doña Mercy is his kinswoman, newly arrived in Mérida."

Zane must have been four inches shorter than the towering blond man, but, with some primordial female instinct, Mercy sensed their antagonism and knew that if they ever fought, size wouldn't determine the winner.

"I've heard of Señor Kensington, of course." Zane's tone and face were carefully expressionless. They moved forward as Doña Elena left them to greet other guests. "Selling guns to the Cruzob must be a very profitable business."

"It is," said Kensington good-naturedly. "As a British subject, I take no sides in these Yucatecan uproars. My factor in Belize will sell you or anyone all the guns you can pay for."

"It takes courage—or gall—for you to show yourself in Mérida," Zane said. "If the Cruzob had taken Tihosuco, Doña Elena's hospitality might not have protected you."

"She wouldn't have had a party," said the Englishman, grinning. "Besides, most of these charming people know me as her kinsman by marriage and as the owner of a large sugar plantation. I didn't know my other interests were common knowledge."

"Those of us who live on the frontier have a lively concern with the source of Cruzob supplies."

"Understandable." Kensington stifled a yawn behind a ruffled cuff. He half-turned his back on Zane, and Mercy again felt as a physical impact the frozen blue flame of his eyes. "But I haven't properly acknowledged my introduction to this lady."

He bent over her hand. His lips shocked her like an extreme of heat or cold. Sheer physical energy seemed to radiate from him. He would consume a woman who was with him much, Mercy thought, and though he smiled at her beguilingly as he straightened up, she feared him.

"I am enchanted, Doña Mercy. Have you formed an impression of Mérida?"

"It's very different."

"From where?"

"The eastern bayou country of Texas."

"I would have guessed the Garden of the Hesperides

40

. . . or at least Avalon." He smiled slowly, deliberately, at Zane, whose face was a taut mask. "May I felicitate you, Falconer, on possessing such a beautiful relative?"

Was there an emphasis on possessing?

"Pure luck." There was an ironic twist to the edge of Zane's mouth. "If you returned to England, Kensington, you might learn you're similarly blessed."

"Alas, if I have a fair cousin, she'll have to find me," said the Englishman, shrugging. "I hope you will be generous and share yours to the extent of granting me this waltz with her."

"Doña Mercy may accept a later invitation if she chooses to, but she's promised me the first dance."

Frost-colored eyes swept from Zane to Mercy, obviously noticing her surprise. "Ah, later, then." With a flamboyant, almost mocking, bow, the large man gave Mercy a last smiling appraisal before he moved on to the loveliest of the dark beauties at the chairs.

Zane moved Mercy into the lilt of the slow, dreamy music. She hadn't danced since the early months of the war, because after that, except for soldiers home on leave, there were virtually no men. The waltz had been considered rather gauche, but she'd loved its intoxicating dips and glides, especially with a strong partner who could sweep her gracefully about. Zane was strong enough, but his dancing was vigorous, rather than polished.

He trod twice on her toes and she caught him staring at Eric Kensington, who was whirling his parter with remarkable smoothness. "Confound this rotten tune!" Zane burst out. "I'm not a dancer, as you've learned, but I'd be shot before I'd let that swaggering Britisher have the first number." He grinned ruefully. "But you wish I had!"

"He's Doña Elena's nephew?"

"The nephew of her husband who was a retired British diplomat. He was much older, but even though he died ten years ago, Doña Elena has not wished for another husband." His voice deepened with mockery. "She should be in a museum as the only one of her kind."

Mercy suddenly wondered what had happened to Zane's wife. She'd assumed the lady was dead, but his bitterness was like a revealing flash of lightning.

When the waltz ended, he escorted Mercy to a chair, said he saw an old friend he should greet, and made his way through the now crowded room to the men who were standing near the windows at the end.

Mercy felt very much on display. She smiled at the young women on either side. They smiled back. One ventured some soft Spanish.

"No hablo español," Mercy said regretfully. That was one thing she was going to have to change! It made her feel lost, almost frightened, not to understand what people were saying.

A quadrille formed next and then came a spirited contredanse, with couples facing each other in rows. Zane was one of a knot of men involved in deep conversation, and Eric Kensington's shining head was nowhere to be seen till the musicians slipped into another waltz and he loomed abruptly before her.

"Though you couldn't save your first dance for me, I think our first one together will be memorable," he said.

Drawing her up as if there were no chance of her refusing, he swept her into the circling mass of flower-tinted gowns and black tailcoats. He was strong and he could dance, his rhythm dominating Mercy till she felt without a will or body of her own, a part of the music.

"You're being admired," he told her. "Men are calling you the Quetzal Lady because your gown shines like the plumage of that sacred bird. The Mayas never killed quetzals, but trapped them for their four magnificent tail feathers, which could only be used by royalty. I have quetzals in my garden, but they are not so beautiful as you."

Mercy could think of no reply. She was both pleased and dismayed that she was being especially noticed. Pray heaven no rumor circulated yet about a man who'd gambled his wife away to Zane Falconer!

"Look at me," Kensington said softly. "Your downcast eyes are charmingly like wings, but I can't guess what you're thinking."

She glanced up, but something in those burningly cold eyes made her swiftly avert her own. "I've made inquiries about your kinsman, Doña Mercy. It's fortunate for him that you're willing to live at a hacienda on the frontier, but not, I should think, so fortunate for you."

"I've little choice."

"Let me give you one, then. Marry me."

That brought her head up. His lips were smiling, though

his eyes were as remote as ever. "An ungallant joke, sir!" she rebuked.

"Consent and you'll find it's not."

"We don't know each other!"

"My dear young lady!" He laughed so uproariously that those around them looked and Mercy was gripped with embarrassment. Where was Zane? Why didn't he rescue her? Sobering, Kensington spoke as if she were a not-very-bright child. "The surest cure for the madness called love is to know the other fully. The very essence of romantic love is illusion, mystery . . ."

"Ignorance?" Mercy supplied.

"Exactly."

Mercy wanted to make some scathing retort, but, thinking back to her infatuation for Philip, she had to admit that the better she came to know him, the less she found to love.

"That's not the way it should be," she murmured, more to her thoughts than to Kensington.

"How should it be?" His tone was an amused caress.

Reflections, feelings, warnings, and imperatives thronged her mind, etched with the hurt and bitterness of Philip's betrayal. But in spite of that, she was sure some men and women did love each other truly and well, that they endured and cherished and made of their communion something marvelous, more than either could be alone. Mercy longed for that, though it seemed unlikely she'd ever find it, buried in the wilds of Yucatán with a man who'd made it clear he wouldn't marry her.

Kensington offered marriage, but in a way that was as insulting as Zane's rejection of it. "Well?" he prompted. "How should it be?"

He'd think her ideas romantic, silly, and female, but that made it all the more important to assert them. Meeting his gaze, Mercy said firmly, "Love is when you *do* know each other and still value and care. It's strong enough to hold while illusions and mysteries vanish, but when phantasms go, then people can love in truth."

"You sound so positive, Doña Mercy. Have you loved like that?"

"No. But I want to."

He lifted his massive shoulders and she felt the powerful beat of his heart next to her face. "Possibly this steady endurance you admire is love, Doña Mercy, but it sounds fit only for the tired or sick or cowards who call themselves realists because they don't dare expect much. What I call love has nothing to do with time and patience and high moral qualities. It's the wild, delicious golden fire that burns when a man and woman desire each other and take their joys."

Some of that fire flickered between them, but Mercy was more wary than ever. A man who didn't even pretend there was more to love than passion! What could a woman hope for from him when she was heavy with child or sick or fading?

"Why do you hold yourself so sternly?" he whispered. "If you left your body soft and natural, would it lead into my kind of love?"

"Love?"

"Desire, then. I want you. You respond to me now and I promise it's nothing compared to what you'll feel when we've learned how to please each other. I'll marry you according to any ceremony you wish."

"I wouldn't dream of marrying in such a . . . a shameless way!"

He chuckled derisively. "Should I have lied? Said I'm ravished by your voice and eyes and crave only to hold your hand?" When she couldn't answer, he said briskly, "I should make it clear that I'm a very wealthy man. The House of Quetzals is fine enough for a duchess, but you needn't be there all the time. We could visit Mexico City, the United States, and Europe, too."

"Why didn't you visit them and find a bride?"

"Till tonight I hadn't seen a woman I wished to marry. I'm surprised at myself."

"You don't *seem* inebriated."

"Only with you."

Mercy didn't answer. As the waltz ended, she looked about for Zane, but he had completely disappeared. "There's a card game downstairs," said Kensington. "From what I hear of him, your kinsman has such luck that he is probably testing it."

Mercy arose. So the Englishman knew the truth about her! But no, surely not. He wouldn't have proposed marriage to one man's winnings and the discarded wife of another. Would he? Mercy felt shaken.

"It's cooler on the balcony," Kensington suggested, noting her confusion. Before Mercy could object, he drew her onto the grille-protected space. Down in the courtyard a fountain played and the air was sweet with flowers.

44

"Now," said Kensington, folding his arms in leisurely fashion, blocking the way to the room, "why won't you marry me?"

In spite of her uncomfortable predicament, Mercy couldn't keep from laughing. "Why ever should I?"

He stared at her, unruffled, considering, like an eagle contemplating a perplexing small bird that it can seize at will. "I should have thought my possessions would persuade most women to marry me, even had I been toothless, decrepit, and foul-smelling."

"You belittle my idea of love," she said. "But I'll never marry unless I believe I've found it." By now she was convinced that Eric knew nothing of Philip, and she had no intention of enlightening him of the fact that she already had a husband.

"You may not love me your way," he granted, taking her hands. "But will you deny that you at least feel something of what drives me?"

He tried to draw her against him, but she resisted. He shrugged and released her but still barred the archway. "Why, Doña Mercy, do you have no mercy? Why are you so cold?"

"We've scarcely met!"

"How can I wait? You leave for the wilds in the morning. If there had been weeks or months to court you, I'd have done so, though with impatience. As it is, there is no time for pretty games."

"You're most . . . flattering. But I must decline."

"Why?" His thick silver eyebrows drew together. "Spare me that lack of acquaintance! I happen to know, Mrs. Cameron, just when and how you became Falconer's kin."

Mercy froze. So he did know. Would he tell her secret, expose her to Doña Elena? She told herself she wouldn't be living in Mérida, that it could mean only a single, terribly public, humiliation, but she felt physically sick as she forced herself to stand erect and meet Eric Kensington's eyes.

"If you know, I marvel more than ever at your proposal."

"When I heard the story last night shortly after Falconer left to claim his prize, I wondered what you'd be like. I was startled to find you at the dance, and even more astonished at you. You're no adventuress, but a lady —and I've a hunch Falconer has promised not to besiege you, though, in your skin, I'd not believe that pledge from any man. Far safer to let me help you obtain your divorce and marry me."

To be whispered and speculated about in dives and gambling places! Shame burned in Mercy like fever, and a vivid, pulsing headache half-blinded her.

"Please," she said, "take me inside."

"If you will consider my offer." He turned at the voice behind him.

"Doña Mercy," said Zane, ignoring the Englishman, "it's time we were going. We will make an early start tomorrow."

Kensington spoke smoothly. "As this lady's kinsman, it's proper you should know that I wish to marry her. Surely you could give her a little time to think about it."

Eyebrows shooting up, Zane looked at Mercy. In a flat, dry tone he said, "Are you considering this proposal?"

Before she could answer, Kensington interposed. "She thinks me mad or up to trickery, I'm afraid. Naturally, I wouldn't have been so precipitous had there been more time. In counseling her, Falconer, I trust you won't fault a rashness born of exigency."

"Whether and whom she weds is altogether my cousin's affair," said Zane. "I can only tell her to remember that part of your wealth comes from selling arms to the Cruzob, who've slaughtered the population of entire towns, from the aged to the babies.

"As *ladinos* have done to them," said Kensington.

"English guns have kept the war alive."

"And protected the Mayas from slavery in their own ancestral land."

"Don't pretend ideals motivate you, Kensington."

The big man shrugged. "I don't. I'm neutral. But lovers of freedom could make a good case for supplying the Cruzob." He smiled at Mercy. "Now you have your warning. Let me have your answer before you leave."

With surprising grace for such a large man, he vanished through the archway. Mercy's headache was now torment, and she leaned against the heavy grille.

"Congratulations." Zane's tone was scornful. "The simple country girl, cruelly victimized by two men, has managed to get an offer from one of the peninsula's richest bachelors. I'm sure I wish you happiness." He turned abruptly.

"Don't!" Mercy cried, pressing her throbbing temples. "I've told him I won't marry him!"

46

"Indeed?" Zane paused under the archway, his tone frigid with skepticism. "He apparently didn't hear you."

"He won't listen! He seems to think I should be delirious with joy at the prospect. And the strangest thing of all is that he knows!"

"What?"

"About Philip . . . the card game."

Zane drew in an explosive breath. "And he still proposed? Incredible!" After a moment, he asked grudgingly, as if the question were pulled from him, "Since you needn't fear discovery, surely you'll accept, won't you?"

"Why?"

"Honorable marriage with a handsome man. Wealth. Position."

"I don't love him."

Zane stared at her, blinked, and burst out laughing. "Good Lord! You told him that?"

"Yes, and I don't see what's funny!"

"His expression must have been." Composing himself, Zane frowned and came to stand beside her, drumming his long fingers on the grille. He seemed to be arguing within himself, then spoke roughly after a moment without looking at her.

"It's only fair to advise you to consider his proposal. Your circumstances are unusual. You're alone in a strange country with no friends or family, and if you go to La Quinta Dirección, you'll meet few marriageable men. Further, your position in my household would probably make you an ineligible match for most Yucatecans of good standing."

The pain in her head was so intense that she wanted only to escape from voices, light, and probing. "I'm aware of all that," she heard herself saying.

"Though it sounds conceited of me, I must make it clear again that I'll never offer you marriage."

"So long as you keep your other promise—not to force me—I still prefer to hold to our agreement."

He thrust back his dark hair with an annoyed gesture. "If it's some foolish notion of honor, debt . . . "

"Philip's debts and your winning have no claim on my conscience."

"Then why?"

"You men!" Mercy blazed, clenching her hands furiously. "Is it past your understanding that some women would rather gladly be free of all of you? I don't love

47

Eric Kensington, and I'd rather work as a laundress or nurse than marry him—or you, either!" she raged as Zane stared, his jaw dropped. "You've offered me a position I'm capable of filling, a way to maintain myself. That's what I want."

It was a long moment before Zane spoke. "Be sure of that. For if you regret your decision once we're at La Quinta, it will be very difficult to leave; in fact, you'd probably have to stay there till next year, when I come to Mérida again."

"I don't intend to change my mind."

"Nevertheless," said Zane heavily, "in view of this extraordinary proposal, I feel obliged to see that you reflect on it. Let me take you down to the garden."

"But . . ."

"I insist."

He slipped his hand under her arm and led her to stairs going down to the end of the balcony. Mercy stiffened but decided not to protest. Cool and quiet might relieve the sense of having a constricting, red-hot band tightening around her head. Zane seated her in the shadows near the fountain.

"I'll be back within the hour," he said. "You're perfectly safe here. No one can see you. This may be the most important choice of your life. Ponder it well."

Mercy closed her eyes, leaned back, and gave herself to softly stirring breezes and to the lulling sound of the water. So good to be alone in a quiet place. Good to escape incredulous questions. Her head felt better already. A deep, involuntary sigh escaped from her.

It was almost as if Zane *wanted* her to marry the Englishman. She was honest enough to admit that she might have been tempted, were it not for Eric's intensity and for the rather alarming premonition that he'd consume her. She'd not enjoyed being Philip's wife. For a good while now, maybe for always, she wanted to be herself, find her own center without being pressured or tugged by a husband.

But she began to feel lucky that Eric had proposed. It was better to go with Zane, knowing that she'd had a choice, and it didn't hurt him to be aware of that, either. He'd have to respect her more than if she'd had no alternative.

There was a soft sound. Mercy sat up to make out

Doña Elena in the dim light cast by sconces above the stairs.

"You're tired, my dear?" The older woman's voice was kind, and Mercy felt a flash of yearning for the mother she had never known. "I asked Zane where you were and he told me you have a problem."

It would have been a relief to confide the whole tangled story, but it seemed impossible to discuss Eric's offer with his aunt by marriage, who'd doubtless be horrified at his impetuosity.

"Zane thinks I may regret going to La Quinta Dirección," Mercy said, moving over to make space for her hostess. "He wants me to be very sure before we start out."

Doña Elena nodded. "Yes, he has cause to fear you might not wish to stay."

"Because of the Indians?"

"Not only that. It's more because of the isolation. The master of a hacienda can stay very busy if he lives on it himself. Most Yucatecan owners do not; they leave everything to overseers and mayordomos. But Zane is different." She lifted her hands prettily, excusing one she liked. "It must be his *norte americano* blood."

"You knew his family?"

"I only saw his mother once when Giles Falconer brought her from New Orleans. Beautiful as a white lily, she was, and, like a lily, she wilted. She died when Zane was a baby. We knew Giles well. Even though my husband was British and Giles had fought against England at the Battle of New Orleans, the two were close friends." She smiled and lowered her voice in the manner of one sharing a scandal. "Giles fought under Jean Lafitte and came with him later to Isla Mujeres, off the Yucatán coast. Giles retired from piracy and went back to New Orleans for his bride, whom he'd loved ever since he was a well-born but penniless young man. What a man he was! He never married after he lost Yvette, but how the ladies of Mérida fluttered when they knew he was coming to town—and not just the widows!"

"Zane is . . . attractive, too."

"Yes, but he's finer spun than Giles. He may have buccaneer instincts, but they're tempered with sensitivity and a kindness he tries to hide. He and Giles before him have treated their Indians well and, fortunately, Giles once saved the life of Crescencio Poot, one of the fiercest

49

Cruzob generals. I'm sure that's one reason La Quinta hasn't been laid to waste."

Mercy had to ask. "Zane's wife?"

"Her father, from the United States, had married the daughter of a wealthy Guatemalan and gone into raising indigo. Ethereally lovely, Consuelo was, but also selfish, pleasure-loving. She wanted Zane to leave La Quinta to his mayordomo and live in Mérida or abroad. To get some peace, Zane began to allow her to spend considerable time in Mérida with an aunt, though he insisted on keeping little Jolie with him. It was only a matter of time till the inevitable. Consuelo ran off four years ago with a handsome Frenchman who abandoned her in Jamaica. Somehow, dying of consumption, she got back to La Quinta. Zane wouldn't let her see Jolie because he'd told the child her mother was dead. He brought Consuelo to Mérida, rented her a house, servants, and skillful nurses, and he asked her aunt to obtain for her anything she desired and to send him the bill. He left then for his hacienda and never saw his wife again."

That explained a lot.

Mercy touched Doña Elena's hand. "Thank you for telling me these things. It'll make it easier for me to fit in at La Quinta."

"I hope you will be happy there," said Doña Elena, her delicate eyebrows knitting. "I think you will be good for Zane, and poor Jolie sadly needs someone to mother her." She rose in sudden remembrance. "I must get back to my guests. Will you come with me, or do you need more time alone?"

Mercy rose, too. "I shall go to La Quinta."

"I'm sorry to hear you say that," called a voice from the balcony, "especially since I'll have to start making detours to that godforsaken region."

"Eric!" exclaimed his aunt. "It's rude to eavesdrop!"

"Informative, too." He sauntered down the stairs to meet them, his rueful grin so infectious that Doña Elena melted, though Mercy stayed on guard. "I don't suppose Doña Mercy told you that I've asked her to be my wife?"

Doña Elena's eyes rounded. She gasped, turning to Mercy. "But you said you were going to La Quinta!"

Eric laughed. "She's rejected me, Aunt, though you seem to find that unbelievable. However, I always succeed at what I decide to do, and I've decided to marry!"

"*Ay de mí,* that won't be difficult, foolish boy! I know a dozen eligible girls who . . . "

Eric interrupted his aunt. "I know only one."

While she watched in dismay, he took Mercy's hands and raised them to his lips. "This isn't the end for us, Mercy without mercy. You'll shimmer one day where you belong—in my House of Quetzals."

With a bow, he left them, passing Zane on the stairs. "You have her for a while, Falconer. See that her plumage is unspoiled when I claim her."

"Doña Mercy is her own mistress," Zane said, but his eyes lit as they came to her.

He waited on the balcony as Eric strode away and the women climbed the stairs. Doña Elena, obviously rattled, excused herself and went through the arch.

Mercy paused in front of Zane, her new knowledge of him making her suspect that the coldness of his tone covered relief, perhaps even pleasure.

"You've decided?"

"I've decided."

He slipped his hand under her arm and she thought he did it with a sort of possessiveness. "Then let's give Doña Elena our thanks and good nights. We'll need an early start in the morning."

5

It was still dark when, bearing a lamp, one of the up-to-now invisible maids brought Mercy a cup of hot chocolate, beaten into foamy peaks and spiced with cinnamon, and a basket with several of the sweet, crisp, flat cakes Mercy had already grown fond of. In spite of the early hour, the maid's glossy black hair was arranged in a looped knot at the back and adorned with a crimson flower. Her long, loose dress was spotless white cotton with red embroidery at the neck and hem. If that was what Zane thought could pass for daily wear at La

Quinta, Mercy was intrigued but doubtful. The garment was so easy and free that it promised wonderful comfort, but such lack of constraints seemed somehow immoral for someone not of the native culture. The girl looked as sweet and fresh as her flower, and she smiled timidly at Mercy's thanks before she went softly out of the room.

While Mercy was at the ball, Vicente had stowed her belongings in packs, and before she'd sought her hammock, she had carefully folded and padded the green satin gown Doña Elena had insisted she keep and put it in the pack Vicente had left for her last-minute things. She dressed quickly in her old gray gabardine outfit and was just finishing her hair when Vicente came for the last pack.

"At least you're not a drag-back," Zane said as she entered the hall. "Can you do a long day's ride and go on next morning?"

"I will."

He glanced at her sharply. "I'm not trying to make a martyr out of you, but I won't smother you with solicitous questions. It's up to you to tell me when and if you need to rest."

"I love to ride." Mercy thought sadly of the pretty bay mare Philip had gambled away. "It's been some time since I've had a horse, though."

"That can be remedied. If you don't like the mare I bought for you yesterday, there are several promising young mares at La Quinta."

So he'd found her a mount, as well as getting the dress. "I'm afraid I've been a lot of trouble to you," she ventured.

"I'd gladly have done much more to find a woman for Jolie." He smiled briefly. "I was beginning to think the only way to get a woman there was to marry her."

Mercy's gratitude withered at its blooming. "Yes, you must be extremely glad you are lucky at cards!"

"You can't say you had no choice."

"You can't pretend that *you* gave me much of an alternative!"

"Why should I when it's to my advantage—I hope—to have you at La Quinta? You've explained why you feel it's to yours, so let's dispense with indignation about the initial circumstances."

He opened the door for her and she walked out.

*   *   *

The straight, stony road was surrounded on both sides by dense, low woods that seemed to cut off any air. Their little caravan of four pack mules, Vicente on his mule, and Zane and Mercy on their horses passed a rich cattle hacienda a few miles from Mérida, but then they had a monotonous time of it till, several hours later, they reached a scattering of thatched huts built around an open square. A few scrawny dogs scampered out to bark, and a woman snatched up her child and ran inside her dwelling, but the half-dozen shirtless Indians lounging beneath a big tree in the middle of the square only stared.

"Five leagues out of Mérida and it's a different world," Zane said, putting Mercy's thoughts into words.

"How far is a league?"

He laughed. "How long is a piece of rope? But we're about twelve miles from the city. Traditionally, the Spanish league is a thousand steps, but you can see the variations—short legs, long legs, uphill, downhill, on the level."

"It's very . . . human, though."

Zane nodded. "Well, yes, it's that." He gave her a swift inspection, as if, Mercy thought angrily, she were one of the pack mules. "Do you need to rest, or can you manage another hour?"

"I'm fine."

"Those sidesaddles must be the very devil. I had a hard time finding one, for the ladies here mostly keep to carriages."

"It's a matter of balance," said Mercy loftily, though her spine ached from the unaccustomed position. She flexed the knee hooked over the projecting sidehorn and shifted her weight as much as possible. "Why is your plantation called The Fifth Direction? Aren't there just four?"

"The Mayas don't think so. From antiquity they've paid a lot of attention to the concept of direction. They believed there was a *chaac*, or rain god, from each quarter and that four other gods supported the sky from the four sides of the world. Red is the color of the god of the east, who was also the bee god, and everything near him was red, even the turkeys, corn, and sacred ceiba tree, with its special bird. The northern god was white; black was the hue of the west; and the south was yellow. Each had a tree, bird, other plants, and creatures. But in the center of all was a fifth direction, where the great

53

green tree of life grew, and in this ceiba perched a quetzal. Green is the color of the fifth direction, and green is the color of corn, which has always been life to the Mayas."

"How do you know all this?"

"Most of it's in Bishop Diego de Landa's history, written in about 1560. It's ironic that he left such a record of Mayan religion, history, and beliefs, because he burned all of their written records he could find in the church at Mani, which we'll pass fairly close to tomorrow."

"Since I'm to live here, I'd like to learn more about the country. Are there books about it at your hacienda?"

"I have Diego López de Cogulludo's seventeenth-century *Historia de Yucatán*, which was republished in 1843. I remember how amused some of my Mérida friends were that the Mayan *batab*, or chief, of Tihosuco, Jacinto Pat, had eighteen pesos and nerve enough to buy the book. They didn't think him such a comic savage when he captured Peto, Tikul, and Tekax; where we'll attend the fair. "He knew the *ladinos* couldn't be permanently and completely expelled, and he negotiated with them, but he was opposed in this and murdered by rival chiefs in 1849."

"What a difference it might have made if he'd lived!"

Zane shrugged. "I doubt it. There was always bitter rivalry among Mayan leaders, and there was never much chance for unity *or* peace. The same Crescencio Poot who owed his life to my father and who is now the chief Cruzob military commander, or 'general of the plaza,' was responsible for the murder of several Mayan generals who were for making peace."

"It sounds so bloody! And confusing!"

"It is, and there aren't many books to help you with it. Until you can read Spanish, you'll learn a lot from the travel books of John Stevens. He journeyed through Yucatán and Guatemala in the early 1840s with his English artist friend, Catherwood, who made wonderful engravings of dozens of Mayan sites. Maybe it'll be interesting for you to learn how the country appeared to an observant New Englander just a few years before the War of the Castes broke out."

Mercy was glad there'd be books at La Quinta. Reading had always been her most unfailing refuge and pleasure. "Can Jolie read?" she asked.

"I taught her to when she was about four. She used to climb up on my lap and get impatient because I was looking at a page that didn't say anything to her," Zane said with pride. "She reads Spanish and English equally well."

"She'll end up teaching me!" Mercy wondered what the child would be like, whether she'd resent a newcomer. Zane clearly adored her. Returning to an earlier subject, Mercy asked, "Do the Indians still remember their old religion?"

"Not the complex rituals celebrated at Uxmal and Chichén Itzá, but the concepts linger. When a Maya plants corn, he prays to the four directions, and each village has a cross at each corner and another in the center, where there's usually a tree. Generally it's the ceiba."

Further questions were driven from her head at the sight of church towers. "Tekoh," said Zane. "We'll rest ourselves and the beasts."

Mercy's relief changed to horror as she identified the white objects above the gateway of a high-walled enclosure they were passing, and she saw more in niches along the top.

"Skulls!" Through the gateway she saw a pile of bones and skulls over at the farthest side, and this struck her speechless.

"It's the custom," Zane said, trying to soothe her. "There's no disrespect intended, but when a family's plot is full they dig up the older dead to make room for the new."

"Is there a graveyard at La Quinta?"

"Of course. But since the hacienda's only forty years old, there's still plenty of room. In your time, unless there's a plague or massacre, there shouldn't be a charnel pit."

The huts of Tekoh were almost hidden by trees and bushes, but as the travelers came even with the huge two-towered stone church on the plaza, several boys ran up and took charge of the horses. Vicente went with them.

"Let's go see if the curate is in," said Zane, escorting Mercy around to the rear of the church. "He has a large region to cover, baptizing, marrying, burying, and holding Mass. And this curate does his best for the people, though Yucatecan priests have been in general a scurvy lot, known for preaching only at Lent, Holy Week, and on their village's saints' day. After independence from Spain,

55

the Church was largely supported by a capitation tax or obvention levied on the Indians. When this was finally abolished, many priests tried to recoup by raising marriage and baptismal charges to an outrageous level. During the early days of the rebellion, one of the important things Jacinto Pat—the Maya who bought Cogulludo's history—demanded that a marriage cost no more then ten *reales* or ten days of labor, and a baptism three."

"And you might add," came a voice from the other side of the gate, "the answer of several rebel chiefs to the churchmen who were asking for peace: *'And now you remember that there is a True God. While you were murdering us, didn't you know that there was a True God?'* " The gates opened and a lean, middle-aged priest welcomed them in with a sweeping gesture. "It is grievous that the Indians whose souls we were charged with could say in truth: *'You were always recommending the name of God to us, and you never believed in His name.'* "

"Padre . . . " began Zane, reddening, but the priest urged them up the flight of steps leading to a building behind the church.

"No need to apologize for facts, my son. I will still take pleasure in offering you refreshment." Serene dark eyes rested on Mercy, and Zane hastily introduced her to the priest as a companion and teacher for Jolie.

The priest, whom Zane called Padre Martín, obviously knew something of Zane's situation, for he nodded and said Jolie should benefit from Mercy's company.

"Even you might," he said with a shrewd glance at Zane, who seemed suddenly fascinated with the thick stone walls of the curate's home.

He brought them into a comfortable room with several armchairs, a writing table loaded with books and papers, and a round table by a deep-set window where more books were stacked. A stately Indian woman, whose handsome face gave not a hint of her age beyond denial of youth, appeared with a tray, served them all hot chocolate, waited till they had drunk, and then inclined her head at the priest's instructions.

"Caterina will take you to a room where you can wash off the dust of travel and rest while a meal is prepared," said Padre Martín.

Gratefully, Mercy followed the woman's swaying white skirt with its embroidered hem down the hall to a small, neat cubicle with a hammock, bench, and washstand. A slight young girl brought a pitcher of water and several coarsely woven towels and filled a copper washbasin. She darted a curious look at Mercy, but she was shooed out by Caterina, who stood in the doorway for a moment, as if to be sure Mercy was content.

"Gracias," Mercy said, trying to make up for her lack of Spanish with a warm smile.

"De nada." Caterina's tone was soft, expressionless. She shut the door. Mercy unbuttoned her dress, slipped it off her arms and shoulders, dipped the edge of a towel into the basin, and sighed with the pleasure of getting clean.

She was dozing in the hammock, her gown still unbuttoned, when there was a tap on the door. *"Sí!"* she called.

Hastily righting her dress, she smoothed her hair and proceeded to the priest's sitting room, amazingly refreshed and so ravenously hungry that her mouth watered when she smelled the beans, tortillas, and eggs filling the three plates on the table.

The paper-thin tortillas were tender and fragrant, not leathery like the only ones she'd tasted before, in Vera Cruz. She flavored the beans and eggs with the dish of sauce set in the middle of the table and ate with more appetite than she'd had since leaving Texas.

Zane and the priest had evidently been discussing Mérida's celebration over the lifting of the siege of Tihosuco. "The government doesn't celebrate victories anymore, just a simple holding-off of the Cruzob." Padre Martín's shrug was philosophic. "For a while it seemed the emperor would send enough troops to subdue them, but from the news that reaches me, he's slipping rapidly from his throne and has no money or men for Yucatán."

"He can't last long now that Napoleon the Third has abandoned him," Zane agreed. "I hope he does abdicate and join his wife in Europe while he still can."

"And you? With Tihosuco given up as too hard to defend, will you stay on at La Quinta?"

Zane frowned. "Of course."

"Why so stubborn? You're the only plantation owner I've known who's lived on his lands."

"If more had, and had taken an interest in their workers, the rebellion might not have come," Zane said sternly.

"That's as useful now as saying that if some clergymen hadn't taken over communal lands, forced the Indians into the Church, and scandalized them with carnally licentious living, there would have been no trouble."

The two men stared across the table and smiled at each other with rueful admiration. Padre Martín sighed. "I suppose we do what we must as individuals, whatever the sins of our groups."

"I'm not foolhardy," Zane said. "Crescencio Poot, old blood-drinker that he is, seems to remember my father saved him when he found him wounded and unconscious in the brush. He renders some protection to La Quinta Dirección. But you, Padre, are the one who should take care. You should let your distant parishioners come to you rather than going so far into the wilds."

"The dying cannot travel. How can I expect the Indians to have faith if I have none?"

"The rebels killed some priests even before they had their *tatich* and their Talking Cross. They even macheted a paralyzed curate in Valladolid."

"And one priest had a harem of Indian women, and another strapped on spurs and mounted an Indian." Padre Martín turned grim. "What is the good of matching outrage with outrage? I endure now and pray for better times for all, including those poor Indians who created their own religion when ours failed them."

Zane gave a harsh laugh. "Those at Chan Santa Cruz, confident of their cross's protection and waited on by *ladino* slaves, wouldn't call themselves poor. This is the first time since the conquest that a Maya could really hold his head high."

The priest sighed. "There you're right, my son. But pride, anyway, is a snare."

"If you had no pride, you'd forget your Indians in the brush."

Padre Martín looked shocked. After a moment's evident soul-searching, he said, "I go to them through the love of our Lord."

"Call it what you will." Zane shrugged, draining his goblet of honey mead before he got to his feet. "I'll tell you this, Padre—I'm glad the Cruzob have their city and their pride, even if it makes my sleep a little lighter."

"In time, some boundaries are sure to be agreed on, and peace will come from the Cruzob and *ladinos*," said the priest.

"Only because each side will despair of wiping out the other."

Padre Martín shook his head at this, though he couldn't repress a slight grin. He walked with them around to the front of the church. The boys and Vicente brought over the animals.

"It's always a joy for me to perform weddings," said the priest, glancing at Mercy with a twinkle.

Zane didn't smile. "Why, then, I wish you a score this week," he said, almost tossing Mercy into the saddle. Mounted himself now, he sounded a bit sheepish. "Thanks for your hospitality, Padre."

"Always it's my pleasure. Greet your small daughter for me." As they started up the long, straight street, he called after them. "Go with God!"

They waved back. There was hostility in the set of Zane's shoulders as they rode on, so Mercy refrained from asking him more about the priest and the war, though she'd have been glad of conversation to distract her from aching, long-unused muscles. At least she wasn't hungry or thirsty now and she felt clean. Drawing all the comfort she could from this, she tried to think of games and lessons for Jolie and put out of her consciousness the broodingly handsome man beside her.

It was dusk when they rode through the gates of a hacienda and were greeted by the mayordomo, Don Raimundo, a light-skinned mestizo who managed the vast sugar cane plantation while the owner, a friend of Zane's, lived in Mérida. Great trees shaded the main house, a two-storied white stucco building with graceful Moorish arches and a crenellated top.

Indians came to lead away the horses and mules and deposit packs on the veranda that stretched the length of the house. This porch was empty except for a few benches, several high-backed, exceedingly uncomfortable-looking chairs, and potted plants. In spite of its grand exterior, the inside of the house was similarly bare. A few chairs, chests, and tables scattered forlornly through the dozen large rooms only emphasized an aura of desertion.

Don Raimundo spoke apologetically to Mercy. "He says the master brings all his requirements when he visits, but since this is never more than a few days out of a year, there's no need for much furniture," Zane explained.

"Tell him I understand," said Mercy, but she didn't.

It seemed to her that if someone didn't care more than that about such a potentially beautiful place, more about the people whose work supported him, he had no right to ownership. Her father had always taught her that owning meant caring for, that the responsibility was at least as important as the benefit.

Within minutes, hammocks had been slung for them in rooms opening onto a rear courtyard. A white-clad young woman with soft, dark eyes brought Mercy a basin and pitcher of water. Mercy washed, took down her hair, brushed it out, and pinned it in a loose knot.

"Dinner is ready," Zane called at her door. There had been constraint in his manner ever since the priest's joking words about marriage, and Mercy was irritated enough to exude a polite chill of her own.

The table was spread on the veranda, which had been hastily tidied up and mopped, for the tiles still glistened in the lantern glow. Don Raimundo was sharing his own meal with them, so Zane had invited him to join them. Or was it to avoid dining alone with Mercy? The mayordomo seemed embarrassed at this democracy, but as two women brought sweet potatoes, chicken in a thick, spicy sauce, a very good corn gruel, and tortillas, he found refuge in food, and Mercy and Zane were hungry enough to match his enthusiasm.

Afterward, there was hot chocolate and a creamy caramel pudding called flan. Mercy still ached from the long day's ride, but it was pleasant to gaze out toward the trees dominating the approach to the house and the white bulk of a church at the far end of the clearing. And from the well, protected by trees, came the soft voices of women fetching water for their huts, which were situated behind the church.

Zane had translated some of Don Raimundo's sparing remarks, but when Zane asked permission to smoke, Mercy decided to seek her hammock. Conversations that had to be interpreted for two people were awkward. Zane was being so formally correct that she longed to kick him, and she was tired. She voiced her thanks and good nights. As she sank into the hammock, nothing ever felt as good.

Mercy was so stiff the next morning that she felt bruised, but the soreness eased as she dressed, though she wondered if the muscles of her back and thighs would ever be the same as before the journey began. After a hearty breakfast of eggs, refried beans, and tortillas, she waited for the rest of their small caravan, standing by an arch of the veranda and watching women visit the well for water and neighborly conversation.

Listening to their laughter and jokes, she felt the lonely isolation of being an outsider, wondered if she would ever belong anywhere, as they did here, and thought she probably wouldn't, unless somehow she got back home to Texas.

There'd be Jolie, of course. Surely, if Mercy was patient, they'd grow close. In time it should be possible to make friends among some of the hacienda women. It wouldn't do to count on Zane, though. Padre Martín's little joke had spooked him like spurs clapped to an untamed colt.

The morning breeze was cool enough to banish her last bit of sleepiness, and, abruptly, it carried a sound different and higher than the soft domestic merriment of the women.

It came again—a cry of distress. The women at the well either didn't hear or didn't respond. Mercy hesitated. The faint scream reached her again, seeming to come from the long stone row that housed the commissary, storerooms, and infirmary. Picking up her skirt, Mercy ran toward it and now she heard a sibilance and a fleshy sound before each cry.

Through the open door of what seemed to be an office, she saw a girl, old enough to have small breasts showing under her white shift, with her thin brown wrists gripped by a stocky, powerful man Mercy thought to be mestizo from the lightness of his skin. A skinny, sallow white man was raising a braided rope. Mercy sprang forward, deflecting the blow.

"Stop it!" she cried. "How dare you beat a girl!"

The man stared at her in shock, shrugged, answered in Spanish, then turned to resume his business. Mercy got in front of him. She didn't know what the thin child had done, but she didn't look more than fourteen, and, apart from the brutality, it was wretched to see the gratification in the men's faces as they manhandled her.

"Didn't they whip slaves in Texas?" drawled a cool voice from the door.

"My father wouldn't own slaves, and I never saw a whipping!" Mercy blazed, swinging toward Zane. "Am I supposed to let this happen because I'm from the South?"

"Wherever you're from, one would expect you to stay out of what doesn't concern you."

Dismayed, realizing the vulnerability of her position, Mercy glanced at the girl, who was trying to stand erect even though blood trickled from her bitten lip and her dark eyes were dilated with shock and pain. Mercy moved close to her, and the mestizo who had served as a human whipping post released wrists so fragile and slim that it seemed a miracle he hadn't snapped them.

"She can't have done anything to deserve this!"

"She may be a thief, a troublemaker, or lazy."

"She's not much older than your own daughter! How would you like her to be treated like this?"

Zane looked from Mercy to the girl. Plainly irritated, he asked the white man a question, then received a flood of indignant self-justification.

"She refuses to marry any of the men suggested for her," Zane explained. "She says she's a descendant of Jacinto Canek, a chief who led an uprising in 1761, and she will never marry a tame Indian and produce more. Such talk and behavior are threats to the tranquility."

"The apathy, you mean," retorted Mercy. "It's interesting that men everywhere have the same answer for spirit or pride in a woman: put a man's weight and hand on top of her, and fill her with babies so that in caring for them she'll forget what was real for her as a person!"

"Unfortunately, that doesn't always work," said Zane with an icy smile that infuriated Mercy till she remembered what his wife had done. "And though you were married, it hasn't gentled your tongue. You might remember, madam, that though I have no wish to constantly remind you of it, I've the same rights over you as the manager has over this girl. You both are in debt-bondage."

Mercy laughed in his face, too outraged to care what he did. "Maybe you'd like to borrow the whip and teach me my place?"

Something leaped between them, a vibrating, magnetic energy that pierced Mercy, making her knees weak. Did Zane feel it, or did anger cause that smoldering deep in those impenetrable eyes that were now the color of the black waters of lakes?

"The girl must obey. Don Raimundo is strict, but not cruel. Once she accepts a normal life, she'll be content."

And her soul would die, the spirit that defied all the power of the hacienda—men who could beat her to death or maim her till it would be a punishment for a man to take her.

"Can you buy her?" Mercy asked.

Reluctantly, Zane said, "I could purchase her debt, which comes from her father, who came into servitude during a great famine. Many people sold their labor for life in those times just for enough to eat. And, since a debt, above what an owner charges for food, clothing, and shelter, can almost never be paid back, it descends to the children."

"Please pay what she owes," Mercy begged. "It can't be the price of even one of those pairs of shoes you bought me! I'll pay you back someday, somehow."

"How, indeed?" he countered. "You labor is mine. Perhaps you have tucked away some family jewel you managed to hide from your slip-fingered husband?"

"My father's medical books."

"You must prize them to have brought them all this way, but I doubt that musty medical treatises would be of value to me." His eyes touched her throat and she flushed as the telltale pulse leaped and throbbed. "There's one thing I could take, but I prefer to have it given, so I won't ask for that." Moments seemed to pass as he glanced lazily from the men to the girl and back to Mercy. "You've demanded that I buy her. You want to save her pride. What about your own? Will you kneel for her? Will you beg?"

Mercy threw back her head. She stared into the mocking, hard-angled face, started to say *I'd sooner die!*, but caught herself.

What did it matter if he got perverse satisfaction from humbling her? To save the girl was the important thing. But, oh, it hurt, oh, it was difficult to sink to her knees.

"Buy her," she said. "Please buy her."

Zane watched Mercy strangely.

"Get up," he said. "I will speak to Don Raimundo."

Twenty minutes later Mercy had salved the girl's back where the skin was broken and they were back on the *camino real*, the girl, Mayel, perched on a scraggly burro that Don Raimundo had thrown into the bargain. He'd been so glad to get rid of an increasingly troublesome problem that he hadn't been much .vexed with Mercy, though he'd warned Zane that the Indian girl would be trouble.

"She can be your maid," Zane told Mercy somewhat dourly. "I hold you completely accountable for her."

"But I don't speak Spanish, let alone Mayan!"

"You'll certainly have to learn."

At least he seemed over his withdrawn mood of the day before. And he had bought Mayel, even if Mercy had knelt for that.

"Who's this Canek that Mayel is so proud of?"

"He was *batab* of Quisteil, a village where a fiesta turned into a riot back in 1761. His real name was Jacinto de los Santos Uc, but he changed it to Canek in memory of the last Itzá king, because prophecies foretold that one of the Itzás would drive all the whites into the sea from where they came. He rallied hundreds of Mayas, but the *ladinos* came down with a crushing force, took Quisteil, and when they caught up with Canek, they marched him and several hundred prisoners to Mérida."

"Then?"

"In the main plaza he was quartered, his flesh torn with pincers, and the fragments burned to ashes to scatter to the winds. Two hundred of his men got two hundred lashes each and had an ear cut off, while eight more were strangled. But Canek's name was remembered. It was used to inspire the Mayas at the start of the War of the Castes."

Mercy felt sick. She didn't think she could ever visit that plaza again. Zane shot her a quick glance.

"I'm sorry. But you'd better understand this country. You can see why Don Raimundo was uncomfortable at having a descendant of Canek's refusing to accept her lot."

"But surely he had other descendants."

"Doubtless. The difference is that this one *cares*."

Maybe that was all the difference with anyone, anywhere.

They were amidst small, rolling hills now, taking a side road toward Uxmal. "It's slightly out of our way," said Zane. "But if you read Stevens' account with Catherwood's wonderful engravings, you'll want to see it. The region is known for fevers, so we won't linger, even though the rainy season seems to be over."

The trees and vegetation pushed densely toward the path, sometimes overgrowing it till Vicente had to hack away vines with his machete. In any case, they had to duck a lot, for the path was cleared for a walking man,

64

not riders. Mercy was glad when they came out into an open field, then was gripped with awe and a sense of desolation as they gazed toward a towering pyramid, obscured with trees and brush and a complex of lower buildings facing it in a quadrangle, their terraces, foundations, and elaborately friezed facades smothered with vines and weeds that grew rank all over the great field.

Some distance away on an elevation gleamed a long white building like an island rising from a sea of green.

"That's the governor's mansion," said Zane. "Stevens and his friends stayed there when they were exploring the ruins. They cleared out enough vines and brush to make pictures of the temples, but it doesn't take long for the jungle to take back anything man does."

Mayel was pointing at the huge, rubble-strewn pyramid, speaking with the sort of delighted shudder children reserve for scary stories.

Zane made some teasing reply and said to Mercy, "She's saying that the witch whose egg-hatched son, The Dwarf, or Magician, raised this pyramid in one night lives in an underground cave near here and will give water to thirsty travelers in exchange for babies, which she feeds to a giant snake."

"Does she really believe that?" Mercy demanded, studying the girl's face, which, now that she wasn't in pain, showed roguish dimples in both cheeks and chin. Her skin was like dark honey, with slim eyebrows winged up, and there was a delicately Oriental look about her.

"Why not? Aren't the old rain gods in the sixth heaven with San Miguel Arcángel, the lords of the wilds in the fifth, animal guardians with San Gabriel in the fourth, wind gods on the second level? And in the first heaven, just above earth, don't village and cornfield guardians keep watch? And the devil's well mixed with the old earthquake god." He chucked at her expression. "Be honest. Which is more fanciful—the old faith, or the conquering one with which it's intertwined?"

Any religion that gave animals and wild places guardians appealed to Mercy. She had never liked the concept of salvation or damnation of individual souls to overwhelm the beauty and terror and power of the natural world, like the marvel of wings and the depths of the ocean. Souls, Elkanah used to say, would fare better if their owners worried less about them and more about their responsibilities and challenges in the living world.

65

She shrugged at Zane's question and stared at the top of the pyramid, its overgrown summit towering against the brilliant sky. "Didn't they practice human sacrifice?"

"Yes, though not on the scale of the Aztecs. Besides, everyone believed the victims went to the highest heaven along with warriors killed in battle and women who died in childbirth."

"They put women in the best heaven?"

Zane nodded. "The Vikings did the same. They and the Mayas considered childbirth a struggle as valiant and important as any war of man."

Mercy had delivered a few babies, though most people had felt it was scandalous for a young unmarried woman to attend a birth. It *was* a battle, though casually accepted as the destiny of a woman. Men seemed to prefer to forget that without the agony of women, their own lordly kind could not be perpetuated.

"Good for the Mayas—and for the Vikings, too!" Mercy said so vigorously that Zane laughed without any of that irony that so often embittered his mirth.

They turned their mounts and within a quarter of an hour were at the Hacienda Uxmal, gloomy and seldom visited by its owner, where they got down to stretch and watered the animals before starting back to the *camino real.*

"Tekax tonight," Zane said encouragingly, as if he guessed how every muscle in her body protested as he helped her into the saddle. "And the next day we'll arrive at La Quinta!"

Mercy was ready. Whatever awaited her there, at least she could get off this animal.

Earlier, Zane had spoken to Mercy about an empty house in Tekax where they could spend the night. Entering its courtyard now, Vicente and Zane unloaded and unsaddled. With her thoughts on the fair they were to attend that night, Mercy watched as Vicente plunked one pack inside the empty house and then turned to Mayel with some direction or other. Promptly, the girl rummaged about among the remaining packs, then brought out the hammocks. Entering the house, Mercy helped her swing these from pegs in several different rooms, and she showed by gesture that she wished Mayel to sleep in her room.

Some Indian boys Vicente had hired to water the animals brought water for the house, and Mayel seemed as glad to wash off the dust of the journey as Mercy was.

Mercy salved the girl's back again, though Mayel indicated she was all right now.

Despite having had a full bath in Mérida, two days of traveling had made her feel thoroughly grubby. There would surely be tubs at La Quinta, and Mercy pictured one, filled with warm water, with great longing. She thought she smelled of horses, and, truly, it would be strange if she didn't.

"We'll eat at the fair," Zane called. "Are you ready?"

"Shall we take Mayel?"

"I suppose so," he said ungraciously, "though I wouldn't be heartbroken if she ran away." He added a few words and the girl's face seemed to bloom. From a hemp sack that apparently held all she possessed, she produced a frayed red ribbon and began to loop it where her hair was gathered at the back of her head.

Mercy raised a hand. "Wait!" she said. *"Un momento!"*

She searched in the pack of materials and trimmings, produced a length of yellow satin ribbon, and cut it with scissors from her reticule. Shaping a huge double bow, she fastened it in Mayel's hair and let her peer into the small mirror Mercy kept with her brush and other necessities.

Mayel's eyes widened. She touched the bow with small, hesitant fingers, then glanced questioningly at Mercy.

"For you," Mercy said, nodding. She'd learn all the Spanish and Mayan she could, but there was no reason why Mayel shouldn't know some English.

Like a burst of sunlight, Mayel smiled. As if making a momentous resolution, she bent over and would have kissed Mercy's hand, except that Mercy caught her in her arms and they embraced. How good and healing it was to give and get affection untinged by stormy tensions of male and female! Mayel was too old to be Mercy's daughter, but she was the right age to be a sister without the competitiveness of being close in age, and as they held each other, Mercy felt free for the first time in years to love another person without fear of betrayal.

Tekax nestled among wooded hills that became low mountains to the south. Its broad streets were full of whites, Indians, and mestizos on foot and mounted on mules or horses, many of the Indians carrying long straw basket-bags on their backs, full of goods to be sold or bartered.

Besides Indian huts embowered by vines and trees, there were many stone houses in Tekax, and those on the plaza were especially fine, one even having three stories and balconies overlooking the street. The church was magnificent, reached by a great flight of stone steps. People thronged in and out, pausing at a table by the door to buy candles that Zane said would be lit at the altar, blown out, and promptly resold.

Tables arranged against the buildings facing the plaza were laden with rings, necklaces, bracelets, earrings, various cloth, brightly framed mirrors, and all kinds of small trinkets. The plaza was full of stands protected by roofs of leaves and small tree limbs where vendors of seeds, breads, and other food sold their items to a constant press of hungry people.

"Tekax lost three-quarters of its population during the war," said Zane, steering Mercy and Mayel through crowds of white-clad Indians and conventionally dressed whites. "But it seems to be recovering, though it's too close to the frontier for much comfort."

"Everyone looks so happy!"

"They are. It's fiesta time. Who can mourn always for what happened ten years ago? But in this very plaza . . . " He broke off. "I'll tell you later. For now let's find something to eat."

It may have been cowardly, but Mercy was glad for his decision, just as she was glad she'd seen the plaza in Mérida without knowing what had happened there to Mayel's forebear.

Zane made a path for them from vendor to vendor. After each purchase, he, Mayel, and Mercy retreated toward the church steps to eat their plunder, first delicious tamales wrapped in cornhusks, which served as holders and could be peeled back as the corn-mush-wrapped meat was eaten, then venison roasted with herbs and wrapped in tortillas, and finally Mercy's favorite crisp, thin, sweet bread, this made with a tempting crusty glaze.

As they were selecting this *pan dulce*, Mercy noticed Mayel glancing wistfully at some poisonous-looking candy. To Mercy's surprised pleasure, Zane's gruff words to the girl must have told her to pick something, for she pointed to some *panuchos* and he paid for them with a few cacao seeds, explaining to Mercy that the smallest coin in Yucatán was a *medio*, worth six and one-quarter cents, and cacao seeds had long been used as money, usually five seeds being equal to one-twentieth of a *medio,* though the value fluctuated.

"As you say," he told Mercy with a reluctant twinkle, "Mayel's not so much older than Jolie. And what longing eyes! Insurrectionists should be made of sterner stuff."

Mercy felt like saying that he himself wasn't as stern as he pretended to be, but she treasured that hint of kindness too much to challenge him. She loaned Mayel a handkerchief to clean her fingers and they moved with the crowd around the plaza, passing, on the far side, a huge circular scaffolding of poles and vines lashed together in tiers and shaded by palm thatch.

"That's for the bullfights," Zane said. "Looks like it'd crash down, but it'll hold the crowds through the fiesta, and then the whole thing will be torn down and used for fuel."

"Bullfights!" exclaimed Mercy. "How horrid!"

"Part of every fiesta." Zane shrugged. "And the bulls are killed only by accident, though they get bloodied up considerably."

"It's a beastly amusement!"

"In both senses of the word, though I don't hold with people condemning what they can have little knowledge of."

They went down a lane to where horses and mules were on sale, but after a careful look around Zane found no animal he wanted.

"Only trotters," he said in disgust. "I thought I might find a pacer for you, but it seems you'll have to make do with what we can find at La Quinta."

When this journey was over, Mercy thought it would be a while before she stopped wincing at the sight of a saddle, but she thanked Zane and was not surprised or even much put off by his growling response.

"I like to ride with Jolie, but sometimes I'm too busy. Then it'll be your duty. Anyhow, I want you to have enough occupations for contentment. I warn you now that I will not tolerate a complaining female!" As they reached the plaza, he slipped her a handful of *medios.*

"Most of the things are for Indians, but you might see something you'd like for curiosity's sake or a trinket for your girl." His keen eyes touched the yellow ribbon. "I see you've already started to spoil her."

"At least it won't give her a stomachache, as that awful-looking candy may!" returned Mercy. "And—and it's undignified for you to dole out money as if I were a child. I know you don't have to give me anything—I'm sure you mean it kindly—but I'd much prefer a small sum granted monthly, as if it were part of a salary."

Their eyes battled. Zane's mouth curved down and she guessed it was on the edge of his tongue to remind her she was a bond-servant. That half-hostile, half-melting, wholly vital awareness coursed between them till she felt as if he held her physically, caressed her with those long brown hands.

"We can do that, of course, though at La Quinta all you needs will be provided for. Any that aren't will have to wait till we make another trip to Mérida. Please consider the *medios* part of your . . . salary."

"You'll make an entry of it in the accounts?"

He lifted his eyes to the heavens. "My God, yes! I'll emblazon it on the wall if you like! Now, have a look around, for the dancing will start soon, and, unless you've an urgent desire to watch, we'd better get back to our quarters."

Mercy found nothing she needed, but she signaled to Mayel to choose a mirror and felt grateful to Zane as she paid for one bordered with red. Jolie must have all the things an indulgent, well-to-do father would have bought her over the years, but Mercy wanted to take some gift to her. As a child, proper or no, she had always loved presents and had tended to appreciate bearers of them.

At last, worriedly conscious of Zane's impatience, she found a table with small carved animals, so handsomely done that the maker must have worked with love, as well as a careful eye. She pointed to a pheasant, a deer, and a jaguar. The old Indian who must have created them looked at them with rather sad eyes and named a sum.

"A *medio* apiece," said Zane. "He'll be happy with two for the lot."

"I'd rather give him what he asks for."

"That is not the way it's done."

"He hates to sell them at all," said Mercy, and she put three *medios* into a hand scarred with work and age. The old man wrapped the creatures tenderly in bits of colored paper. Mercy thanked him, hoping he'd understand that she admired his art, and for the moment something flickered in those melancholy eyes set deep in the wrinkled face.

He muttered something. Zane made a curt reply and drew Mercy away. "What did he say?" she asked, holding onto Mayel's hand as Zane hustled them through the packed street.

"He said you were as gentle as a deer and that he would pray the jaguar would not harm you. It was pretty clear he considered me the jag!"

Mercy burst into helpless laughter. "I should think you'd take that as a compliment."

"If he knew you," returned Zane, "he'd know it was the other way around."

Vicente had obtained milk and served them mugs of frothy hot chocolate before he went off to the evening's festivities. Mayel almost fell asleep while drinking hers, part of the *panuchos* still clutched in her hand. Zane shooed her off to bed and came to watch Mercy wash the drinking mugs and stand them upside down to dry on the window ledge.

"All this must seem heathen to you," he said, his eyes glowing in the candlelight. "Are you afraid, Mercy?"

She stared at him. What was wrong now? Had he decided he didn't want her at his home?

"That was the plaza where *ladino* troops won back the town from the rebels, whipped them, and then hurled them from the second-story balcony of the municipal palace to bayonets waiting below. They say a young boy begged and cried, but they tossed him down, too."

"Don't!" cried Mercy, putting her hands out.

"But that was nothing compared to when Crescencio Poot marched into Tekax with several thousand men in 1857. He and his Cruzob macheted and killed over a thousand people—babies, the elderly, whomever they came upon—and then drank and raped and looted through the night. Poot had them out the next morning and away with their spoils of cloth, liquor, weapons, utensils, and gunpowder. It took five days to bury the dead." Zane strode to the window and gazed out toward the merriment a few streets away. "I'm glad my father was dead by then, that he never knew what the Indian he had saved did to helpless, unarmed people."

Mercy felt sick. The spiced, rich food she'd enjoyed now made her queasy. Zane turned and caught her hands.

71

"Let me send you back," he urged. "Vicente can take you. This isn't your country. It's not right to take you where such things happen."

"You say La Quinta hasn't been raided."

"Poot can't live forever. He's assassinated many in his time. Someone will likewise blot him out." He gripped her shoulders. "Go now, Mercy. I'll pay your way back to Texas—New Orleans, if you'd prefer. But I was mad to dream of taking you to La Quinta."

"I've no place to go." Mercy realized it was true. "I've no one left. You've offered me a home and work, Zane. Are you reneging?"

His eyes narrowed. "No, just giving you a chance."

"Thank you."

"Not at all!" he said savagely. "Whatever happens, don't blame me!"

He gripped her wrists and pulled her to him. His mouth took hers and seemed to drink from her, drawing out her strength, but when his hands cupped her breasts, stroked them till they tingled and her body screamed, she managed somehow, desperately, drunkenly, to pull away.

"You promised!" she gasped.

His face was a ruthless, jeering mask. He took a long step forward, as if to seize her. She shrank away.

"Oh, damn you!" he grated. "Go sleep with the child! You're a married woman, and you manage to look like a violated nun!"

He swung out. The door banged. Mercy heard the click of his boots outside. She knew he'd ease his frustration with some soft body, or at least with wine.

All she could do was go to her hammock . . . and think of him, achingly hungry for his lean, hard fingers and his wildly sweet kisses, which made her forget everything else.

She stiffened with shock. Dear God! She was falling in love with him—a man who distrusted women, who was resolved to treat them only as a convenience.

Mercy fought back tears. She mustn't let him guess she cared, mustn't let him have what was nothing to him but honor to her. Someday he might change. Meanwhile, she must resist his power, armor herself against his appeal.

Where was he now?

She remembered the coquettishly lovely mestizo woman, a beautiful Creole who'd smiled at him from be-

72

hind an older woman's back, and she writhed inwardly as she pictured him in someone else's arms. He'd find a woman, of course he would, and he'd forget all about her as he sated himself.

Mercy gave a few self-pitying sobs, but she quickly derided herself into drying her eyes. She'd never let him know how she felt! Never! Not unless . . . unless he asked her to marry him. . . .

Rejecting that insane delusion, she tried to make her breathing match the steady, even sound of Mayel's. Her eyelids grew heavy. She gave a last protesting sniffle and then slipped into dreams.

It was a silent group that left Tekax the next morning. Vicente behaved as if nursing a dolorous headache, Mayel kept stealing glances in her mirror, Zane had dark hollows under his eyes, and Mercy, wondering where and how he'd spent the night, was afraid she knew.

They came through Peto, a garrison town defending this southern point of the frontier, its fine old church and gracious colonial buildings dominating the plaza, which Mercy was sure had its bloody history of looting, takings, and retakings by Cruzob and *ladinos* She didn't ask and was glad Zane didn't seem to feel obliged to tell her. Probably he felt he'd given her full warning last night, a final chance, and now she could take what came.

Turning east from Peto, leaving the *camino real,* they took a road squeezed by thick growths and vines. It was past noon when they rode into a small village and swung their hammocks in the roadhouse, a structure intended for use by the priest when he came or for the occasional traveler or official. A couple of Indians brought glossy green leaves from what Zane said was a breadfruit tree. Its fruits were edible and so were its nuts and sap, while the evergreen leaves made fine provender for livestock. The animals were led off to water and then hobbled to munch on breadfruit leaves while their owners rested and partook of tortillas and beans, the only food quickly available.

Their rest was brief, though. Fleas assailed them, seconded by mosquitoes, and they were forced to retreat outside. It was scarcely worthwhile hunting for trees for their hammocks, so they rested against the packs for an hour and then were on their way again.

Welted by mosquitoes, it took Mercy a while to recognize a different tormentor, but as she began to itch in new spots, driven almost wild with the urge to dig ferociously at the bites, Zane gave her the first sympathetic glance he had spared that day.

"*Garrapatas*," he said. "My father called them chiggers."

Mercy groaned. "I thought they felt familiar!"

Zane grinned. Either he was feeling better after whatever his night's occupation had been, or he undertook to take her mind off their tiny but maddening attackers by filling in some of the background of the War of the Castes.

After losing many warriors in battles against the *conquistadores*, the Mayas had lost thousands more of their number to smallpox, other plagues brought by the invaders, and from starvation when forced from their cornfields, but gradually the Indians increased again. They were obligated to work one day a week for the owner of the land on which they lived and planted, but that was not too arduous. Six months of labor would produce the thirty bushels of corn to feed a family and another thirty bushels to barter for salt, cloth, and gunpowder.

It was only after independence—when the former colonies, free of Spain's restrictive rules, could grow sugarcane and other crops—that labor on some haciendas became unremitting for those Indians who had gone into debt during a time of famine or need and thus became virtual slaves.

During the sporadic separations and wars with Mexico after independence, Santiago Iman, a captain in the militia, promised the Indians that if they'd join him against the Mexican forces, he'd put an end to the obventions or payments they had to make to the Church. Iman armed the Indians who answered his appeal and Yucatán drove the last Mexican troops from the state in 1840.

"Strange things went on," said Zane. "Yucatán even hired three ships of the Texas Navy to patrol the waters between the peninsula and the Mexican mainland. Did you know that?" Not waiting for her reply, he continued. "It would have been Texas—it was then, had been ever since the Texans defeated Santa Ana in 1836 and gained their freedom from Mexico."

Mercy nodded, smiling as she bit back the impulse to inform this arrogant man that she knew the history of her own state very well, indeed.

"Well," Zane went on, undeterred, "when Santa Ana returned from his defeat in Texas, he sent an expedition to Yucatán. So, once again, the Indians were given promises—a lower Church tax, the gift of new lands—if they'd help fight the Mexicans. They did. It was at this point that the Texas Navy was hired to harass the Mexican fleet. With this help, the Yucatecans successfully fought off a forcible takeover by Mexico. Shortly afterward, however, due to the economic realities, I guess, the Yucatecan leaders felt compelled to send a commission to make peace and arrange for an advantageous reunion with Mexico."

Zane shook his head. "And for that," he continued, "everyone was happy—except the Indians, who never got the land they had been promised. But then, during the Mexican-American War in 1846, Yucatán became angry at Mexican indifference to its exposure to the American fleet, and again there was revolt against Mexico."

"No!"

"Yes. And once again the Indians were promised land, lowered taxes, and given guns. Native troops helped take Tekax and Peto from Mexican troops and then took Valladolid in January, 1847, running amok and slaughtering civilians. That was when the Indians first tasted blood—some say quite literally that they ate human flesh during the sacking. They knew they could fight, knew they could win. They began to ask why they should fight *ladino* battles for promises that were never kept."

"Small wonder."

Zane nodded. "Mayan leaders took counsel and sent to Belize for guns. While trying to track them down, government forces looted and burned the ranch of one of the leaders near Tepich. A white officer violated a twelve-year-old Mayan girl, the first rape of thousands to occur during the war.

"A few days later Indians killed every one of Tepich's score or so of white families, making exception only for rape in retaliation for what was done to the Indian child at the ranch. Then the *ladino* troops took the village and burned it, killing the Indians, defiling their shrines, and filling the well with stones. That was the start of the War of the Castes, and the fate of Tepich was repeated bloodily in many other towns and villages."

"Of course I've heard of the Mexican-American War,"

said Mercy, "but I didn't know about the other war till we got to Yucatán."

"And I'm sure you didn't know that in 1848 Yucatán's Governor Santiago Mendez sent letters to Spain, the United States and Great Britain, offering 'domination and sovereignty' over the state to the first power willing to help Yucatán put down the rebels."

"Incredible!"

"Incredible politics is the rule in Yucatán," Zane said wryly. "When Mendez's offer wasn't accepted, he resigned and the new governor hit on the profitable idea of selling Mayan captives into Cuban slavery, a practice that continued for years, and the Mayas sold were often peaceful—easier to catch than the rebellious ones. Through all this you must remember that most of the rebels were *huits,* or 'loincloths'—Mayas who still lived pretty independently in the wilds. The subjugated Mayas who'd served the *ladinos* for centuries in towns and haciendas didn't join the Cruzob and were often slaughtered along with their white masters."

Mercy glanced at Mayel. Did the girl know all this, or did she only remember garbled half-mythical stories of Jacinto Canek? And Vicente, who served so silently and well—behind that smooth, dark face, what was he thinking?

The woods grew denser and in places the branches thrust so low that they had to dismount and lead their animals. Mercy was never sorry to do this. Her mare had a jolting, ragged gait, and Mercy was even stiffer and sorer this last day than the one before. She welcomed the distraction of the blackbirds calling, "What chee-e-er!" And orioles flashed through tall ceibas, while humming-birds flashed blue, green, and purple as they flew here and there.

Golden cassia shone like a yellow blaze through the forests, and Zane told Mercy that the tree that stood out against the green with its dark red bark was called the *indio desnudo,* or "naked Indian." Everywhere were orchids growing high in the trees, some a brilliant yellow, others red or blue, while air plants, looking like upside-down pineapple stalks, flaunted red and blue flowers.

She pulled in her breath in delight at the sight of a handsome bird perched on a breadfruit tree, swinging two long tail feathers that were striped most curiously from about halfway down to right above the fan-like flaring tips. Its frog-like croak contrasted with its beautiful colorings of green, blue, and turquoise.

"Is that a quetzal?" Mercy inquired.

Zane shook his head. "They're found only in the high cloud forests. You're looking at a mot-mot. But we do have several kinds of birds with the green and red coloring of the quetzal, though they lack the fantastic tail plumes and rather bushy head and wings. Look at that iguana sunning itself on the big rock yonder!"

Mercy couldn't discern the creature till it moved its head and shifted the four-foot-long reptilian body that blended perfectly with the grayish-white limestone outcropping.

"They may crash down from trees where they've climbed after birds or eggs," said Zane. "But they're completely harmless and very good to eat."

"People eat snakes, too," said Mercy, shuddering. "But I've never cared to try it!"

"Wait till you're hungry," Zane said and grinned.

They rested for an hour that afternoon. In spite of weariness, Mercy could scarcely stay quiet. What would La Quinta be like? Could she make a place there for herself? Most of all, what would Jolie be like? Mercy was much more concerned with these questions than with safety from Cruzob raids.

Glancing at Mayel, she thought the girl looked forlorn. Mayel had refused to fit the mold of hacienda life, but it had been familiar and she could have no more idea than Mercy of what La Quinta would offer of joy and grief. Their eyes met. Mercy smiled, trying to promise wordlessly that she'd look after the girl. Mayel dimpled, relaxed, and burrowed her head against Mercy's arm, the mirror still gripped in one hand, but there was no one to whom Mercy could turn for reassurance. If she voiced her doubts, Zane could say, truthfully, that he'd given her every chance to choose a different course and that now she must make the best of it.

Philip's handsome, reckless face flashed through her mind. What kind of man was he, to gamble away his wife and leave her to whatever use her owner decided? Anything, anything at all, was better than being married to someone capable of that!

Sunset threw a red tint over the arched stone gate carved with the name of the hacienda. Through it, Mercy caught her first glimpse of the white stone house with arches running its length. A small chapel, with its bell and cross, stood to the left, with a row of stone buildings between it and the approach to the house. To the right was another long stone structure divided into what seemed to be storerooms and a commissary, and beyond these were other buildings and yards separated from the main house by breadfruit trees and coconut palms.

A huge ceiba dominated the center of the front grounds. It was ringed by carved stones piled several feet high, and the ground in the raised bed was covered with marigolds. Walks of pebble mosaics led from it to the house and in the other three directions. An old Indian at the gate ran out to kiss Zane's hand. Several boys, responding joyously to Zane's greeting, took charge of the mules while other followed toward the house.

Suddenly, as Zane rode under the ceiba, a small human form hurled itself precariously down into his arms, startling the horse so that it went dancing, but neither Zane nor his impetuous welcomer seemed to care.

"Papa! Papa! I thought you'd never come!" Winding brown, thin arms around him, the child hugged him with ecstatic force, her golden head close to his dark one. "Did you bring me something? Show me!"

Getting off his horse, Zane laughed with so much love and pride that tears stung Mercy's eyes. Her own father had once hugged and loved her like that, but never again ... never again. She would never even see his grave.

"I brought you a lady," Zane told his daughter, reining so that Mercy could come level with them. "Doña Mercy, this is Jolie. Jolie, Doña Mercy will teach you all you need to know about growing up, and she will do your lessons with you."

Violet eyes stared at Mercy with such adult, feminine antagonism that Mercy inwardly recoiled. It was as if the girl's mother was present in that look. It was a relief to hear a child's voice speak pettishly.

"I don't want to grow up, Papa! And I like to do lessons with you! Just with you!"

"I've taught you all I know," he joked, apparently untroubled by her reaction. They had reached the house now. He sprang down easily, gave Jolie a final hug, and set her down before he helped Mercy to dismount. Then he said a few words to Vicente, who nodded and took Mayel through an archway at the side of the house.

Jolie claimed her father's hand as soon as he stepped back from assisting Mercy. She almost dragged him up the broad flight of stone steps. Mercy followed, admiring the plants and vines that grew in urns or stone troughs placed by the arches and against the walls of the tiled veranda, though only humorous self-mockery kept her from shedding a few hasty tears behind Zane's broad back.

Jolie didn't like her—she wouldn't have liked anyone who threatened her complete possession of Zane. So there went the fanciful dreams of a child pathetically eager to be mothered and loved. May as well embrace a cactus! Jolie shot a challenging, curious look over her shoulder.

Mercy met it directly and dropped one eyelid in a slow, deliberate wink. Jolie scowled, turned around, and walked faster.

I'll still be here when you turn around, Mercy thought. *You may not love me, but you'll learn some things.* She thought even more vehemently: *And so will your father!*

6

There were four great doors opening into the house, each carved with a tree, and an arched center entrance of wrought iron leading to a narrow courtyard that ran back to a joining wall at the end. Doors opened off this garden court, and as Zane motioned for Mercy to precede him through the gate, a stately woman stepped from the last door on the right.

Appetizing cooking aromas came with her. Graying hair was plaited into a thick, single braid, and her loose white dress was spotless, worked with green at the neck and hem. Her broad face lighted up at the sight of Zane, who swept her close and kissed her cheek, speaking a few sentences in Spanish before he turned to Mercy.

"Chepa was my nurse. She's housekeeper now and oversees all the running of the house, though she also does most of the cooking herself. She'll take you to your room and see that you have whatever you need. We'll dine in an hour." He spoke slowly to the older woman. "Chepa, this is Doña Mercy."

Chepa's black eyes flicked to Jolie's annoyed face, then rested on Mercy with vigilant intentness. *What will you be to us?* inquired that anxious, though wise and steady, gaze. *Do you bring La Quinta a blessing or a curse?*

"Welcome," she said and crossed the tree-shaded court to a door next to the one Zane was now opening, with Jolie still clinging to him.

The room was exactly right for its furniture, large enough to hold without crowding a tall chest, an armoire, a velvet cushioned chair with a matching footstool set near a small bookshelf with a reading lamp, a washstand behind a red-and-gold-lacquered screen that also sheltered a copper hip bath, and the most beautiful bed Mercy had ever seen.

The headboard's deep Oriental curves built to a graceful peak, and the red lacquer was designed with intricately delicate golden tendrils, flowers, and birds. The coverlet was crimson, quilted with golden leaves. There were no pictures, but a large oval mirror framed in red and gold hung over the washstand, and gold and red flowers were painted in a border around the doors, one large window. and at the top of the white walls, the colors mellowed with age.

"Water," said Chepa, signaling that she would have it brought for the tub and stand. "You . . . want . . . what?"

"Gracias. Agua is *todos."*

There was going to be a weird mix of Spanish, English, and Mayan around here, but instead of sniggering at her effort, Chepa looked pleased and seemed to search for words.

"Welcome," she said at last, again.

"Gracias," said Mercy.

A boy came with her packs just as two young women brought pails of water. They filled the porcelain ewer on the stand and poured the rest of their sparkling burden into the tub, standing so they could watch Mercy from beneath their eyelashes. Both wore flowers in their shining hair and looked like flowers themselves, with bright embroidery edging their white shifts.

The moment they were outside the door, Mercy could hear them giggling and chattering. No doubt she looked strange and hampered to them in her full skirts and long sleeves. *Also grubby!* she thought, catching her reflection in the mirror. She took her dresses and one cloak from the pack, hung them in the armoire in the hope that some wrinkles would fall out before dinner, and, with a sigh of anticipation, stepped behind the screen to undress.

Glowingly clean after soaping, rinsing and toweling, Mercy put on her last clean drawers, chemise, and petticoat. One of her first sewing tasks must be to make new underthings. Hers were patched and mended till patches and thread, not the original cloth, held them together.

The blue calico dress was less wrinkled than her gray poplin. She slipped into it and wore her old black shoes, because any of the fine new footwear Zane had purchased would make the gown look even more faded. She brushed her hair, promising to wash the travel dust out of it tomorrow, coiled it high on her head, and told herself that at least she was clean and neat.

It didn't take long to put away her things. She hesitated over the little carvings, then ruefully tucked the pheasant, deer, and jaguar into a drawer. Jolie would scorn presents now and any clear overtures. Her confidence would be painfully won, if at all.

Mercy didn't know where dinner would be served, but she decided there was nothing wrong in exploring a bit. Opening the other door, she found herself in a hall that ended with a door just beyond her room. There was another door between her room and a wide arch leading to what appeared to be a large and spacious sitting room. Across the hall were two other doors. Mercy neither saw nor heard anything. Stepping back inside her room, she went out through the courtyard.

Good cooking aromas tantalized her. Those, along with a hum of muffled laughter and talk, must have come from the kitchen. Mercy knew this wasn't the time to get acquainted there. She walked to the entrance and stood on the long porch. It was twilight. The storerooms and commissary were dark, but lamps shone from the opposite row of buildings. Like a guardian, the great ceiba bulked against the distant walls and gate.

"Are you glad the journey's over?"

Mercy whirled at Zane's voice. He stood in the entrance of the right side of the house, silhouetted against the glow of a lamp on a desk. Bookshelves lined the walls, there was a long trestle table littered with books and periodicals, a huge leather chair, and a jumble of pipes on the stand beside it. It was clearly Zane's lair, his office and place of relaxation.

She couldn't see his expression, but his tone had a note of sympathy, or Mercy's need made her imagine it did. So far from home, from her people, language, and places she understood—but she'd been betrayed by her husband, her last link to the past. And it *was* past. Elkanah lay in Pennsylvania's soil, their land was sold—there was nothing to go back to.

Yet she missed the common history, shared opinions, and familiar places. If Philip had been willing, they could have made a future, forged strong again the links broken by war. That was over now, though. She was bound to this man she couldn't see, whose face was hidden in the shadows, but whose body called to her, this man who seemed to have only bitterness and contempt for women he might desire.

She loved this man.

But he mustn't know that—not now. He would use her and throw her aside. Someday, perhaps, if he came to trust her, she might win something from him beyond casual lust. If he loved her, she wouldn't care that much about marriage vows. What she couldn't endure would be for him to use her till he grew tired of her, only to defuse sexual need, and deny her any part of his thoughts and heart.

"I'm glad the traveling's over," she said, then risked some of the truth with a shaky laugh. "It's like falling down a well and hitting bottom. I'm a little dazed."

She knew the moment she'd said it that it was an unfortunate simile. "So you're trying to find a way out?"

"No! I just meant that I'm groping, trying to find out where I am, what I can do."

"You needn't fly into it all at once." He sounded almost kind. "Get acquainted with Jolie and Chepa, have the women start sewing those dresses, and look over my books and see what can be used for Jolie. For a classroom, you might want to have what was my room when I was a boy. It's right across the hall from yours, and there's a globe, atlas, and many of my old books."

"Did you have a tutor?"

"Father sent me to a Virginia military academy for two years starting when I was twelve. I couldn't stand it any longer than that, so I made sure my teachers couldn't, either." He grinned and the light from the window caught his turned face, giving her a heart-stabbing glimpse of the handsome, high-spirited boy he had been. "I got most of my education from a staved-up prelate friend of my father's, a renegade priest who taught me Latin and Greek and history when he wasn't clutching a bottle or a woman."

"What a preceptor!"

"He married a mestizo beauty in Valladolid and died defending her and their baby during the first sacking of the town."

There was nothing to say to that. It seemed that all things here came back sooner or later to the war, just as in her own country. At least a generation would have to die before some of the horror and grief and hatred could subside.

Zane changed the subject, as if he, too, wanted to forget constant looming threats and bitterly mourned losses. "If you need help with your little waif, Chepa can talk to her, but, of course, the sooner you can speak both Mayan and Spanish, the better. I've put Mayel in a small room next to Chepa's behind the kitchen so she'll be available when you want her."

If Mercy was fearful and uncertain, what must Mayel be? She knew the language and Chepa seemed kind, but such a young girl must surely feel lost and very alone. Mercy resolved to look in on her after dinner and let her know someone cared about her.

"Thank you," Mercy said.

Silence deepened between them. She grew tremblingly aware of the magnetism—the male energy and force—that radiated from him in an aura that touched her own. Did he feel it, too? Surely he must! And though it was primitively physical, there was more to it than that—a wild elemental clash of powers seeking to fulfill themselves, seeking to merge, to create a new identity.

"When I've seen to urgent matters, I could show you some of the countryside," he said. "There's a little village not far from here with a Mayan priestess and quite a remarkable hidden wellspring known for its virgin water."

"Virgin water?"

"Water from cave drippings or deep, secret sources. It's hard to find, so, like blood, it makes an acceptable offering to the spirits."

Zane strode to the edge of the tiled porch and looked out over his inheritance, hands behind his back, shoulders hunched slightly forward. "What," he said abruptly, "do you think of Jolie?"

Startled, Mercy searched for an honest but inoffensive reply. "She's beautiful."

A gesture of his hand dismissed that. "I know well enough how she looks."

"She seems to have a high intelligence."

He nodded encouragingly. "You'll find she does." He waited. There'd be no dodging his intent.

Mercy lifted her chin and took a few deliberate breaths. "Jolie seems spoiled, selfish, and absolutely of no mind to learn anything from me!"

Spinning around, Zane caught Mercy's hands and brought them to his lips in a laughing salute. "Good! If you can be both tough-minded and truthful, you have a chance with the little imp! She can twist me around her little finger in spite of my resolves, and Chepa is as helpless."

"I can't do much with her if you don't support my authority."

"I'll support you." His tone was surprisingly grim. "If she doesn't learn some discipline and patience, she'll be just like . . ." He broke off, but Mercy was sure he feared the child might be like her self-indulgent and faithless mother.

A bell rang and he motioned for her to precede him into the courtyard.

Dinner was served on a terrace at the back of the house, entered from the center court. The paving extended to four large trees, reaching in crescents halfway around them. A door from the kitchen opened onto this porch and another was at the far end, but there was a long expanse of white plastered wall and on it was a fresco, lit now with twining leaf sconces.

In brightly painted relief, a tree gripped a fearful monster in its roots, while its trunk was level with men hunting and planting corn and women spinning cotton and patting tortillas while children played among flowers and butterflies. Above this terrestrial scene, the branches spread and on either side were patron figures with a great sun above all.

"That represents the Mayan creation myths," said Zane.

"It's lovely," Mercy responded, utterly beguiled.

"It's silly fairytales and super . . . superstition!" Jolie

tugged at her father's arm. "Let's eat, Papa! I got so hungry, but I waited for you!"

"You've gone to bones!" he gasped, squeezing a chubby arm. "Quick, then! Sit down before you faint!"

He assisted her into a chair scaled to her size, chuckling, but her golden eyebrows knit furiously and she looked on the verge of tears.

"Don't treat me like a baby!" She darted Mercy an edged glance. "I don't like it in front of strangers!"

Zane's indulgent smile faded. "Doña Mercy isn't a stranger, Jolie."

"To me she is!"

Except for coloring, father and daughter looked very much alike as their wills clashed. Their mouths hooked down in the same fashion and the angle of their eyebrows was identical.

"I knew you needed someone to teach you manners," Zane said to the small mutineer. "I'd no idea how much! Now, you will beg Doña Mercy's pardon."

Mercy felt a tug of sympathy for the embattled rebel. "I'm a stranger," she said, "but I won't be for long."

Neither Zane nor Jolie responded to her smile. "Apologize," ordered Zane.

Jolie hung her head, her lower lip trembling, though it thrust doggedly forward.

"Oh, Zane, it's not important!" Mercy protested.

"Allow me to decide that. Jolie?"

"What if I don't?"

"By God!" Zane rocked back, between laughter and exasperation. "You young hellion, you have the gall to sit there and ask?"

"You never spank me," said Jolie in a matter-of-fact tone. "If you send me to bed without supper, I'll starve myself all week and you'll beg me to eat! So what will you do?"

Zane looked thunderstruck at this cool appraisal, but he had the sense to refuse idle threats. "Maybe I'll *do* nothing," he said, "but I'll be displeased with you, and very much ashamed."

Her shoulders hunched, Jolie was silent for a long moment.

"Doña Mercy," she said in a whisper, not looking up, "I beg your pardon."

Mercy wished she dared to put her arms around the

child, but the proudly stubborn set of the whole strong little body forbade any such gesture.

"Please, let's forget it," she said. But from the grim look on Zane's face as he seated her and from the way Jolie kept her eyes lowered, she knew it would be a long time, if ever, before Jolie forgot.

It was an uncomfortable meal. Zane, probably with wisdom, made no effort to woo or make up with his daughter, and he ignored her refusal of all the food except for some delicious-smelling turkey. This, Zane explained to Mercy, was pit-roasted in a native way that was also used with deer, small pigs, and iguanas.

"You may want to watch Chepa make *pibil* one day," he said. "It makes even tough meat tender and is a perfect method for cooking on a hunt or journey if one has the time."

There were yams, small, succulent green-corn tamales, tortillas, and crusty rolls. For dessert they had thin pumpkin seed cakes glazed with honey.

Chepa herself had brought the turkey, still nested on the steamed banana leaves in which it had apparently been cooked.

"How did you know I was coming in time to make *pibil?*" he had asked her, appreciatively inhaling its fragrance.

"I made deer *pibil* last night," Chepa admitted, smiling. "It can be eaten cold, after all. And if you hadn't come tonight, I had a young pig selected for tomorrow. Shall you, the master, not have a good meal when you return from a journey?"

"The meals are always good," Zane assured her.

"This bad one doesn't think so." Chepa touched Jolie's golden hair, gave her a sharp glance when the girl stared at her plate, then moved off to the kitchen with a regretful lift of her shoulders. Chepa, evidently, was used to Jolie's temper.

A graceful young woman Zane called Soledad served the other foods and cleared everything away before fetching the pumpkin seed cakes and foamy hot chocolate. Jolie made up for her earlier abstentions by consuming three cakes and two cups of the rich, spiced hot chocolate.

"Bed for you now," said Zane, rising.

"Thank you, Papa, but I can go by myself."

"But . . ."

"I'm not a *young* child anymore." Jolie had a quaint, almost archaic, manner of speech that probably came from living with adults and using three languages. Back straight, arms at her sides, she stiffly offered her cheek to be kissed. "Good night, Papa. Good night, Doña Mercy."

They both said good night. She vanished through the gate, small, lonely, gripped by a pride and resentment that seemed too fierce for her.

"I've most deeply offended Her Highness," said Zane, forcing a smile. "But I suppose it is time I stopped tucking her in."

"I'm sorry to have caused trouble."

Zane shrugged. "Clearly, I should have had a woman here years ago, but at first, I . . . well, to be blunt about it, I wanted nothing to do with the whole tribe of adult white females. It's just been the last year, when I had visions of Jolie's growing out of being a child, that I knew I had to get someone."

"You could send her away to school."

"Laugh if you want to, but that would break both our hearts."

It was indeed time for a woman to be at La Quinta, a woman he could love, have a life with when Jolie married. But he seemed utterly set against his own needs, except for the crudest physical gratification. Mercy despairingly believed she might change the daughter's blighting attitude long before she did the father's. He had given all his tenderness and protective love to Jolie. Mercy understood this especially well since her father had done the same with her. As far as she remembered, he'd never thought of remarrying.

Trying to imagine her reaction if Elkanah had brought home a wife, Mercy gave a rueful shake of her head and laughed. "It's hard for a doted-upon daughter to have another woman in the house, even when it's her own mother. I'm sure I'd have made life difficult for any lady my father might have brought in, though by the time he went off to war I was beginning to realize that he needed someone his own age. And, of course, if he were still alive, I'd be delighted now for him to marry."

"There's no question of my marrying." Zane's cold words were a slap.

Mercy flushed. "I . . . I'm aware of that. I only meant that I can sympathize with Jolie."

"That should help, but it won't serve to be soft with

her. She can be as implacable as a tyrant if she senses irresolution."

"A family trait?" Mercy asked sweetly.

Zane stared at her, poured out liqueur, and offered her the tiny crystal goblet. "You may do," he grudged.

"I'll try."

Their eyes met and held. His hand closed over her wrist and pressed warmly against the pulsing so that she felt revealed to him, nakedly exposed by the speeding pounding of her blood.

"It's not too late." His voice was husky, reaching to her depths.

"Too late for what?"

He drew her to her feet. "Let me show you something."

Moonlight whitened paving stones through the walled courtyard, past a fountain, and out among trees that had the unmistakable scent of citrus.

"Lemons, limes, and oranges," said Zane. "In the spring their blossoms perfume everything. Bees go crazy trying to collect all the pollen."

He'd kept her hand in his, her arm tucked up through the bend of his elbow. It was wonderful to be close like this. But even while she felt herself expanding, flowering like one of those blooms he'd mentioned, she was afraid this shared moment would end in bitterness.

She wouldn't be his mistress, not unless he loved her.

They passed the orchard, a row of coconut palms, and struck a path leading into thick woodlands where the moon couldn't reach. Zane knew the way, though, and he drew her along.

In ten minutes they stood in a clearing and Mercy stared at a curious square tower no more than twenty feet high, with dark windows facing them like blind eyes.

"Come," urged Zane, drawing her across the eerily lit open space and inside the building.

He let go of her, fumbled for a moment, and struck a match, quickly lighting a small Phoebe lamp. The soft yellow glow illuminated a large, low-ceilinged room with a circular staircase winding up the center. There was a fireplace, an open-faced cupboard with a few glazed plates and mugs, a small, flower-carved trestle table and bench, and over by a window were two chairs and footstools.

The round table between them held a lacquered tray with a decanter and lacquered cups. The floor was stone, but bright straw mats softened it. The air was musty but not unpleasantly so, for in the damp smell of disuse lingered a wistful trace of roses.

Zane lit a candle, handed it to Mercy, and indicated the stairs. "Have a look."

Lifting the hem of her skirt, she ascended with care, for there were no banisters and the stone steps narrowed to a point at the end so that she could step only on the broader part. The staircase was designed to be a support for the second story, around which her candle flickered as she stepped onto solidly hewn planking, caught in a breath of wonder.

The high chamber looked Moorish, sparsely furnished, yet luxurious. Long narrow windows had the squared-off arch distinctive of Mayan architecture, because, Zane had explained, they never learned how to make a full arch and instead built converging sides as close together as possible and then closed the tip with a flat piece. The walls were stark white except for floral traceries around the windows, but the ceiling was painted in brilliant geometric designs, with a predominance of purple, dark green, and azure radiating out from a many-petaled flower in the center.

A couch was positioned directly beneath the flower, covered with purple silk and bolsters and cushions of every color. Spotted hides were scattered around the floor. There were several beautifully carved chests, a stand built to hold a large onyx washbasin and brazen ewer, and an airy, high-backed wicker chair cushioned with turquoise velvet.

The high chamber was for the bed, and the bed was for love. Feeling Zane close behind her, Mercy felt as if her blood were slowing, heavy as molten gold. Her breath came quick and short, seeming not to reach her lungs, turning her dizzy, faintingly weak.

"If you'll be my woman," Zane said, and his voice seemed to come from far away, strained and odd, as if he, too, were having trouble with breathing, "you could live here and I'd supply whatever you wanted for a pastime —books, a horse, music, or painting equipment."

"And Jolie?"

His long mouth tightened. "I'll find another teacher for her, someone older and plain. Why waste you on her when she's going to fight you every inch and detest you for the reasons that make you so desirable to me?"

"But you say you haven't found anyone who'll come here."

"I haven't tried that hard. Now that I see how spoiled Jolie's getting, I'll get a suitable dragon if I have to advertise in the New Orleans papers."

"You wouldn't want me to see Jolie?"

"You'd have a housekeeper. There'd be no need for you to be at La Quinta."

"You mean that you don't want your mistress besmirching your daughter."

He scowled. "It can't distress you to avoid a trying and perhaps impossible task. I'm no sentimentalist. My daughter's behavior can only make her distasteful to you."

"Working with her was the position I accepted when I refused Mr. Kensington's proposal."

"I told you flatly there's to be no proposal—of marriage—from me."

"And you promised not to force me into your bed."

"I'm not forcing you." He laughed suddenly and his eyes shone incandescent. "You want me. Your breasts hurt, don't they? I can take that ache away with my mouth; I can pierce that inflamed swelling so you'd be honey-sweet and peaceful and sleep happier and sounder than ever in all your life." He didn't touch her, but his voice and eyes burned into her depths. "Why deny what you want, too? You'll have a luxurious life and I'll be generous. When you go back to the States, it can be as a well-to-do woman."

"And I can open an elegant brothel like many a retired whore?"

For a moment she thought he would strike her, and she willed herself not to flinch. "I wouldn't advise it. Some goaded customer would slit your lovely throat ear to ear!"

Bowing sardonically, he stood back to let her descend. "This is where you lodge your paramours?" She couldn't keep from asking the question.

"It's none of your damned business, but I've only kept one woman here, and she wasn't mine."

Jealousy flared in Mercy. She pictured another woman on that couch, smiling at Zane with outstretched arms and a compliant body. "A nun, I suppose!"

"Very near it. She's Xia, the priestess in the village that I mentioned before."

"And you made that tower for her?" Mercy asked in a disbelieving tone.

"In daylight you'll see how ridiculous that is," Zane said with a harsh laugh. "The tower is part of an ancient ceremonial site that spread over several miles. My father rebuilt it and kept his concubines there after my mother died, but I've had no such use for it myself. Nor, in case you're wondering, have I used the women of La Quinta. A few nights in Tekax have always cured my restless seasons."

"Then I wonder why you'd risk the possible difficulties of having a mistress you couldn't just use, pay, and forget till the next one of your seasons."

"I'm not a young stallion to go rutting off when the devil drives me. The convenience of having a woman close at hand rather than a day's ride away is beginning, I'll admit, to counterbalance my liking for solitude, but not," he added grimly, "to the extreme that I'll marry, in case you hope to price yourself up to that!"

If you loved me, that would be enough. Nothing else is, unless you do.

"I'd hate the life you offer," Mercy said. "I'd be doing nothing useful, existing only for your . . . diversion. No amount of money or luxury could make such a waste of myself worthwhile."

He stared at her, shock changing to mockery as his long mouth quirked. "And what was the mystic and high purpose you fulfilled in marriage with Philip Cameron?"

Stung but unsubdued, Mercy snapped, "I learned that I need more than to be some man's convenience! Wouldn't the prospect of only"—she cast around for some withering description—"standing at stud disgust you?"

"Doña Mercy!"

"Wouldn't it?" she pressed.

"I'd enjoy a chance to find out." His eyes danced, the cleft deepened in his chin, and he looked younger than she'd yet seen him.

"Not if that was all you could do. A married woman at least has a house to take care of, cooking, and usually children. Her time can be full and useful. Your mistress needs to be a stupid, sloth-like creature who could spend all day sleeping or preening. No woman of intelligence or ability would live in such a harem-like manner."

"You," he said grimly, "make the virtues of a stupid,

91

sloth-like, but amiable mistress shine by comparison! You stole your tongue from an adder! One might as well take a thorn bush to bed. So go to your virtuous sleep, madam, but take this with you!

He crushed her to him, ground her breasts cruelly against his hard body, forced his loins against hers, and took her lips savagely, bruisingly, thrusting his tongue deep into her mouth. From struggling futilely, she went limp, supported only by his arms, ravished by the onslaught till, if he had thrown her on a bed, she could not have resisted.

As she went softly and yielding, his hands gentled and his lips moved over hers so softly that she trembled. "Good night," he said, drawing away, steadying her till she had control of herself again. "As soon as you've settled in, you may start pursuing your Calvinistic ideal of duty and work. I wish you joy in it!"

He bowed, his dark hair falling over his forehead so that she longed to push it back, turned abruptly, and strode to a door opening off the veranda.

Her hand going to her lips which still felt the force of his, Mercy fought back tears. Why? Why was he so obstinate?

Was he so mulish he'd never admit he craved a single mistress to give him the security and closeness he'd failed to find in marriage but could never find with casual, infrequent couplings?

He wanted closeness without risk, the solace of love with none of the pain. He wanted to be the center and source of a woman's life, and to pay for that in money and things.

Not with me, Mercy vowed, not with me.

But she knew if he really chose to use a little force, break down her defenses as he had just done minutes ago, he could have her.

Once.

If that does happen, if he does take me—and God knows he can if he's ruthless, for I love him and my body cries for his—then I must go away. To live as he wants me to in that tower would destroy the person that I want to be. His slave I may be, but I won't be his body servant!

Mercy thought of going to see how Mayel was, but there were no lights in the rooms behind the kitchen. The girl must be asleep.

And Jolie? Had she cried that night with self-pity and

hate for an interloper? What would happen if she remained adamant, refusing to be friends?

Mercy sighed. Journey's end. She was at the center, the fifth direction, and what would happen now?

7

Mercy awoke to a presence and saw Mayel, golden in the light that streamed through the window. The girl had the yellow ribbon at the back of her hair, and the shine in her large, dark eyes made her look like a different person from the whipped, rebel debt-slave of two mornings ago. She put a tray with a covered pot, cup, and crisp, sweet bread on the bedside table.

"*Buenos días,* Doña Mercy."

"*Buenos días,* Mayel." Mercy searched for words. "*Como estas?*"

There followed a torrent of words and gestures, none of which Mercy understood, except for "*buenos*" and "*está bien,*" repeated many times. She sighed, realizing again that she must learn two languages before she could enter fully into the life of La Quinta. But there was no mistaking Mayel's happiness. She was like a shrinking thorn plant that had suddenly burst into leaf and flower.

"She says the wonder of La Quinta is what it *doesn't* have," said a scornful voice from the window. Curled into the ledge that was large enough for a bench sat Jolie, her pointed chin digging into her knees, her tousled curls a bright blaze. "There's no jail, no whipping post, no *administrador* or assistant mayordomos, and the *chichan cuenta,* a little bill, is an honest charge that is paid off regularly so that a *nohoch cuenta,* a big bill, doesn't accumulate and make the workers debt-slaves."

"I'm afraid I still don't understand much of that."

Jolie shrugged as if to say Mercy's dullness of wit was no surprise, nor any concern of hers. "Most haciendas are run by an *administrador* who often lives in Mérida or

Campeche or Valladolid, like the owner. He visits the holdings of his employer and sees that the mayordomo is running things at a good profit. The mayordomo lives at a hacienda and sees to its day-to-day operation with the help of overseers called assistant mayordomos. We don't need those. Our people don't have to be whipped, because if they work well, they get wages besides what they charge at the store. They elect their own field bosses, and Macedonio, the mayordomo, and Papa do all the managing."

"But the . . . what did you say? *Nohoch cuenta?*"

Jolie patted back a yawn. "I can't explain it all," she said, swinging off the ledge like a stretching cat. "It's time for my breakfast."

She slipped out of the room, leaving Mercy to wonder how long the girl had been sitting there and watching her. Why was the thought of being watched while asleep so disturbing? Because one was exposed, defenseless?

Mayel pointed to several white native dresses spread on the chest and conveyed by words and gestures that Chepa had sent them for Mercy.

"*Gracias,*" Mercy said and nodded when Mayel glanced at the door, as if asking permission to go.

Propping up pillows, Mercy luxuriated as she slowly nibbled the crisp, sweet bread and sipped hot chocolate. Except when she was sick, it was the first time she'd ever eaten in bed, and though she didn't intend to make it a habit, this morning it was most pleasant to pamper her travel-sore body and savor the spicily delicious drink.

She'd best take comfort where she found it—from this indulgence, from Mayel's joy—for it would be a long struggle to win Jolie, and a different and infinitely harder struggle to keep from being Zane's woman in the tower. In that she had to fight herself. If he had spoken love words to her, wooed her with sweetness, made it more than lust, she'd have succumbed to him last night, even knowing how deadening such a life would be, cut off from normal contacts, devoted to serving only one need of this stormy, complex, terribly cynical man she loved.

She was lucky that he'd been honest. Of course, that was so he wouldn't have to feel guilty or responsible for her, but it showed him to have some conscience. And apparently he was a kind and just master, one who toiled on the place with the men causing his prosperity.

Sipping the last of the hot chocolate, Mercy stretched,

winced, wondered when the numb feeling would leave her buttocks, and got to her feet. Small knives seemed to jab through her legs, thighs, and shoulders. Thank goodness she hadn't had to mount and ride today! Although she loved horses, she didn't care if it was weeks before she got on one again.

She hobbled to the chest, grimacing, and examined the white dresses, fine cotton worked with bright embroidery in broad borders around the skirts, sleeves, and simple round necks. One had flowers, another birds of every color perched among leaves and vines, and on the third shift-like garment fluttered yellow butterflies, some hovering between neck and toe.

With a soft cry of delight, Mercy put two dresses in the armoire and began to dress in the third one.

When she entered the courtyard half an hour later, it was with shyness and the fervent hope that she wouldn't encounter Zane till she was more accustomed to the airily loose garment.

Her camisole and drawers slightly distorted its flowing lines. Petticoats would have bunched grotesquely. Mercy was sure native women wore nothing at all under the garment, a stupefying thought that had a forbidden seductiveness when she imagined for a second how comfortable and free that would make her.

Utterly shameless, too! It was all very well for women who were used to such unrestricting ease, but, even with her vestigial undergarments, Mercy felt naked, nervous without yards of material swathing her legs, without the confining tightness at the waist, throat, and shoulders.

Feet were another matter, though. She wiggled her toes happily in the sandals that had been placed near the dresses. As a child she had gone barefoot with her father's approval, though visiting ladies had warned her that her feet would spread to the "size of a fieldhand's," and during the war it had been no privation to be shoeless in warm weather. Sandals were an item of native dress she could eagerly adopt, and she added them to hot chocolate, the sweet breads, and fresh tortillas as admirable features of this new life.

Hesitating in the sun-splashed courtyard, she decided to let Chepa know she wouldn't need more breakfast. Then she should go to Zane's library-office and see what was suitable for Jolie's lessons. Surely, after an absence, he'd be out looking over his fields and attending to anything urgent that had come up. Mercy wished for him to see her in the charming butterfly dress, yet she dreaded the way she was sure his gaze would go through the cloth and make her nipples stiffen and thrust against the butterfly wings. . . .

She mustn't think that way! It was hard enough to hold him off with her whole will set on it. She couldn't, if she let herself dream of him, live through in memory her response to his alternately cruel and tender mouth, his hard, overpowering body.

Forcing him from her mind, she moved quickly toward the kitchen, called a greeting, and was welcomed at once by Chepa, who smiled at the dress.

"Muy bonita." She looked approvingly at the way Mercy had drawn her hair back from her face and knotted it low at the back in a semblance of the Yucatecan style.

Mercy thanked her for sending the clothes and breakfast, using as much Spanish as she could while Chepa suggested, supplied, or corrected words. Then she decided to give Mercy a lesson, touching utensils or other objects and giving their Spanish names.

The kitchen was a large room with a fireplace, several long tables, wall niches ornamented with copper luster pitchers, and open cupboards that held handsome glazed blue-and-white stoneware. An array of utensils that looked like a torturer's equipment hung from cast-iron hooks. One wall shelf, incised with floral designs, held an assortment of objects somewhat resembling narrow-handled mallets with decorated round tops.

"Molinillos," Chepa said. Taking one down, she placed it in a pan and twirled it briskly. "Makes hot chocolate good."

So that was how it got that wonderful frothiness! Mercy decided to learn the trick, but not today. Chepa was busy, and, besides, Mercy was eager to see the rest of the house and as much as possible of the hacienda. Still, she had a last thing to express.

"Mayel happy *aquí*," she said. *"Muy, muy bien!"*

"Mayel look like daughter of me." Chepa's eyes grieved for a moment. "Daughter dead."

"Oh, I'm sorry!"

"Last, youngest child," said Chepa, "like *mariposa.*" She touched an embroidered butterfly on Mercy's shoulder. "Your papa and mama with the good God?"

96

Elkanah would have snorted at that question from a minister, but not, Mercy thought, from this aging, simple woman who remembered so wistfully a flown-away butterfly daughter.

"Yes," she said.

"Then heart not ache for home. You like room?"

"It's . . . *bonita!*"

Chepa smiled at what must have been a misuse. "Was of Don Zane's mother."

Mercy was glad to hear it. She'd hoped it wasn't the faithless Consuelo's, but there was no predicting Zane. She thanked Chepa for showing her the kitchen and went back into the courtyard.

The dining room had a fireplace carved with jaguars at one end, a fine, high chest with many small drawers, more open cupboards gleaming with silver and blown glass, and in the center was an immense table, its trestles carved with deer, javelinas, doves, and pheasants. A dozen chairs, all but two arranged against the wall, had needlepoint cushions and their high backs were carved with the same creatures. The two pulled up to the big table looked lonely. Mercy was glad her first meal had been on the porch.

Outside Zane's office she listened, heard nothing, then came softly around to peer in the window fronting the veranda. She jumped and smothered a shriek as a warm, long hand gave her bottom what was almost a pat.

"Too tempting to resist," chuckled Zane. "When you lean forward, you elevate your . . . uh . . . interesting portion in a most revealing way."

"No gentleman would . . . "

"Have I ever claimed to be a gentleman?" His white teeth flashed in his tanned face. Her flesh still glowed from that brief, fleeting pressure. "I'm a pirate's son, remember! Do you like your Indian smock? I was thinking of your comfort, but my concern's been even rewarded by a most pleasant sight. It would be even more delightful without those absurd things you have on underneath."

Flushing hotly, Mercy crossed her arms over her breasts, so conspicuously marked by the butterflies, and she wished her heart wouldn't pound till it made those same butterflies rise and fall tempestuously.

"I . . . I'm not here to feed your lascivious fancies!"

"But dear Doña Mercy, how can you prevent it?" His

eyes sparkled. If he'd spent a restless, frustrated night, it didn't show. "Even in those cramping, yet voluminous, dresses you brought from Texas, you could whet a man's appetite. Now that I can actually see the flow of you from shoulders to ankles, don't think I won't be dreaming."

"Dream all you want, but don't touch me!"

Though he didn't move forward, he seemed to loom overwhelmingly close. Mercy stepped back, pleading with a blindly outstretched hand.

He dropped a kiss on it. "Do I frighten you that much?" he asked softly. "Never mind, then. Regain your composure while you look through my books. I must spend the rest of the morning with Macedonio, but perhaps this afternoon you'd like to see the village and learn something about the planting of hemp—that's our major crop."

"Can we walk?"

He stared, then laughed. "Yes, if you'd be more comfortable, I must see if I can find you a smooth-gaited mare for when you recover. We'll have our noon meal on the veranda."

Nodding, he moved off in his long, easy stride, which was deceptively fast. His taut-muscled thighs were slim, but his shoulders were as broad as they could be without seeming out of proportion. His wife must have been a fool to prefer another man, at least on physical grounds, and Mercy felt instinctively that before her treachery embittered him, Zane would have been an excitingly zestful, yet sensitive, lover.

Would he ever be again? Would he ever trust anyone enough?

Absently stroking the curve his hand had touched, Mercy opened the heavy door and went into the library, which smelled fragrantly of tobacco, leather, and books.

A good smell—his smell. Breathing it in, Mercy closed her eyes for a moment, gave herself an admonitory shake and began to read the titles of the books. Some were in Spanish, but most were in English. There was Carlyle, and also Darwin's *Origin of Species,* one of the last books she and Elkanah had read together, discussing its theory of evolution and natural selection, views that had infuriated clergymen, though Elkanah said forthrightly to his Presbyterian friends that he found the faith in a gradual change for the better, considerably more edifying than the doctrine of predestination, with souls damned before they were even incarnate.

Tennyson, Poe, Balzac, Hugo, Dickens, Thackeray, Browning—all the authors one would expect where there was a love of reading, but there were others that surprised her: Walt Whitman's *Leaves of Grass*, which had stirred such commotion; Thoreau's *Walden;* Emerson; John Stuart Mill; and FitzGerald's *Rubaiyat,* this last being one of the few non-medical books Mercy had brought with her.

Finding these books that she had read before was like finding comforting old friends in a totally unexpected place. Mercy touched them lingeringly even as she sorted out books she wanted to read as soon as possible to gain more knowledge of Yucatán.

Bernal Díaz del Castillo's history would have to wait for her to learn Spanish, as would the de Landa and Cogulludo, but she set aside W. H. Prescott's *The Conquest of Mexico* and John Stevens' travels through Yucatán and Guatemala, with the marvelous engravings by Catherwood.

Now, where should she begin with Jolie? Perhaps she would not plan a curriculum until she'd gained some knowledge of Jolie's special achievements. Narrative poetry might be a good start—Longfellow or *Idylls of the King;* or perhaps some of Browning's character portraits. Mercy decided to look over the books in Zane's boyhood room before taking any more from the office, and she was rising from the footstool when something moist, hairy, and pliable poked between her arm and ribs.

Gasping, she sprang up, staring at a narrow-nosed creature the size of a very large cat with a fluffy, dark-ringed tail the length of a rust-colored body poised on stubby legs. Its pert, intelligent face had small, round ears. It made a gently inquiring mewling sound, but it showed neither fear nor aggression.

Mercy, after her first alarm, laughed at the thoroughly winsome, puzzling beast. "What are you?" she asked as it moved its tail gracefully to and fro. "You look like a mix of raccoon, possum, monkey, and cat, with maybe a little anteater thrown in."

"Flora's a coati," said Jolie from the door. "She's very clever and kills snakes." Somewhat hopefully, gauging Mercy, the girl added, "When coatis get angry, they lash

99

their tails and hiss and *leap* with their claws and teeth on whatever has upset them."

"They'd have a hard time leaping without their teeth and claws," said Mercy, smiling. "What a charming animal! Is she grown up?"

"She had four babies last spring and they still live in part of the old ruins out behind the stables. We hope they'll stay and keep the snake population down."

"We had lots of snakes in Texas," Mercy said. "Coatis would be very popular there. Would you like to come to the room your father used to have and see how we can use it for your lessons?"

Jolie didn't answer but trailed along, having picked up the coati, which peered over the child's shoulder while its tail almost brushed the floor.

Leading the way through the large sitting room without giving Mercy a chance to notice more than a massive fireplace and heavy, carved furniture, Jolie went down the hall and opened the door opposite Mercy's. "When I was little and got lonesome, I'd make believe I had a brother who slept here," Jolie said. "And I pretended I had a sister in Grandmother's room."

"You don't pretend anymore?"

"I decided it was nicer to have Papa all for myself." Those violet eyes might have been made of glass, they were so hard. "I got so I didn't mind the empty rooms between us. But I don't like for you to be there."

"No, I'm sure you don't. But there doesn't seem to be another convenient room." *Only the tower in the woods, with its high chamber.* Mercy glanced around the high-roofed cubicle, trying to get some sense of the young Zane.

The high, narrow bed's posters were almost as wide as it was. There was a desk and chair, washstand, and shelves along the wall filled with books, birds' nests, wooden whistles, clay flutes, rattles, and all kinds of objects that must have come from old Mayan sites, things like incense burners, effigies, bowls, and carvings. In one corner stood a sort of drum made of a hollow log with a lengthwise slit in the top, and above the desk hung several bows, quivers of arrows, feathered lances, and a number of machetes and knives.

Mercy sighed. It would be a distracting classroom. She's always be catching glimpses of Zane lugging in some treasure or sprawled on the bed reading or dreaming. But if they put a screen in front of the bed and turned the desk like this, put the globe there . . .

"Don't you go moving Papa's things!" cried Jolie, planting herself and Flora between Mercy and the desk. Flora gave an obliging hiss and swung her tail back and forth.

"Papa will move his own things," said his voice from the door. "You may help, Jolie, or go to your room."

After a second's pout, Jolie put the coati on the window ledge. In short order a screen had been found and the furnishings were shifted, making a small but adequate space for studying. Jolie was thumping idly on the log drum, which even at that level gave out a hollow resonance.

"Go wash," Zane told her somewhat irritably. "And put Flora outside before she breaks something."

Jolie gave the peculiar drum a last tap. "If you don't like this anymore, Papa, why don't you give it to me?"

"And have you call up your fellow rebels?" He grinned. "Hurry, now, or those *panuchos* I smelled will be cold before you get to the table."

"Panuchos!" Jolie ran out with the coati slung over her shoulder like a fur piece. Zane turned to Mercy.

"So you think my old bed should be hidden?" He shook his head, chuckling. "If you knew the dreams I indulged in there in my randy youth, I doubt you'd consent to be in here at all!"

"You seem to have had the usual warrior longings," Mercy said, glancing at the bows and lances.

"More than longings," said Zane. "At sixteen I was actually a captain, fighting alongside Colonel Cepeda Peraza for a return to liberal federalism—a restoration of liberties. This was back in 1853. We took the northeast and captured part of Mérida before we were driven out and had most of our commanders shot. Cepeda survived, however, and is in fact living in Mérida now. Anyway, cholera struck our retreating men, the Mayas had flared up again, and after we stopped their advance, those of us who hadn't died from wounds or the black vomit were glad to go home. Some Mayas who'd fought for us were sold into slavery in Cuba, with the profits going to an old crony of Santa Ana's."

Slavery. War. Plague. Was it the same everywhere? Mercy could think of no response. After a moment, Zane touched the log drum. "Those months cured me of delusions about glorious battle. There was no more time for

101

buglers to play the *oracion* over the dead, only the *ataque* and *deguello*—that means throat-cutting, no quarter. I've heard it was sounded at your own Alamo. But I've heard bugles enough for my whole life. And if I hear one of those drums booming through the forests, it disturbs my sleep for longer than the noise warrants." His gaze touched the books Mercy had selected. "Those will get you off to a good start, though they'll contain nothing of the War of the Castes or the empire. Perhaps it's better to learn about ruins, which have, after all, survived the downfall of Mayan civilization, Spaniards, invading Mexican armies, and constant Yucatecan rebellions."

"Ruins are interesting, but they have no life."

"Well, you'll see the village this afternoon," said Zane. "That'll be reality enough."

"Panuchos!" shouted Jolie.

Zane laughed and stood aside to let Mercy precede him.

Panuchos were plump, fried tortillas filled with beans, shredded turkey, onions, and a bland, green paste that Zane said was avocado. These were delicious but so filling that Mercy could barely finish one, and she declined custard and mangos, content to sip tea.

Jolie started on a second *panucho*, but after a few nibbles she said plaintively, "I'm all full, Papa."

"So, yes, you may take the rest of your *panucho* to Salvador, but don't lure him away from his work and get him in trouble."

Excusing herself prettily in a way that suggested Zane had taught her better manners than he guessed, Jolie hurried off with a second tortilla wrapped around the *panucho* for security and warmth.

"Who's Salvador?" Mercy asked.

"He came close to being a Mayan Christ," Zane said slowly. "It was the most grotesque thing I ever saw—a three-year-old tied to a tree to die while he was worshipped with incense and drunkenness. When everyone was quite drunk, I got him down and brought him here. I tied a branch of copal, the incense tree, in the bonds that held him, so when the village awoke next day a miracle was proclaimed, and that copal branch is displayed to this day on the altar."

"But why would they do such a thing?"

Zane shrugged. "Child sacrifice isn't new among the

Mayas. They offered the gods what was pure, virgin, and after the Spaniards brought their faith of a crucified Lord, a number of children were put to death like that. But Salvador's torment came from different roots. The *maestro cantor* of the village, who surely was insane, thought to create a Mayan savior for his people, and for this he chose the son of his young sister, Xia, who was already skilled in the use of herbs and in giving cures."

"She didn't consent!"

"She was drugged and placed against the foot of the tree. I couldn't interfere while the worship-orgy was going on because I was alone, on a hunting trip, and I would simply have gotten killed without saving the boy. But sometime later I went back and did as I have told you. Then after talking with Xia enough to be sure she loved her child and hadn't agreed to the martyrdom, I told her how I'd taken Salvador and that he was now being fostered by Macedonio and his wife. He doesn't know she's his mother It would mean death for both of them if the villagers found out he didn't turn into a sacred copal branch. Xia's used the reverence paid to her to become a real power in her town. Two years ago her brother died, and I suspect she put him away with poison."

"You sound as if you admire her!"

Raising an eyebrow, Zane considered. "I suppose I do —as one admires any beautiful, deadly thing."

"Is she ... beautiful?"

"Like the rarest orchid." Zane hesitated. "She lived for a while in the tower a few years back when her village was plagued with smallpox and people blamed her for not curing them. When the sickness waned, she returned with enough corn to get the people through the season of no harvest, so she regained her status."

"You gave her the corn."

"There was plenty here. Should I starve people because a madman led them to kill a child?" Zane added gruffly, "It wasn't unselfish. When I'm shorthanded, that's the village where I hire extra workers. I'll take you there some day when you feel like riding." He grinned. "Be sure to act properly impressed if Xia invites you to view the miraculous copal branch."

"It's a great pity when miracles depend on the trickery of men like you!" Mercy retorted.

"But what if there'd been no trickery?"

Mercy couldn't repress a shudder. "I'd rather see Salvador than the copal branch!"

"You'll meet him this afternoon," said Zane. "Come to my office in an hour." He walked with her through the courtyard and left her at her door.

Lying down with a volume of Stevens, Mercy read about his 1843 impressions of Mérida, including a description of a bullfight, and she was grateful Zane hadn't taken her to one. The tale was fascinating, but she caught herself dozing off. The journey had left her weary, as well as stiff.

Rousing guiltily, she saw by the gold-and-red clock on the mantel that an hour had passed. Slipping into the butterfly gown she'd laid across the chest, she decided her hair was passable, so she slipped on sandals and hurried through the courtyard to the veranda, where she almost collided with Zane.

"Rule number one in tropical climate," he chided, laughing as he checked her, "never hurry. You'll just run into those who don't, and you'll all wind up in a heap!"

"I didn't want to be late," she said, flustered even more by the careless way he slipped his hand beneath her arm.

"Are you trying to make me think you're that freak, a conscientious female?"

"Women," she snapped, "would be more responsible if they were given more control over their lives. Why should they be conscientious when legally they're classed with children and lunatics? Men use every method of bribes and coercion to make women feel trivial and then complain because they sometimes are!"

"Yet you cling to your fetters," Zane mocked.

"What do you mean?" Mercy demanded.

"That gown would fit naturally and you'd be more comfortable without those absurd undergarments."

She gasped, blushing, then tried to struggle away from him, but his warm fingers closed more firmly around her bare arm and he smiled jauntily down at her as he brought her through a walk between the main house and the row of buildings on its right.

"At least you've the sense to wear sandals, and I suppose we must make allowances for the strange things women are taught." His dancing, dark gray eyes brushed along her body. "However did you escape corsets?"

"Sir!"

"I'll show you the factory and drying yards later," he said, switching smoothly to business as they came out by a small chapel with a graveyard behind it. Oval white huts with shaggy thatches, almost obscured by vines and bushes, were arranged around a well, with a ceiba tree and cross close by. Pigs squealed, turkeys gobbled, chickens pecked about the clearing, and even at this siesta time a few women were working in patches behind their dwellings. Several burros roamed the common and babies napped in hammocks under thatched shelters attached to the backs of most houses. A large front and back door let Mercy see straight through the houses that had no windows.

"Mayas have made huts like this—of wattle and sticks plastered with lime—since back before the conquest," Zane said. "Materials are always at hand to make another. One reason the Cruzob were hard to defeat was that they could move quickly. Hammocks weigh almost nothing, and they had few clothes or other possessions. They carried corn for food and seed, of course, and as much other food as they could, but they were so poor that this was practically nothing. With a machete, gun, and corn, they could start again almost anyplace."

"Have any of your workers joined the Cruzob?"

"The Cruzob fight mostly as village groups under their local village chiefs, or *batabs*. The only man I know of who went to them married into a Cruzob village, which is unusual in itself. Villagers tend to be clannish and they viewed outsiders with suspicion even before the war."

"What are those little huts near the larger ones?" Mercy inquired.

"Those are for worship. Each family has a personal cross that's handed down to the eldest son and kept in its own shrine. Each cross is dedicated to a saint or to the Holy Cross and is believed to have guardian powers. Some are stronger than others. The cross of some fortunate family may grow so powerful that it becomes the main cross for a whole village."

"It must be a good feeling to have a special guardian."

"The Mayas needs all the help they can get. A drought, rot, or hail can cause starvation. Workers at La Quinta, of course, don't have to depend on their crops to live, but corn is such a holy thing to them that I think they'd grow it even if they didn't need it. They call it Grace of God and believe mankind was created from cornmeal. When priests said that Jesus was the 'bread of life,' it was easy for the Mayas to link him with their own maize deity."

"Does the village exist of itself, or only for the hacienda?"

"It was here when my father raised La Quinta from the stone of ancient ruins. He contracted with the *batab* for laborers, and though most of the men work for me, they are not required to. Most of them are harvesting their main corn crop right now, but when that's done they'll come back to the hemp, or henequén, which requires work all year."

"You get along with the *batab?*"

Zane laughed, skin crinkling at the edges of his eyes. "You bet! Macedonio is a *batab* as well as a mayordomo."

"Convenient."

"It does simplify things. But he was elected by the village, not appointed by me. He won't serve as *batab* for life, and there's a Council of Elders and several assistant *alcaldes* with specific duties. A scribe keeps all the village documents locked in a chest: land treaties, royal grants of common land, quaint, circular painted maps several hundreds of years old, wills, and genealogies. The scribe's supposed to be elected, but since he's the only one who can read and write, he usually holds the post for life and passes it down to his son."

"May I look in the church?"

In answer, Zane escorted Mercy across the village center and into the small church, with its stone floor and crude benches. There was a crucifix at the altar, and along the walls were small shrines with statues of saints so crudely carved and painted that they must have been made locally by someone with more piety and devotion than skill. The exception was a large plaster image of a sweet-faced woman draped in brilliant blue and rose. She had more candles and flowers than all the other saints put together. Zane paused before her with a smile.

"One thing you'll approve of—the main fiesta here is for Santa Yñez in January. She's the village patroness. And *she* has a patron to watch over her offerings and see that her feast is properly celebrated. The patron has twelve helpers to assist in service and guardianship to her,

106

and several other of these saints are potent enough to have their patrons and twelve assistants."

"But it's Santa Yñez who watches over the fifth direction?"

"You remember well," Zane said approvingly. "And every year there is a main fiesta. This one has plenty of liquor, food, music, and fireworks, and when possible there's a bullfight."

Mercy couldn't repress a sound of dismay. Stevens' description of the bleeding, pitiful bulls made her hope she would never have to see such a spectacle. Zane shot her a strange, testing look.

"Never mind. You'll enjoy the dancing, at least. Now, let's go past some cornfields on our way to the henequén fields."

8

The cornfields were scattered in clearings hacked and burned from the wilderness, the stalks growing wherever a seed found enough soil to root in the thin, shallow, rocky earth. A plow would never work here.

"After the proper prayers and offerings," Zane said, "a man takes a pointed stick and makes holes wherever he can. A field uses up its fertility in three years, so the work of cutting a new field is done in one's spare time and the burning of the dried wood takes place in the spring. Tricky business. If the wood's too green, the burn won't be thorough enough to let sunlight reach the planted crop, but if a man waits too long, the rains may start and the wood can't be burned. Generally, the *H-men* predicts the weather and people follow his advice."

"*H-men?*"

"It means 'he who knows.' He can do some curing and foretell the future with grains of corn or sacred stones, but mainly he's supposed to help obtain a good harvest. He may study his Count of Days, which shows cycles of weather and events, but I'm sure he relies more on when flying ants swarm or the frogs croak."

"Do you think that lore came down from the old Mayas?"

"I'm sure it did. Mayan religion is almost totally aimed at producing plentiful crops of corn, and these homespun rites are what linger after the complicated astronomy and theology of the priest kings is forgotten."

"But how did people plant and harvest during the war?"

"As best they could. There was no time to clear and burn fertile new fields, so they had to sow their seed hastily in worn-out soil and hope enough would come up to keep them from starving. Often they had to choose between eating seed corn and starving when there was no crop or going hungry, even starving, while waiting for the corn to grow. And many Cruzob starved, though the fortunate got by on what corn they could salvage, roots, and berries. During the worst times, there was only a little game because it had been hunted close to extinction."

Mercy admired the ripened ears of the stalks, which were higher than her head. "Then a crop like this must make everyone happy."

"Yes, especially since we feel fairly sure the Cruzob won't attack and steal it. After the harvest is in, each man will put up an altar in his field and offer food and drink to the spirits in thanks for the crop. The gods take the vital, spiritual part of the sacrifice, but after the proper prayers, people can feast on the material remains of the offerings."

"That sounds like a system that ought to benefit both gods and worshippers," said Mercy, smiling.

"It's all a part of *tamen,* harmony with heaven, which is the Maya's state of grace. Corn is sacred. Growing it is a religious, as well as practical, act. Grain was sacred, of course, in that without it life on land would cease. The soil that nourished plants was holy, too, then, a first altar. Civilized man got a long way from those simple facts, but he was as ultimately dependent on crops and the animals living off of them as were the Mayas, whose life revolved around the cycles of the buried or resurrected corn."

They walked now along a path worn through weeds and thick growth that was higher than Zane's head. He said it was an old cornfield. No breeze could reach them, and the afternoon sun blazed down almost like summer.

Mercy was glad to come out of the dense, airless field into a vast clearing.

Rows of blue-green agave with broad-bladed leaves tapering to dagger points grew as far as Mercy could see. Machetes flashed as barefooted men with rolled-up white trousers and shirts worked up and down the field, cutting off leaves, trimming the edges, and piling them into bundles that were carried to the ends of rows to be hauled off by mules that pulled carts along a movable track.

"This is henequén," Zane told her. "Each plant has forty-two leaves, and each plant is worked every four months, at which time the twelve largest leaves are cut. A worker must count to be sure he cuts that dozen. Henequén requires year-round attention. Besides collecting leaves, weeds have to be kept out, and there's still the work to be done at the drying yards and factory."

"Is it a profitable crop?"

"Perhaps the best for Yucatán's stony soil. I think it'll eventually be the most important product of the region, but many owners won't try it because it's seven years before the plants can be harvested. That ties up capital for a long time with no return, whereas sugarcane's second year's harvest generally pays all the costs of getting started, and after that it may return annual profits of up to seven hundred percent."

Mercy stared. "Then why doesn't everyone plant sugarcane?"

"Because, sweet Mercy, comparatively little soil is good enough to nourish it." Zane touched a henequén leaf with his boot toe. "*This* can grow almost anywhere, and as trade expands, so will the need for rope and twine."

A wave of premonition swept over Mercy. She thought of what she had heard about some Southern plantations, and she remembered Mayel being whipped.

"You pay your workers," she said. "But if debt-slavery's so common here, won't it increase, and won't the debt-slaves be driven mercilessly, to increase the owner's profit?"

"Once initial costs are recovered, it's easily possible to pay a decent wage," said Zane.

"Possible, but will men who live in Mérida all year care what goes on as long as they have sufficient money to indulge their cultured whims?"

Zane's mouth thinned angrily. "Do you expect me to change human nature? In time, debt servitude will be forbidden, but I find it strange to hear someone from the South so troubled about slaves."

That stung, flicking the raw, proud flesh of Mercy's mingled guilt and defensiveness about her homeland, which she loved, while knowing it had planted the wind of bondage and reaped the whirlwind of defeat and ruin. She turned away, staring blindly.

"I beg your pardon, Mercy." The touch on her hair was so light that she wasn't sure she hadn't imagined it, except that a sort of healing warmth spread through her. "Any person has plenty to account for without being held responsible for the sins of his group or race."

"As long as people are enslaved or killed or despised because of race or group, the other thing follows," Mercy said. "But I won't wear sackcloth and flagellate myself for Simon Legree."

Zane laughed. This time, unmistakably, he did ruffle her hair. "You're expiating your crimes by being Jolie's teacher."

Jarred into the realization that she was indeed a bond-servant, totally dependent on this man's decisions, Mercy moved away from him. That he had so far refrained from physically subjugating her made the way she felt about him all the more dangerous. One could hate and scorn a ravisher. But how to resist a captor whose cage was so spacious and beautiful one never glimpsed the bars, who made her hunger for him till yielding would be even more a giving in to her own desires?

She must fight herself, as well as him. It was easy to think it didn't matter, that such indulgence would harm only herself, and Elkanah was no longer on this earth to care. But to be Zane's plaything, to choose an existence in the tower only to serve his sensual desires and her own—that would be the death of her as a whole person, living and working in the world.

Jolie needed a teacher for many reasons, the least of which was academic. Mayel should know someone cared about her. La Quinta was a small world where Mercy could work and learn. She wanted life, rather than the self-centered, confined enchantment of being a man's isolated mistress.

But if he loved me . . . if he loved me and let me stay at the house and be part of La Quinta . . .

"What a long face!" teased Zane. "This is hard work, true enough, but nothing like plantations using debt la-

110

borers. The stint on those is from two to three thousand leaves a day, and workers are flogged for failing to cut that many, for improper trimming, for being late—for almost anything. That big Chinese coming up the row is Wei, one of the elected foremen. He doesn't beat men, but he checks to see that the trimming is done properly and that the right number of leaves are being cut."

"If workers are treated so badly, you'd expect them to revolt, especially after the War of the Castes."

"The plantation workers are mostly tamed by three generations of servitude. As I told you before, not many of them rebelled. It was the wild backwoods Indians or those who had just recently been forced to serve the *ladinos* who hoped to drive the whites out."

Wei, who towered over the Mayas, came forward, removed his straw hat, and bowed to Zane and Mercy. Zane spoke to him genially, evidently explaining Mercy's presence, for the big man with the braid bowed again before he went back to his inspections.

"Wei is the son of my father's old cabin boy," Zane said. "He has a pretty young Indian wife and two beautiful children. In a few generations, his bloodline should be indistinguishable. Whether whites care to admit it or not, there's a good deal of Indian blood in some of the best families, and everyone knows how generously white men have passed on their characteristics to their unacknowledged offspring."

"You sound exactly like my father," Mercy said. "He used to make people furious by asking why, if white blood was superior, that a small proportion of black classified a person as a Negro."

Zane looked genuinely shocked. "That's not exactly what I meant. And I'm surprised he'd talk about such things in front of you."

"He talked of whatever was on his mind." Mercy felt a stab of longing. "He thought that even a child could understand a lot. I can't remember his ever telling me that I was too young to ask something or that it was bad to wonder."

"Then he must have spent an unconscionable amount of time answering questions!"

"He never seemed to mind."

Zane had stiffened, gazing across the field. "Jolie!" he shouted.

A small figure some distance down the row stepped out

from behind one of the big plants, and there was a telltale gleam of metal as she passed a machete to the boy beside her. Her sandaled feet scuffing reluctantly, she came toward her father, head down, lips pouting.

"I want to be able to do whatever Salvador does," she said, attacking first. "You always say, Papa, that the owner of a plantation should know about and be able to do every kind of work needed to run it!"

"You don't yet own La Quinta, little slippery tongue, and you never will if you hack open an artery with a machete."

"But . . ."

"You're not fair to Salvador," Zane said sternly. "If you got hurt, he'd feel he was to blame, though Lord knows I'd never hold him to account for your foolishness. You're getting too old now to follow him around as you did when you were little."

"You want him to just be another worker," Jolie accused. "But you know he's different! He wants to be an *H-men* and learn how to produce good crops. That's why he's working even though he's so young!"

"He's eleven," countered Zane. "Some boys of twelve support widowed mothers and younger children. But I admire his energy." He called the boy, who came forward quickly.

No taller than Jolie, this child Zane had saved from crucifixion had warm, brown skin, shining black eyes and hair, and the happiest smile Mercy had ever seen, though he seemed worried about his friend and stood defensively in front of her.

Zane spoke pleasantly but firmly. Jolie opened her mouth to protest, but Salvador silenced her with a look and answered Zane quietly. Zane nodded as if content and asked a few questions. Salvador replied in a respectful but decided way, shaking his hair back from his eyes. His face lit up with delight at Zane's next words. Jolie gave a glad cry and hurled herself upon her father, giving him a rather sweaty, dusty hug.

He commanded her to change into clean clothes and stay away from the henequén harvesting, then ordered her off with a kiss. Salvador ducked and seized Zane's hand, and he would have kissed it, but Zane warded him off and, in a gruffly kind voice, told him to go back to his task.

"Amusing, isn't it?" Zane asked as they turned toward huge yards where yellow-white fiber was spread over long rails. "Jolie obeys Salvador and, indirectly, I obey her. So that makes a barefoot eleven-year-old Indian the real power at La Quinta."

"Hardly that. But what did you say to make them so happy?"

"I said our *H-men*, Victoriano Zuc, has no sons and might be glad to have an apprentice. The ironic thing is that the boy's own mother could teach him more than anyone else. It must be from her that he inherits the tendency."

"And perhaps the incense he breathed along with prayers when people thought he was dying. Does he know about that? Does he remember at all?"

"I don't know. He had nightmares when I first brought him here and curled up by Macedonio's wife like a whimpering, scared puppy. But Chepa gave him some potions and told him a lot of stories, and I think what he remembered became for him part of a dream or witch tale. He's never seen his mother since then, though, when she took refuge in the tower, she asked me to bring him by so she could look down at him."

"He's such a handsome, sparkling child. She must wish she could have him with her."

"They resemble each other. If she tried to pretend he was some orphan she'd found, some jealous or suspicious person might start raising doubts. Then this time neither she nor Salvador would likely get away."

"Couldn't she take him a long way off, to Mérida or Campeche?"

Zane's eyebrow twitched. "And give up her authority? No. Xia loves her son, but she'll never again willingly be in a position where she'll be at the mercy of others. Men took her son and gave her power—a bitter, loveless compensation, but one she's come to consider her due."

Prefer influence to her child? Mercy hoped she'd never encounter the woman. She sounded like a beautiful, soul-deadened husk, yet Zane seemed to admire her.

As they passed the drying yards, Zane explained that the thick, long leaves were fed into a rasping machine that shredded them. This rasper, developed after the government had offered a reward to someone inventing a mechanical stripper that could replace the slow, laborious hand-rasping process, separated a powdery, green waste from the stringy fiber, which was hung to dry till it changed from pale green to golden and then was sorted according to quality, bound into bales, and sent by mule cart to Sisal for shipment to Europe and the United States.

A glance inside the factory at chutes, turning wheels, and sharp-toothed machinery was enough to intimidate Mercy. To her, the noisy machine seemed possessed by some malevolent giant insect mind of its own, and the farther away she could stay, the better. They peered into the warehouse, which smelled like rope, and into the store, where several women were buying clothing, blankets, or food.

"Most haciendas charge such high prices that a worker's wages never are enough, and he goes deeper and deeper into debt. The owner gives him credit enough to eat so he can go on working, but never enough to pay his debt and leave."

"My father used to say that to pay a man only enough to eat and barely survive was almost worse than slavery, since no one felt obligated to take care of such a laborer if he got sick or too old to work."

They were under the ceiba at the front approach to the house. Zane stopped abruptly. "Damn it! Must you always be quoting your father?"

Recoiling as if she'd been slapped, choked by hurt and anger, Mercy couldn't speak for a moment. When she could, her words came out in a rush in spite of her effort to speak calmly. "I'll never mention him again—to you!"

Hurrying toward the house, she heard his footsteps crunching deliberately behind her, closer with each long stride. She couldn't run. He caught up with her before she reached the steps.

"Forgive me," he said.

Mercy couldn't reply and inwardly reviled her trembling lips.

"I'm sure your father was a wise and estimable man," Zane said in a conciliatory tone. "But it's exasperating to have him quoted so often."

"I doubt you'll ever be the source of such annoyance," Mercy snapped.

Zane chuckled. "That's probably what irritates me— along with the feeling that you're trying to make me feel as if your father were at my back, with dueling pistol leveled, to make sure I treat his daughter with more propriety than I really want to!"

Mercy had to laugh at that and forget her anger, but

after Zane went into his office and she continued through the courtyard, she had to wonder if much of his comparative forbearance didn't stem from having a cherished daughter of his own. For whatever reason, Mercy was grateful.

Chepa called to her from the kitchen. "I make *cochinita pibil*," she said. "You see?"

A door on the opposite side of the kitchen led into a side yard where a boy was tending a pit of glowing embers a little more than a yard long and about half as wide and deep. On a high table, Mayel was stirring onions, mint leaves, pork rind, and salt into what was obviously the blood of the small pig lying on the bed of banana leaves while Chepa finished drenching it with a mixture of things she pointed out to Mercy: oregano, tabasco peppers, black pepper, the juice of bitter oranges, and a red-orange pulp whose name Mercy knew she could never pronounce.

Mayel held a rinsed membranous bag, which Chepa stuffed expertly with the onion mixture, touching her own ample stomach and pointing to the membrane so that Mercy knew that one was the pig's. Chepa called to the boy by the pit, and he began lifting out smoldering wood, ashes, and stones with a small shovel. He put damp henequén fiber on the remaining stones, and on this Chepa arranged banana leaves, the stuffed stomach, and the little pig, then covered them with more leaves and damp fiber. Smoking branches, ashes, and stones went over this. A last layer of the soaked hemp was tamped down by earth.

"Ready tonight," Chepa said. *"Muy buena."*

Feeling somewhat queasy, Mercy praised the seasonings. She had never liked to prepare meat from a recognizable animal and hadn't eaten flesh at all when living alone. Philip had jeered at her for her squeamishness. She had scolded herself for failing either to avoid meat altogether or else to have the hardihood to face up to its origins.

Back in the kitchen, already tidied up by one of the pretty young women who was now making tortillas, patting the corn dough into round, thin cakes to be baked on the large, flat stone occupying the rear of the grate above the cooking fire made on a conveniently raised stone foundation, Chepa urged Mercy to have a cup of hot chocolate. When water, chocolate, and spices in a saucepan came to a boil, Chepa selected an elaborately carved *molinillo* from the rack and twirled it in the boiling liquid till it began to foam. She took it from the fire, let the foaming stop, then put it over the heat again and spun it till the foam threatened to overflow. One more time she did this before taking the beverage to the table, twirling till the chocolate pleased her critical eye.

Chepa poured the hot chocolate into two blue-and-white mugs and handed one to Mercy, taking the other herself as she sank into a cushioned leather chair with the manner of one who's earned a rest. That chair, in a corner where she could watch the whole kitchen, the cooking court, and the inside courtyard, was clearly her throne, from whence she regulated the preparation of meals and the running of the household. Everyone moved briskly when she spoke, but she exuded goodness and said nothing when the tortilla-maker divided the remaining hot chocolate with Mayel.

Mayel, not used to a kitchen in which such largesse was routine, shot a nervous glance at Chepa, who smiled and nodded. The girl's face gleamed. She drank in a neat, concentrated fashion that reminded Mercy of a blissful kitten's innate fastidiousness. Already she seemed less scrawny, and she didn't always flinch when someone came near her. When she grew out of her coltish boniness, she'd be unusually beautiful.

She hadn't wanted to marry the man selected for her by the mayordomo of the hacienda near Uxmal. Would she find someone here who wouldn't disgrace the blood of Jacinto Canek? Mercy shrugged the thought away. She was by no means sure that marriage was the happiest thing for women, though economics and custom forced them into it. Zane had given her guardianship of Mayel. She'd see that the girl wasn't compelled to take a husband.

It was ironic to have control over another person's fate while she had so little over her own. Of course, it had been better to come to La Quinta by choice. Zane had been mightily impressed that Eric Kensington had offered his bond-slave marriage. It must put him more on his honor to keep his promise not to take her forcibly.

The great trouble was that it wouldn't take that much force.

Wrenching her wayward thoughts from the hard curve of his mouth, which *could* soften when he looked at Jolie, from the long, steel-muscled hands that weakened her the most when they were gentle, and, most of all, trying not to remember that dark granite of his eyes that was some-

116

times almost black, other times smoky, Mercy smiled at Chepa.

"Delicious!" she complimented, savoring a last taste of hot chocolate.

"*Deliciosa!*" Chepa laughed. "Close to same. Many such words."

Mercy thanked Chepa, then said, with reservations, that she looked forward to the *cochinita pibil* that night. She was just leaving when a young woman appeared in the doorway, holding a choking, gasping child in her arms.

Chepa at once opened a cabinet and got a hunk of what looked like resin from a jar. Putting this in a chipped pottery bowl, she lit it and held it for the youngster, a handsome but pitifully thin four- or five-year-old, to breathe.

A number of times after she tried to take over her father's duties, Mercy had asthma patients inhale steam. Sometimes it helped, but often she was helpless to do more than brew soothing teas, try to rub some of the spasmed tightness from the sufferers' backs, and pray they would catch their breath. It was an illness that terrified her.

Therefore, she watched in fascination as the boy gradually stopped choking. In a few minutes he coughed up phlegm, which Chepa caught in a bit of hemp fiber. Zane had explained that fiber too sunburned to be of commercial use was saved for pit-baking, cleaning machinery, scouring, and other odd jobs. A basket of the hemp was under the high table, and now Chepa used up several balls as the boy alternately drew in the aromatic smoke and brought up mucus.

Perhaps twenty minutes later, the child was breathing without the frightening wheeze that had wracked him at first.

Chepa patted his thin cheek, took an elixir from the cabinet, and gave it to the mother, along with some instructions. Murmuring thankful-sounding words, the woman left with the child.

Sadly, Chepa shook her head.

"But you helped him so much!" Mercy said.

"Till next time." Chepa sighed and then brightened. "Salvador was bad sick, same thing, when El Señor bring him. Last few years not much." She showed Mercy the remnants of the fragrant resin. "Copal help."

"Copal?" Mercy echoed.

117

Wasn't that the incense burned at Salvador's near-martyrdom? "What was the medicine you sent home with them?"

"Sarsaparilla with *chia* and *tlatlacizpatli*. Also, if copal no work, *toloache* smoke good, but it make one see monsters, colors, things not really there. Better copal—if it work."

"Don't sick people go to the *H-men?*"

Chepa gave her majestic shoulders a tiny shrug. "He make cure for witch sickness, find lost things, and knows about corn. But snakebite, machete cut, fever, bad cough, baby borning—people ask me." She looked sad. "Old secrets. Father taught me. I was teaching daughter. Maybe now teach Mayel."

Diffidently, because she didn't want to ask for knowledge forbidden to outsiders, Mercy said, "My father was a doctor, a healer of the sick. He taught me some things. Could you tell me the ways of your medicine?"

Chepa turned so that Mercy couldn't see her face. When Mercy had almost decided the woman hadn't understood, she turned and gazed for a long time into Mercy's eyes.

"I teach," Chepa said.

For the next hour she showed Mercy and Mayel leaves, seeds, roots, and dried flowers, conveying their uses with signs when her English failed, correcting Mercy's pronunciation of each name till it was recognizable.

"I show plants growing," Chepa promised. "Then you tell apart better."

"I'll have to write it all down," Mercy said. "What a lot there is to learn!"

"Much more," Chepa said, an expansive motion of her arms embracing all directions. "The good God made a cure for all hurts."

Possibly, if one knew what. Mercy was dazzled at the contents of the little cupboard, especially by the pain-killers and anesthetics.

Besides *toloache,* there were various morning-glory seeds, cacti, leaves of the white *sapote,* and the roots and seeds of several impossibly unpronounceable plants. *Epazote,* or wormweed, would purge worms, as well as season food; mint-like salvia, borage, and steeped willow leaves were used for fever. The flowers and bark of the Mexican magnolia, *yoloxochitl,* helped heart ailments,

118

and for the *garrapatas*, or chiggers, that had so plagued the journey, a dressing of agave gave relief.

There were treatments for gout, colds, pneumonia, diarrhea, constipation, and to increase the flow of mother's milk. "I can even," announced Chepa, "pull tooth, no hurt."

Mercy stared at this. Having a tooth pulled out was such a wretched and bloody experience that no one did it until infection or pain drove them to it. "You mean you give *toloache* or copal so the person doesn't feel the pain?"

Chepa shook her head. "No hurt. I show someday." She giggled, a strange, girlish sound from her regality. "*H-men* wants to know. Never tell him. He has his things, and I have mine."

So there was a little professional jealousy there. How Elkanah would have reveled by talking to Chepa! Mercy thought a bit ruefully of the medicaments she'd brought with her, naturally assuming she might have to nurse the ignorant peasants. Even so, there might be a few things Chepa would like to add to her pharmacopoeia.

Mercy complimented Chepa's skill and supplies, thanked her for the instruction, and crossed the court to her room, eager to review her father's notes and go through her medicinal packets.

She thought she heard a door close as she entered. No one was there, but the cushions on the window ledge looked as if they'd been nestled against. Mercy paused, then got out the small carved animals she'd bought at Tekax. The deer and pheasant she placed close together on the window ledge, then positioned the jaguar in the corner far enough away not to be a suggested threat.

Surely Jolie would like them, and if they weren't a direct present . . .

Mercy had still not fully unpacked. She put her few remaining pieces of jewelry in a lacquer box on the chest, except for the black coral necklace Zane had given her. This she fastened around her neck. The sewing materials went on a shelf in the top of the armoire, where her dresses hung with a drooping shabbiness accentuated by the somber beauty of the quetzal dress.

Doña Elena's dance seemed an eternity ago, yet was less than a week had passed. Had Eric been drunk, to offer her marriage, especially knowing that she'd been wagered by her own husband on the turn of a card? The

119

Viking had seemed sober enough. Perhaps he'd just wanted to annoy Zane.

A sort of chill fire shot through her as she remembered Eric's searing mouth and his cruelly inescapable embrace. In her heart she knew that his wish to have her was more than an accident, more than a perverse whim to anger Zane. But surely he was in Belize by now, or soon would be, and there was no reason why she'd ever see him again unless they met by chance in Mérida next year.

Mérida. Next year. Both seemed worlds away.

This is the fifth direction, she told herself. *This is where you start.*

And already she *was* starting. She had at least a sketchy idea of henequén production, the workings of a village, *cochinita pibil,* and a treatment for asthma, as well as a glimpse of Chepa's other remedies. The schoolroom was arranged and some books were selected. Now all she had to do was capture her recalcitrant pupil, who'd rather help her friend cut henequén than behave like the master's daughter.

At least Jolie was capable of loyalty and affection. How delighted she'd been when Zane hinted that Victoriano, the *H-men,* might take an apprentice!

Mercy caught her breath in sudden inspiration. If Salvador thought the white man's learning might be useful, and if Zane would let him study with Jolie, that might be a way of making the studies palatable. Mercy had no wish to sit opposite a glowering, spoiled girl and try to penetrate a locked mind. Even less did she want to have to appeal to Zane to compel a semblance of compliance.

Cheered by hope that Salvador would welcome all the knowledge he could get, Mercy reached the bottom of her pack and took out her father's letters, books, and a small bundle. The bundle contained her medical remedies: sassafras' pungent bark; mint, which she knew could be found here; mountain pinks and the bark of dogwood root, for fever; horehound and mullein leaves for croup; garlic for influenza and bronchitis; dried pomegranate rind for diarrhea and dysentery; dandelion roots and yarrow for upset stomachs.

They were like old friends, remembrances of home, of her father explaining their use, and her efforts to ease his patients with them after he was gone. She held up another packet.

Rue.

The next was rosemary. *". . . that's for remembrance."*

And in the last packet were dried violets, sweet-smelling, having many uses. But her mind flew back to Ophelia's grief for her father. *"I would give you some violets, but they withered all when my father died."*

Mercy put down her head and wept, but it was more purge than grief. These violets might be withered, but beautiful flowers grew here. Though her abilities were slight compared with Chepa's, and possibly even with Victoriano's, she would use them and improve, for her father's sake, if not her own. She would use her life in a way that would make less bitter the waste of the years he could not have, and in spite of his agnosticism and her own doubts, she prayed that he might somehow know. And she wouldn't be Zane's mistress unless he loved her and let her do her part at La Quinta. She wouldn't live shut up in a tower, sealed away from life, for any man, and one who would ask that couldn't truly care about her, anyhow.

She remembered her father's favorite words, from Marcus Aurelius: *"And art thou unwilling to do the work of a human being, and why, then, do you not make haste to do that which is according to thy nature?"*

Feeling a closeness, a sense of communication, as if Elkanah were watching her and smiling, Mercy opened his letters and began to read them.

9

Her father's letters alternated in their tone: outrage of a man whose colleagues seemed criminally careless and obstinate to excitement over a newly discovered substitute for a medicine kept from the South by the blockade; helplessness in the face of death, maiming, and agony.

If I come home, I'll study hypnotism, for to stop pain is wonderful. Don't think I'm driven out of my

121

wits, dear Mercy. An Austrian physician named Mesmer used the technique, which goes back to at least Paracelsus. I look at the sick, wounded, and dying, those who cannot escape their torment, and I'd sell my soul to give them ease—not even healing, just an end to pain.

And:

There's no such thing as "laudable pus." The hogs who applaud this are surely responsible for much gangrene, probing wounds and operating with dirty hands. They're the same death-dealers who come from a patient ill with some loathsome or contagious disease and, unwashed, deliver a baby, killing many a new mother with puerperal fever.

But Mercy studied most carefully the notes he'd added to Dr. Francis Porcher's *Resources of Southern Fields and Forests,* a treatise published in 1863, at the urging of the Confederate surgeon general, to give substitutes for unobtainable drugs.

To replace quinine for malaria, there was dogwood, poplar, and willow bark steeped in whiskey. Elkhanah noted wryly that the last ingredient made it a popular medicine. Poke was used for neuralgia, itch, and syphilis. For the almost universal bowel ailments that probably killed more men than any other cause, there was blackberry, sweet gum, and willow.

When scurvy threatened, doctors were advised to ask the men to bring in greens, poke, dandelions, mustard, wild onion, pepper grass, and such. Elkanah noted that he had more faith in this preventive than in most of the cures.

Only the deepening of twilight, till she could no longer make out the words, alerted Mercy to the time and where she was. First she put the books on the table by the chair. Then she tucked the letters and herbs into a small chest by the window. This done, she changed into the flower-embroidered dress, pinned her hair back in a loose knot, and decided it was cool enough for a shawl.

As she entered the courtyard, Zane stood under the arch. His scowl disappeared when he saw her. Mercy's heart lifted at that. He must have some softness for her, to spend time as he had that day introducing her to the plantation, to refrain from simply exercising his rights as her master. If she were patient, went about her tasks with Jolie, and stuck to her resolves concerning him, wasn't it at least possible that someday his bitter disillusion might fade and make him risk loving again? If he'd love her, she'd never hurt him. But there was no way, now, to convince him.

"You're late," he growled, but there was eagerness in his eyes as he stood back to let her precede him to the table.

The *cochinita pibil* was succulent. Zane complimented Chepa, echoed by Mercy. The sauce made a tasty flavoring for the rice. Zane told Chepa that after she'd saved enough *cochinita* for next day, she could give the rest to whatever people in the village had no one to hunt for them. This was evidently the practice of La Quinta, to avoid tainted meat and provide animal flesh for villagers.

Jolie, who'd been subdued during the meal, refused a dessert of spiced custard, but she asked for a second mug of hot chocolate, complaining that her first one hadn't been foamy enough. "You go and twirl it, then," Zane suggested.

To Mercy's surprise, Jolie trotted off happily beside Chepa. "She likes to be in the kitchen," Zane explained. "It's where she spent much of her time till last year, when she decided that as a young mistress she shouldn't behave like a scullery maid."

Mercy couldn't help laughing. "So now she cuts henequén! Your daughter isn't getting to be a prim and proper sit-on-her-hands doll, Zane."

"Neither are you," he retorted somewhat grimly. "So it would seem I've at least found her a compatible teacher."

"If she'll listen to me." This was as good a time as any, so Mercy plunged in. "Zane, could Salvador study with her? Surely it would be an advantage for you to have a man around who was educated in both Mayan and white ways. If he becomes the leader you seem to think he will, it should be useful to give him the broadest knowledge possible."

Zane frowned, turning his cup. "Doesn't it occur to you that Jolie and the boy are getting too old to continue their unusual friendship? Boys only a few years older than Salvador are often fathers."

It was Mercy's turn to stare, but she recovered after a moment. "They must feel like brother and sister."

His mouth twitched. "Incest is an old and honorable tradition, at least among noble or royal lines."

"You twist everything!"

"I point out facts you'd prefer to ignore."

Biting her lip, Mercy tried a different attack. "Maybe they shouldn't be together indefinitely, but I'm concerned with getting Jolie into the classroom."

"She'll do as I tell her."

Mercy gasped with exasperation. "You can send her body, but she can leave her mind in the kitchen or the field—anywhere but a place she detests."

"It's up to you to capture her interest."

"You should know that's impossible," flared Mercy, "since she's as stubborn as you are!"

"And you're devious, sweet Mercy, for all your plain speaking." The corner of Zane's mouth twitched. "You began this gambit by suggesting that Salvador's education would benefit me. Now it develops that you're simply trying to wheedle Jolie into the classroom."

"That's one reason, but it seems a shame not to teach a child that anxious to learn. Who can tell? He might help bring peace to this country."

Zane shook his head, as if in mute wonder. "You do argue a case! Now the future of Yucatán hinges on my decision. Try it, then. But I'll keep an eye on the situation."

"I'm sure they won't elope for a few years," Mercy teased, then winced at the slip the instant it was out. "I . . . I'm sorry."

"You may be sure I'll guard my daughter better than I did my wife."

"Would you want a woman you had to imprison?"

His eyes reflected the yellow light of the candle, though shadows dimmed his face, so that it gave the impression of being a disturbing, not-quite-human mask.

"Aren't you imprisoned, my dear?"

The deep, suggestive timbre of his voice made her heart leap so that the flow of blood through her veins felt edged with flames. "You mean I'm your bond-servant?" she almost whispered.

"I mean you sometimes want me as much as I always want you," he said with a short laugh. "But propriety, the laws you've been taught, make you punish us both."

124

If you would love me . . . if you would let me do the work of a human being . . . She couldn't bare her feelings to him. Then, indeed, she would be undefended. "I won't live shut away in a tower like a one-woman harem," she said. "I've a mind and capabilities that will atrophy if they're not used."

"I enjoy your mind, contentious as it makes you," he said. "And what of your capability for joy, for possessing and being possessed? Won't it wither away if you don't use it?"

"I'd rather it did than overgrow and crowd out everything else," Mercy said, though she ached at that thought. Would it be possible to be near him like this for years and still deny him, deny the smoldering, tingling honey-fire that danced through her at the mere sound of his voice?

He made a disgusted sound. "I'll bet you had heroines when you were growing up!"

"I still do."

His eyebrows arched up sardonically. "My God, you admit it! You are a freakish wench, though I'm almost afraid to call you that. If I hadn't won you from your scapegrace husband, I'd vow you came out of a convent."

"Yet you've behaved as if I came from a brothel."

"I've come to believe that's where most women, by instinct, would be most at home."

"There'd be no brothels if men didn't want to escape from women they consider too good and pure to be in them."

He flinched. "Little sharp-clawed devil! Just who, on heaven or earth, merited your admiration?"

"Joan of Arc," said Mercy defiantly. "Florence Nightingale. Marie de France, Aspasia. And among men I would name Saint Francis, Jesus, Moses, and Pelagius—and my own father."

"Of course, your father!"

"Of course!"

"Joan of Arc," considered Zane. "She was a virgin witch-warrior who chided the king of France and her own judges. Yes, I can see why you'd like her! Florence Nightingale's a termagant, though I suppose that's forgivable in view of the lives she's saved. Aspasia was the whore of Pericles."

"She was his *companion!*" Mercy corrected him

125

fiercely. "And her home was the center of cultural and civic life! She helped Pericles write his speeches, and though she was publicly humiliated and tried for her life, without her the Golden Age might have been brass."

"Oh, no doubt Pericles was simply her mouthpiece and she really composed those lines President Lincoln borrowed so successfully for the Gettysburg Address," derided Zane. "The attainments of the other lady elude me, but I'm sure you'll dispel my ignorance."

"Marie de France wrote poetry."

Zane looked startled. "And for that she has a place in your temple?"

"Yes."

Zane considered a moment. "I don't know her. Could you remember a few lines?"

"She's talking to her dead love in the poem I like best. Perhaps he was William Longsword, the bastard of Henry the Second and Fair Rosamund, though Marie herself may have been Henry's half sister.

> "Hath any loved you well down there,
>   Summer and winter through?"

She continued with the tapestry-like words, shimmering with love and grief.

"There we have it!" Zane exclaimed, leaning forward. "You feel a bit ashamed, but you revere beauty and love!"

"I'm not ashamed!" she retorted. "Love is far different from lust."

"Some day—or night—you must enlighten me," he drawled. "But let's return to your heroes. Why Moses and Pelagius?"

"Both of them took mankind's part. Moses told God that if He wouldn't forgive the sinning Israelites, then Moses' name, too, should be taken out of God's book. I can't stand all those wretched religious men who were always ready to send everyone else to hell as long as their own souls were saved! Pelagius opposed Augustine, teaching that men could win salvation through their own efforts and weren't essentially evil. It's too bad Augustine won that battle and fastened the millstone of original sin on Western civilization. People might act better if they thought they were better."

Zane didn't speak for so long that she thought she had

made him angry or had estranged him with her revelation. Strange, she and Philip had never talked like this, and she had missed it, for Elkanah had given her his pungent views on almost everything and listened with questioning interest to her opinions. Tonight, carried away, she'd spoken nakedly of things important to her. Maybe Zane didn't like that. Maybe he didn't believe her or thought her a fool.

"What *have* I brought home?" he said at last. "I begin to understand why you rescued Mayel. How is your waif?"

"Happy." Mercy hesitated to compliment him, but she decided it was only fair. "She's excited about all the things La Quinta *doesn't* have—a whipping post, jail, assistant mayordomo, or *administrador*."

"I don't need those," Zane said roughly. "The production of this plantation is far ahead of those using debt-laborers, and I've no wish to let a manager oversee *my* land and skim off profits."

He was determined to seem cold-bloodedly practical. Yet he had bought Mayel, the plantation hummed with busy contentment under his direction, and he'd rescued Salvador at some risk to his own life.

Mercy waited just a moment and then raced on, following a thought that had just popped into her head. "Zane," she said, holding her breath, "do you think it would be possible to include Mayel in the school, too?"

Zane sighed, passing a hand across his brow, then stared hard at her. "Now you want my daughter to study with that Indian wench, as well?"

"That 'Indian wench' is a descendant of Mayan royalty."

"Mayan royalty. Ah, yes." He sighed again. "And why not?" he said finally. "Perhaps it would provide a more school-like atmosphere. Perhaps it would even divert young Salvador's attention from Jolie, and hers from him. Yes, go ahead and try it out, Mercy. But don't forget—I shall keep a sharp eye on the venture."

Mercy couldn't stop the smile that stole across her face. "Well," she said quickly, "Mayel should be pretty busy, then. Chepa wants to teach her about herbs and healing. She says Mayel reminds her of her daughter."

Zane groaned. "*Every* scrawny thirteen-year-old with big eyes reminds Chepa of her daughter!"

"What's wrong with that?" bristled Mercy.

127

"Nothing," muttered Zane. "I don't need to ask how Chepa relieved the boy's asthma that day, or about the wonders of her cupboard."

"You must know *toloache*," Zane said. "They call it jimsonweed in the United States."

"But I thought that was poison!"

"Aren't lots of medicines when used improperly? *My* father used to say anything that could cure could kill, too."

Chuckling with that dart, Zane went on to say that Aztec and Mayan physicians had been far ahead of their European counterparts at the time of the conquest.

"For a start, the Aztecs were fastidious. They bathed daily, whereas Europeans might go year in, year out, without more than an accidental dunking in the rain. The streets of Tenochtitlán were cleaned every day by a thousand sweepers, and human waste was collected and transported to farms. The Aztecs forbade the dumping of garbage into the lake or canals at a time when European streets were open sewers and 'romantic' Venice stank to high heaven. But the Spaniards changed all that. It was much like the Vandals descending on Rome."

"Clean habits alone have made deaths from childbirth far less frequent," Mercy said, surprised and delighted to learn such things from Zane.

Zane nodded. "In fact, mothers had a steambath before delivery and then again not long after. And you know about the pain-killers, which were used in childbirth and for other things, as well. Horrible as human sacrifice was, the victims were certainly drugged so that they felt nothing. Some even danced ecstatically before they mounted the pyramid."

At Mercy's shudder, Zane added cynically, "The Spaniards were so shocked by the sacrifices that they imported the Inquisition to carry on the sort *they* understood —they went about the holy task of slaughtering the majority of Indians in order to convert the remnants. Why be appalled, Mercy? All nations practice human sacrifice."

"They can't! They don't!"

"What else is war?"

"Why, war is . . . when two sides don't agree with each other and try to settle a question by force."

"So men die for federalism, the Union, the Confederacy, the Queen of England, democracy in Greece, or the Republic of Yucatán. That's not sacrifice?"

"That's fighting. You were a soldier. You must believe in fighting."

"Fighting for one's home, village, or immediate territory is an instinct we have straight from our animal nature. But when we translate this into dying for abstracts or political entities far removed from the victims' lives, then they are human sacrifices, as surely as if their hearts were torn out on an altar to obtain the blessings of the gods on the nation." Zane shrugged. "Perhaps it's necessary, but as long as the strongest of a country's young men are periodically consecrated to defend some nationalistic posture, we should think of this as what it is."

"My father didn't believe in slavery or even care much about the phenomenon of states' rights. He joined to take care of the sick and wounded."

"So we might call him a *humane* sacrifice."

"I suppose you *could* say . . . "

"I wonder if you know that the first warfare was waged in order to get sacrifices for the gods without having to kill members of one's own group. Early man, it seems, believed that some human life must be offered up to obtain prosperity and safety for the greater number. It was natural enough to prefer to immolate strangers, especially if they disputed a water source or had better land or prettier women."

"Are you saying that religion was really the first cause of war?"

"I say it's probable. Then tot up the Crusades, the wars of Reformation, Islam's conversions by scimitar, and all the murdered heretics—and the pile of corpses doubtless exceeds that of those dead in secular wars. And now that Catholics and Protestants hate each other less bloodily, mankind can battle over political and economic systems, which are the new religions." He made a gesture of disgust. "You gave me a poem," he said after a moment in a voice that had gentled. "Shall we walk a little? I'll give you some singing words from a Mayan prophet, Chilam Balam, who wrote not long after the conquest. Many towns have copies of his works, which they use as scriptures of sorts."

Would he take her back to the tower? Mercy's feet slowed as they reached the gate of the rear courtyard, but this time Zane, placing his hand beneath her arm, took her the other way. The moon rose stealthily, veiled by snatches of clouds, and the leaves splattered exotic shadows like those of Marie de France's poem. *The long, quaint, odorous leaves like hands* ...

They came to a semi-clearing where ruined stone walls gleamed eerily. A serpent's gigantic head opened massive fanged jaws where it guarded a black overgrown entrance. Before she knew what he was doing, he lifted her easily and enthroned her on the serpent.

" '*My son*,' " he said in a strange, deep voice that made her flesh creep, " '*go bring me the green blood of my daughter, also her head, her entrails, her thigh, and her arm . . . it is my desire to see them . . . set them before me that I may burst into weeping.*' "

"What does it mean?"

"Her blood is wine, the entrails are an empty beehive, and her head is a jar for making wine This is part of a very long ritual called the Interrogation of the Chiefs." He spoke now in a normal voice tinged with laughter. "Did you think I was about to make *you* a sacrifice?"

Primitive, unreasoning fear had flowed through her, there in the ruins with Zane's face a mask in the silver light and his voice so creepily resonant.

"For all I know, you turn werewolf at certain times of the moon," she said crossly, trying to slip down.

His arms imprisoned her. "I thought you liked being on a pedestal," he said mockingly.

"A pedestal's not of much use if I'm still within your reach!"

"Would you really want to be past it?"

An odd breathlessness choked her. Before she could answer, he turned her palm up and kissed it, his warm lips moving to her wrist, lingering on the pulse.

"I can feel your blood course," he murmured. "And it isn't green, but it may be honey-wine. There are other words for you from the works of Chilam Balam: '*Son, bring me a very beautiful woman with a very white countenance. I greatly desire her. I will cast down her skirt and her loose dress before me.*' "

His arms closed, bringing her down against him so that to gain her feet she had to slide the length of his hard-muscled body. He was trembling as much as she was. This gave her a thrill of power mixed with fear. If he lost control . . . did more than woo and blandish . . .

In the desire and yearning sweetness of the moment,

she wished he would follow the words of the Mayan prophet and strip off her clothes and possess her utterly.

He touched her face, caressed her throat and breasts, and kissed her with a violent hunger that aroused an almost unbearable need in her. She yielded her mouth fully, accepting and answering his thrusting, quivering tongue, putting her arms around him for the first time.

If he sank down with her now . . .

But he tore his lips away, unclasping her hands while he stared into her face. "Come with me to the tower. Oh, sweet Mercy, come to the tower."

Not a word of love. And the tower had come to mean now the same thing to them both—a place where she would exist for his pleasure, living only to gratify him. And though she craved that pleasure, too, she would not take that road in life.

"No."

He stared at her, his eyes reflecting the cold, frosty glint of the moon, then roughly took his hands away from her so that she nearly fell. It was hard, hard, to take back her full weight, to smother the sweet flowing of her body and being toward him.

"It won't work," he said from between gritted teeth. "I won't offer you marriage, whatever whore's tricks you use to drive me crazy!"

Whore's tricks? Mercy shook with outrage and frustrated desire. "You brought me here! You pulled me into your arms and kissed me and . . . "

"But you have the mouth as sweet as honey-wine warmed in the sun and the breasts so soft that my hands ache to touch them and the softness where I long to plunge this hard, throbbing sword you create but will not sheathe."

He spoke softly, as if dreaming, in contrast to his earlier outburst, but Mercy was so hurt and angry that she scarcely heard him. Whirling away from him, blinded by tears, she turned to run down the path, but she stumbled over a vine.

He kept her from falling and imprisoned her arm firmly in his long fingers. The first time he spoke was at her door back at the house.

"Sleep well in your virtuous bed!" With a curt bow, he strode away.

Heedless of the coverlet, Mercy threw herself across the bed and sobbed with wrath and humiliation. *Whore's tricks!* How dare he, when he'd suggested the moonlit walk, beguiled her with incantations, and kissed her as he had!

She'd never go to his tower—never!

But there was a heavy, dull ache in her stomach that persisted as she undressed and washed. Savagely scrubbing the palm he had kissed, she took vindictive satisfaction in the certainty that *he* was aching, too. And it was supposed to be worse for men. Good! She was glad that *something* was!

She barely saw him during the next few days, except at meals, when he was formally polite. Chepa had brought three of the best seamstresses of the village to start sewing the materials brought from Mérida, and she had translated while Mercy explained what she wanted. One of her old dresses would serve as a pattern, except for the blue-gray satin dress, which could be styled like the gleaming quetzal gown.

The blue challis for Jolie could be a miniature copy of Mercy's, though she felt it advisable to disguise this by the use of different trimming and a very broad sash. Jolie was intrigued with the cloth and trimming, and since the women worked in the sitting room, where there was plenty of room and they could chat, she was constantly gleaning scraps for her various dolls, tying those around them in startling gypsy-queen combinations.

"Would you like to make your doll a ball gown out of this?" Mercy asked when she found Jolie eyeing the blue-gray satin. "You'd need to sew and hem it, though, or it'll unravel."

"I don't like to sew," Jolie sniffed. "Chepa will do it for me."

"Chepa's very busy."

"She does whatever I ask her!"

"But *should* you ask her?" Mercy asked pleasantly.

Jolie scowled, pouted her Cupid's-bow mouth, defiantly snatched a jumble of scraps, and flounced out. When Mercy went to her room a little later, the pheasant and deer were gone from the window ledge, but the jaguar had been moved to the center, facing out, as if in a threat. There was no doubt of the positioning's hostility and virtually no doubt about who'd done it. Staring at the small, snarling jaguar, Mercy gripped her arms close to her body as a sudden chill assaulted her.

The spiteful jealousy of a child—she mustn't let it upset her. Lessons had to start soon. From that contact, they'd form some kind of relationship, but it looked as if trust would be a long time in coming. As for affection . . . Mercy sighed.

Gazing at the jaguar, she laughed whimsically and tied a bit of blue ribbon around its neck in a fancy bow. Its snaring countenance now seemed playful.

"School starts tomorrow," she said to the jaguar, then went in search of Jolie before she was tempted to delay class a few more days.

After hunting through the house and courtyards, Mercy followed Chepa's suggestion to look for the child in the stables. Built of stone, these were set some distance from the eastern side of the house, with several corrals adjoining. Here, too, were the wagons, and several carriages, which, though they were polished and new looking, didn't appear to be in use.

Mercy caught a glimpse of silver and leather through a half-door, and she couldn't resist peering in at pegs holding hackamores; bridles, plain or embellished with silver and precious stones, with bits from cruel spade to gentle snaffle; and dozens of saddles resting on wooden blocks.

Here were double-rig saddles Mercy knew from Texas, Spanish single-rig saddles, a few pad-like English saddles, and several sidesaddles. These were variously either completely devoid of ornamentation or embossed and decorated from moderate to extravagant levels with conchos, nailheads, and stitching that was often of silver or even gold. The stirrups ranged from plain metal or wood to embossed round or eagle-billed ones decorated with rosettes and conchos. A small sidesaddle gleaming with silver had to be Jolie's. Saddlebags hung in the far corner.

It was a museum of horse gear, well oiled and cared for, the odors of horse and leather pleasantly nostalgic to Mercy, though her father had never owned more than four horses. Far more than any housework, she had enjoyed perching on a sawhorse in the straw-strewn stable, working oil into the saddles and bridles and usually giving her father's boots a treatment, as well.

Suddenly a long, cinnamon, dark-ringed tail waved beneath her. Mercy jumped back and other jerking tails joined the first one until there were four coatis hissing and spitting.

"Oh," said Mercy, laughing, though she was careful not to make any abrupt motions. She kept her distance. "You must be Flora's babies! How handsome you are!"

"They don't know what you're saying," Jolie said rudely, darting from around the building with Flora parading before her. Flora's half-grown brood retreated to the protection of her soothingly undulating tail. "Do you go around talking to animals?"

"Don't *you?*" asked Mercy.

That scored. Jolie's violet eyes widened, then narrowed. "But you're grown up!"

"There are all kinds of grown up. I like animals just as much as I ever did."

"They don't like you."

"Flora does." Mercy bent down and stroked the matriarch between neat little ears. "Her babies were frightened when I sprang out of the way. I think they'll be friends when they get used to me."

"They may scratch you with their claws and bite you with their teeth!"

"You're fond of that idea, aren't you?" Mercy said. "It sounds like something out of a witch tale."

"When I grow up, I shall be a witch," Jolie announced darkly. "I'll live in the sacred cave at Xia's village, where the virgin water is, and have a whole pack of coatis—a jaguar, too."

"Will they get along?"

"They'll have to! I'll command them, and I'll have magic."

Mercy remembered waving a paper fan as a child and half-believing she controlled the wind with it. "That sounds a lot more interesting than living in a hut with a cat or two. Maybe you could write a story about it."

Jolie dug a toe into the dirt. "I don't have time."

"You can have lesson time for it," said Mercy.

Jolie's golden curls bounced as her head tilted back, defiance in every line of her small body.

"I thought Salvador might like to study with you," Mercy continued. "If he wants to be an *H-men*, surely the more he knows, the better."

"You'd teach Salvador along with me?"

"Yes, and Mayel, too. It'll be more interesting for you and probably for me, too. Of course, until I learn more

Spanish and Mayan, or until Salvador and Mayel know more English, you'll have to translate, but that'll be good practice for all of us." Mercy added frankly, "Since I have to learn two languages, I'll be studying hardest of all, I imagine."

Jolie's brightening face dimmed. "Papa won't allow it."

"I've already asked his permission."

"And he said yes?" demanded Jolie incredulously, her blonde brows rising.

Mercy nodded. "We can try it, at least. It was hard to convince your father, and I expect that he'll stop by sometimes to be sure everyone's studying. Do you think you can find Salvador and Mayel and tell them we'll start in the morning after breakfast and study till noon?"

"Victoriano may not like Salvador's taking lessons with an outsider."

"Surely you or your father can explain that Salvador will be a much more valuable helper if he knows English and something of the world beyond La Quinta and Yucatán."

"Then Victoriano may get jealous and want lessons, too," Jolie said, smiling. She scooped up Flora, and the coati hung over her back like a plump fur stole. "I'll go ask Salvador. But, mind you, I won't make him come if he doesn't want to. And you could tell Mayel yourself, couldn't you?"

She skipped off, followed by the young coatis, indeed resembling some child witch with her familiars. Mercy drew in a last sensuous inhalation of leather, horse, and oil smells before she started back to the house. She had conditionally won this first skirmish, but she suspected she was in for a long, wearying battle.

At least Jolie didn't shock her. She remembered too well her own roguish "Why not?" reveries in childhood, that curious amoral period when nothing seemed ordained except vhat she chose. At that age, which was Jolie's now, she would have loved to be a witch!

Mercy went through the sitting room, smiling and admiring the various garments in progress. It gave her the feeling of being someone's frightfully spoiled mistress, though, except for the satin Zane himself had bought, none of the gowns was extravagant. It was just that having so many new things at once, including underwear, was a never-before-experienced luxury that made her feel vaguely guilty, as if she didn't deserve them.

But she hadn't deserved to lose her father or Star or to have Philip sell the farm, and certainly she had not deserved to be wagered and lost at cards. There was no reason why she shouldn't enjoy the clothes, her pretty room, Chepa's excellent cooking, and the well-run household as long as she did what Zane expected—well, not *everything* he expected, but as much as she could for Jolie.

10

What to teach the daughter of a plantation owner, the descendant of a warrior chief, and the almost-crucified son of a Mayan priestess? Arithmetic, of course, demonstrated with pebbles for Salvador and Mayel. They should not take long to catch up with Jolie, whose mastery of adding and subtracting was at best shaky. And Salvador could already count to thirty, the number of leaves left on a hemp plant after the twelve largest ones were cut.

Jolie could read both English and Spanish quite well, so she read classics, history, poetry, and did compositions, while Mercy worked with Salvador and Mayel on basic English or practiced with them the Spanish she was learning herself. With this last, they got Jolie's patronizing help.

Geography mixed with history took wings when Mercy hit on the idea of relating the Mayan ruins, which they took for granted, to the pyramids of Egypt, ziggurats of Babylon, mosques of Arabia, and the great cathedrals of Europe. And she found another sphere of comparisons in the tree that the children knew as the ceiba: this was the same tree that supposedly grew in the Garden of Eden, that was called the *yggdrasil* in Scandinavian myth, was known as the banyan in India, and that formed the basis for both the stylized menorah of the Jews and the pagoda of the Chinese.

Mayel found the language hard, but she practiced shyly during other hours, anxious to please Mercy. Salvador was eager and quick, learning English much faster than Mercy was acquiring Mayan. Jolie, proficient in speaking all three and reading two, basked in her role as translator, though she was not inclined to study anything that didn't come easily. She had an agile, broad-ranging, but undisciplined intelligence.

Zane stopped by for a few minutes every morning, listening from the door but not interrupting. Mercy had not seen him alone since that walk to the moonlit ruins, and she wondered if he meant to ever after be distantly polite but avoid any real contact.

On the third day of lessons, though, during the noon meal, he asked if she'd like to meet him at the stables at about three o'clock. "Wear something you can ride in," he warned. "I may have found you an acceptable horse."

"A . . . a horse?" Mercy had missed her spirited but sweet-tempered mare more than, truth to tell, she missed the man who'd sold her—sold them both, for that matter.

"Not a mule." Zane sounded irritable and she noticed with a little shock that he was looking tired, hollow around the eyes. "I'd thought this filly might do for Jolie in a few years, but there's no use having her be riderless that long. Besides, the mare Jolie has now should do her fine till she's twelve or thirteen and has more weight and strength in her wrists."

Jolie had been staring almost open-mouthed. Now she sprang up and ran to Zane. "I'm strong enough for a big horse, Papa! Let me try!"

"And how would Piñata feel if she knew you were so anxious to have another mount?"

"I'll still love Piñata, but I've had her since I was a small child!"

"All of two years," he answered solemnly. "Piñata's a nice pony with sense enough to keep you from breaking your neck. You may have your pick of the new colts this year, and it'll be ready by the time you are."

"I'm ready now!"

"You're not," he said sternly. "But have your dessert and we'll go look at the colts when you've finished."

"No!" she screamed. With a stamp of her foot, she glared furiously at Mercy, tried to speak, then fled when her voice failed her.

Mercy gazed in dismay at Zane.

His jaw clamped tightly and he rose, excusing himself. "I'll see you at three o'clock," he said, then turned to go.

"Oh," protested Mercy, "I don't think I should have that mare now."

"It was stupid of me to mention I'd thought of holding her for Jolie," he admitted, "but there'd have been little sense in it, wasting several years of a horse's riding time. Far better that she choose a colt. And she will, as soon as she gets over her tantrum."

"But . . . " Mercy bit her lip. She'd gotten Jolie to her lessons, but they'd reached no rapport yet. This might make understanding completely impossible.

"Jolie's spoiled," Zane said. "I'm just realizing how much. You, of all people, must know I can't give in to her against my better judgment."

True enough. It was just a shame he'd let slip his previous half-plans for the horse. Mercy dreaded repercussions, and, though she'd longed to have a horse again, she'd rather have done without than have gotten one this way.

"At three," said Zane and strode through the gate.

She read Stevens for a while, finally forgetting her distress at Jolie's resentment in fascination at the traveler's account of Uxmal and over details of the villages and countryside such a short time before the War of the Castes would bring such violent changes. When her ornate little clock pointed to two-thirty, Mercy dressed in her fullest skirt, the old gray gabardine, tucked the black coral necklace she always wore out of sight, fastened her hair back neatly, and went to the stables.

Zane was there before her, watching a boy lead a dainty little chestnut mare around the clearing. Already saddled, the mare was brushed and burnished till she gleamed like new copper, and the way she tossed her head was archly feminine. Mercy thought with a pang of the mare Star, which Philip had sold, the companion she'd never see again, and she felt disloyal to be so thrilled at this mare's grace and carriage. But she couldn't resist approaching gently and speaking.

"Beauty," she whispered, stroking the silken muzzle with its twitching nostrils, "oh, you beauty!"

"Her name's Castaña," Zane said, strolling up and inspecting the mare with a critical gaze that flicked to Mercy.

"She matches the color of your hair." He smiled wickedly. "She's sweet-tempered, however, and doesn't require a heavy rein. Her gaits are smooth. It's a joy to mount her."

Blushing furiously, Mercy shielded her face against the mare's glossy neck. "If you like her so much, you should keep her."

"She's too light for me. I'd wear her down if I rode her much."

You'd wear down anyone or anything, Mercy thought, but she judged it wisest to avoid double meanings. She luxuriated in stroking the mare and murmuring to her.

"Let's see you handle her," Zane proposed. He gave her a hand up and scowled as she hooked her knee above the sidesaddle horn. "Do you know what I'd do if I were an enlightened female?"

"I'd love to hear!"

"I'd get some of that material made into divided skirts," Zane said, "even trousers. Damned if I'd ride to one side like that! Any fool can look at a horse and tell how it was meant to be straddled."

"Indeed!" flashed Mercy. "Then one can only assume that the fool of a man who invented sidesaddles hated women!"

"Probably." Zane's eyes sparkled with mischief. "To men, at least, the shape of the body or object suggests its natural use, the best way of grasping and using it. Now, this can be varied for piquancy or the novelty of experiment, but there can be no doubt that the best way to ride and control a horse is with a leg on either side, just as a similar position . . . "

"I think I *will* ask for some divided skirts," Mercy interrupted. "If you don't mind, I can't think why anyone else should, and it would be such a relief!"

"Take the mare around to the clearing," Zane said. "Then, if she and the gear all suit you, we'll go for a ride."

It was a delight to feel the intelligent, sensitive response to the slightest pressure of the reins. Castaña loped and cantered and single-footed till Mercy longed to turn her loose on a broad expanse where they could stretch out and skim the earth, the way she used to do with Star.

"She's no hacienda breed that only knows how to trot," Zane approved as he signaled Mercy to halt near the stable.

Zane's raven-black stallion was led out for him and

the boy opened the gate near the stable. They skirted the corrals and picked up a narrow track where Zane led till they emerged on what was a fairly good but somewhat overgrown road.

"The way to Tihosuco and Valladolid," Zane said. "Or one could go south from Tihosuco to Chan Santa Cruz."

"The Cruzob holy town?"

Zane nodded. "Myself, I prefer Tulum, on the coast, about a day's ride from Chan Santa Cruz. The castle is on a cliff above the water, and from it you can watch that incredible blue-green water surge over the white sands to break on the rocks. My father used to take me there. He never got over his love of the sea. But the region belong to the Cruzob now. Tulum used to be a center for the worship of the setting sun; the ancients made pilgrimages there. They believed an underground tunnel led from there out beneath the sea."

"It sounds beautiful—and fearsome."

"Both. But I wish I could show you the sea. Those Caribbean waters have to be the clearest in the world. Pure white sand can be seen under the waves a long way out, as if one were looking through a gigantic liquid sapphire. There are palms and clumps of purplish periwinkles, and fantastic coral reefs often make pleasant, sheltered spots. My father also took me to a place called Akumal, Place of the Turtle, which had a beautiful curving, sheltered beach. We'd hired a native boat to sail us to Isla Majeres, where Lafitte had headquartered, and to Cozumel, another pretty island. We grilled our catch and swam and lay on the sand. At night the stars and moon were so close that it seemed we could touch them. I'm glad my father didn't live to the time when he couldn't visit the sea. He had a good death—he had heart failure while breaking in a new horse, and he was dead when he struck the ground."

Mercy didn't know how to respond to that. After a long moment, she spoke, softly. "You miss the sea, too."

"Yes. But it was a holiday for me, a special time, not a home, as it was for my father till he settled at La Quinta. I'm sure if it hadn't been for me, he'd have gone back to sailing after my mother died." Zane gave her a sheepish glance. "I blasted you for talking so much about your father," he said gruffly. "It would seem it's your turn."

"I like to hear about your father."

"No need to be polite."

140

"But I do! It makes you seem more . . . human."

His mouth twitched. "Even the devil was young once. Shall we try your mare's canter here, where the road is broad enough?"

At the end of an hour they turned back toward La Quinta. "Xia's village is about ten miles down that side road," Zane said and pointed as he swung Kisin around. The black horse was named for the old god of earthquakes, who was also, Zane had said, the Mayan devil. "I'll take you there soon if you'd like to go. As I warned you, La Quinta's isolated."

"I'd like to see the village, of course," said Mercy, stroking Castaña's neck, inexpressibly happy at being on a fine horse again and at having stayed on good terms with this unpredictable man for a record length of time. "But La Quinta has everything essential. I don't mind that it's not close to a city."

"Give yourself time," Zane said with an edge of bitterness. "My wife loved it at first, but within six months she was calling it a prison."

"People differ. You, for instance, are the only plantation owner anyone seems to know who tends to his own lands. And though nearly everyone else uses debt-laborers, you don't."

"Good business in both cases."

"Perhaps. But practice reflects attitude."

His dark gray eyes raked over her jeeringly. "And you want me to believe that you, too, are an exception?"

The stinging jibe brought angry words crowding to her lips. She swallowed them, then waited till she could speak with dignity.

"Believe what you please."

She pushed Castaña ahead, but Kisin soon came up even. "Are you saying that *you* could be happy at La Quinta, never long for society, shops, or the company of other women?"

"Chepa's the most interesting woman I've ever met. I doubt if I can even start to learn everything she knows."

Zane shot Mercy a strange look. "Learning—that's important to you, isn't it? But you'll miss women of your own kind to talk to."

"Why? I've never had them. I talked with my father."

Zane scowled. "Oh, yes, your father."

They rode past the corrals in silence. Boys came to

take their horses. Zane, springing down easily, lifted Mercy from her saddle, holding her off the ground for just a second longer than necessary.

"The mare seems all right. Will you keep her?"

"She's wonderful. I'll very much appreciate the use of her, but, of course, Jolie should have Castaña in a few years if she still wants her."

"Jolie will be enamored of the colt we select when she gets over her pouting. It's not good to ride a horse you don't own. I give you Castaña."

"She's too valuable a gift for me not to feel indebted."

His lean face broadened with a smile. "Marvelous! How many gifts will it take to mortgage you so completely that you become . . . grateful?"

"I already am."

"Yet not enough."

"What you ask has nothing to do with gratitude. You speak of loneliness! I'd die in that tower."

His eyes smoldered over her till she felt consumed by licking, tiny flames. "Even if I came to you each night?"

Her lungs constricted and her body yearned for him so fiercely that she could barely whisper. "You expect me to trade what I can learn and be and do for existing to gratify your lust?"

"Plenty of women would be glad for the chance." His raw laughter mocked them both. "Not for my personal charms, possibly, but I pay well."

Mercy stared at him, angry, yet sorrowful. Why did he shut himself away from all feeling? "You pay money for whores, but a lover costs trusting and risking hurt."

He eyed her with a sardonic curve to his lips. "You have so much experience? I had supposed the scarcely trustworthy Philip to have been the only enjoyer of your favors."

She said nothing. He didn't want to understand, so he'd always be able to twist or evade her words. She turned toward the house, but long, hard fingers closed on her wrist, swinging her around.

"Has there been someone else?" he queried, his gaze probing her like a dark steel blade.

She tried to wrench away, could not, and threw back her head. "My life before I became your . . . your bond-maid is none of your business!"

"By God, it is! If I've let you withhold from me, by your pious, innocent tricks, what you've given others . . . "

142

He dragged her to the wall between the great house and Macedonio's, imprisoned her with a bent arm on either side, and pried up her chin with one hand. "Have you been with other men than your spineless husband? Has your purity all been deceit?"

"If I'd loved another man . . . if I'd taken him, I still wouldn't think I'd deceived you!" she blazed. "Loving's different from being bought, from indulging an animal need!"

"*If* you loved—*if* you'd taken!" Zane gripped her shoulders till they ached. "Plainly! Have you had a man other than Philip?"

Trembling with outrage and the treacherous response of her body to his hands, Mercy said between her teeth, "That, Zane Falconer, is none of your business! You didn't win my past!"

He spun out and away from the wall, hustling her with him. Mercy hung back, digging in her feet. "Where . . . where are we going?"

"To the tower."

"You said you wouldn't force me!"

"That was when I thought you to be chaste."

"Why have you let one woman shape the way you judge all of us?" she cried. "My husband served me badly, too, but I hope I have enough sense to blame him personally, not every man in the world!"

"You are a prisoner of your past, too."

"How?"

His mouth twitched. "You insist on a wedding ring, which brings us back to the question: Have you been with anyone but your husband?"

Mercy swallowed, but his grip was inexorable. "There . . . there was no one else," she muttered.

He gave a harsh laugh. "How quickly your brave defiance yields to whimpering!"

"If I outweighed you by eighty pounds and was a foot taller, I might make you whimper, too!"

"Or blench." He stopped, looking down at her.

A tear squeezed from her eye, and though she blinked angrily, he saw it and wiped it away with the ball of his thumb. "Mercy, Mercy, why are you so stubborn? We both know I can do with you whatever I will."

"You can rape me—once."

He raised an eyebrow. "How would you limit it, my sweet, when you can't prevent it? You're too tough-minded to kill yourself for your 'disgrace,' and you'd find it damned hard to kill me."

"I'd get away from here."

"And swap me for starvation or perhaps slavery in some *batab*'s hammock at Chan Santa Cruz?"

"If you break your word, whatever happens to me is on your conscience."

"You think I have one?"

"I know you do."

He put his hand out deliberately, fondled her breast, and watched her eyes as the nipple tautened and her body flexed involuntarily.

"That gives you the dimmest idea of what else I have," he said, his face strained and cruel. "I want you till it sometimes crowds everything else out of me, including what you call conscience. Don't push me too far, Mercy."

He released her so abruptly that she stumbled backward. He gave her a crooked smile. "Besides," he finished softly, "I'm not convinced, however you protest now, that once I took you, you couldn't be resigned to some sweet bondage. Philip was your husband, but did he make you shudder with rapture, beg for more? Did he ever drive you out of that funny, sober, righteous mind of yours?"

She stared at him, shrinking. He whirled away and shouted toward the stables. In a moment a boy reappeared with Kisin. "Tell Chepa I won't be home for dinner," Zane called over his shoulder.

Stunned, Mercy watched him vault into the saddle and go back the way they'd come. Where was he riding? Xia's village? Mercy tripped as she walked back to the house, feeling exhausted, holding her breath to try to quell the throbbing ache in her loins. The black coral he'd given her seemed to jab into her throat.

He had Xia. She had no one. How long could this go on?

She stopped in the sitting room, went around examining and praising the sewing work, and managed to explain the divided skirts she decided to have made from challis and the gray-blue poplin. These must be full enough not to cling, but they shouldn't be cumbersome, either.

One of the women had arthritic hands, and just that morning they had been bothering her so much that Mercy suggested she stop sewing. Now the woman was stitching more briskly than anybody. When Mercy asked with sign language and a few Spanish words what had happened, the woman smiled and pointed out to the veranda to where some bees hummed around a morning-glory vine. She then touched several red welts on her hands.

"Poison from bee kills poison in hands," Chepa explained, coming in. "Ants can help, too."

There was no doubting the cure, though it seemed extreme. Mercy told Chepa that Zane wouldn't be home for dinner, and, finding it difficult to bear the housekeeper's troubled expression, she passed on to her own room.

For a while that afternoon, she'd been happy and Zane had seemed to be, as if he felt more for her than the ready lust he'd admit to. It was as if he kept trying to persuade himself that she deserved nothing else, that no woman did. And just as she wouldn't be his unless he loved her, he wouldn't lie to cajole her into bed.

He thought, of course, that she was intent on marriage, but hurt and angered as she was by him, she didn't think he'd use that kind of deceit. If he ever said he loved her, she could believe him.

But his wife had scarred him deeply, so deeply he might never again trust enough to love. Maybe the only way he could feel safe with a woman kept over a long period of time was to lock her in the tower and share with her only his eroticism, not his life. Mercy knew frustration over her might drive him to install some woman there, and she hoped she wouldn't know about it, though a secret like that would be hard to keep quiet around La Quinta.

Changing into a dress embroidered with birds, Mercy was brushing out her hair when a reflection in the mirror made her gasp.

Turning, she stared at the jaguar on the window ledge. Blood was smeared around its carved fangs, and it was posed with its forefeet on a green-and-red object.

Mercy put down her brush and moved slowly to the window. It was real blood on the small animal, most of it coming off when she picked it up. Its prey was a bird, surely a quetzal, made from clay covered with bits of green and red feathers. There was more blood on the throat.

A grisly little charade. Jolie had gone to considerable trouble to arrange the surprise, and the ribbon with which Mercy had changed the wild cat into a pet one was wadded in the corner, also smudged with blood.

Perhaps it was childish, but Mercy felt uneasy at leav-

145

ing the tableau. She washed the blood from the jaguar and newly modeled quetzal and perched the bird on the jaguar's shoulder.

Jolie made a hasty meal of it when she learned that her father wouldn't be at the table. As she reached for several honeycakes, already on her feet and mumbling excuses, Mercy lightly touched a cut on the end of the girl's finger.

"Did you hurt yourself?"

Jolie yanked her hand back, as if burned by Mercy. "It's just a scratch!"

"A jaguar scratch?"

"You'd better be careful!"

"I'm not afraid of such tricks, Jolie, but I don't like them, either. I don't want to forbid you your grandmother's room, but I shall if you keep this up."

"It's more my room than yours!"

"In a way, perhaps, but it's where I'm living."

"I wish you'd never come," said Jolie with quiet hatred, her violet eyes narrowed. "You're in between my room and Papa's, and now you stole my horse!"

Whirling away, she vanished through the gate, leaving Mercy to sip hot chocolate and brood. Had it been wise to force the issue with the child? It had seemed best to get it over with while Zane was away. He was already irritated with Jolie, and his sudden attempts at discipline were likely to cause more problems than they cured.

But why, Mercy wondered, did she feel so lonely and forlorn because he wasn't there?

Zane didn't appear for breakfast, but he came to stand in the doorway during classes and listened with his dark head tilted to one side while Mercy explained that well-born Chinese girls had their feet bound to make them tiny and admired, though the bandages had a maiming effect and virtually crippled the select victims.

"Corsets are just as bad," Zane snorted. "How any woman whose waist has been squeezed to sixteen inches can have a healthy baby is beyond me. But the deadliest blight of all is the way we bind minds—tight, tight, no chance to think, and once all sense of proportion is warped and intelligence hugs its fetters, it doesn't matter much if the body's twisted, too."

"It's interesting that women undergo most of their mal-

146

formations in order to be more attractive to men," observed Mercy. "At best, men have some ideal of feminine beauty, and woe to the female in that society who's too thin or too plump, too tall, short, or shaped differently from what men have decided they want!"

"I'll be my own shape," said Jolie, protectively tucking her feet beneath her. "I'm glad you're back, Papa. I don't like for you to be away."

"If you get nervous, you must tell Doña Mercy."

"I'm not nervous," she said, dismissing Mercy with a glance of veiled disdain. "It's just that the house doesn't feel right when you're gone."

"Come, minx, don't turn an overnight trip into the voyage of Ulysses!" He tousled her shiny hair and left the room.

As he passed, Mercy saw on his muscular brown throat a small oval of tiny, regular marks, and near it was the raised welt of a scratch. Xia, or whomever he'd gone to, had given him a tumultuous night. He could now ignore Mercy till his male tensions started building again; and that thought made her so angry that she would have enjoyed scratching him herself, but not from transports of passion.

When lessons were over, Jolie lingered for a moment. "Would you like to see the old maps and genealogies of the village?" she asked. "This afternoon, the scribe is going to show them to Salvador and me. Victoriano has arranged it."

"That would be interesting," Mercy said, startled at the overture. "Yes, I'd like to see them, if you're sure it's all right."

"It's arranged," repeated Jolie. She didn't smile but wore a look of fierce determination. Had she decided, however grudgingly, that she'd better make peace with Mercy? "Salvador and I will wait for you by Macedonio's at three o'clock."

"Thank you," said Mercy, smiling into the taut little face, hoping this would be the start of a tolerance that might warm to friendship. "I won't be late."

"Neither will we," Jolie said. Snatching Salvador's hand, she pulled him after her.

Zane and Jolie, on good terms again, filled the noon-time conversation with a discussion of the colts Jolie had announced she was eager to examine. It really did seem

147

that she had decided to adapt gracefully to the situation, though her gaze flicked hurriedly past Mercy when she looked her way at all.

"I'll be busy going over accounts with Macedonio this afternoon," said Zane as they rose at the end of the meal. "But if you wish to ride, I'll tell one of the men to accompany you."

"Thank you, but I won't have time today," Mercy said. "I'm going to visit the scribe with Salvador and Jolie."

"He's showing us the maps and genealogies!" Jolie said.

"Good!" Zane slanted Mercy a surprised but pleased glance. "But I think, Doña Mercy, that I didn't yet advise you against riding alone. Never do that. If I can't escort you, I'll send a reliable man."

Though Mercy loved solitary jaunts, it wouldn't have occurred to her to ride alone in this region, but she found the prohibition a trifle galling. Still, with his eyes holding hers, there was nothing to do but nod agreement.

"I'll meet you at three," she promised the child, and she went to her room while father and daughter drifted through the courtyard, their laughter floating back.

Mercy watched them through the window, the black head and the gold one. Each was the only blood relative the other had in the world; their closeness was both tender and alarming. *That's how Father and I were,* Mercy thought with a surge of pain. *Can I ever be that close to another man, ever trust one?* At least she could understand Jolie's possessiveness and give her room and time to accept an outsider. From this afternoon's invitation, that acceptance might come sooner than Mercy had dared to hope.

Lying down with Stevens' travels, she read till it was time to join the children.

Sóstenes Pec, the scribe, was a withered old man whose hands shook as he opened the rawhide-covered chest in the village's public building. He said something in Mayan to Victoriano Zuc, the *H-men,* and the only Indian male Mercy had yet seen who could be called fat. His skin looked woman-soft, and he had a trilling, rather high-pitched, voice.

In Spanish so slow and simple that Mercy could follow the gist of it, Sóstenes explained that he had learned to read and write from his father, who had learned from his father, who had studied with the priests in Tekax. The priests had destroyed all the old Mayan hieroglyphic manuscripts they could find because the hieroglyphs were so bound up with old gods and .beliefs. Still, the Spaniards hadn't tried to replace the Mayan language with Spanish, but had taught the sons of priests and leading families how to write Mayan words in European script, so nearly every village had a scribe who could do this.

Carefully, Sóstenes displayed documents concerning land and then a number of more or less handsomely ornamented genealogies. He spread out his own, painted on very thin bark, which showed a many-branched tree with a man and woman on either side of it. These, he said, were his great-grandparents, and on the branches were written the names of their descendants.

Next he exhibited a round map, also on bark, marking Mérida as Tihoo and showing Mani as the center of the country, according to the old Mayan tradition. Another map showed the village and surrounding region. There were royal grants of common land, several land treaties, and bills of sale.

Victoriano, who either spoke no Spanish or pretended not to, took Salvador to one side with several of the documents and, with Sóstenes' help, apparently explained to him some important facts about the village. Jolie pressed a small pointed finger on a symbol a short distance from the village on the map that Mercy was studying.

"This is what's left of a temple with a big jaguar. Would you like to go see it? It's near a wellspring in a cave that's supposed to go way down underground, maybe all the way to the sea."

"How far is it?" Mercy asked, hoping the expedition would be feasible. She was eager to respond to these first hints of acceptance from the puzzling, haughty, yet vulnerable little girl.

"Oh, half an hour, maybe," Jolie said and shrugged. "We wouldn't be late for dinner. Salvador's already been there. We can let him study with Victoriano while we go on."

"All right."

Mercy thanked Sóstenes, praising the care that had been taken with the priceless old records. She said goodbye to Victoriano while Jolie, in Mayan, must have explained to him and Salvador where she was taking Mercy.

Flora was waiting outside the council building and

149

greeted them with delighted whimpers, pacing along beside them as they took a narrow path leading out of the village. They passed several cornfields where men were harvesting and one place where an Indian was clearing a new field, alternately using an ax and machete, depending on the size of the tree or bush.

"This all must have been part of the old city," Jolie said, kicking at the round-edged stones of what had been a wall. "Papa says it covered several miles, but there's not much left of it now except this jaguar shrine and the tower behind the orchards." She shot Mercy a weighing glance. "Have you seen the tower?"

"Yes." Mercy tried to avert questions about the circumstances. "It would be a great place for Rapunzel. Do you know that story?"

"The name of my grandfather's *chère amie* was Rosamunda," said Jolie with disconcerting directness. "He never loved her as he did my grandmother, but Chepa says a man should not live without a woman. Did Papa show you the tower?"

"Yes." Mercy's cheeks were hot. It was ridiculous to be interrogated like this by a child, but refusing to answer would make it seem she had something to hide.

Again, that strangely adult violet gaze touched her, then veered away. "Xia lived there once, you know."

What a grotesque conversation! But the only way Mercy could think of to manage it was to be matter-of-fact, to register no shock for the benefit of those sharply inquiring eyes.

"Yes, so your father said."

"Did he tell you she was *his chère amie?*" queried the girl, her eyes narrow violet slits.

Mercy's breath caught with stabbing pain. "That's none of my business," she contrived to say coolly after a moment. "And this is an improper subject, which we'll not discuss again. However, since you plainly know more about such things than you should, let me assure you that I'll never live in that tower!"

Jolie nodded and sighed. "That's what Xia said. She said you'd make Papa marry you."

Was there no way to end this absurd and wildly indecent exchange? "Your father doesn't intend to marry," said Mercy in a crisp tone. "And since I've never met Xia, I'm amazed that she'd say such things, especially to you."

150

"She doesn't think I'm a baby," snapped Jolie. "She knows I can understand things."

With supreme effort, Mercy held her peace, but she had a vastly uncomfortable flash of how an older woman possessed of a priestess' lore, if not supernatural powers, could work on the mind and senses of a child like this. If Xia *had* said those things, and Jolie's crudities had the ring of truth, the woman had to be in love with Zane. And even if he'd never marry her, she at least had his body, which Mercy must deny.

Jolie scooped up Flora and set her over her shoulder. "There it is," she said, pointing. "See the jaguar? Around on the other side there are signs carved on the stone."

The jaguar was really two seemingly male and female heads and torsos connected by one smoothly massive shared lower body. The heads faced in opposite directions. Dominating the rubble of walls and fallen arches, the double beast had evidently been kept cleared of creeping vines and plants by some devotee. A short distance away water gleamed from a limestone grotto that led into a dark hole.

Mercy was moving around to see the glyphs Jolie had mentioned when there was a cracking sound, scrambling, and then a cry.

11

A few feet away, Salvador lay sprawled in a hole, which he had evidently fallen into. A snake with a yellow-marked head so deeply pitted that it seemed to have four nostrils was struggling in a litter of branches and leaves. With a hiss, Flora shot past Mercy and landed on the snake's back, tearing it open with suddenly lethal claws, ripping out its entrails.

Mercy snatched up Salvador, lifted him clear of the hole, and put him on the ground in front of the jaguar, flinching at the marks on his leg.

151

"Cuatro narices!" Jolie was wailing. "It's poisonous!"

"Run for Chepa and your father!" Mercy ordered.

She'd never tended a snakebite, but she remembered a treatment her father had used, repudiating as worse than useless the popular remedy of whiskey. *"Don't let the person run or spread the poison through the blood,"* he'd warned. *"And get the venom out—quickly."*

"Salvador," Mercy whispered, "Salvador, be quiet."

Jolie plunged away with a terrified moan. Mercy had no knife. Suddenly she thought of the sharp black coral around her neck. Slipping it off, she selected the sharpest piece, gritted her teeth, and cut a cross over each fang mark. Clamping her mouth over one incision, she sucked and spat, sucked at the other and spat again, then returned to the first cut.

Salvador didn't move or cry, but his body was trembling. When she glanced up, his dark eyes watched her with a trust that made her suck again, though by now she should have most of the venom out. Her mouth felt strange. Father had said it was important not to have cuts or sores in the mouth. She spat several times, rinsing with the flow of saliva. She decided to start carrying him. She didn't know what more, if anything, Chepa could do, but waiting here was just too frightening, and the minutes she could save might be vital.

Lifting the boy, staggering under his weight, she talked to him softly as she labored along the path, assuring him in mixed Spanish and English that most snakebites didn't kill, and, anyway, most of the poison should be out.

Sweat had broken out on his face but he smiled. *"Gracias,"* he whispered. His eyes closed. Mercy plodded on, her back and arms aching, praying for someone to hurry. Flora, having devoured all she wanted of the snake, stalked regally before them.

Mercy, obsessed till now with trying to treat the bite, began to reconstruct. Salvador must have finished his lesson with Victoriano and run ahead to surprise them, hiding behind the jaguar in the shrine, which was probably a favorite retreat of the children's. When he'd bounded out, he'd fallen into the hole, where the snake was resting.

In another second, Mercy would have stepped on that deceptive covering of leaves and branches herself. If she'd been bitten, would Jolie have been so stricken? Would she have run as if devil-possessed for help?

Mercy pushed such thoughts away. The cornfields were deserted, but the village must be close. She hoped Jolie had called for help as she ran through. Gasping for breath now, Mercy felt so dizzy that she wondered if she'd swallowed and absorbed some of the venom.

A small calloused hand brushed her cheek. *"Lo siento,"* murmured the boy.

"Está bueno," Mercy encouraged. "Chepa will help."

She heard a confusion of voices ahead. Victoriano appeared, followed by Sostenes and a dozen excited women. Victoriano snapped an order that melted away the group, except for the scribe, and he took Salvador from Mercy's exhausted arms, examining the cuts Mercy had made, scowling, and shaking his head as she tried to explain to Sostenes in garbled Spanish what she'd done.

If the boy died, it was plain that the *H-men* would blame her, but before he had a chance to try his remedies, Chepa trotted into the village, moving with astonishing speed for her ample build, and gathered Salvador to her bosom, dismissing the *H-men* almost as curtly as he had sent away the curious women.

Victoriano drew himself up and seemed ready to blast the housekeeper when Zane, followed by a white-faced Jolie, strode into the clearing. Again, Mercy told what she'd done.

"It sounds reasonable," Zane said. "I'll carry him, Chepa. You go ahead and make your brews."

Easily lifting Salvador, he spoke with courtesy to the *H-men* and scribe and moved off with such long steps that Mercy and Jolie had to run to keep up.

"You sucked out the poison," he said over his shoulder. "Little fool, to take such a chance! Are you sure you didn't swallow some?"

"I spat it out."

Zane glared at her as best he could while keeping one eye on his route. "You look awful! Chepa will make you some tea, too, and put you to bed! Sucking fer-de-lance venom! Your father was crazy to tell you such a thing!"

"He thought it worked better than anything else."

"For the victim, maybe! But how about you? What if you have a canker or hollow tooth or . . ."

"Don't yell at her, Papa!" Jolie gave his arm an admonishing tug and darted ahead. "I'll bring some water so Mercy can rinse her mouth."

Relieved of Salvador's weight, Mercy breathed less painfully, but her head throbbed. Still, she kept up with Zane till Jolie intercepted her with a gourd of water and insisted she swish it thoroughly around her mouth. When this was done, Jolie grasped Mercy's hand and they hurried to the kitchen.

Zane held the boy while Chepa measured herbs into an earthenware pot. Water must have been boiling for some other use, for a kettle of it was ready and she poured some of this over the leaves and dried blossoms.

"Open your mouth," Zane commanded, scowling down at Mercy.

"I don't have any sores," she said crossly.

"Open," he advised, "or I'll do it for you."

He would, too. Rather than be handled like a horse put up for sale, Mercy opened her mouth as she had done when her father was examining a sore throat. She gasped as Zane, still holding Salvador, deftly pulled up the edge of one lip and then the other, scanning her gums and her mouth's inner flesh before he gave a relieved nod and took away his big but oddly gentle fingers.

"Doesn't seem to be any way you could absorb poison, as long as you didn't swallow it. Sit down and keep still. We'll tend to you as soon as we've got the boy settled."

Mayel brought in a lizard, which Chepa cut in half with one swing of a heavy knife. While one side squirmed, she clamped the other on the snakebite and held it in place with a broad twist of hemp fiber, which she entrusted to Mayel while she strained out the pungent tea. Sweetening it with honey, she told Zane to hold the cup for Salvador, then poured a mug of the brew for Mercy. Discarding the lizard poultice, Chepa applied the remaining half and had Mayel keep it tightly pressed to the bite while she looked at the small half-corpse and nodded in satisfaction.

"Not much poison. Doña Mercy get nearly all." She beamed. "Good healer. You show me."

"I'll be glad to," said Mercy with a shaky smile. "This tea is very good."

"Make sweat," said Chepa. "Make sleep." She took the gruesome bandage off Salvador and handed it and the other piece to Mayel with directions to bury them deep in the ground. Doña Caterina, Macedonio's wife, and foster mother to Salvador, rushed into the kitchen and was given her foster son, along with nursing instructions. She carried him off, accompanied by Mayel, who bore a pot of the herbal brew.

"Will he be all right?" Jolie asked tautly. "Will he, Papa?"

"He should be good as new in a few days," Zane promised. "You can go see him for a few minutes now and then, but don't be pestering his mother out of her wits. All he needs now is rest and Chepa's tea." Staring down at Mercy, he said grimly, "Now we'll take care of you."

"I'm fine," she insisted, finishing the bracingly aromatic drink.

"You'll lie down, cover up, and have broth or soup tonight," Zane decreed. "Chepa, help me put Doña Mercy to bed."

Before she could evade him, he swept her into his arms and started through the courtyard, trailed by Chepa and Jolie. Feeling ridiculous, Mercy tried to deny the comfort of being cradled against his strongly beating heart.

"I can walk!" she argued.

"Not till I say you can." He placed her on the bed and waited behind the lacquer screen while Chepa helped Mercy out of her dress and into a nightgown and tucked her in snugly with a blanket and extra coverlet from the armoire's bottom drawer.

All this time Jolie stood by the window, gazing fixedly at the jaguar. Now she ran to the bed, seizing Mercy's hands.

"I . . . I knew the snake was there! I tried to kill you! If Salvador dies, I'll get a lot of snakes to kill me!"

As Mercy stared in shock, Zane grasped his daughter and spun her around. "What did you say?"

She tried to move her lips several times before any sound came out. "I took Mercy to the jaguar shrine. I knew a *cuatro narices* was in the hole. It was covered enough to trap it, but a person could crash through." She shuddered convulsively. "Oh, Papa, beat me! Do something! I feel so wicked!"

"You didn't find the snake and do all that yourself," Zane said in a hoarse voice after a frozen moment during which Chepa gave a disbelieving cry. "Who helped you? Salvador? If so, we should have let the young devil die!"

Jolie frantically shook her head. "Salvador didn't know, Papa! He . . . he likes Doña Mercy. That was one more reason I . . . I hated her."

Zane grasped Jolie and shook her till her golden hair bobbed. "Who was it? Who put the snake there?"

"Zane!" Mercy cried. "Come here, Jolie. Sit by me and we'll talk about it till you feel better."

"Feel better!" Zane exploded, the curve of his nostrils etched white. "This is no prank! A French convent may be what you need, Jolie, before it comes to prison!"

"Come here, Jolie," said Mercy again, and this time Zane released her.

The child clambered up beside Mercy, buried her face on her shoulder, and sobbed heartbrokenly. Zane paced and swore and Chepa seemed to be muttering prayers or invocations.

"I . . . I don't like to tell," Jolie said at last. "But it was so bad I guess I have to, don't I?"

"I think so," said Mercy. "I can understand your wanting to get rid of me, Jolie, and I don't think you knew what it would really mean. But a grown-up would."

"Xia did it."

"Xia!" choked Zane.

He flexed and unflexed his hands while Jolie blurted out her halting story. She met Xia every week at the jaguar shrine to be instructed in magic. The last time she had spilled out her feelings of jealousy, how much she wished Mercy weren't at La Quinta.

Xia had suggested a way to cure that, a way that would seem an accident. "She said if it didn't kill you, it might frighten you enough to make you go away," confessed Jolie, avoiding her father's eyes. "And she said if this didn't work, there were other ways. . . ." Sturdy arms tightened around Mercy. "I didn't really want to kill you!" Jolie wailed. "I . . . I just wanted you not to be here!"

No one spoke for a long time. Mercy felt sick at the depth of Xia's hatred. It was easy enough to understand, shocking as it was, how a clever woman could play on and influence an admiring young girl who was fiercely resentful of an intruder. Jolie didn't truly comprehend death, but Xia did.

"I'm leaving your punishment to Mercy," Zane told his child heavily. "But whatever she says, I'm tempted to send you to school in France, or at least in Mérida. You need control before you do serious damage to yourself, if to no one else."

Jolie was mute, though she'd shrunk closer to Mercy at

each of her father's words. Mercy didn't know what to do. Jolie was remorseful now, but how long would it last in a child who could connive at murder, a child who'd proved an apt pupil of a deadly woman?

"What do you think, Jolie?" she finally asked.

"I've been bad," whispered the child. "If Salvador gets well, I'll try to be very very good. I . . . I don't want to be a witch! And I never want to see Xia again!" Her arms gripped Mercy tighter. "Please stay and help me. Help me be good."

Mercy held her close and soothed her. "You don't have to be so good that we'll think you're sick," she said. "But maybe you could help Salvador's mother while he's sick and learn to make his tea if Chepa will teach you."

"I teach," Chepa vowed, eyeing her adored nurseling with a severe expression. "Teach plenty!"

With pathetic dignity, Jolie turned and looked at Zane. "You won't send me away, Papa? I'll go if you say so. I'm too bad even to be alive. But I don't know what I'd do away from you and La Quinta."

"It's up to Mercy," Zane said.

That was harsh. Mercy would have given much to spare her small former enemy. "I can't teach you as much as the nuns, Jolie," she said, "but I think in a few more months you'll have greatly improved my Spanish."

"Thank you! *Mil gracias!*" Jolie rocked Mercy with an energetic hug and then went off with Chepa.

Zane stalked over, frowning as he pulled the covers up tighter around Mercy's chin. She was growing drowsy from the tea and warmth. "You live up to your name," he said. "I hope you won't be sorry." His dark head was close to hers as he brushed a kiss on her hand, but by the time her dulled senses registered what was happening, he had left the room.

She slept till Jolie brought her a bowl of soup, followed by Zane with a candle and more tea. "I don't think I need that at all," Mercy said, smothering a yawn. "I'm not the least bit sick. How's Salvador?"

"Sleeping and a little feverish," Zane said. "The leg's swelling some, but Chepa's poulticed it with *toloache* and turpentine. The tea will help him sleep and ease the pain."

"I'd like to go see him."

"Wait till morning." Mercy started to rebel. Zane stopped

her arguments with a sip of the hot, honey-sweetened brew. "Even if all you're suffering from is a fit of nerves, rest won't hurt you. And Chepa's tea will send you off to sleep like a baby."

"But . . . "

"You think it's self-indulgent, even sinful, to be in bed when you're not racked with fever and ague," Zane chided. His eyes danced and he added so softly that Jolie, who had strayed over to the jaguar in the window ledge, couldn't hear, "Beds have sweeter uses, but have a lesson now, teacher, in the restorative effects of slumber."

This son of a pirate was capable of locking her in, and Chepa's potion must have had a lingering effect, for, by the time she had eaten her soup and, under Zane's watchful gaze, drunk the fresh tea, Mercy was glad to accept Jolie's hug, Zane's amused wishes for sound sleep, and cuddle back into her nest of pillows. She'd be up in the morning; everything would return to normal, including Zane. But tonight it was lovely to feel his concern and drift off while feeling safe and warm in his protection.

She was awake at dawn, full of energy. She dressed and before breakfast went to visit Salvador. Jolie was already there, standing by her friend's hammock, puffs of fatigue around her eyes. She was feeding Salvador bits of fresh pineapple as if he'd been a fledgling, while Doña Caterina baked tortillas on a flat stone.

Rising to greet Mercy, the mayordomo's gentle-eyed wife thanked her for helping the boy and made Mercy understand that his fever had subsided and that now he was hungry, a good sign.

Chepa came in to apply a new dressing and clucked approvingly at the appearance of the leg. It was red and puffy around the fang marks, but Mercy had seen bee stings that looked worse. He balked at the tea Chepa tried to give him.

"He'd like to have lessons today," Jolie explained. "Can he, Doña Mercy?"

Mercy looked at Chepa, who shrugged. "He keep leg up till swelling gone. Maybe lessons good—make him ready to drink tea."

Doña Caterina was glad for Salvador to have company while she did the laundry. So it was agreed that after breakfast class would be held by the hammock, after which both Jolie and Salvador would have Chepa's sedative brew and rest.

Zane stopped in and somewhat grudgingly approved the plan after a shocked look at Jolie and an almost insultingly thorough inspection of Mercy.

"I suppose lessons will keep you out of trouble," he said. "And we can't keep you drugged all the time. But, Doña Mercy, if you're not too tired this afternoon, I'd like to take you riding."

Mercy had hoped to take Castaña for at least a quick canter. A ride with Zane, in his present obliging temper, would be wonderful, dangerously bittersweet, as such joys must be unless he changed his views. She told him she could be ready at any appointed time.

As they carried the globe and a few books to the mayordomo's house, Jolie told Mercy that she'd confessed her responsibility for his accident to Salvador and that he'd forgiven her after a hard scolding for trying to get rid of Mercy in such a horrible way.

"No one else has to know, do they?" inquired Jolie anxiously. "That would be so awful!"

Relieved that Jolie's mood of extreme self-flagellation was passing, Mercy refrained from pointing out that ambush with a fer-de-lance wasn't exactly admirable. "I think everyone knows what they need to," she said. "Let's help Salvador get well and forget the whole thing."

Jolie glanced up, her brow furrowed. "There's still Xia." As a cold glow of warning touched Mercy, Jolie added, "Papa's going to talk to her, though."

So, it seemed, was Mercy. When she met Zane at the stables shortly after lunch, he gruffly asked how long it was going to take her to get some decent riding clothes, said he'd never known a boy so eager to learn that he begged for lessons while he was sick, and then, as Castaña followed Kisin along the road they'd taken the day before, he announced that they were bound for Xia's village.

"I considered quietly wringing her neck," he said dryly. "But I think knowledge of what she almost did to her son and a few other things I intend to tell her will ensure her good behavior."

"But why flaunt me at her?"

"To grind the point into her so that she won't forget." The bleakness in his eyes faded as he grinned. "Besides, I promised to show you that miraculous branch of copal

159

that was crucified in place of Salvador, and I doubt, after this visit, that either of us is likely to visit Xia again."

Did that mean he was giving up his mistress?

"Why are you frowning?" Zane asked.

Mercy hesitated.

"Out with it!" Zane said impatiently. "I'd rather tell you the brutal truth about anything than leave you to jump to your own weird conclusions."

Smarting at the goad, Mercy said coldly, "When you told me that Xia had taken refuge in your tower, you said she wasn't . . . yours."

"She wasn't . . . isn't . . . never could be. Xia belongs to herself and perhaps a dream of power."

"But you . . . you were . . ."

"We had each other, if that's what you mean, but the idea of Xia being any man's kept woman is laughable."

"Indeed?" asked Mercy frostily. "I thought you believed that capacity was universal in women."

"Some snake venom stayed on your tongue," he retorted. "Xia would have maintained an *alliance* with me, but I need something different from a woman."

"Like subjection?"

His long mouth clamped tight. "You want to quarrel. I won't indulge you, madam."

He sent the gleaming black horse into a canter. Mercy held Castaña back, nursing her wrath, though she felt like crying over the way their relationship, so comforting and close last night, had gone sour. Xia might not have agreed to be his dependent mistress, but she certainly must love him to attempt murder.

A chill ran down Mercy's spine, which she stiffened resolutely as she followed Zane down the turn-off to her enemy's village.

Xia had golden skin and eyes, black hair dressed in a high coil, and her smiling cat-like profile was like that of an Egyptian queen. Her sandaled feet were carefully tended, as were her tapering fingers. Her white cotton dress was embroidered all over with hummingbirds and flowers.

She invited them into her house, sending a girl for hot chocolate. Luxury was manifested by a table with two chairs and several handsome chests. On the top of one were books, including several manuscripts in Mayan European script.

Greeting Mercy in beautiful Spanish that made her acutely aware of her clumsiness in that tongue, Xia chatted of the harvest till their hot chocolate was finished, at which time Zane asked if Mercy could see the shrine.

"If she likes." Xia rose and led the way past the council house and common, where several hobbled burros grazed and the boy who'd taken the horses stood feeding them cornstalks.

This village was about the size of the one at La Quinta. Though sounds of children and hushed voices came from some of the huts, no one came out to stare at the visitors. The little church was cool and dim, its saints along the wall enjoying their offerings. There was the bleeding, crucified Christ and his sorrowing mother. But on the altar lay the object that made this church different, gave it a special sanctity, and brought the devout on pilgrimages.

The copal branch was the length of Mercy's arm, broken off with two stubs jutting out. Flowers were heaped around it, sweetening the thick, musty air.

And for this branch and the power it gave her, Xia had given her son. Mercy gazed at it in mingled fascination and horror. What if Zane hadn't been there that night seven years ago when Salvador hung on a cross! Zane was right. Xia was not a yielding woman . . . unless, perhaps, with him.

In front of the church Zane turned to the priestess. This time he spoke in Mayan. Xia's slim, sensuous body contracted. Then she stood perfectly still, her face expressionless except for a twitching at the corner of one eye.

When Zane had finished, she asked one question, one question only.

Zane replied in a word.

"Come," he said to Mercy.

In minutes they were mounted, leaving the ring of huts. Mercy ventured a half-glance around. Xia still stood in the church doorway, her figure as bright as a bedecked idol's against the interior darkness.

"What did you tell her?" Mercy had to ask. Frightening though the woman was, there was something in her stillness that cried out with torment.

Zane looked straight ahead. He'd been courteous in

161

front of Xia, but he was clearly in an evil temper. "I told her she had almost killed her son. I told her to keep away from my daughter. I told her if harm comes to you, even by apparent accident, I'd flay her pretty hide off her body and drape it around that copal limb."

Mercy sucked in her breath. She didn't ask any more questions, though she suspected that last terse query of Xia's, and his one word, had been the end of their "alliance."

In a few more days, Salvador seemed as healthy as ever, though two small scabbed pits formed on the bite. Now that Jolie was trying to help Mercy with Spanish and Mayan rather than make her feel stupid, Mercy's progress began to match that of her pupils.

She learned from Chepa, too, almost daily observing a new treatment or helping concoct and administer those she had seen before. Mayel had an aptitude for herbs, and Jolie found it interesting in fits and starts.

When Mercy's divided skirt was finished, Jolie wanted one. She was also pleased with her blue challis dress and insisted that she and Mercy wear their matching outfits for dinner the day they were finished.

"Please, Mercy, do my hair the way you wore yours when you were my age," Jolie urged. "Only please remember that I'm not a *young* child!"

Repressing a smile at this favorite loathing of Jolie's, Mercy did her best to tame Jolie's thick, wildly curly crown into sedate, long ringlets tied back in a bow. Jolie clapped at herself in the mirror.

"Now I look like someone from your country! Don't I, Mercy? If you didn't know, wouldn't you think I was from Texas, or even New Orleans?"

"Yes," said Mercy with a twinge. However truthfully she'd told Zane she didn't miss the society of a town, she *did* miss her country, familiar faces, and a sense of belonging. But as she tried to love and remember her father without futile mourning, she was trying to feel like that about her homeland. The day might come when she should go back, but till then she wanted to remember it with love and gratitude, but not the melancholy that would taint life at La Quinta and keep her from being as much a part of it as was possible.

Once, loosely quoting scripture, Elkanah had told her that the Jews in Babylon had been told to pray always for Jerusalem but also to "pray for the city where you are." The home of the heart and the home of the body—each required a different tribute.

Zane complimented their dresses and Jolie's hair, but he had little else to say. Fortunately, Jolie was at full bubble. Savoring a delicious lemon soup made with chicken broth, Mercy wondered if seeing them dressed alike had called up a memory of his wife. Since the visit to Xia, he'd been so distantly polite that Mercy was beginning to think she'd imagined his concern and kindness after Salvador's accident, or that Chepa's tea had made her hallucinate.

She'd thought she didn't like fending him off, but she liked his cool indifference even less!

Days had developed a pattern now, except for Sunday, when Chepa hustled Jolie and Mayel off to church. There was breakfast, then lessons till lunch, then private time to rest or read, and then learning cures from Chepa or having a ride, often with Jolie, whose Piñata was a plump, taffy-colored little mare with coquettishly long eyelashes. Zane sometimes joined them, but when he didn't Vicente rode behind, armed with a machete and a shotgun.

Mayel filled the bathtub every evening and kept the room dusted, but Mercy didn't really want a maid. So, apart from the time spent in school, the girl was usually with Chepa, who treated her as if she were indeed the daughter she had lost. Mayel, not forced to battle to defend her proud descent from Jacinto Canek, flitted about the house like a diligent butterfly, and her laughter tinkled like a silver bell against Chepa's resonant belly laughter.

After her bath, Mercy put on fresh clothes for dinner. As the nights cooled, dinner was served in the dining room, where a small fire crackled in the fireplace to take away the chill, though the days remained warm. It was not quite warm enough for the native cotton dresses within the shaded house, at least not for Mercy. Chepa and the other women simply added shawls. With a sigh, Mercy reverted to "civilized" clothing, though losing the unmatchable comfort of native dress was compensated for to a degree by the pleasure of having her first new clothes in years. The gray-blue satin dress was done, too, but it hung wistfully in the armoire next to the quetzal gown, awaiting an occasion or the advent of those rare guests Zane had been so emphatic about wishing to impress.

Christmas was coming, though the weather and green foliage made it hard to believe. Last Christmas hadn't been joyful, what with Philip berating her reluctance to leave the States and thus preventing him from accompanying Jo Shelby or the other leaders to Mexico, but Mercy's eyes misted and a lump swelled in her throat when she remembered Christmases before the war. Father's patients had brought turkey and hams, bacon, plum puddings, brandied fruitcakes, and pies, convinced that a wifeless man would have no holiday cheer unless they provided it, which they did with such excess that Father usually gave away most of the largesse to families in need. And there were parties with eggnog and mulled wine and carolers. . . .

Mercy tried to bring her thoughts back to the present, but memories of Philip lingered perversely, probably because she almost never thought of him consciously. It was as if by that treachery of wagering her fate on a game he had excised himself from her surgically, but the angry hurt that welled in her now made her suspect the betrayal had been so callous, so unspeakable, that she'd merely sealed over the ugly abscessed wound in order to function.

Had he gone back to the States? Or joined Maximilian? Mercy hoped with fervent bitterness that she'd never see him again. She turned her concentration to what she could give the people closest to her at La Quinta.

Jolie had explained that Christmas day was a religious festival here, and that instead of on that day, gifts were exchanged on Epiphany, the Day of the Three Kings, which fell on January 6. But as Mercy had always used Christmas to remember friends—with small gifts like potpourri, dried fruit, nuts from the woods, winter bouquets of grass, pods, and air-dried flowers—she decided to do the same now.

Chepa would get the fluffy shawl, Mercy's one remaining luxury from before the war; ribbons would be perfect for Mayel, along with a necklace from the store; there would be a shirt from the same source for Salvador, plus a book of proverbs and fables in simple English that she was making for him. Jolie was a problem, and for the first time Mercy regretted the absence of fashionable shops. Then she remembered the soft toys of her youth and decided that a plump blue challis coati with button eyes could serve as both pillow and cuddle companion.

As for Zane . . . Handkerchiefs?

Mercy grimaced at the thought. For a reader, a book was always good, but, again, there were no shops. She'd noticed, though, that his books were marked with scraps of paper or string. If she could find enough bark of the kind used for maps and genealogies, she could make a supply of durable bookmarks, decorated with his initials, or . . . why not a ceiba, the tree of the center and fifth direction, for the owner of La Quinta Dirección?

Immensely pleased with the thought, she went to Chepa to find out what bark to use. She found her mentor with a middle-aged woman whose jaw was swollen.

"Good you see this," said Chepa. "Secret in my family. Victoriano want to know. I teach Mayel, instead." She smiled at the girl, who handed her a small vial. Chepa applied something to the patient's tooth, then spoke to her quietingly. "Now we wait for the tooth to get soft," she told Mercy. She added with a twinkle, "You no believe."

"If you can pull teeth painlessly, you could make a fortune in a city!" Mercy said. "What's in the vial?"

"Rattlesnake poison and vinegar."

"Rattlesnake poison!" Mercy was too close to the encounter with the fer-de-lance to entertain any feeling but dread for serpents. "You put venom in this woman's mouth?"

"On bad tooth." Chepa's tone was equable. "I use, father use, grandfather, back and back. No one ever die."

Mercy hoped she wouldn't have to choose between a toothache and this miracle method, but the patient showed no signs of distress or alarm. While they waited, Mercy asked about manuscript bark and was told that the inner bark of the fig tree had been used as paper by the ancients and that there were several of the trees growing near the tower.

Perhaps twenty minutes had passed when Chepa reached into the woman's obligingly opened mouth and wiggled the tooth. Then, without wrenching or tugging, Chepa seemed simply to lift the tooth out. She held it for Mercy to see before she gave it to the patient, who thanked her and obediently sipped the mint tea Mayel handed her.

Mercy shook her head. "Astounding!"

"Very old secret, but I teach you if you want."

"How do you get the poison?"

"Kill snake. Cut off head, and when really dead, take out fang."

Mercy shuddered. "Thanks very much, but I'd rather you did the tooth-pulling."

"Why, Doña Mercy!" came a voice from the door. "You should always learn anything you can! You never know when it'll be useful."

Eric Kensington filled the entrance so hugely blond and overpowering that even Chepa gasped. But what stopped Mercy's heart before it lunged and speeded, what made her brain whirl as if she were going to faint, was the man beside him.

Philip—Philip, her husband.

12

He smiled, his blue eyes as frank and cheery as a boy's, though the lines in his face seemed deeper. He came forward, his hands outstretched.

"Mercy, love! I've come to take you home!"

How could he? Walk in like this, grinning, actually seeming to think she'd welcome him! So enraged that she felt as if she were flying apart, exploding into thousands of tiny bits, Mercy put her hands behind her.

"You . . . you're a fool if you think I'd go anywhere with you ever again!" she shouted.

Philip stopped. The pupils of his eyes swelled and he flushed, but when he spoke his voice was soft, cajoling. "That—what happened—was all a wretched mistake, darling. I was drunk. When I came looking for you, you were gone. But now that I've found you, thanks to Kensington, I'll take such care of you as you can't imagine. I know now how much I need you!"

"If you come a step closer, I'll vomit on you!" It wasn't a threat; she was truly sick to her stomach, her whole being full of revulsion.

Philip's lips twisted. "Why, you little bitch!" he said under his breath. "You're my wife, and you'll do what I say!"

"That's enough, Cameron!" Zane's voice cracked like a whip as he thrust past Kensington. He must have been behind them listening. "She *was* your wife, but you made her my bond-slave. Keep your hands off my property!"

Philip spun around, but before he could argue the big Englishman interposed. "I beg your pardon, gentlemen, but this is scarcely the way to settle such an important matter. You've got to put us up for the night, Falconer, unless you want a bad name for being terribly inhospitable, so why don't we go have a drink and discuss this properly?"

"We've already discussed it, as you damned well know, Kensington. I said if Doña Mercy greeted her husband fondly, perhaps I'd let him purchase her bond. Since it's clear she hates the sight of him, there's nothing more to say."

"But she's my wife!" Philip cried.

"I have an overriding claim." Zane gestured for the men to precede him. "You're welcome to spend the night, of course. You may sling hammocks in the sitting room and Chepa will bring you food. Under the circumstances it would be awkward for you to have meals with the household."

Philip's weakly handsome face contorted. "By God!" he blurted out. "If you . . ."

"Come along, Philip," ordered his companion. He flourished a bow to Mercy. "I'm sorry it appears we shall not improve our acquaintance on this occasion, madam. But there'll be other times."

Dazed, Mercy stared after them. It was as if a loathsome, chained monster had broken loose in the murky depths of buried agonies and dreads and now glided toward her with Philip's smiling deceitful face attached to its gross vileness. She began to shake. Chepa held her till the spasm ebbed, then made her sit down with a shawl around her and drink the rest of the mint tea brewed for the patient.

"Tell me," she suggested. "Not good to keep angry-afraid inside."

So, alternately sobbing and storming, Mercy poured out her hurt and rage, telling how her husband had insisted on coming to a foreign country and then had gambled her away. "How can he look me in the face?" Mercy choked, clenching her fists. "How could he possibly think I'd forgive him?"

"Bad man."

Mercy shrugged wearily. "Maybe not *bad*—terribly weak. And that's worse! Give me a bad person any day. At least you know what to expect."

For some reason, she thought of Eric Kensington, who was certainly not weak. But she didn't know what to expect from him, either. Why, if he was interested in her himself, and the shine of his silvery eyes today had said that he still was, had he brought Philip and supported his claim?

"I witch him," Chepa suggested, as if discussing seasonings for a stew. "He die, little white rooster. Then you not wife."

"Oh, no!" Mercy cried instinctively.

"Why not? He make you tremble, make you sick."

"But he'll go away. Please, Chepa!" The woman looked unconvinced, and Mercy searched for words to prevent her from acting secretly. "My father would be grieved if I asked for someone's life."

"He was soldier."

"Only to keep men alive."

Chepa meditated. "The old ones say man has to make real, true face, real, true heart," she said at last. "Make by self, with acts. Only few do this. Most take face, heart, from other people. Husband make no true face. Kill him, kill only unshaped mud."

Mercy shook her head. "I can't do that, Chepa. I'd fight him if he tried to take me, if Don Zane had allowed him to. But you must promise not to bother him, or I *will* be sick with worry!"

"Should have done, not talk," Chepa grunted, then gave a heave of her massive shoulders. "So, white rooster live. Now you take bath. Dinner ready soon."

It was strange to sit at the big table with Zane and Jolie and know that Philip and Eric Kensington were across the courtyard in the sitting room. Though the turkey was piquantly stewed in a pungent black sauce that Mercy would usually have relished, she could only nibble. Jolie, obviously instructed not to pry, kept shooting curious glances at Mercy. Zane talked steadily, as if determined to reduce the visitation to an unimportant incident, while answering some of the questions he must have guessed were gnawing at Mercy.

"Kensington says he had business in New Orleáns and encountered Philip there in a gaming house. When it developed that Philip's luck had turned and he'd recouped his fortunes, except for his vanished wife, whom he continued to lament, Kensington told him where you were and even offered to detour to La Quinta on his own journey home to Belize."

"I don't believe it!" Mercy flashed. Then she added bitterly, "Of course, I can't really believe he's here, either."

"Not for long," Zane assured her grimly. "They've promised to be up and away by dawn. It seems Cameron will go along to Belize and take passage from there to the United States."

"Perhaps I should ask him to divorce me," Mercy pondered. "If I ever decided to remarry, if might be hard to locate him."

Zane chuckled. "In his righteous indignation, he did say that he might divorce you on grounds of desertion."

Mercy gaped incredulously, then burst into laughter.

"Are you hysterical?" asked Jolie worriedly.

Smothering her last hiccoughy giggles in her napkin, Mercy shook her head. "No, Jolie. I'm just thinking how funny it all would be if it weren't so ugly. If he knew I wanted a divorce, he wouldn't think of it, but probably he imagines I'd hate the scandal. As if being gambled for and given to the winner leaves a woman much concern about what people say!"

"I hadn't noticed that you were exactly crushed and humble," Zane remarked. He went on to news he had gleaned over an obligatory drink and cigar.

Maximilian had been persuaded not to abdicate and had bone back to Mexico City, though the Juaristas gained ground daily. "The United States is sending arms and ammunition to Juárez," Zane continued. "Secretary of State Seward has given the American ambassador to the Juárez government authority to use U.S. land and naval forces in any way short of actual invasion that might help drive out the French. It's only a question of time for the emperor unless he decides to join his poor, mad Carlota."

"She *is* mad?"

"The pope's refusal to support her husband seems to have permanently overturned her mind, though she's said to have rational moments."

"So she won't be coming back."

"Only in her wild fantasies."

After a silence, Zane said that Philip was ranting about that fall's elections, which had given the Republicans two-thirds control of each House, so that Reconstruction was now certain to be ruthless and to grind the vanquished South even more cruelly into the dust. Mercy ached for her homeland and wondered miserably if there would ever be a time when she could feel again that the United States was her country, not just the South.

"It's been an upsetting day for you," said Zane as they were sipping hot chocolate after the meal. "Chepa will bring you a restful brew, and when you wake up in the morning, Cameron will be out of your life forever."

But not out of her thoughts. His reappearance had opened the sourly festering wound she'd foolishly considered healed. Until the putrescent matter drained, she could have no peace.

Jolie gave her an especially warm hug that night and Zane walked her to her door. "Good night," he said. "Don't let this distress you. Tomorrow it will seem like a bad dream."

A nightmare. Mercy thanked him and went inside. The shuddering began and lasted even after she was in bed, with the covers up to her ears.

But Chepa came. The tea was hot and Chepa's hands were comforting. Gradually, the trembling stopped. Mercy fell into sleep like a heavy stone in black water.

She awoke to a brutal grip prying her jaws apart. She tried to scream but was stifled by cloth stuffed so deep in her mouth that she gagged. She fought, trying to dislodge the obstruction enough to shout, but a blow against the side of her head knocked her senseless for a moment. She roused at being swung over a man's shoulder, and she kicked and beat with her hands.

"Damn you!" It was Philip's threatening whisper. "I'll tie you hand and foot, then!"

Tossing her back on the bed, he tore a sheet and bound her cruelly in spite of her struggles. "You still belong to me," he panted, "and I'll take you away in spite of that fool Falconer!"

Mercy tried to cry out, but the gag stifled the sounds rising in her throat. She still couldn't believe this. She had felt so safe in Zane's house, so secure in his protection. And what would Philip do with her now? Why did he want her?

It wasn't out of love that he'd traveled here, but she was astonished that spite and bruised conceit could move him to such effort. Certainly he'd never have come without Wellington's company.

Too baffling, too hazy. The truth was that she must somehow get help before Philip dragged her away; otherwise, she wouldn't be missed till morning, and that might be too late—too late for Zane to find her.

Philip lifted her again, grunting at her weight, gripping her painfully at the knees while her pulse thumped in her head, which hung downward. Dizzied, she fought for consciousness and gathered her strength as they moved down the hall.

If she could suddenly shift all her weight to one side, topple Philip over, or at least make enough noise to wake up someone! Trying not to alert her captor before the last minute, Mercy concentrated, then put all her effort into a mighty sideways lurch, powered by a desperate wrenching of her whole body. She fell partly against the wall, thus making only a muffled sound, but Philip swore loudly as he toppled against a piece of furniture.

She rolled away, hoping to hit something that would crash. Philip stumbled across her, caught his breath in fury, located her head, and struck her.

Lightning exploded in her brain. She knew nothing till Zane's voice pierced her swirling fog, along with the glow of a candle.

"Cameron!"

Philip sprang. The candle that Zane put down flashed against a blade. Zane sidestepped, caught Philip's uplifted arm, and wrested away the knife.

Quite deliberately, he drove the knife into its owner's throat, yanked sideways. Philip crumpled, face down in spreading blood. Zane stepped past him without a downward glance, then knelt by Mercy and removed the gag.

"Close your eyes. He's an ugly sight," said Zane as he untied the strips at her ankles and wrists. "Did he hurt you?"

"Not much. Oh, Zane, how dreadful!"

For a moment, he held her close before he said brusquely, "Don't shake like that. It's over! Come, I'll put you in my room while yours is being . . . cleaned up."

Strong arms lifted her. Mercy clung to Zane. "It's so . . . awful! I hated him . . . I never knew how much till he came, but . . . "

"He's dead. He deserved it. He'll never bother you again." Kicking open the door of his room, Zane put Mercy on his big high bed and held her as he might have consoled Jolie. "Maybe in a way it's better. At least you don't have to wonder what he's doing or feel linked to him. Your life with him is finished."

Eric Kensington appeared in the doorway. "What's going on? My God! You've butchered Philip!"

Zane wrapped the coverlet around Mercy and got to his feet, crossing to the door. "He tried to abduct this lady. Did you know of his intention?"

"Of course not!" Kensington's surprise and indignation seemed real. "He was downcast and was still drinking when I went to sleep, but I'd thought he was resigned to traveling with me to Belize and from there taking a ship to the States."

He came to stand in the room, his eyes dwelling on Mercy. "I must abjectly beg your pardon, Doña Mercy. I may be overly sentimental, but the thought of reuniting you and your repentant husband made me forget that, in fact, you might not desire that. I should not have meddled. Believe me, if there's any way to make amends, I'd be grateful to atone."

"You can take the body out with you and bury it— off my land," Zane said thinly. He studied the big man and Mercy watched them both, sensing the male antagonism that vibrated between them in spite of Kensington's apparent contrition.

Both were tall, but Kensington must have been four inches taller than Zane's more than six feet, and he was probably twenty pounds heavier, massive through the shoulders. Both were in prime condition, though Zane seemed lighter on his feet and quicker. Zane was like a rapier, while Kensington was a broadsword.

Both could kill. Dark steel eyes clashed with those of molten silver.

The edge of Kensington's mouth bent down and he

172

shrugged. "I can see that having her husband's grave on the premises might disturb Doña Mercy," he said softly. "It's a pity to see a quetzal hide like a wounded dove. Therefore, I'll see to the corpse's removal. My servant can bundle it up if you've some old sacking."

Horrified at hearing a man spoken of as if he were refuse. Mercy asked if he couldn't be wrapped in a sheet. Zane gave this order to Vicente, who'd run in barefooted, rubbing his eyes, along with Chepa, who piled more covers on Mercy and made her drink brandy from the decanter by Zane's bed.

Kensington stood on the threshold and bowed, his golden hair shining even in the light from the one lamp Zane must have lit before going to Mercy's room. "There's no way I can express my regret at the unpleasantness this has caused you, madam. Thinking only to make you happy, I've brought you pain. Most of all, I'm sorry that when you remember me, it'll be with disagreeable associations. But life is unpredictable. I hope I may find a way to please you."

"It seems most unlikely," said Zane, "since Belize is far away and La Quinta is far off the road to Mérida."

Kensington raised an eyebrow. "Who knows? Since the start of the War of the Castes, many people have found Belize a refuge. I wish you continued immunity from Cruzob forays, Falconer, but there could be a time when you or this lady would welcome British protection." His eyes on Mercy, he smiled. "Believe me, Doña Mercy, I am always at your service. Should, heaven forbid, any mischance befall Mr. Falconer, be mindful that you have a friend."

"That won't be necessary," Zane cut in. "My mayordomo has instructions in case of my demise. It's nearly dawn, Kensington, and the men have readied your horses. Chepa, will you make this gentleman some breakfast so he can be on his way?"

"I make you some tea," Chepa told Mercy, then went out through the courtyard entrance.

"Thanks for seeing that I get an early start." Kensington smiled. "Farewell, Doña Mercy." His eyes lingered on her so that she felt cold in spite of the heaped covers and began to tremble again.

"Have a safe journey, Kensington." Zane stared at the Englishman till he bowed a last time and strode away.

Closing the door, Zane crossed to the bed and looked down at Mercy, a muscle twitching in his lean jaw. "It seems you have an eager protector. He could scarcely propose it more plainly than he did in front of me, but I'm sure his old offer of marriage still stands. Now that you have no husband, you should consider it."

"Do you want me to . . . to go away?"

"We're discussing what you want," he said harshly. "Do you want to leave with Kensington?"

"No!"

Bending, he caught her face between his hands. "Why not, if marriage and respectability mean so much to you?"

"I don't love him."

Zane let her go as if her flesh burned him. "Love! A trumpery word women use to justify whatever they do and break a man to their use! And you won't admit to passion, will you, honest need of the body? No, it has to be love and legal binding and a hook through a man's nose!"

Shrinking back on the pillows, Mercy gazed at him, fighting back tears. He reached for her, then whirled, grasping his hands tightly behind him. "Who'd believe I've had you at La Quinta all this time and not taken you?" he asked savagely. "I can't believe it myself! I'm not made of iron, Mercy. If virtue's paramount with you, you should take Kensington, for if you stay here, someday I might not be able to stop myself." He'd been speaking with his back to her. Now he turned violently. "Do you understand that?"

"What?"

"If you stay here, tempting me just by your softness, your sweetness, the way you move and walk, sooner or later I won't be able to stop."

Their eyes met with tingling, frightening, ecstatic shock. If he had lain down with her then, Mercy could not have opposed him, but he went out of the room, as if devil-driven, just as Chepa came in with tea.

"Your room ready now," she said, holding the cup so that Mercy had to drink. "Don Zane say I have hammock by you for some nights if you afraid."

Chepa made her finish all the brew. "I want to get up," said Mercy. "It's nearly daylight. I can't sleep after . . . "

"Lie down," Chepa said. "Close eyes. I rub neck and back. Get up then if you want."

174

With her face down against sheets that had the clean male smell of Zane's body, Mercy shuddered as Chepa's hands, for a second, reminded her of Philip's. She heard again that stifled choking. But as she tensed, Chepa kneaded at her muscles, working them into place as the herb drink gradually soothed her mind.

She never knew when the stroking ceased.

Her rest was deep and sound. When she awoke, she gazed at the carved headboard a long moment before she realized she was still in Zane's bed and why. Light streamed through the shutters, gilding a huge mahogany armoire, a leather armchair and reading table, and a chest of dark wood inlaid with what looked like bone in a running pattern of incised leaves.

What held Mercy's gaze was the small cabinet with open hinged doors and a curved top that stood in a large wall niche. Inside the cabinet the madonna stood on a crescent moon, wearing a crown of silver, as did her infant son. Behind them was a painted blue sky spangled with stars, and around the niche were painted roses. It was charmingly feminine, the only touch of grace in an austere chamber. Mercy was sure it had belonged to Zane's mother, but she would have expected him to close the doors of the little shrine; she was glad that he had not.

The clock struck eight. Mercy pressed her face and breasts against Zane's pillows for a moment, then remembered he must have slept here with his wife, the woman who seemed to have made love a lying mockery to him.

Mercy grimaced as she slipped from the huge bed and went barefooted to her room. Why had he let one woman determine his view of all the rest? Perhaps he was changing slowly. At least now he wanted a rather permanent mistress instead of occasional satiation with the whores of Tekax or Mérida or whatever strange gratifications he'd shared with Xia.

The door of Mercy's room was open. She hesitated, took a deep breath, and stepped inside. Her bed was immaculate, the torn sheet replaced. There remained nothing to show a man had seized her there in the night.

A pleasantly astringent smell filled the air. A handful of herbs was charring in the fireplace. Chepa's purification? Mercy smiled, but she was grateful.

*   *   *

Vicente and Chepa must have kept their silence, because knowledge of Philip's death never filtered out. Jolie remarked that the big golden man had looked like a Viking, which led to geography, stories of the far-sailing dragon ships, and the possibility that Quetzalcoatl, the fair god expected by the Mayas to reappear on earth, had been, in fact, a Viking.

His name, which meant Plumed Water Serpent, could easily derive from the prow of a typical Norse vessel or wings on a helmet. Though Quetzalcoatl had been just and beneficent, the Spaniards, who'd been taken for him since, were not. And again, Maximilian's blond hair and beard had made some Indians believe he was their returned savior.

Zane happened in during this discussion and said softly from the schoolroom door, "Did you know he burned himself to death along this east coast? I believe it was at Tulum and that he's the diving god shown on the temple mural there, uniting heaven and earth."

"Why did he do that, Papa?" asked Jolie, her eyes wide.

"He got drunk and dishonored himself so terribly that he believed he must die. So he put on his robe of quetzal feathers and his turquoise mask, which he wore because he was very ugly, and he journeyed to the east. There he set himself afire and his ashes rose to the skies. They say that's when all the brightest birds were created. He descended to the Kingdom of the Dead, and on the fourth day he rose into heaven and became Venus, the Morning Star and the Evening Star, male and female, and god and man."

Jolie put it into Mayan for Salvador and Mayel, who had been, with eager puzzlement, catching what they could. Then she regarded her father with solemnity. "Is that true, Papa?"

"Some of it, I think. There must have been an ugly fair-skinned stranger who became a good king and tried to end human sacrifice. This made the priests angry and they may have conspired to make him sin so terribly he would want to end his life. His descent into hell and ascent to heaven? Who knows, child? It's the common legend of all great heroes."

Jolie considered, her golden eyebrows arched. "Mr. Kensington might be a Viking, but I don't think he's good like Quet ... Quetzalcoatl."

"The Vikings also sailed to Russia," Mercy added. "And they raided England so ferociously that there was a prayer against their fury right along with pleas for protection from battle, murder, and sudden death."

"That's more like Mr. Kensington," Jolie said and nodded. Zane had left them. The girl took Mercy's hand and pressed it to her warm little cheek. "You look sad, Doña Mercy. Are you sorry you didn't go with your husband?"

"No." Mercy's throat felt scalded and she had a flash of Philip when they were young, galloping beside her down the walnut land, smiling as he fed her wild strawberries and kissed her the first time. "No. I couldn't go with him. But I am sad."

"He wasn't a Viking," said Jolie. "But he didn't seem old enough to be your husband. He was like a boy."

Mercy thought that was probably the truest epitaph that could be made for him.

She had nightmares for the next few nights, but Chepa would come from the nearby hammock to quiet her, and by the end of the week it all seemed like a horrid dream. She couldn't be glad about Philip's death, but it had cauterized the wound of his betrayal, cleanly searing it out so that this time as it healed, it healed clean.

Philip was dead. An act of his had brought her where she was, but she'd stayed by choice. She was, more than she'd ever been, in control of her fate. Zane allowed her that power, of course. Even if, as he had warned, he took her now by force, she'd chosen to run that risk rather than go with Eric Kensington.

Zane was seeing to the clearing of some new land for henequén and was gone from morning till night until the sixteenth of December. On that day, work slacked off for the long holiday season, which would last for almost a month until the village's patroness, Santa Yñez, had her fiesta during the third week of January.

On the first night of the nine-day festival of Los Posadas, Mercy went to the village with Chepa, Mayel, Salvador, and Jolie. They followed the procession of pilgrims carrying a litter that held images of Mary riding on a burro, Joseph, and an angel. Singing and carrying candles, the group moved toward the church, where they sang a song begging for lodging at the inn.

From inside the closed door, the villagers posing as

177

innkeepers sang back a refusal to each pleading, till at last the pilgrims said that Mary would be mother of the Holy Child. At that, the innkeepers threw open the door and welcomed in the travelers. The holy figures were placed on the altar and everyone knelt to pray. Then women brought out sweet bread and various cakes and candles. The villagers spilled onto the common. and dancing began to the music of a ukulele-like instrument, drums, and flutes.

The young people danced in pairs, in each the man with his hands behind his back and the girl coquettishly lifting the edges of her skirt as they faced each other. When they passed, they lifted their arms and clicked their fingers rhythmically. Mayel was drawn into the dance. She looked entrancing in a festive embroidered cotton dress that had belonged to Chepa's beloved lost daughter, and a yellow ribbon perched like a great butterfly at the back of her coiled black hair.

Sóstenes and another man brought out a gay paper-and-tinsel star *piñata* and a child was blindfolded and given a stick. He tried to hit the *piñata* which the men held out of reach on a rope, and after flailing wildly for a few minutes, his place was taken by a girl, then by another boy, till at last a little girl of perhaps four was allowed to hit it, shattering the paper sides so that candy and a mass of small trinkets and toys rained down to be scrambled after by the children.

A *posada* was held each night, but Mercy didn't go again till the ninth night, Christmas Eve, when the villagers, shortly before midnight, said nine Ave Marias and sang to the Virgin as an image of the Infant was placed in the manger on the altar.

There followed a midnight Mass chanted by the *maestro cantor*, an old layman who knew most of the ritual and presided over the village's religious life. It had been years since a true priest had visited the hacienda, but even before the war, a year or two often passed so that when the priest came, he often baptized children at the same time he married their parents.

A feast was served in the council house. Zane appeared for none of the celebration, though Chepa told Mercy that he had, as always, supplied the *piñatas* and the festive meal.

Jolie was falling asleep as she ate, so Mercy roused her

enough to half-carry her home and get her to bed. Covering the girl up to her chin, Mercy gazed down at the smooth angel's face and lightly kissed the golden hair, giving thanks that Jolie had come to accept her, and for being allowed to take part in the *posadas*, even though, at this season, she felt especially far from home.

Blowing out the lamp, she turned to the door and almost collided with Zane, who steadied her with quick, hard hands and spoke softly before she could be frightened, drawing her outside and closing the door.

"You didn't know I was watching, did you?" He had been drinking and his words tended to slur. His fingers dug into her arms as he gave her a shake. "You . . . kissing my child. Madonna."

Frightened, Mercy tried to pull away, but he gripped her tighter, then gave a choking little laugh. "Been waiting. Thought when you came in I'd give you my present and brandy . . . get you drunk, get you to bed. My Christmas present. But I'm drunk."

"Zane . . . "

"You always stop me. Why is that? Why do you always do what stops me?"

Weakened by his hands, upset at his drunkenness, Mercy couldn't answer. Suddenly he opened her door and thrust her roughly inside.

"Merry Christmas, Mercy. My big present is leaving you virtuous. But there's something else for you on the bed."

He almost slammed the door. Shaken, her breasts tingling with arousal till they hurt, Mercy leaned against the wall, clamping her jaw tight to keep from calling after him. She yearned for his mouth, the strength of his arms, the force and sweetness and wildness of his lean, well-muscled body, so racked with need that it threatened to sweep away all reason. But some small whisper of sanity persisted in the storm.

To be his while he thought as he did would mean a sealed existence in the tower, a life apart from that of La Quinta. If she let passion turn her into a slave of his body and her own, she'd betray herself far worse than Philip had done.

Father! Father! . . .

Elkanah's kind, sad eyes seemed to caress her, helping her ride out the strongest moments of temptation. When she could breathe again, she lit a lamp and moved to the bed.

There on the pillows lay a book bound in red leather. She opened it and read on the hand-lettered title page: *Cures from the Badianus Manuscript, an Aztec Herbal of 1552.* Turning through it, she read of treatments for everything from skin ailments to poor flow of milk after childbirth. There were pages of herbs in color. A magnificent treasure! Mercy touched it lovingly, thinking how Elkanah would have studied it.

Tomorrow she must make sure the gift hadn't been a drunken whim; but for tonight she would sleep with it close to her pillow.

Since everyone had been up late the night before, Christmas day was quiet. Mercy still intended to give her gifts on Christmas rather than on the Day of the Three Kings, so she put the plump blue coati on the still-sleeping Jolie's pillow. Then she came up softly behind Chepa to wrap her in the soft shawl and said to her, *"Feliz Navidad!"* And Mayel exclaimed over the parcel of bright ribbons and several necklaces.

Salvador admired his new shirt, but he was utterly enraptured with the handmade book of proverbs and fables. That left only Zane. The sweet, spicy smell of fresh-baked sweet bread and hot chocolate announced breakfast, so Mercy took the carefully decorated bookmarks along to the dining room and put them at Zane's place as Jolie ran up to her frantically.

"The coati! It's so soft and cuddly and just beautiful! Thank you, Doña Mercy! Salvador and I have something for you, but we'll give it to you on the Day of the Three Kings."

"I don't know if I can stand the suspense that long," Mercy said and laughed.

Zane came in, a bit heavy-eyed, but apparently with no memories of last night. He smiled with surprise and appreciation as he looked through the bookmarks. "The tree of the center," he said and nodded. "Handsomely done, Doña Mercy. My library will take on elegance once I'm not marking places with tamale husks, bits of sisal, wood slivers, and scraps of paper. Thank you very much."

"You're welcome. And thank you for the book of cures.

But are you sure you want to give it away? It must be very rare."

"The only one of its kind," Zane confirmed. "A doctor friend of my father's translated it into English for him and got an artist to copy the herb pictures from one of the few copies of the old Aztec manuscript. I'm sure no one else would get as much pleasure from it as you will."

"There's nothing I'd rather have," Mercy admitted, not sure that she should allow herself to be persuaded.

"Not even diamonds?" Zane teased.

Only you . . . but how can I say that? "It's the most wonderful present I've ever had," she said honestly, and they sat down to breakfast, beamed over by Chepa, in her luxurious shawl.

It was a peacefully happy day. That afternoon, Zane suggested that he take Mercy and Jolie riding, and they got home just in time to freshen and change before a dinner of *cochinita pibil*, tamales, yams, seasoned rice, pumpkin seed cakes, and caramel pudding.

A fire crackled in the hearth. It wasn't needed for warmth, but it cast a cheerful glow that made them linger at the table long after the dishes were cleared away, and even Jolie had all the hot chocolate she could drink.

"I know I'm too big to sit on your lap, Papa," she muttered sleepily. "But can I, for a little while?"

"Oh, I think we can manage that," Zane said and laughed. "But from the way your eyelids droop, I think I'd better carry you to your room!"

She didn't argue but caught Mercy's hand. "Will you come tell my coati good night? His name is Carlos."

"Why did you decide to call him that?" asked Mercy as they crossed the courtyard to Jolie's room.

Jolie yawned against her father's shoulder. "That's what I called my pretend-brother before I knew Salvador."

Zane was commanded to admire the blue challis animal. When he'd done so to Jolie's satisfaction, he went to his office and Mercy slipped into her own room.

It had been the happiest day she'd spent in Yucatán, the happiest in years. The long ride that day with Zane and Jolie and the shared evening meal had made them seem almost like family. Mercy sighed, beginning to undress. Tonight, however, she and Zane wouldn't share the big matrimonial bed—any bed at all.

181

Putting on her nightgown, she was picking up her hairbrush when she noticed a small packet beside it on the chest. How had that got there? A surprise from Zane or Jolie?

She opened the paper, staring at the gleaming jade that was smooth and cold in her palm. A quetzal. A slip of paper had fallen to the floor. With strange, fated knowledge, she bent down for it and held it in fingers that trembled.

"Sometime, someplace."

That was all. It wasn't signed. No need for it to be. Eric Kensington must have paid someone to put the gift in her room. The quetzal seemed suddenly to burn her hand. Opening the chest, Mercy dropped the exquisitely carved jade in a corner and covered it up.

She held the brief note over the lamp till it caught on fire and burned, but as she flicked away the burned flakes she seemed to hear the big Englishman laughing sardonically.

Nonsense! He was on his way to Belize. Zane had made it plain that he wasn't a welcome guest. Arranging for this quetzal to be left in her room was a final touch of bravado, a swagger before accepting the inevitable.

Mercy put the *Badianus* copy by her pillow and kept touching it for reassurance, but it was a long time before she fell asleep.

13

On the Day of the Three Kings, Mercy awoke to find a row of pottery jars on the table by her bed, each painted with a different herb. When she peeked inside, each jar held leaves, bark, or seeds. Here was the start of a Mayan apothecary, and there was also a small horn flask, which she unstopped, puzzling at what appeared to be plain water.

"That's virgin water," called Jolie from the window

ledge. "Salvador and I climbed way back in the cave above the jaguar and got it where the stalactites drip. Holy water, Mercy, the kind the old ones offered to the gods!" She was dancing up and down with impatience. "Come see what the kings left me!"

There was an elegant French doll with a complete wardrobe, a baby doll with a hand-carved crib, a heart-shaped locket, a blue velvet riding cloak lined with dark blue satin, and several books: Hawthorne's *Tanglewood Tales*, Dickens' *A Tale of Two Cities*, and a recent book that Mercy had heard of but never read, *Alice in Wonderland*, by Lewis Carroll. Zane must have specially ordered some of the gifts and combed Mérida for the others, yet it was the homemade blue coati that Jolie hugged even as she crooned over the beautiful dolls.

This day of gifts was mostly for children, but at breakfast Zane thanked Jolie for the initialed handkerchief she'd put in his boot. And Mayel exhibited a bracelet, which Chepa must have left on her window ledge. It was Mayel who'd painted the herbs on Mercy's pottery, and she flushed with pleasure when Mercy brought the jars for Zane to see, while Chepa announced that Mercy must learn where to find all the substances so she could keep her "medicine chest" supplied.

Zane raised an eyebrow at the horn flask of sacred water, but for Jolie's sake he didn't question the propriety of giving a mortal the due of gods.

Epiphany was only ten days past when the village began to hum with preparations for the fiesta of its patroness. Santa Vñez. There was dancing, and some years bulls were brought in for fights, but Zane had been quietly discouraging this custom. and to Mercy's relief there would be no tormenting of bulls during this fiesta.

She wasn't expecting the conclusion of Saturday night's festival. After the young couples had danced to exhaustion, thirteen men entered the clearing. They wore turkey-feather headdresses and each man held a turkey tucked under his left arm by its feet. While musicians in the center played on flutes and drums, the performers circled and danced, and Mercy realized with a rush of nausea that they were wringing the turkeys' necks.

Starting to back away from the spectators, she was stopped by Zane, who stepped out of the shadows. "You eat turkey," he reminded her.

"I don't know if I ever shall again!"

Zane smiled. "Why, doubtless you'll enjoy some of the broth made from these birds! Come, Doña Mercy! Shouldn't you have the courage to face where your food comes from?"

Thus challenged, she conquered her squeamishness and watched till the dance ended and each man placed his turkey on the ground before him. The leader walked around, stirring each bird. One gave a flutter and there were jeers and shouts from the crowd.

The careless dancer hung his head and the leader beat the turkey against the man's skull till it finally expired. Mercy gritted her teeth, though she couldn't keep from flinching at each dull thud. When the leader tossed the turkey down, the dancers began to pluck the birds, jumping and yelling, while the air was full of feathers. Mercy had seen more than enough. With a defiant glance at Zane, who watched her amusedly, she worked her way out of the shouting throng and hurried to the house.

The main village feast was over. Santa Yñez should be pleased with the expense and labor in her honor, and Victoriano had made offerings of corn gruel to the gods for protecting the village and its cornfields. Life at La Quinta went back to normal and men who needed new fields for that summer's planting hurried to finish clearing their patches.

Mercy was busy teaching and learning all she could from Chepa about herbs and healing. Often now, when Chepa was busy, Mercy took care of fevers or nosebleeds, diarrhea or intestinal upsets. She rode Castaña nearly every day, usually with Jolie. Vicente was most often their escort. Zane, though polite, was avoiding Mercy.

This was the only blemish on her contentment, but there was no answer, since she was sure that Zane would interpret any overtures on her part as a yielding, an invitation to possess her on his terms.

Then, at the end of January, a messenger came from Colonel Cepeda Peraza, Zane's old commander. He'd slipped out of Mérida a few weeks earlier and was now commander of a revolution against the empire. Would Zane fight with him for Yucatecan independence and bring any armed men he could find?

The messenger, a young mestizo with only a hint of fuzz above his upper lip, went to bed right after dinner. He had to make an early start the next morning. Jolie slipped out of her chair and went to put her arms around her father.

"You won't go, will you, Papa?"

He considered heavily. "Yes," he said at last, "I think I must."

"But La Quinta's so far from Mérida!"

"Yet that's where our laws are made and where the present imperial authorities have arrested a number of my Republican friends and sent them to the penal colony on Cozumel." Zane's lips thinned. *"That* matters."

Jolie regarded him seriously. "I thought you said you were too old to be a soldier."

"I'm sure every man who ever was quickly decided he was either too young or too old," Zane teased. "But if Peraza can fight one more time for Yucatecan liberty, I suppose I have to join him." Jolie's mouth quivered and a tear slid down her cheek. Zane swept her onto his lap. "It shouldn't be for long, sweetheart. With French troops leaving Mexico, the empire's bound to fall, and shortly. The fighting will center around Campeche and Mérida. You'll be in no danger here."

"I don't want you to go!" Jolie wailed, clinging to him. Mercy, her hands clasped tightly in her lap, silently echoed that cry. But she knew if a man didn't fight when he believed he should, he lost something of being a man.

Zane's eyes met hers above Jolie's head. "Honey," he said in the Southern way he must have learned from his father, "I don't want to go one bit! But Doña Mercy will be with you, and so will Chepa, and with luck I might get home before it's time to plant corn."

He produced a handkerchief, and after Jolie had trumpeted into it, she swallowed hard. "When . . . when are you going, Papa?"

"The day after tomorrow."

She wound her arms even tighter around him. Mercy ached not only for this parting, but in remembering how she'd said almost the same things to her father nearly seven years ago.

He'd never returned. But that had been a long war, and he'd lived through many battles before he died at Gettysburg. Zane had been to war before, and he'd be careful. Surely he'd come home. He had to!

But she knew very well, of course, that loved men die as fast as friendless ones, and Zane would be cautious, but he'd do his duty. Murmuring some excuse, she fled from the table, escaping through the back court toward the orchards and the tower.

It was dark but the path was good. She'd come this way instinctively because she wanted to be alone while she fought the waves of desolation that almost overwhelmed her.

The tower loomed dark and lonely. She moved slowly to the door and tried it. The device that raised the bar on the other side lifted. She hesitated on the threshold only a moment before she went in.

If Zane didn't come back, how bitterly she'd regret not having been his! It made a tremendous difference—that he was going away. In his absence, she'd have to be more concerned than ever with Jolie and the affairs of La Quinta. Mercy pressed her hands to her waist and loins, then made a decision.

Tonight she'd go to Zane. She wanted that, craved at least one time with her love. If for him it was lust, well, that was his concern. She wouldn't ask for guarantees or conditions. This would be for now.

When he came back, if he came back, then they could fight the battle of where she belonged. She was as resolved as ever not to be his concubine. She was equally determined to send him away with all the sweetness she could give him of her body, while she would have, whatever else happened, the memory of him.

Heartened, she turned to go, then stared at the dark figure in the doorway with just a thrill of alarm before Zane said, "I love you, Mercy. It's you I love."

Dawn was approaching when they left the tower. In the upper room, he had seared away with his passion the shame Philip had caused with his sadistic demands. She had never dreamed a man could enter a woman with such sweet, throbbing ferocity and stroke her to ecstasy with his long, supple fingers, alternately sensitive and ruthless, as if he knew what rhythm her needs demanded even before she did. He kissed her in her most secret places and made her feel she was opening like a flower, tremulously exposed to his lips and tongue, flooded with warm honey-wine. And she tried to anticipate his wishes, to make him so happy that he, too, would forget that other faithless loved one.

They fell asleep, and when they awoke he was ready

to take her again. She, in spite of being swollen and tender, welcomed him hungrily.

"We should go," he said after the last time, running his hand along her cheek and throat. "I've got to get ready, make some kind of sense . . . God knows how I shall! Will you meet me tonight, Mercy?"

"Yes! Oh, yes!"

He took her face in his hands and kissed her gently. "Tell me, love, had you decided to have me even before I came?"

She laughed huskily, tracing the cleft in his chin, glorying in being able to lavish the warmth of her love. "I had decided, sir, to demand you take me to bed! I couldn't let you leave without that."

He laughed, too. "And I had sworn to say I loved you even if you didn't want to listen. I couldn't leave you without that."

He kissed the tears from her eyes as they came down from the tower.

One more night to discover and delight each other, to try not to think of the separation that had, ironically, brought them together. They slept to awake embracing, and they pleasured each other till they drifted into sleep, closely entwined, as if they could become physically part of each other.

"Will you marry me when I come back?" Zane asked, his head on her breast in the dawning while he caressed her throat and face and shoulders.

"Are you sure you want that?"

"Yes," he said somberly. "I thought it would be enough to keep you for my hidden love—and I've loved you for a long time, though I tried not to admit it. But I want you in my home, in my life, to mother Jolie and the babies we'll make, to be with all my years. I suppose that's why I could never quite force you, though I came close to it several times, especially when I was trying to convince myself that you were a mercenary wench who thought only of iron-clad marriage vows for security's and convention's sake."

She smoothed the lines in his tanned forehead and kissed the sun wrinkles at the corners of his eyes. "If you'd said you loved me, I don't think I could have resisted. But I couldn't have been happy in the tower, shut away from everything else."

187

With a rueful chuckle, Zane pulled her up. "I guess it took a revolution to shake us out of our pride enough to tell the truth. And now I have to go, my love! But at least now in the nights, till we can be together again, I can know how you feel in my arms and go to sleep remembering."

He kissed her tears. Before he left that morning with Vicente and a score of young men who welcomed a chance to see the world beyond La Quinta, even if it meant battle, he put his mother's wedding ring on her finger.

"I didn't give this to my first wife," he said. "I must have known, in the back of my mind, that she wouldn't be the woman I could treasure and love more and more all my life."

His last kiss was for Jolie, but his gaze lingered like white-hot steel on Mercy before he inclined his dark head, signaled to his men, and rode through the gates.

Mercy was so grateful and happy to know Zane loved her that it eased some of the pain of missing him, but Jolie moped about for a week, sticking to Mercy's side, except when Salvador wasn't wanted by Victoriano and she could roam with him. Chepa tempted her appetite with her favorite foods, but moving Flora into her room seemed to comfort her most, and Flora seemed glad enough to escape her nearly grown brood, though she graciously visited them several times a day. Mercy lengthened school hours a bit. Jolie was encouraged to spend evenings after dinner reading or chatting in Mercy's room.

Zane had told Jolie that he meant to marry Mercy, and Jolie approved of this. "I hope you'll have a baby girl, though," she mused, her violet eyes dreamy as she cuddled Carlos while Flora lay at her feet. "I don't think boys are as amusing to dress and take care of. Do have a girl, Mercy!"

"I'll try," Mercy promised, though her wish was for a boy with Zane's eyes and mouth and hair.

"You should have twins," Jolie decided, "a boy and a girl. Then you'd have it all over with."

"That would be time-saving," Mercy said, smiling. "But I'm afraid there's no way of controlling it. What shall we read tonight?"

"The Cheshire cat?" Jolie rustled through the pages of

Alice. "I wish Flora could learn how to do that—just fade away to a grin!"

"Then you couldn't hug her."

"I guess not, sighed Jolie. "Things and people have to be *there* before you can touch them." Her voice quivered, but she cleared her throat and plunged into the story.

February came and the new cornfields were cleared, with the brush and trees drying till the time came to burn them. Macedonio seemed to be faithfully supervising the laborers in the henequén fields and told Mercy that the new land was being planted. Apparently Zane had told him Mercy would be future mistress of the hacienda, for the mayordomo treated her with even greater deference than previously.

Mercy and Jolie rode almost daily, accompanied by one or another of the men at the stable. Jolie also spent considerable time with the colt she'd picked, a handsome little gray with a black mane and tail. Mercy kept a sort of journal-letter for Zane in case there should be an unexpected chance to send it. He'd promised to send messages whenever he could but he had warned her not to expect them.

"If I should be killed, Vicente or one of my men will come at once to tell you," he'd said. "Otherwise, consider me well and try not to worry. This shouldn't take long."

It seemed, already, very long. But somehow hour followed hour and day passed into day, busy, but every moment was made long by wondering where Zane was and what was going on in the world beyond La Quinta.

One night after Jolie had been tucked in with Carlos in her arms and Flora cuddled against her knees, Mercy was describing this in her long letter to Zane. He might not see it till he came home again, but it helped to share things with him and believe that wherever he was bivouacked, he was thinking of her, too. She'd finished an account of the day and sat remembering those nights in the tower, tremendously grateful that they'd been together at the same time she was sick with longing.

She didn't recognize the faint scratching at her door as more than the rasp of limbs outside until it grew insistent. Chepa or Mayel would have knocked, and no one else ever came to her room after nightfall except for Jolie.

Nervous simply because this was so unusual, Mercy went to the door and called softly. *"Quién es?"*

"Xia," came the answer. "I have news of El Señor."

Xia, here late at night? But Mercy, though full of misgivings, would have opened to the devil if he'd had word from Zane. Unbarring the door, she held it open. Xia slipped in like a forest wraith. She was wrapped in a shawl of purple with deeply fringed edges and her topaz eyes shone in the lamplight as she surveyed the room before turning to Mercy.

"El Señor has been wounded and carried to a village a few leagues from mine. If you want to see him, I'll take you there."

"Wounded?" Mercy echoed.

"In the thigh. It seems to be healing." Xia spoke in slow Spanish that Mercy could follow without much difficulty She grimaced, watching Mercy with plain dislike. "He asked for you constantly till I promised to come, but I shall be happy to tell him you chose not to leave your comforts."

"I must call Chepa. She might know of some herbs . . ."

Xia shook her head decisively. "I had enough trouble persuading the *batab* of the village to let you come and persuading him to shelter El Señor till he's well enough to be moved. I've seen his wound and you must know I have some skill in such things. Chepa could do nothing. Leave a note for her if you wish, and let's be on our way" —the proud, full lips compressed scornfully—"unless you're afraid to walk with me in the woods."

"How do I know this is true?"

"You don't." Xia shrugged, turning. "I'll tell him you lacked the courage to come to him and that he must get well enough to hobble home before he can see you."

"Wait" Mercy breathed deeply.

She wrote a note to Jolie, asking her to tell Chepa what had happened, and pinned it on her bed. Then she changed into outdoor shoes and put on her cape.

"We could get horses," she suggested.

"The way to the other village is too overgrown for horses," Xia said. "It's much faster on foot." She set off at a swift, flowing pace that compelled Mercy to hurry in order not to lose track of her. They slipped out through the rear courtyard and went past the orchards and the ruins where Zane had brought her one night, then picked up the road that ran from behind the stables.

Questions crowded Mercy's tongue. Where had Zane been fighting? Was the revolution over? Was he all right except for the thigh wound?

"Who knows?" responded Xia to everything but the last query. This she answered peevishly by saying that he must have a fever to call so insistently for Mercy, who certainly couldn't nurse him as well as she, Xia, could.

She went at such a pace that Mercy had to save her breath for walking. Soon they turned off the road and headed for Xia's village. Trees and brush pressed in around them. Vines caught at Mercy's cape and hair. It was exceedingly dark and only the white hem of Xia's dress and the soft glide of her sandals assured Mercy that the priestess was still in front of her.

Had she been a fool to come? Xia had tried to kill her once. Why not finish the task while Zane was gone and then lie to him? Mercy took some comfort in the note left on her bed, but she was distrustful and increasingly frightened. Xia could take a few steps off the path and abandon her, then get rid of her in any one of a dozen unpleasant, untraceable ways. Yet how could Mercy not have followed her, when Zane might be at the end of his journey?

Xia seemed to slow down a bit and hesitate. Mercy stopped, breathless, pressing a pain in her side. "How much farther?"

"This will do."

Mercy's heart turned over. She knew the voice even before the tall, broad figure before her seemed to blot out everything. Whirling, she tried to dodge into the woods. Hands so powerful that they muffled her struggles brought her against a muscular, dense body that made her feel smothered, helpless, insignificant. She writhed till she could jerk her head downward, then sank her teeth into his hand.

Eric laughed, opened her jaws with his thumb and forefinger, and set his mouth brutally against hers in an assault as deliberate as a physical beating, embracing her so tightly that she was pinioned. She couldn't breathe, couldn't move. Her mind darkened in panic.

"Well, now, my sweet," he murmured, lifting his head, "you must write your good-bye note to Falconer, and then we'll be on our way."

"You must be mad!"

"Probably. I can't believe I'd go to this trouble for

a woman—finding your worthless husband, bribing him to buy you back so he could hand you over to me, and now this stratagem!" He laughed gaily. "Whether I'm bewitched or it's become a matter of pride, of scoring over Falconer, I'm going to have and keep you as long as I desire." His palm curved over her breast, completely covering it. "But first you'll come along to my camp and compose a letter that'll convince your recent owner that you've seen the advantages of going with me."

Mercy's knees were so weak that she'd have fallen without his encircling arm. "Maybe you can drag me to Belize," she said, "but you can't make me write a letter."

"But of course I can." Eric sighed as if grieved to have to demonstrate. "How sad it would be if Falconer returned to find that his only child, such a winsome little golden one, had been strangled in her sleep one night."

Mercy gasped. "Kill Jolie? You . . . you couldn't!"

"I could," he said silkily. "What you must understand, Mercy, is that I have no conscience—not a wisp. I could have that girl, who's apparently dear to you and certainly her father's pet, killed with no more compunction than if I'd shot a deer for dinner."

Mercy believed him. He read this in her silence and made a sound of approval as he drew her off the main trail.

"Be happy," mocked Xia, a trilling voice from the night. "When Zane comes home, I'll forgive his affronting me for your sake. Don't worry about him. He'll be consoled."

Silvery, taunting laughter echoed in Mercy's ears. She'd been tricked. She had known all the time that it might be a ruse, but she hadn't been able to risk ignoring Zane's distress. She'd have to write the abominable letter, and when Zane read it his ingrained distrust of women would incline him to believe it. Besides, it might be months before the revolution was over, and by then Mercy felt as if she would be dead, or so used by Eric that Zane wouldn't want her.

Numbly, guided by Eric's hands, she stepped into a clearing. Eric called an order and in a moment a light flared, dimly revealing its location inside a stone hut. Two horses and half a dozen men stood by the building.

Eric stooped to enter the thatched hut, drawing her after him. On a stump, worn smooth with use and lit by a candle, lay paper, a steel pen, and a small inkwell. Eric indicated a stool.

"Compose your letter, my love. Then you'd better write another for that housekeeper who seemed to dote on you."

His head almost reached even the highest peak of thatch. He sat down on a crude bench, crossing his arms, while the splendidly built black man who must have lit the candle brought him a flask.

"Some wine?" Eric asked, offering her the embossed silver container.

Mercy shook her head, staring at the paper. Was there some way to code the truth into her message?

Head thrown back, Eric drank thirstily, wiped his lips on a fine linen handkerchief, and watched her with eyes the shade of snow reflecting shadow.

"Perhaps I should spare you the difficulty of creation and tell you what to say. Yes, that would be best. You might otherwise cleverly inject a word or two that'd set Falconer wondering if you'd gone with me willingly."

"I'd rather . . ." Mercy began.

Those cold eyes touched her. "Sweet Mercy, learn at once that your 'rathers' have nothing to do with what happens. If you'd accepted me in Mérida, if I could have thought you cared for me, no doubt I'd have been softly indulgent so long as you pleased me." His voice dropped to a purring. "You chose Falconer over me, preferred being a servant in his house rather than mistress in mine. I am obsessed with you, I will have you, but you've no power."

The pupils of his eyes seemed to spread, darkening the strange quicksilver of the irises. "Write," he commanded. "And since I don't know what you ordinarily called him, best dispense with a salutation. *'Eric Kensington has been kind enough to escort me to Belize, where he will pay for my passage to New Orleans in return for certain favors. This seems a small price to escape the wars and revolutions of this unhappy country. Thanking you for the courtesies you have shown me, I remain your appreciative but homesick Mercy.'* "

Mercy scratched off the last word. Eric came to look down at the page, then nodded with satisfaction. "Rather good, if I do say so. 'Courtesies' could cover anything that passed between you. I'd enjoy trying to make him think you'd fallen in love with me, but this quiet, practical tone's more convincing, don't you think?"

When Mercy didn't answer, Eric tilted up her chin. "You will answer when I speak."

"You may not like what you hear."

He smiled. "If I don't, you'll like it less. Can the housekeeper read?"

"No."

"But Jolie can." He pondered a moment. "It should suffice to tell her you've found a way to go back to your own country. You may, if you wish, express your affection and say you'll miss her."

Writing a few sentences, Mercy ended by asking Jolie to give Chepa her thanks for many kindnesses and to give her love and farewells to Mayel and Salvador. *"Please forgive me for going away like this,"* she ended, while Eric towered above her. *"I'll always love and remember you."*

"Touching," Eric said, taking the letters and folding them. "I'd believe it myself if I didn't know better. Now Thomas will take these back to your room and exchange them for the note you left when you thought you were going to your lover."

Too despairing to respond to the jeer, Mercy stared at the candle. Eric gave the letters to the lithe black man, who went quickly out. Dropping to one knee, Eric brought Mercy around to face him.

"Was he your lover?"

"Yes!" With a wild surge of hope, Mercy raised her head and unflinchingly endured Eric's gaze. Perhaps he wouldn't want another man's mistress. "I was his, and I'm glad of it! I love him . . . "

"And you hate me," Kensington finished, his eyes smoldering like white-hot ash. "That should make your training interesting." They stared at each other, hunter and quarry. Eric's voice thickened. "Take off your clothes."

Mercy didn't move. Her bones seemed to have melted; she was surprised she didn't collapse in a soft, formless mass. Eric set his hands on the high collar of her old gabardine dress and ripped it to the waist. As she raised her arms to shield herself, he gripped both wrists and held them behind her as he tore off her camisole.

Half-fainting, she moaned and struggled as his fingers cupped her breasts, then toyed with her nipples. His

194

teeth nipped her from breasts to belly. He tossed her garments aside, put her down on a couch of blankets spread on fragrant leaves in the corner, wrenched off his own clothing, and held her arms above her head while he thrust and battered his way into her tightly constricting body.

Deep within her, he moved back and forth on his knees astride her, his free hand stroking her as if claiming, branding.

"Narrow as a virgin," he said. "At least it'd seem you've had no one since Falconer chose to play the noble ass and go join Peraza. Open your eyes."

She kept them closed, turning her head as far as she could to one side. Eric's grasp closed over the bottom part of her face, bringing it around. "Look. I want you to see me on top of you, to get it through your skull that I'm your master."

When she still defied him, he lowered himself and rammed savagely in and out. Each thrust of his swollen, pulsing hardness made her want to scream with pain. Would he tear her apart? As suddenly as it had begun, the staccato lunging smoothed into lazy, almost contemplative, strokes.

"Look at me," he whispered.

She couldn't bear another onslaught without crumbling. She opened her eyes and slowly met his. He was bronzed to the waist, as if he was often without a shirt, and the crisp, curling hair on his chest was even brighter than that on his head.

"Feel me inside you," he told her. "You must want me. You must be ready to receive me."

As if he derived great excitement from her upturned gaze, he increased his tempo till he paused with a violent shuddering. Her bruised vitals felt the pumping flow drain rigidity from that part of him that had driven into her so cruelly.

And all the time he simply watched her.

Mercy awoke in a hammock, not remembering where she was till the aching between her thighs brought back in a stabbing rush all that had happened. Gray light showed that the hut was empty.

Sitting up in a rush, a trapped creature discovering its tormentor was at least momentarily gone, Mercy gnawed her lip as she stood, wincing, and gripped the blanket closer as she saw her torn clothes crumpled by the bench.

The wan light was choked off as Eric filled the doorway. "There's a dress for you on that peg in the corner. I picked it from the things Thomas brought. It would seem odd for you to leave your belongings, so I had him bring your clothes and personal items. Your hairbrush is on the stump. If you need anything else, we'll dig it out of the packs tonight."

Bending to avoid the ceiling, he reached her in one long step and kissed her deeply, as if he drew from her some rich, subtle nourishment. He put his hands on her beneath the blanket and caressed her till she trembled in dread and shame.

"What, my dear, so eager?" he mocked, raising his lips slightly from hers. "Control yourself. When we rest at noon, you may show me what you enjoy. I'm certain I can introduce you to some new pleasures." He pressed the heel of his hand hard against her stomach. "Inside you feel like wet, warm velvet. I can scarcely wait to be there again, but I'm also eager to get you home, where we can have a proper bed."

Taking the blanket from her protesting hands, he sucked in his breath as he looked at her.

"It seems I can't wait."

He forced her to the fallen blanket.

Mounted on a glossy black little mare, Mercy had to crouch against its mane most of the time to keep from being caught by vines and low branches. Eric, ahead of her, led his big bay thoroughbred, which he told her he'd gone to Kentucky to examine and buy.

"I'm particular about what carries me," he'd said as he lifted her into her saddle. "It takes stamina to bear my weight and pace. Add to that my being hard to please and you might see why I think no journey's too long or price too high for what I've determined suits me."

Mercy couldn't answer and was thankful when he moved ahead to take the reins of his horse. Excruciatingly sore and nauseated, she'd forced down the hot tea Eric insisted she have and had eaten a bite or two of sweet bread. Eric had tried that morning to woo her a bit, but he quickly lost patience with her rigid body and took her swiftly.

"At the House of Quetzals, there'll be baths, lotions— all the luxuries that make loving an art," he'd said while she was dressing. "By the time we get there, you should appreciate them."

She longed to say that nothing would make her welcome his passion, but she was fast learning that angering him was a costly gesture. If she was to preserve her sanity and health for the time that must surely come when she could escape, she'd do well to spare herself.

Thomas walked ahead of Eric, clearly on alert. The other men followed behind Mercy. They kept to a narrow jungle track that finally came out on what Mercy judged to be the road to Tekax.

How wonderful it would be if Zane and his score of armed men came trooping along it! But he was probably in the north helping his old commander plan the capture of often-besieged Mérida. Mercy sighed. When he read her letter, and that might not be for months, would he hate and despise her? Or would his heart make some excuse for her and leave him sad?

Eric looked back at her with that uncanny way he had of seeming to guess her thoughts. "Peraza's massing men for a push on Mérida," he said. "But the men who remember Carlota, danced with her, and received decorations will fight for the empire with more conviction than usual in Yucatán's purely political joustings. Until the War of the Castes, when butchery became the rule, political prisoners were seldom shot, but there'll be executions after this revolution, whichever side wins." He chuckled while Mercy tried to keep all expression from her face, hiding the fear for Zane that her captor's mocking words stirred in her. "How would you choose, Mercy, *mia*? For Falconer to return and read your message, or that he have a heroic death sweetened by the memory of you?"

Her scorn must have shown clearly on her face.

"Actually," Eric said, shrugging, "if he dies, it'll probably be from dysentery or yellow fever. I can't imagine why, having soldiered as a pup and knowing the danger of it, he let himself be urged away from you and that plantation he takes such pains in running. Lucky for him he's rich enough to be considered eccentric, or he wouldn't be received in society."

Mercy couldn't restrain an incredulous laugh. "Society he mixes with a few days a year after a hundred-mile journey?"

"In your eyes, of course, he's far too superior to mind

what people say." Eric made a deprecatory flourish with a hand surprisingly graceful and well shaped for such a big man. "But when he wishes to marry again, my dear, the opinions of the *mamas* and *dueñas* of Mérida will have paramount importance if he wants one of their daughters. For all he's the son of a pirate, Falconer knows that."

"He was going to marry me!" Mercy couldn't keep from crying.

"Ah," mused Eric in a tone of sympathy. "Is that how he breached you?"

"It wasn't like that!"

"No? It's curious, then, if his intentions were so lofty, that he went off to war without going through the ceremony. What if you had a child, especially should the father be killed?"

Mercy disdained to tell Eric that she and Zane had come together only after, and because of, his decision to join Peraza.

"Especially if Zane dies, I should want his baby," she retorted.

Eric stopped in his tracks and faced swiftly around. "Are you in that condition?"

Strange that she hadn't even thought of that before. It *was* possible, but after last night she didn't think any beginning life could have survived. "I don't know," she said, pleased to goad him.

He turned and strode onward. "I wouldn't mind getting a child from you, though naturally I won't marry another man's mistress. If you give birth, we'll have to check dates to see whether to keep it or give it to a wet nurse."

"I'll keep any baby I have!"

"Get it first and then we'll argue," he advised.

They went on and on till the aching where he'd used her merged with saddle weariness and a drumming headache. When they stopped at noon, she was so plainly ill that Eric swore, slung a hammock for her between two breadfruit trees, and gave her a mug of tea before he had any himself.

"Once we're into British territory, I don't care how indolent you are," he said. "But I pray to heaven that you don't prove to be a delicate wench!"

"I suppose you could always feed me to the crocodiles."

His eyes narrowed. "I should get a doctor and see that

you did what he advised," he said grimly. "Don't try to play fragile with me, Mercy, for if I find you're shamming, I'll take it out of your lovely hide."

He set Thomas to making broth from doves one of the men had shot and compelled Mercy to sip that and eat an orange before he let her sleep.

14

It would be six days till they reached the Rio Hondo, a calm jungle river dividing Yucatán from Belize and Guatemala and which would put them within miles of Eric's plantation. They swung south before reaching Tekax or Peto and took a wide detour around Chan Santa Cruz, the holy city where the Talking Cross gave orders through the *tatich*.

"He's a mestizo, Bonifacio Novelo," explained Eric. "And though Yucatán is constantly protesting, the British have little choice but to treat the Cruzob as a *de facto* nation. Besides, what are these squabbles and wranglings to us? We don't care whether those with wood to sell or money to buy our guns are *ladinos,* mestizos, Indians, or Creoles."

"They aren't English," summed up Mercy caustically.

"How well you put it," said Eric. "But whatever your opinion of British condescension, the population of Belize is tremendously varied and free-shifting, with color no barrier to marriage and position. Whites are only a small fraction, far outnumbered by Negroes, mulattos, and Carib Indians who revolted against their French masters and fled here, close to five hundred Amoy coolies who were brought here last June to work in lumbering, some sepoys deported from India after their rebellion failed, and even some Confederates like your late husband.

"Then there are perhaps ten thousand refugees from the War of the Castes, some *ladinos,* some Cruzob, with every range in between. Most of them live in the Corozal region, which has been raided frequently during the last few years by Cruzob and Icaiche Mayas. The Icaiches are supposed to help fight the Cruzob, but they'd rather plunder across the Hondo."

He went on to tell her that just before Christmas some men of the Fourth West Indian Regiment were sent to repulse Marcos Canul, the Icaiche *batab*, but instead were defeated and chased all the way to the city of Belize. During January, the Icaiches continued their invasion, demanding rent for the disputed border and Belize itself. The governor of the crown colony kept his barge ready to sail and panic was widespread. A militia was organized to aid the West Indian detachment and they set out with "rocket tubes" to subdue Mayan villages that had supported the invasion.

The zooming of these fiery missiles into easily kindled thatched villages quickly restored order, but the Icaiches were still on the roam.

"And as soon as the militia is withdrawn, the Icaiches will be back," Eric growled. "Belize protests to Campeche, since Canul, as a *batab*, is actually considered a local official of the Campeche part of Yucatán. Campeche, which can't do anything about Canul and his Icaiches, promises to try while complaining that Belize isn't English but really belongs to Yucatán, and that people who sell guns to rebels shouldn't howl when the guns are turned on them."

"I can't see how they'd feel that way," said Mercy dryly.

The pack trail they'd come down had grown steadily worse, often little more than a tunnel through dense jungle and swamp along which the horses had to be led. Either the journey left Eric with little inclination to dalliance, or he'd been alarmed by Mercy's near-prostration the day they started out, for, while he'd treated her as well as the grueling traveling allowed, he had not even kissed or fondled her since that morning assault in the hut.

She was almost beginning to hope that he'd decided he didn't want her when, during a noon stop, he cocked his head at her. A week's stubble made him look more than ever like a wild Norseman, but his white shirt was clean and his supply of linen handkerchiefs seemed inexhaustible.

"I don't want you to think, sweet Mercy, that you no

longer attract me. Nor must you think that the way I took you first is my accustomed mode with ladies. I thought it wise to teach you an initial lesson through your body, which, if learned solidly, needn't be repeated. When we reach the House of Quetzels, I want to show you that I can be as tender and sensitive a lover as you could ever wish for."

"A tender, sensitive man wouldn't treat me as you have."

His eyes glinted. "Well, Mercy, *mia,* you may have me however you choose, but you'll have me." He rose and lifted her to her feet with that effortless strength before which she was helpless.

On the sixth day they passed through desolated Bacalar, unmolested by the small Cruzob garrison kept there to protect the Rio Hondo trade route.

At the Hondo, a boat manned by eight blacks waited at a small wharf beside several thatched open shelters and warehouses. Thomas and their previous escort took the horses and packs overland while Eric handed Mercy into the pitpan.

"These are what the Indians were using when the Spaniards came," he said. "The design can't be improved on, but mine is a bit more luxurious than most."

Mercy nearly smiled at that. Forty feet long, tapering from about six feet at the center to narrow ends, the pitpan was hollowed out from a mahogany trunk. Handsomely carved posts supported a wooden roof above cushioned seats, and there were curtains to protect passengers from sun and storm. Two of the blacks steered from behind with rudder-like motions of their oars, while the others sat two on a seat and plied paddles, as long as they were tall, beginning a rhythmic chant as they set the boat in motion.

Forest on either side; sun glinting off the water; the voices of the boatmen. Reminded of Cleopatra's barge, Mercy could have enjoyed the excursion if she hadn't been compelled to it and didn't dread the end. Eric seemed content to relax and look from her to the sparkling water, radiating a kind of satisfied peace.

He was the buccaneer sailing home with his loot. Mercy avoided his quietly triumphant eyes and stared at the water, glimmering like broken fluid shards of mirror, until, almost mesmerized, she fell asleep.

*　　*　　*

She awoke while being picked up lightly. Eric sprang with her from the pitpan to a dock at which other boats and barges were tied up. Striding along the planks that shook under his weight, Eric held her high against his chest and kissed her on the mouth.

"Soon," he said, "soon, my love. There've been many women at my house, but none like you."

His mouth was hard, insatiable. Mercy tried to slip down. "I can walk."

He chuckled. "But I wish to carry you. See? There's my House of Quetzals for my quetzal woman."

"I'm no quetzal woman!"

"But you are, for the quetzal is precious and rare."

"And caged?"

"You'll see."

The house before them was built of beautiful woods, cedar, mahogany, and some she didn't know. making a spectrum from ivory to near-black, with rich shades of red and dark brown predominating. Stone was used for the foundation and trim. It was a sprawling two-storied structure of many verandas, guarded by giant palms and other majestic trees.

Like a conqueror with booty, Eric raced up the steps with her through the doorway, where there stood a tall black in a spotless white jacket with a blood-red sash. They went through a passage, with doors opening on either side, and out into a court formed by the L of the house and thick plantings of bamboo and palm.

Here, among trees, vines, rioting bougainvillaea, poincianas, hibiscus, and poinsettias, hung a number of cages. Each held what could only be a quetzal, with iridescent tail feathers gleaming, the brilliance of green and crimson unbelievable.

Though the ornate brass cages were large, the birds wouldn't fly. All perched so morosely that Mercy asked falteringly, "Are they alive?"

"Of course." Eric put her down at last, but he kept his big arm around her. "These are all male. Females aren't showy."

"But they live in cloud forests!"

"These don't."

"Isn't the climate bad for them? They don't look very happy."

He regarded her with amused scorn. "Happy? Birds? My dear girl, you're wildly sentimental! Birds don't have

202

feelings. What they do possess is instinct, their nature."

"It's the nature of a bird to fly."

Mercy's voice shook. He stared at her in true astonishment. "You're crying over them! Why? They have the best food and are safe from predators. Can't you just think of them as living jewels?"

"I hate this garden!"

His jaw set. "Do you? Well, then, it's time you saw your chamber."

"My cage?"

"You could consider it your frame, your setting. I created it for you."

"For yourself, you mean," she corrected bitterly.

"By God," he said slowly, drawing her inside, "do you need another lesson? Shall I rape you in the hall so the servants can watch?"

She didn't answer. He gave her a slight shake. "Well?"

There was nothing to do but say, "I'd like to see the room."

He picked her up again. Laughing exultantly against her hair, he ran with her up the curving staircase. Mercy closed her eyes.

It was a large, airy room with a balcony overhanging a view of the river and with windows with shutters that were open to let glossy leaves and fronds form a second sun-spangled curtain outside. The floor was covered with woven grass matting with Persian rugs scattered about, and the walls were of polished, fragrant wood. There were several gracefully curving bamboo chairs padded with turquoise velvet, an inlaid rosewood chest, a writing desk, and an immense bed of intricate brass filigree wrought into birds and leaves. It was mounded with pillows and spread with an iridescent green satin.

A door stood open to a small mirrored room with shelves and rods, obviously intended for clothes, and an arch revealed an alcove with a shell-shaped brass tub and an assortment of ewers, towels, and soaps.

"If there's anything you wish changed, tell me," Eric urged, clearly pleased with his handiwork. "The bellpull will bring your maid, Celeste. She'll unpack for you and help you bathe." His gaze traveled to the huge bed. "Rest a while before dinner. I don't want you tired tonight." He brushed a light kiss on her cheek and left quickly, sounding the bell as he went.

Mercy stood in the center of the rustically luxurious room. He had gone to great trouble to make ready her . . . frame? Setting? She was caged just as surely as those birds in the court, far from their high cloud forests, unable to fly. But she could plan. Sooner or later, there had to be a way.

There was a shy rap. "Come in," Mercy said. She wasn't going to take out her frustration and anger on the servants.

A girl with warmly perfect *café-au-lait* skin and up-swept black hair stepped in and curtsied, her bangles and earrings tinkling. "I am Celeste, *madame*. You require a bath?" She spoke English with an upper-class accent. The effect was charming.

"I'd love a bath, Celeste." The girl was so graceful and sunny that Mercy smiled in spite of her weariness and fears. Celeste smiled back.

"The water is being brought, *madame*. May I assist you in disrobing?"

"Thank you, I can manage."

Celeste's face clouded. "I have not displeased *madame?*"

"Of course not!" How could she explain that she didn't much like being waited on and shrank from being naked in front of most people? It was different with Zane. "It's just that I'm accustomed to looking after myself."

"I can, perhaps, brush your hair?"

Celeste seemed so perturbed at not fulfilling what she expected of herself that Mercy sat down and was soon lost in the sensuous pleasure of having her hair brushed free of tangles and dust. Six boys of about Salvador's age came in with pails, which they emptied into the tub, their eyes gleaming with suppressed mischief as they stole sideways glances at Mercy. They wore white cotton trousers reaching just below the knees and red sashes, but their bared upper bodies shone cocoa, copper, yellow, and shades in between.

They exited to return in five minutes with refilled buckets, three of which Celeste commanded to be left on the bench by the tub.

"It might be useful if I scrubbed your back?" persisted Celeste.

Mercy sighed, beginning to unbutton her dress. "Would you wash my comb and brush? And it would be a great help if you poured water over my hair after I wash it."

"Excellent, *madame!*" Celeste vanished with the brush and comb and there were sounds of unpacking, but she was back in plenty of time to rinse the lather from Mercy's hair and help her towel off, massaging Mercy's scalp till it tingled.

In her dressing gown, Mercy walked barefoot across the grass matting and carpets to the bed, grateful to see that Thomas had brought her books, including the *Badianus* excerpts, which lay on the chest. Someone had placed a tray of freshly cut fruit on the small lamp table, along with a large crystal goblet of pineapple juice.

Persephone, Mercy thought with a superstitious chill. *She ate the fruit of Hades and could never again live the whole year through in the bright world of her mother.* But there was no mother to look for Mercy, or father, either, and Zane might not even know for months that she was gone from La Quinta.

Thanking Celeste, who stood waiting, as if to be given further orders, Mercy went to stand on the balcony facing the river and slowly sipped the sweet, delicious liquid.

Going back to the great bed, she simply could not get into it, tempted as she was by down pillows and snowy linens. She took one pillow and lay down with it on the floor.

She awoke to feel someone watching her. She raised her eyes to Eric, who stood looking down from what seemed a giant's height. He motioned to a servant, who put a tray on the table by the chairs, set two places, and went smoothly, silently, out.

"Is the mattress too hard for you, my love?" Eric's tone was courteously interested. "Too soft?"

"I don't know."

His eyebrows lifted. He was clean-shaven, smelled of bay rum, and wore a soft white shirt and white trousers. "Don't know? Haven't you tried it?"

What had he done to her during those hours in the hut near La Quinta that, even after the intervening ten days of considerate restraint, made her shrink inwardly, evade his real question? "I . . . just felt like lying on the floor."

He laughed unpleasantly. "No doubt—because you knew that bed is where you'll lie with me. If necessary to rid you of that misgiving, my sweet, I'll take you on the floor and, indeed, all over the house so there'll be no place without memories of me. Stand up."

She did, but she instinctively took a step backward. Eric's eyes dilated. He gave the impression of moving, though he stood perfectly still before he suddenly turned to the tray and lifted a silver tureen cover.

"Ah! Turtle soup. You'll find it superb. And here's broiled lobster. We have two men whose sole duty it is to alternate in bringing seafood daily from the coast, and fishing's good in the river, too. Pierre, the cook, learned his skills in Paris. I think you'll find him able to conjure up even Texas dishes you might have a nostalgic feeling for."

That seemed possible if she were to ask for the Louisiana Creole and Cajun dishes that were common in eastern Texas, but she wondered what he'd do with corn fritters and poke greens. Eric ladled soup into porcelain bowls broadly banded with gold and seated Mercy in the fan-backed bamboo chair.

Pouring a pale, sparkling wine, Eric shook out his cut-work napkin and broke open a small crusty roll with the inimitable odor of having been fresh-baked.

"Is the soup to your taste?"

She was, in fact, hungry, but his cool assumption that she'd so readily be on almost honeymoon terms with him outraged Mercy. She would *not* be cosseted and beguiled by luxuries or masterfully cajoled into enjoying this life.

"I have no appetite," she said.

"Have you not?" Their eyes locked. "You'd better find it, Mercy, *mia*. You'll need stamina tonight, I expect to make up for what I denied myself on the trail from esthetic considerations and sympathy for you."

"Sympathy!"

He nodded. "I'm trying to exercise patience with you. Rape has its charms, but it grows repetitive. Love's sweeter variations and delights require a willing partner."

She stared at him, wordless, gripped with disbelieving hatred. Could he think she'd ever do more than he forced her to, ever want to pleasure or be pleased by him? He sighed and laid his hand on her throat. It was like being claimed by a great tawny cat.

" 'Willing' may be too sanguine a description for the moment, but I shall at least have compliance, and that without dark looks and sulking. Eat now; it'll make you feel better."

"I told you . . ."

"There's an alternative," he cut in. "I wouldn't dream of exhausting a dinnerless lady with the diversions I have in mind, but I can derive considerable satisfaction from alternate amusements."

"I'm delighted to hear it."

"Are you?" he smiled. "But, of course, I expect you to share the rather special entertainment." He considered. "When girls are whipped in the courtyard, sometimes the quetzals scream along with them. But sometimes I prefer to watch just one at rather close quarters. The writhing and play of muscle is more intimate that way. Have you a preference?"

"You . . . whip women for no reason?"

"My amusement is the best of reasons. Don't look so appalled, my dear. *I* don't whip the girls. It's done by an expert who won't break the skin."

"I suppose one shouldn't be surprised if you slept with the women under your power," said Mercy between clenched teeth. "But to use them this way! It's horrible! Disgusting!"

"Oh, I enjoy them when I feel like it. All the house servants, male and female, are the handsomest to be found. They don't think me such a monster as you do. They're not overworked, they live well, and whether I whip a girl or rape her, she gets her pick of baubles at the store." While Mercy tried to fit this into her understanding of this man who was presently all-powerful in her life, he went on thoughtfully. "I could call in one of those boys who fetched your bathwater. There're two of them, I think, whom I haven't sampled yet."

"B-boys?"

"You don't know about one of the most ancient and celebrated kinds of love?" he asked mockingly. "I could have sworn that Philip had predilections that way."

With the humiliated shame of new half-comprehension, Mercy remembered that night when Philip had been so drunk and the degradingly inexplicable and painful way he'd used her. Now Eric was saying that, of course, males could be used like that, too.

"So?" inquired Eric. "Fond memories recast in a different light, or perhaps they weren't so fond? Don't judge the departed too harshly, sweet. Perhaps like myself and any number of potent men, he found it an interesting side dish, but in the main preferred fairly basic delights."

207

There was nothing to say. Like Zane, he controlled the daily lives and fates of humans on his estate, but where Zane had governed himself and used his conscience in the treatment of his workers, Eric had no law higher than his whim.

"So what shall we have?" he asked, as if consulting a menu. "A whipping here or in the courtyard? One of the boys? Sometimes they screech the first time, but, like women, they soon get used to it."

"I think I'd rather die than live with you forever."

He chuckled. "Enchanted with you as I am, Mercy, I doubt I'll want you that long, since Zane's already had you. In two or three years I might see just what he'd give for you, though I've a feeling he'll be sticky about my leavings. If he was serious about marriage, I fear that's one dream you'll have to give up."

"I don't see how I could go to him or any other decent man after what you seem to have in mind. I hate to think what I'll be like after two years with you!"

"So little confidence in yourself," he mused. "Well, love, don't let it fret you. There'll always be a pensioner's corner for you here, or I could surely find you an English husband in Belize City, one who wouldn't know your amazing background. But why talk of the future?" He got to his feet in the graceful, easy fashion that always surprised her because he was so large. "I'll ring the bell and by the time Celeste comes, you must decide about the evening."

She caught his arm. "I'll do what you want."

"Good girl." He gave her cheek an approving caress, sat down, and began to eat with a voracity that was frightening.

Mercy concentrated on her own food and wished the meal would never end.

After one of the innumerable servants had removed the dishes and left more wine and fruit on the table, Eric untied the sash of Mercy's dressing gown and eased it off her shoulders, letting it drop to the floor. He watched her for a moment, his breath quickening and his eyes seeming to film, before he carried her to the bed.

He took her quickly, as if he couldn't wait, so swollen and hard that she bit her lips to keep from screaming till his fluid pumped into her and he rolled off and lay beside her with one arm flung across her body.

Tears stung at Mercy's eyes. To mind the physical pain seemed ignoble under the circumstances, but she wondered how long she could endure simply that part of her captivity.

"I still hurt?" he asked gently, his fingers rubbing away the few tears that had squeezed out in spite of her pride. "Never mind, love. You'll fit me better every time, and I can do some nice things for you that will feel wonderful."

He began to stroke her. She went rigid. "I . . . you needn't bother!"

"But I want to."

Rising, he came back with water and cloths, cleansed her aching, plundered parts, and then rubbed scented oil on her from neck to toe, working it in with firm, sure strokes that gradually eased away her resistance and made her relax to a surprising extent. He turned her over, then oiled her back and artfully kneaded her shoulders, buttocks, and thighs. It felt so good that the only way she could accept it was to remind herself that she was helpless against his fancies and had better get any help from them that she could.

Everything seemed to be melting into the warm, flowing caress of powerful hands that turned her over again and began to smooth her breasts, brushing the nipples, traversing with strong, solid motions her vulnerable-feeling stomach and loins till even that unprotected area stopped tensing.

Maybe that's all he's going to do, she thought drowsily. Languor deepened with each soothing stroke. Then something damp and sensitive was following the hand as his tongue played around her navel, teased her nipples, and urgently but salvingly invaded the place he had breached so roughly.

Mostly his tongue flicked where she wasn't sore, playing over a small, exquisitely tender place that Zane had found, too, but which had been a fusing, indistinguishable part of the rapture to which he could bring her.

With Eric it was different—she had no wish for *him*—but the arousal demanded discharge, with the tension mounting unbearably till she flexed her thighs, trembling, as his tongue probed the wounded but now desirous entrance to her depths.

Flames of pink and gold exploded within her. Eric seemed to drink, suck from her some essence. She cried out irrepressibly as the tautness drained, leaving her soft, spent.

"Sleep now, my love," he said, and he held her in his arms.

She awoke caressed in the dim light of early morning. Almost before she remembered where she was and with whom, Eric finished preparing her and slowly, carefully, penetrated, stopping when she tightened, thrusting a fraction deeper when she relaxed.

"I'm within you," he said at last, "to the hilt, sweet Mercy. Shall we see if you can like this just a little?"

He kept up a soft rhythm for a while, but she was determined not to respond, horrified and angry at herself for his easy victory last night. As if he read her thoughts, he gripped her flanks, raised her to fit him as tightly as his size would allow, and hammered till that instant when substance spurted from him in pulsing jets that she felt like a muffled heartbeat in her loins.

"You're tougher than you think," he told her, panting as he collapsed beside her. "You won't break from my usage, and in time you'll rise to meet me and thrust back, wanting to feel me as deep as you can."

She didn't answer. How was she to fight him when the price was the torture of others? And if she had to be quiescent under his hands, how could she prevent her body from responding to his skillful, questing tongue?

There was no way, probably, though she doubted his prediction that she'd ever respond to his practice of the normal mode. With one careless arm, he lifted her on top of him and held the back of her head so that, resting on the pillows, he could see her face.

"Moral quandary?" He laughed, stroking her breasts and thighs. "How are you going to reconcile what your body does with your top-lofty ideals and love for your errant cavalier?"

Despairingly, she wondered what Elkanah, who understood human souls but ministered to bodies, would have said. He would never have told her to hate or despise the wonderfully made and vulnerable body for responding as it was intended and designed to in order to continue the race. If she'd been given a choice, it would be different, but she'd had none.

"Loving Zane has nothing to do with what you can

make me feel," she said. "I won't blame myself for that any more than I will for eating and drinking."

"Fortunate Mercy!" he chided, frowning humorously. "To enjoy the pleasures of sin while wearing a martyr's crown! Possibly I shouldn't have used that leverage but instead held you with force till you opened in sheer, hungry wanting."

"That wouldn't have happened as long as I could fight," she said blightingly.

He shrugged. "There are potions. And sleep is perhaps the best drug of all, for then prohibitions of mind and conscience sink under the ocean of primeval needs. You couldn't stay awake all the time. I could have you well on the way to flowering ecstasy, my dear, before your brain could warn you it was no dream of Falconer, but me in the questing, joy-giving flesh."

"You have what you went to so much trouble to get in disregard of what I felt or thought or wanted," she said stiffly. "I don't see why you should consider it now."

"But it's what you think and feel and want that make you my quetzal woman, my rare, precious one." He spoke in a lightly bantering tone, but she believed him. "I'm not a fool, Mercy. There are a dozen women at this hacienda as beautiful as you. They bloom like flowers, fragrant, exotic, ready for my hand. In spite of my rather frightening reputation, any number of society mothers in London or New York, not to mention Mérida or Mexico City, would give their daughters to me because of my wealth, though the girls, I think, wouldn't come for that alone. But none of them has had for me that strange lure that Falconer must have sensed, too. There's a strength about you like the flashing of a blade, a core of being. At that core, you are kind. Truly, Mercy."

She stared at him, frightened for the first time that she might be stripped of her loathing for him. "You're wrong," she said. "If I ever have the chance, I won't be kind to you, and I will show you no mercy at all."

"That's the flashing blade," he mocked, though the pupils of his eyes contracted to a point. "But you could never wield it except to save someone else."

"You'll see!"

It flashed into her mind for the first time that she might find a way to kill him. He was right. Sleep did disarm. Even a giant lay helpless. At this moment, there was a knife beside the fruit.

He picked it up and cut for her a section of pineapple. "In case you should determine not only to harden your heart against me in case of my misfortune, but to do away with one you can quite justifiably consider wicked, I have entrusted Thomas with an order. He will carry it out if he lives because he loves me." Eric raised himself on the pillows and regarded her with tolerant good humor. "Are you curious?"

"I had thought of cutting your throat, so perhaps you'd better tell me."

He laughed in delight. "You are indeed my rare one! What became of the quetzal I bribed one of the maids to leave in your room at Christmas?"

"I dropped it in a chest."

"But the giver's not so easy to dispose of, eh?" He grinned. "I've instructed Thomas, in event of my death at your hands or in any suspicious way hinting at your involvement, to kill Falconer if possible, or his daughter."

Mercy drew away from him. He only chuckled. "I reckon that I've thought of everything, Mercy, *mia*. There's no way to thwart me without bringing destruction to others. If you'd quit beating your wings against the cage, you could enjoy the mansion."

With a stifled gasp, she turned away from him.

"Why don't you sleep as late as you can?" He shrugged mildly. "Come down for breakfast when you're ready. I've an accumulation of business, but I'll acquaint you with the house today and we might even go riding."

She pretended to sleep while he dressed. She sensed him standing over her, and she fought to keep her breathing regular. His hand trailed over her from throat to flank, as if affirming possession before he covered her and left.

But Mercy couldn't sleep. Light spilled through the shutters now and she abhorred the comfort of the huge bed in which Eric had not only taken her, but had exacted blind tribute from her body. She almost wished he'd remained the brutal attacker of that first night, a man she could hate physically, detest as a complete ruffian.

Eric, though, was subtle, highly intelligent, and complex. She felt transparent with him. Just as he was intrigued by something other than her body, she had to contend with much more than his. Since he was ruthless and she wasn't, he could control her. All through his subjection of her, he'd never threatened her with death or whipping, though his rapes had been calculated to break her resistance and implant fear.

A formidable adversary.

But she was Elkanah's daughter, and she had been Zane's love. As long as Zane lived, there was a fragile hope they might be reunited. After losing her old life and identity, she'd been able to make a place for herself at La Quinta.

Just as she held out against Zane's early wish to seclude her in the tower, she must keep inviolate here her own center, her own fifth direction, which was another way, probably, of naming that essence Eric craved. Instead of putting her inside a tower, he wished to storm and carry the citadel within her. It would take all her courage, endurance, and inventiveness to withstand him.

But it was at least a challenge, better than the bleak, trapped hopelessness she'd known with Philip. Mercy tossed off the light coverlet and sprang up, ignoring her aches. She opened the shutters and looked northeast, across the Hondo and Cruzob territory toward La Quinta.

What were they saying about her there? Chepa would be puzzled and sad; Jolie must feel betrayed. But at least she had Salvador and Chepa till Zane came home again. Mercy couldn't bear to imagine what he'd think when he read her letter.

Mutely, she prayed he was well, and Jolie, too, and all at La Quinta. She hoped that somehow she might be able to see them again. And then she turned from the river and began to check exactly which of her belongings Thomas had brought, much as a shipwrecked person would inventory tools for survival.

Her clothing was in the small room, and, though that wasn't of vital importance, it helped to remember how Zane had insisted she get the gray-blue satin, and that Jolie had a dress of the same blue challis and slept at night with a stuffed coati of that material. Here was the black coral necklace, the sacred virgin water, and, defiantly, she wore the ring Zane had given her.

Besides the *Badianus* copy, there were her father's letters and the few books she'd kept of his. It was like finding lost treasure to open a box and find the herbs and medicines Chepa had given her along with what she had taken from Texas and what she'd collected at La Quinta.

Thomas had done well, and when she had a chance, she'd thank him, though it was ironic to be grateful to someone for breaking into her room and taking her effects.

The sight of the herbs reminded Mercy that Eric was virile, and as often as he seemed intent on having her, she might experience the common result. In one of Chepa's jars were dried flowers of the dwarf poinciana. Mercy resolved, though with revulsion, that any time her flow was late, she'd immediately purge herself with the brew Chepa prescribed for women who had more children than they could care for.

Fortified by this decision, the means to carry it out, and the presence of the objects she most prized, tangible links to her loved ones and skills, Mercy washed, cleansing herself thoroughly of Eric's male odor, and dressed in the prim gray-blue poplin with white collar and cuffs.

She brushed her hair severely, pinned it in a coil, stood a moment behind her door summoning courage, and then entered the larger household, where for a time she must live.

15

Thomas was in the hall and came forward, bowing, as Mercy reached the bottom of the stairs. "I trust madam is rested from the journey," he said as formally as if he hadn't, nearly two weeks ago, waited outside an abandoned hut for Eric to finish raping her before that journey started. His sable skin startling against white shirt and trousers, Thomas wore a green sash. Mercy guessed him to be in his twenties, slender but strongly built. He had an aureole of tight-curling black hair and the stern face of a warrior, except when he smiled.

He did so when Mercy thanked him for collecting her books and herbs. "Madam must be at home here," he said warmly. "Will you have breakfast in the courtyard, or on the terrace, or in the dining room?"

Not the courtyard, with its captive birds. "The terrace,"

Mercy decided, involuntarily noting fine paintings that made the broad hall a gallery. The hardwood floor was polished to gleaming. Mercy noticed that two pretty mulatto girls, who dropped curtsies to her, were applying wax to furniture that bore the sheen of unremitting care.

"Would madam perhaps wish to talk with the cook about what she desires?"

"All I want is coffee and a roll."

Thomas looked stricken. "Pierre hoped, I know, to tempt madam with his crepes."

She was at war with Eric, not his people. "Tell Pierre I shall be happy with whatever he has at hand," Mercy said, yielding, and she followed Thomas through a side corridor to a terrace that faced the river and was shaded by palms.

After seating her in a bamboo chair by a bamboo table, Thomas departed and returned quickly with coffee, saying that her breakfast would be served in a few minutes. Then he glided off, reminding Mercy of one of Aladdin's efficient genies.

She sipped the pungent coffee, stirring in the first cream she'd had since coming to Yucatán because there were no milk cows at La Quinta. The river reflected the sky. It didn't seem much of a barrier to resentful Mayas, who felt the land claimed by Britain really belonged to them.

Pondering escape, she wondered if she could find her way home even if she didn't fall prey to swamps, crocodiles, or Cruzob. It seemed unlikely. Unless she found an accomplice, she'd better stay where she was and hope for some other way out of her elegant prison.

With bustling flurry, Pierre swept onto the terrace, shooing a boy ahead of him with a tray. *"Madame!"* cried Pierre, bowing so deeply she pitied his plump belly. "Pierre Chandel, your most devoted servant!" He kissed her hand so that the waxed tips of his gray moustache pricked her. He had curly gray eyebrows, thick hair of the same color, Delft-blue eyes, and a pink complexion that glowed like a baby's. "It is my duty—*mon plaisir*—to prove that there is civilized cuisine even at this barbarous end of the earth. One must improvise, of course; one must substitute. But there are advantages. Wait until you taste *ceviche* made from conch with fresh-squeezed lemon! Or a dessert of fresh coconuts, pineapples, and bananas, or fresh fruit *crèmes*, or pig pit-roasted in the native manner! The seafood is a marvel: lobsters of fourteen pounds, stone crabs, shrimp, and such fish! And great turtles and turtle eggs! With lemon, butter, and parsley, the humblest fisherman can dine like a king off an endless variety of sea bounty. And we have geese and ducks, as well as chickens and turkeys. If you had only tasted the smoked goose I prepared at Christmas with side dishes of oysters and shrimp!" He paused for breath and beamed enormously. "But I prattle while you must be famished. Your pardon, *madame!* You have a particular fancy this morning, or may I surprise you?"

He so obviously craved to do the latter that Mercy smiled. "Surprise me, please, Pierre." With a flash of foreknowledge, she added, "But not with too much. A roll and coffee is all I am used to."

Pierre answered with an eloquent snort, bowed, and rushed away. He must have had mixtures ready for cooking, for in twenty minutes he returned with a retinue of three boys who held trays while Pierre himself arranged the repast on the linen table mat he spread on the table.

"Omelet with slivers of ham and green peppers," he announced, setting down a covered dish by the heavy, crested silver. "Crepes with toasted coconut and rum sauce, and a fresh fruit parfait. Enjoy it, *madame!*"

He was gone in the happy oblivion of duty done while Mercy stared at the beautifully served repast with something like horror.

All this work to make one meal for one person seemed almost sinful, though, at least, thanks to the plentitude of fruits, food plants, and fish, she didn't need to feel she was depriving anyone of food. Some of her father's patients had lived just as self-indulgently, of course, but she had acquired from him a feeling that no person should consume in worldly goods and comforts more than a reasonable share, and that was based to a degree on what they contributed to the world.

But the food was before her, it smelled tantalizing, and she uncovered the perfectly done omelet. She finished it, ate two of the incredibly thin, delicate crepes, and was finishing with the fresh fruit and coffee replenished from the silver pot when Pierre returned.

His face fell at the sight of the remaining crepe. "Too much rum, perhaps? *Madame* does not like coconut?"

"They were superb," Mercy assured him. "But I wouldn't be able to move if I ate that one. Let me have it later."

His Delft-blue eyes bulged. *"Madame!* A warmed-over crepe is like a dowager trying to be a *jeune fille!* Never will it happen while I'm in charge of Monsieur Wellington's kitchen!"

"What, a difference of opinion already?" Eric sauntered through the French doors, pulled up a chair beside Mercy, and poured coffee into the extra cup on the tray. "A tragedy, Pierre?"

"Madame suggested I serve her a warmed-over crepe!"

Eric shook his head. "I share your horror, Pierre, but you must understand that *madame* lived through a war that must have considerably reduced her gustatory expectations."

He polished off the crepe while Pierre moaned. "But, *monsieur,* it is cold now! You cannot possibly . . ."

"Excellent," said Eric, using Mercy's napkin. "I wish to show *madame* around the house, Pierre, but when I resume my labors with McNulty, she can visit your kitchen and you can discuss her preferences."

His sensibilities still outraged, Pierre bowed huffily and took himself back to his dominion. "Temperamental, but worth it," said Eric, grinning. "I could never endure it here without him. However, I'll have a word with him if he fattens you up too much with his sauces and pastries." Appraising eyes went over her, as if summing up her attributes. "You could stand a little flesh, but not enough to hide the wonderful modeling of your bones."

"I'm not a prize racehorse or piece of sculpture," Mercy said.

"Indeed, not," Eric agreed with a twinkle, rising and helping her up. "But you won't stuff yourself in the hope of disgusting me. Quaint little puritan that you look to be in that gray gown, it molds your breasts and trim waist."

"My father always warned me about the health risks of overeating."

"Not to mention the artistic ones," murmured Eric. "Shall we begin with my office, love? You might as well meet McNulty. French cook and Scottish accountant! Took me five years and as many men to hit upon McNulty, but in his way he's as invaluable as Pierre."

"You seem well served."

"I go to great trouble to see that I am," he replied blandly. "I'm never content till I'm sure I have the best."

Passing down the hall, he opened the first door on the right and let Mercy precede him into a large book-lined room with a smaller one adjoining, where a freckled man with thinning red hair glanced up from a ledger. His bow to Mercy as he rose was curt. Clearly, he was absorbed in his work and didn't care to be interrupted.

"Mercy, this is James McNulty," said Eric. "James, this is Doña Mercy."

"She's no more Spanish than I be," said the wizened man, adjusting his spectacles to view her. "A sonsie lass with Scottish blood, I'm bound!"

"Scottish-Irish," Mercy admitted, "with a streak of Welsh."

McNulty nodded approval before he peered at Eric. "Now, sir, there be no way I can sort out the payments to those howling Icaiches for logging rights until you sit down and explain it all to me!"

"In an hour, James, you may go at me till you're satisfied," Eric promised.

They left the Scotsman to his work. Eric had three desks in his main office, each surrounded by files and bookcases. "It helps me not to get mixed up," he said and laughed. "The desk to the right has all the material on logging, sugar's in the middle, and the left one concerns cattle and domestic matters."

"Don't you deal in guns?"

"I'd certainly be wasting a great frontier location if I didn't," he said after a moment. "It's a profitable sideline, but though the estate began as a logging concern, sugar now provides much of the income." He gazed out at the river. "I haven't done badly for the black-sheep younger son of a Midlands baronet."

Mercy grimaced. "Are all younger sons black sheep?"

"It's the only way they get to amount to anything," returned Eric imperturbably.

The library was across the hall, with a scatter of pipes and the smell of tobacco to indicate that Eric spent considerable time in a massive leather chair by a reading table strewn with rare editions and periodicals in several languages. There was a glittering array of decanters and bottles on a sideboard, and one wall was fitted to hold rifles, shotguns, and small arms, all well oiled.

Next to the library was a music room. White magnolias were reflected on the polished top of a grand piano and an organ that might have graced a cathedral filled one wall. A violin lay on the blue velvet-cushioned window-seat overlooking the leafy courtyard, and a rosewood harp inlaid with ivory sat by a gilt-legged needlepoint bench. In a large recess behind it was a portrait of a very young woman, her fingers on the strings of a harp exactly like the real one. She wore an off-shoulder gown of dark green satin, and her rich chestnut hair was tied back with a ribbon of the same color.

Mercy's scalp prickled as she stared into remarkably lifelike eyes that seemed much too sad and wise for such a young face. The hair, the skin, the eyes! It was like looking into a mirror that gave back a not-quite-true reflection that prompted one to look closer and see the face was longer, the mouth classical, and the chin pointed. But Mercy looked enough like the woman in the painting to have been a sister.

"That is Alison." Eric sent his fingers across the harp strings, eliciting a sound like a cry of pain. "My half-sister."

"She's in England?"

"In the family vault. Holy ground—even though she was a suicide."

Mercy gave a cry, full of pity and a kind of eerie dread, as she stared at the grave, sweet countenance. "Why? Why would she do that?"

"She was going to have my baby." Eric gripped Mercy's wrists and made her face him. "Don't look like that! How can you know? Our mother died when Alison was five and I was three. My father—her stepfather—left us to nannies and servants who generally ignored us when they weren't actually abusive. Father drank to excess, and females of propriety couldn't stay long in his employ. So Alison both sistered and mothered me. Each was all the other had to love, to huddle against on lonely nights, or seek comfort from when Father buffeted us about. I was sent off to school, of course, but Alison had a governess, some improvement over the slattern nannies, and music was her joy and deliverance. Even Father would often ask her to play.

"When I was sixteen, I came home at Whitsuntide to find that Father had betrothed her to a man of his own age. Alison was distraught. I held her and promised to

219

think of something. We were innocent till then, but as God may judge me, if there is a God, our loving was as natural and sweet and inevitable as the opening of a flower. Father caught us one day in the attic, where we'd used to play as children. He stunned me with his walking stick and beat me senseless. When I came to, I was gagged, tied hand and foot, and Father's estate manager and a groom were taking me to Southampton.

"There they paid the captain well to keep me locked in a cabin till the ship reached the West Indies. The captain, honest in his way, delivered a letter from my father that disinherited me in the best sanctimonious style while bemoaning that a poor widower who'd devoted himself to his motherless children should be so disgraced. He enclosed one hundred pounds, adjured me to try to drag myself from the morass of heinous crime, and said if I cared at all for Alison's peace I would never come again to England, or even try to communicate with her—that she would be married to the worthy Christian gentleman selected for her before I could read the letter."

In spite of her need to hate Eric utterly, a picture of a battered, despairing boy separated from the only person he loved and dropped into a strange country came so powerfully to Mercy that she almost touched his hand. "Did you ever see her again?"

He shook his head. "It was a month before I got back to the Midlands. My father was so drunk he didn't even know me. I had to get the story out of the governess who had stayed to take care of him, and share his bed, I would reckon, when he was capable. Alison had told the worthy gentleman about me. That, quite predictably, shocked him into bleating like a sheep, and he hastily retreated. Alison, the governess said, had hoped my father would exile her, too, and that somehow she could find me. But he found another man, this one debt-ridden, ailing, and as old as the first, who, for a sum, would marry her and acknowledge the child. It was to escape him that Alison took arsenic that was kept to poison vermin. My sister, to die that way! But it was my fault, my piggish, selfish fault! She was goodness to me all my life, and that was how I repaid her."

"You . . . were very young."

"So was she—and much more innocent. I had heard talk at school, had been to a few public women." His gaze turned inward. "I took Alison's portrait and harp and worked my passage to Sisal, for I remembered hearing that one of my mother's many brothers was a merchant in Mérida. He gave me a position, and after that I seemed fortune's darling. But nothing really mattered."

"Did your uncle and Doña Elena know?"

"My uncle was something of a family skeleton himself for going into trade, and he simply assumed I was a kindred spirit, which was true enough. I'd have smothered in England. We've Viking blood in my mother's line, and it surfaces in every generation. I've distant cousins scattered from Canada to Texas and from the Transvaal to New Zealand."

"I suppose you can't all stay in England."

"If everybody had, we'd be standing on each other's shoulders," said Eric. "Meanwhile, Belize is a fairly unusual place. Though it's been claimed by the British since the time of Elizabeth, they've always been a tiny minority here. The first to arrive were mainly British Navy men who traveled up the rivers cutting dyewood. Do you know of it?"

Mercy shook her head.

"It's very valuable wood, the price for which has risen steadily since its discovery by the Dutch in the 1600s. They found it produced a superior, non-running dye. Later, when the settlers came, they were prevented from growing more than subsistence crops of dyewood or anything else, in accord with a treaty with Spain. But all that has changed since Mexican independence and since Yucatecan refugees started bringing in sugarcane cuttings in the late Forties. I have two hundred acres in cane, and McNulty advises that I plant more as soon as the mahogany is cut."

"Can't you leave the trees?"

"When they command such a price?" Eric turned abruptly from the harp and led Mercy across the hall to a sitting room furnished with what she thought was Regency with some Chippendale: two striped Grecian couches; plush chairs; a teapoy with brass inlay; a variety of drum, pillar, and claw tables and stands. "Useless room," said Eric, though he regarded it with a certain contemptuous pride. "The only time it's used is when the governor visits or when an Englishman accompanied by his wife comes this way, which is damned seldom."

A large dining room with tapestry-upholstered chairs,

221

a massive oak refectory table, sideboard, and several oak china cabinets took up the remainder of the bottom floor, except for a small room with French doors opening onto the terrace. Two plain comfortable chairs were pulled up to a small round table with a bowl of fruit in the middle of its sparkling white cloth. There were books, pipes, and metal containers, which Eric said contained biscuits, candied ginger, nuts, and other tidbits in case she got hungry between meals. He added, unnecessarily, that he spent most of his waking time here or in his office or library. A walkway led from this room to the kitchen house, a separate structure.

Upstairs was a huge room used for storage, repairs, and sewing. The room was equipped with two Singer sewing machines. Mercy had seen the hand-cranked machine designed by Howe, a Boston watchmaker's apprentice, which could make two hundred fifty stitches a minute, outdoing what a good seamstress could accomplish in five or six times that length of time, but Eric assured her that these Singers were far superior and that sewing for the whole household was done on them. On their floor, there were two guest bedrooms besides Mercy's.

"And this is where I sleep," said Eric, drawing her inside yet another room.

He took her slowly, almost contemplatively, in the canopied four-poster bed, watching her face, with a gentleness more unnerving than his violence. Dear God! Did he try to imagine she was Alison? That story had made it impossible for her to hate him with clean, undiluted purity, but it made her angry with him, too. Instead of making him compassionate, tragedy had turned him into a conscienceless exploiter of people and land. Instead of his love making him respect hers for Zane, it made him pitiless in grasping for a husk of what he'd lost.

As if sensing her rebellious thoughts, Eric again, with his probing, skillful tongue, won from her that involuntary tribute of cresting, blind, shuddering release before he entered her, drivingly this time, and reached a convulsively trembling climax, after which he seemed to doze for a few minutes, one gold-haired bronzed arm flung over her.

"Will you rest?" he asked, his eyes still closed. "Or will you visit Pierre?"

"I'll see him," she decided.

222

They washed and dressed and went downstairs. She wondered if she'd ever understand this man who was her captor.

The kitchen was the most surprising room in the house. Herbs grew in long boxes set on every windowsill. Amidst rows, shelves, and cupboards of enamel, copper, and cast-iron cooking vessels and utensils, bins and barrels and containers of foodstuffs, was a long, heavy table centered with shelves of seasonings, measuring cups, bowls, spoons, and knives. A fireplace situated in a small side room was equipped with spits and grills, but the pride of the cook's heart was a fearsomely impressive system of fast oven, slow oven, pastry oven, steam closet, hot closet, and bath boiler all in one imposing stove fired in the center.

"The first of this marvelous invention was shown at the great exhibition in Hyde Park in . . . yes, 1851, I am sure, *madame!* It cost Monsieur Kensington a small fortune to have it shipped here, but he's often told me it was worth it, yes!"

The pantry was almost the size of the kitchen and resembled a grocery. All of the tinned delicacies were imported, and there were bins of flour, rice, beans, and sugar. Crocks of butter, cream, and milk were stored in the coolest corner. Next to the pantry was a tile-topped counter for cleaning and dressing game and fowl, with a large basin equipped with a drain.

"You could cook for the queen of England," said Mercy.

"I could!" Pierre wasn't one for false modesty. "But this is better. Monsieur Kensington leaves the kitchen to me." He gestured at the half-dozen helpers who were going about various tasks. There were two boys of perhaps fourteen or fifteen, two young men, and two middle-aged women. "They do what I say, but none can argue over the correct way to prepare *faisan à la flamande* or *galantine de poulard.*"

"Neither will I!" Mercy laughed.

Pierre couldn't quite cover his look of relief. "But *madame* must be pleased!"

"I'm sure I will be. I like fruit and vegetables, I am very fond of cheese and eggs, and I've come to like tortillas."

"I don't serve those, not me!" When Mercy glanced at the woman making the flat cakes, Pierre said, "Those are for the servants."

"Well, maybe I can have one now and then," Mercy said. "Please make whatever you judge best, Pierre, but remember that I can't eat as much as Mr. Kensington."

"When *madame* has had time to sample my creations, perhaps she will tell me her favorites?"

Time. Mercy thought again of the food of Persephone. But she must endure, and for that she must eat. Of course I will," she told Pierre. "Thank you for showing me your wonderful kitchen."

He bowed her out and began calling orders for what Mercy feared was the start of the noon meal. Going back to the house, she stood on the terrace, reluctant either to go to her room or wander about.

What was she going to do here? She wasn't the mistress of the house and hadn't the slightest wish to meddle in what was obviously a smooth-running arrangement. She enjoyed cooking, but Pierre was lord of the kitchen, and, anyway, she was determined not to seem in any way to be assuming a permanent and contented place in the mansion.

She could spend some time daily in keeping a journal and recording all she had learned about Yucatán and Belize. Here, as at Zane's, there was the incredible luck of a good library. She could continue learning Mayan and Spanish, for there were both Mayas and mestizos among the house servants. But these pursuits, interesting as part of a routine, couldn't be enough.

Since she was a child, Mercy had felt needed and important, keeping house for her father and then, during the war, filling in for him as best she could. Continuing to help the sick while keeping a garden and trying to manage a house and cook meals as Philip liked them had been more than she could sometimes manage. She'd never get in *that* position again—trying to satisfy an emotionally infantile man who could only demand but never give. At La Quinta, she'd taught the children and learned medicine from Chepa. She'd been useful there, a part of things.

Now the need to work, even if she could find something that didn't intrude in someone else's sphere, was frustrated by a resolve *not* to fit in here, *not* to become part of Eric's establishment.

Had she been a painter or writer, she could have been busy without supporting Eric's ménage, but those weren't her talents. If she had a gift at all, a prime concern, it was healing.

She frowned, suddenly arrested. With all that sugar and logging and the people required to maintain the House of Quetzals, there *would* be sick and injured.

Even if there was a doctor, she could be helpful while learning what he knew. Her father had never had time to follow up on home care, diet, and such things. There'd surely be something she could do. She'd ask Celeste. It wasn't the kind of thing Eric seemed likely to approve of, but once she learned his routine she could pretty much know what hours would be her own. Those hours could help her remain herself, linking the present with her father and Chepa. But at the moment she was driven to walk down to the river and look away toward La Quinta.

Where was Zane? Was he safe? Would he believe that letter? Even if he didn't quite, how could he guess what had happened to her? It hurt to be thought faithless, not only by Zane, but by Jolie, Chepa, Salvador, and Mayel.

Strong arms fitted around her, hands cupping her breasts. "So here you are, sweetheart!" Eric turned her around for his kiss. "Let's see what Pierre has for luncheon. After our siesta, I'll show you some of the plantation."

He swept her along with him, but she looked back over her shoulder at the sunlit water and in the direction she hoped to travel again toward the man who was the center of her loving.

The mare brought around to the terrace for Mercy was a pale tan color, so beautiful that in spite of Mercy's determination not to be blandished by any of Eric's gifts, she couldn't restrain a cry of admiration as she stroked the velvety muzzle and touched a mane that would have suited Pegasus, the winged horse of the Muses.

"I've seen buckskins," she said, "but never one this color."

"She's a palomino," Eric explained. "A color, not a separate breed, though there's lots of Arab in the ancestry. It means 'like a dove.' I broke this one in myself, though I had her ridden by a lightweight. Her name is Lucera."

The saddle was a mellow rust color stitched with gold.

Eric helped Mercy into it before he mounted his big bay stallion.

"My land stretches from the river to highlands, from about sea level to over two thousand feet, so it has great variety," he said proudly. "I have cattle in the regions unsuitable for cultivation, and I have experimented with coffee and tobacco, but sugar is my main crop, apart from mahogany and dyewood."

"Are your workers slaves?"

Eric shot her an amused glance. "They aren't likely to leave. They're all in debt to me. But slavery was abolished in all English dominions in 1840, and the owners in Belize freed their people a year before that. I wonder if you're aware, delectably self-righteous one, that one of the reasons you Texans wanted independence from Mexico was that their constitution had forbidden slavery."

"Then why do they still have it?"

"Debt-slavery is at least legally different, though the results are the same. And slavery in Mexico and the West Indies has always been bizarre in that blacks were imported to preserve the Indians, who never stood up well to grueling, heavy labor. My cane fields are worked mostly by refugee Mayas, but I use blacks as much as possible for the mill and refinery."

They passed gardens and orchards, corrals and sheds, pastures for horses and dairy cattle, and at a distance from the road, in a swampy place, scores of immense black pigs rooted and wallowed. The way twined through stands of trees, new growth, Eric explained, since the original mahogany and dyewood had been felled, used now to fire the boilers, which demanded tremendous amounts of wood in addition to the fibrous refuse of the cane.

"Besides needing lots of workers to plant, cultivate and harvest the cane, it takes more to cut wood and run the mill and refinery. All these people have to be fed, so the community busied with sugar is a small village with a management separate from the rest of the estate. The mayordomo, chief overseer, and refinery master are all *ladinos* who fled the War of the Castes and know how to get the Mayas to work."

Remembering the hacienda from which she'd rescued Mayel, Mercy didn't like the sound of that, and she liked less the sight of the whipping post situated near the store in the clearing around which the workers' huts and small private plots were scattered.

"I hope that isn't used," she said to Eric.

He looked at the post, a lopped-off tree the height of a man, and shrugged. "Surely you've heard the adage that the Indian hears through his back. I don't interfere with Don Gerardo as long as he keeps production up."

"Why, that's worse than maltreating people yourself! It lets you profit by such tactics without having to accept direct guilt!"

"I could stand the guilt." He smiled coldly. "I lack the time. My workers are unusually well fed with plenty of meat, cheese, and eggs. They have Sundays off and the wages are better than average."

"So, perhaps, are the prices at your store!"

He shook his golden lion's head. "Mercy, Mercy! I'm a businessman, a proprietor, certainly not a saint, but not the villain you'd like to think me, either. I run a plantation, not Utopia. Indians have never gotten more for their labor than a living. They get a comparatively good one from me. It's not my fault that they spend more than they earn."

Thinking of his cook and fantastically equipped kitchen, the daily delivery of seafood, the servants whose purpose it was to keep his house as he wanted it, the quetzals caged so far from their cloud forests, Mercy choked with indignation.

"How can you say that? How can you seem to think so many people exist just to make you rich?"

"I think it because it's so," he said without anger. "Do compose yourself, my dear. Here comes Don Gerardo."

The mayordomo, a handsome middle-aged man with a narrow moustache, greeted them profusely, expressed his delight in meeting Doña Mercy, and his thankfulness that Señor Kensington had returned safely from his journey through the Cruzob-ridden jungles.

"I had prayed the emperor would send armies from Mexico to crush that vermin, but it seems the French troops have all sailed and the emperor cannot even defend himself," lamented the mayordomo. "Now, with Marcos Canul raiding even British territory, what safety is there? Nineteen years ago I fled Tekax, and now I begin to think I can never go home! Not," he added hastily, "that I wish to leave El Señor's profitable employ."

"If you should, I can replace you," said Eric equably.

227

"We'll just have a look at the mill and refinery before riding past the nearest fields, where you will be so good as to accompany us in case there are questions."

Don Gerardo bowed and declared his pleasure at their further company. Leaving him to have his horse brought around, they proceeded toward the refining center adjacent to the mill, where mules powered hardwood rollers that crushed the cane, sending the juice into troughs that ran to the boilers, kept bubbling by Negroes who kept the fires stoked with wood replenished by loads brought up by glum-looking burros.

The refinery director, Don Manuel, portly and sweating, explained to Mercy, at Eric's request, how after enough boiling of the syrup, sugar crystals began to form. These were separated from the remaining liquid, which was molasses, and refined into white sugar.

As they rode past the refining kettles and platforms, a smithy, and woodworking shop, Don Gerardo rode up on a handsome sorrel and they approached the fields, which stretched away to the jungle.

The greenish stalks flaunted tassels that grew twice as high as the heads of the men cutting them off at the ground and tossing them into mule-driven carts to be cut into manageable hunks by other men with sharp knives. When one of these carts was full, it creaked back to the mill.

"Cortez probably planted the first sugarcane in this hemisphere," said Eric. "New plants will come up from the stubble of the cut ones, so I get two or three harvests before replanting." At a word from him, Don Gerardo called the nearest man, who brought a cutting of several joints. Holding it for Mercy's inspection, Eric showed her where the dormant eyes, or buds, were. "The eyes are placed downward as the cutting's planted lengthwise and covered lightly. The eyes root and start new plants in just a few days, but we won't replant till the rains start in late May."

Eric started to toss the cutting back to the waiting Indian, paused, and frowned. The young man was dressed in rolled-up white trousers like the other hands, but there was something different about the way he stood and held his head. A gold earring glinted in his left ear. He had a hawk face, sloping forehead, slightly hooked nose, and broad, high cheekbones.

"Who is this one?" asked Eric.

"*Señor,* he's *batab* of one of the small Mayan sub-groups, neither Icaiche nor Cruzob." Don Gerardo tugged nervously at his moustache, then added with venom, "It's my belief he's allied with the Cruzob. However that is, perhaps you'll remember that he and some of his men came to buy guns a few months ago."

Eric nodded. "It's coming back. They didn't have enough money, but this man was afraid that Icaiches would overrun his village unless it had guns."

"So he asked to stay as hostage for payment."

"And I said I didn't need hostages but could use another field hand," finished Eric, gazing at the tall man, who looked straight back. "I see his people haven't redeemed him. He was a fool to count on their love."

"They will come," said the *batab* in Spanish. "They are not *dzul*. whites, to sell anything for money."

"Dog!" snarled Don Gerardo. "Kiss El Señor's hand at once and beg his pardon, or you may need to buy a new skin!"

"He owns my labor, not my worship," said the young *batab*.

Gerardo raised his metal-tipped braided quirt but Eric stopped him with a shake of his head. "Why begin something that couldn't end till he'd be too ruined to work for a couple of days? A *batab* opposed to the Icaiches might be valuable I'll think about it." He studied the Indian in gauging fashion. "What is your name?"

"*Señor.* I am Dionisio Caamal."

"We'll talk again. Dionisio."

With the slightest inclination of his head, the Indian turned back to his furrow, slicing the two-inch-thick stalk with a seemingly effortless sweep of his arm.

"*Señor,* with all due respect, insolence cannot go unpunished!" burst out Don Gerardo. "Let me order a whipping for that one, or the workers will all be infected!"

"He may be worth more to me with his pride," said Eric. "I think, had you used your quirt, he would have cut your throat in the next instant, and, though he would, of course. have died immediately, that couldn't help you."

"I have overseen such dogs all my life, *señor.* He needs to be beaten till he crawls to kiss the lash."

Eric stared at Gerardo till he glanced down and licked his lips. "Such wisdom and management techniques helped bring on the war that sent you scuttling across the Hondo," Eric said in a stinging tone. "You will excuse us now. And perhaps you should keep a record of whippings and the offenses. I've told you that judicious punishment may be necessary, but I won't tolerate indiscriminate abuse." His frosty eyes glared at the mayordomo. "You understand?"

A flush darkened Don Gerardo's sallow face. "Yes, *señor.*"

"Good. I'll expect a report monthly; and if there's nothing to report, I'll congratulate you."

"So long as El Señor doesn't blame me if production falls off and there are incidents . . . "

"Ah, but I shall," said Eric sweetly. "You have authority to punish when necessary. My mayordomo must have judgment; it is what sets him above fieldhands and overseers."

Don Gerardo bowed with a choking sound as they rode on.

"Will his reports be honest?" Mercy asked.

"I think so. But to be sure, I'll also ask for such an accounting from the overseer, who'd be very happy to succeed to Don Gerardo's job."

"Do you really have a plan for that young *batab?*"

"It's possible. I'll confess the Icaiche raids are too close for comfort, and I hear the militia will be disbanded in a matter of weeks. When that happens, Marcos Canul is sure to come south of the Hondo again. If Dionisio would undertake to kill him, it'd be worth a goodly number of rifles."

Mercy remembered the proud stance of the *batab*, the fearless way he had confronted his master and mayordomo. "I don't think he'll kill another Maya for you," she said, "even if they are enemies."

"You're a romantic, love. For rifles in this country, men do many things." As if startled by a sudden unwelcome thought that persisted after an incredulous attempt at dismissal, Eric turned in his saddle to scan her narrowly. "Are you making a hero of him? Listen, my sweet! Mayas rape white women more out of hatred than lust, and, don't forget, that's how our handsome young chief would serve you if he got the chance!"

Angered past caution, Mercy laughed in his face. "How do you rape me? With hate? Lust? I tell you, Eric Kensington, that I don't see any difference!"

"Let me refresh your memory." Seizing the reins of her horse, he dismounted and tied the horses outside a storage shed they were passing. He brought her out of the saddle, dragged off the divided skirt and her drawers as he carried her inside, spilled her down on a heap of old sacking, and spread her legs apart.

He was so swollen that she felt she would break apart as he entered her and then rocked back and forth with savage, jolting thrusts. "I hoped your first lessons taught you what rape was!" He panted, gripping her wrists. "But since your memory's bad, doesn't this seem different from the way I took you this morning and last night?"

"It's all rape!" she shouted at him, strangling on rage and pain. "It's all rape because I hate you, hate you . . . "

A blow from the side of his hand dazed her. "Say you love me!" he gasped, shaking her. "Say you love me!"

Her head lolled. She felt as if her neck were broken, as if it were somebody else to whom this was happening, but from within herself, though her body cringed, she found the strength to cry against the closed, blind look in his eyes. "I hate you! I always will! It's Zane I love!"

He circled her throat with one hand, and his fingers tightened till the world went black.

16

Several times she was conscious of being carried, handled, of voices she knew she could recognize if she tried. It was too much effort. She didn't want to know them, or where she was, or even who. Her throat ached. Her head hurt. Best to drink whatever they gave her and sink back to soft darkness.

"*Madame*," insisted a gentle voice. "Pierre begs that you have some of the creamed crab he's made especially for you, and a bit of lovely jelly—in three colors it is! Please, *madame! Monsieur* has gone riding and Pierre is in utter distraction with no one to taste his food!"

Mercy opened her eyes and smiled shakily at Celeste. "Is it dinner time?"

"Indeed, *madame*, and past!"

It was deep sapphire twilight through the windows, and the glow of the bedside lamp was muted by its azure glass shade. Mercy tried to sit up. Immediately her head seemed occupied by a pounding drum.

It was so easy to lie back and sleep. At that moment it even seemed desirable to shutter the windows during the day and live in that great bed, pretend to be sick when Eric came, and drift in and out of dreams. She still had in her mouth the taste of brandy someone had forced down her. Between brandy and sleep, she might escape Eric by lying in this chamber.

And she might cease to be herself, too, atrophy till there was no chance of ever finding Zane. Mercy lifted her feet off the side of the bed. She mustn't let Eric cow her, but she would have found it hard to go downstairs if Celeste hadn't said he was riding. She had been undressed and put to bed in a loose peignoir. With Celeste's help she slipped into underthings and one of her native dresses.

"Tell Pierre I'll have a little food on the terrace, but not too much," she said, brushing her hair, unable to tell in the dim light if there were bruise marks on her throat.

"I understand, *madame*."

Celeste went out quietly with a consoling backward glance. What did she know? How had Eric explained Mercy's condition? Not that he had to explain. If he had killed her, there was no one to demand that he explain.

I have only myself to rely on, she told herself as she plaited her protestingly curly hair into one thick braid and let it hang down her back. But she remembered Dionisio, knew there was at least one other defiant soul on this estate, and somehow that cheered her, made her feel not quite so alone.

He could die or she could die without the other knowing. They might never meet again. But Mercy had felt a closeness with him that day, gloried in his pride, and she knew she'd never forget him.

Mercy touched her cheek, swollen where Eric had struck her, decided there wasn't much she could do to hide it, and went downstairs.

Lamps burned in the halls and a few were scattered around the terrace, but Mercy reached the table before she saw she wasn't alone. Eric rose from a chair in the corner, came forward, and took her hands before she could retreat.

"I thought you might come down if Pierre's grief and my absence were presented to you," he said lightly, but strain showed around his eyes and mouth. "I . . . I'm sorry, Mercy, *mia*. But when will you learn not to madden me?"

Strange, but she almost laughed. "Probably when you learn not to make me angry."

He kissed her eyes and mouth, then the throat that still pained from his grasp. "It seems I must learn," he said huskily. "You're too small and fragile for such handling. I'll have to master you by other means. Come now and sit down before Pierre has apoplexy!"

After dinner he played the piano for an hour while Mercy lay on the chaise, pretending to read, but actually listening. He played with vigor and sweep, stormily, and she wondered if he ever imagined that Alison stepped out of her portrait and played her long-abandoned harp.

He shared Mercy's bed that night, but his kiss was brief, and though he held her in his arms, it was protectively. Only who was there to protect her from Eric himself?

The next day at dinner Eric had considerable news, garnered from an English logger from Belize on his way to cut mahogany on lands rented from Marcos Canul.

The emperor was rallying for what could only be defeat in Mexico, deprived of the support of his poor, demented empress. In Yucatán, Peraza's forces were growing as he gained daily support in the north. Mérida would soon be under siege, if it wasn't already in that familiar and unhappy state.

"And there's a joke from your country, love," Eric concluded as Mercy wondered if Zane was safe and if he found winning more to his taste than losing. "Secretary Seward seems about to get his wish! Alaska! Can you imagine that frozen wasteland? It's got a new name: 'Seward's Folly.' "

"Was there anything else?" Mercy asked wistfully. It seemed so long ago since she left Texas! But the news she hungered for would scarcely filter to this crown colony—how her neighbors were, what had happened to the farm, what was really happening with Reconstruction.

Eric frowned, trying to remember. "The government's

233

setting up reservations in Indian territory for what are called the Five Civilized Tribes and making a reservation for the Sioux in the Black Hills. And they say buffalo cover the plains and that hunters are going after them thick and fast. If I weren't so busy here, I'd be tempted to go up and see that western country. And I'd take some of those cattle that're being butchered in Texas for their hide and tallow up north, where they'd fetch real money."

"It's a long way to a railhead," argued Mercy.

"Cattle can walk and men can drive them." Eric shrugged. "Would you like that, Mercy? To go home?"

He seemed to mean it. Mercy's heart leaped. Then she remembered Zane. Where he was would always be her center now; she'd never be at home without him.

When she didn't answer, Eric swore. His gaze fell on the gold band on her finger. "Will you satisfy my curiosity?" he asked in that leashed way she had come to dread. "I've assumed that ring was Philip's, but you aren't the type of woman to wear a ring for convention's sake. Where did you get it?"

"It . . . it's an heirloom."

"Your mother's?"

"No." Why couldn't she lie?

"Your father's?"

She shook her head.

Eric's breath went from him in a sigh. "It must be Falconer's—belonging to his sacred mother, no doubt. I'm sure he kept nothing to remind him of that trull, his wife, except the child."

"It's his mother's."

"So you believe he meant to marry you," said Eric in a pitying tone.

"I know he did."

"Such faith, and from one who should know better!"

"It wasn't the way you think at all!" Goaded past keeping her secret, Mercy fought to steady her voice and hold back tears. "Zane . . . we weren't lovers till two nights before he left, after Peraza's messenger came."

Eric's eyebrows rose. His gaze probed hers. "Is this true?"

"Why should I lie?" Mercy asked bitterly. "You've treated me like a whore! Why should I care what you think?"

"I've treated you like the one woman I've had to have."

She shuddered involuntarily. Eric muttered something, grasped her hand, and slipped off the ring. Mercy leaned forward, catching at his large, hard fingers, trying to pry them apart. "Give it back! Please, let me have it!"

"So you can consider yourself married in all but fact to that pirate's son?"

"I . . . I won't wear it if you'll only let me keep it."

He shook his head. "I know so well the use of shrines, sweet Mercy. However, I won't throw it away. It'll go in my vault, along with deeds, wills, mortgages, and other important items." She knew that begging would make him more adamant, perhaps anger him into throwing the ring away, but she couldn't hide her intense sense of loss.

Springing up from the table, she ran blindly into the hall, groping for the stairs so she could go to her room and vent her helpless wrath. Eric seized her by the shoulders, turned her against him, and stood immovable as a rock while she sobbed and beat at him.

"I'll give you another ring," he said when her outrage was spent and she fell stonily quiet under his hands. "I can marry you as I offered in the beginning, now that I know you didn't live complaisantly as Falconer's concubine. From what you say, it's possible he meant to marry you. I can see how you might feel, with some justice, that I owe you a husband."

She stared up at him, unable to believe her ears. "I don't just want a . . . a husband! It's Zane I love!"

"An unfortunate predilection, Mercy, since I love you."

"Not me, God help you! A likeness to your half sister!"

"That drew me to you at first. But I have glimpsed a fire in you that Alison was too gentle and young to have. That's why I hunted for Philip all the way to New Orleans and brought him to La Quinta in the hope that Falconer might feel obliged to sell you back to your repentant husband."

"But you meant to buy me from Philip."

"Exactly, though I thought you to be Falconer's woman. How did he resist, or is he softer toward tears than I? I couldn't marry his mistress, but I meant to keep you as long as that sweet fire warmed me." He passed one hand lightly over her face. "It hasn't warmed me yet, but one day it will. You will love me. A woman, in time, must love the man who delights her body, protects her, and sees to her needs."

Mercy stayed mutely defiant. He drew her against him so that she heard the steady, strong pounding of his heart.

"She comes to love the man who fathers her children," he finished. "That's how I'll have you at last, Mercy, if not before. A baby will fill your heart, preempt first place. Loving the child, you'll love something of me that will lead you to forget what's past and gone."

She thought of the dwarf poinciana flowers, but she knew better than to tell him she would use every means in her power not to be with child by him. A primitive part of her nature told her that the instincts and biological drives of a mother were directed at the child's safety and good. Even if she kept from developing a feeling for Eric, having a child by him would make it harder to find a way back to Zane.

"Why," asked Eric abruptly, "did you never conceive by Philip?"

"He was at the front for a good part of our marriage, and then when he came home . . ." Mercy fell silent, hating to remember those drunken fumblings, her pain and humiliation. "It . . . just never happened."

"I suspect he didn't come to you often."

Mercy averted her face. In spite of all that Eric had said and done to her, she found it shaming to discuss sex, and especially her relations with Philip.

"Blushing, sweetheart?" Eric laughed softly. "Never mind. "I'm in no wild hurry, but if you don't root one of my seeds by Christmas, I'll think myself a poor planter! And if there's some problem with how you're made, we'll find a doctor who can set it right."

Would a doctor be able to tell she was using a draft? Christmas was a long way off. Mercy refused to worry that far ahead. "When a baby starts, you'll want to marry," Eric said. "But why not do it now? We could go to Belize City this week. The governor's my friend. He'll give a reception and do all the honors. You've never been to Europe, have you? We could go to Paris or Rome, stop in London. And New York has wonderful shops, if you'd enter Yankeeland." His face glowed with eagerness. "Let's do it, Mercy! You won't be sorry!"

It was strange that she should hate to dash his excited boyish planning when he had forced her from her love's house in a way that would surely cost her Zane's trust.

"Well?" Eric persisted.

"No, I can't."

He was very still. Only his powerful heart pumped its secret rhythm against her cheek. "I'm going to take you upstairs and have my pleasure with you," he said at last. "I'm going to give you pleasure, too, however you fight it, for that lovely body craves what I can do. Why not protect yourself, be able to go anywhere with pride?"

"I could never be proud again if I did what you suggest."

He stiffened. Fear made the flesh seem to move on her bones. She knew how swiftly, ferociously, he could attack. His strength and size were such that even when he was trying to be gentle, he sometimes hurt her. But he only swept her up and buried his lips against her throat.

"Then we must make a baby! That'll change you!"

He used her skillfully that day, coaxed and brought her twice to that shivering, tremulous pulsing during which he entered and prolonged her sensations. Then with an inexorable, hushed intentness, he strove for and reached his own summit, his steel-muscled body locked over her so quietly it seemed she could hear him pumping into her.

Let me not get a baby, she implored in the sort of desperate prayer that wells out of human impotence, made without any clear idea of to whom it's directed. *Let me not conceive, but if I do, let the poinciana work. . . .*

Eric liked to watch her bathe, to watch Celeste rinse her with clear water and help her dry off after she stepped onto the soft wool mat. One day he brought a crystal flacon. After Mercy was toweled dry, he told Celeste to rub the perfumed oil into Mercy's skin.

Though she was embarrassed at being touched all over, lingeringly, by another woman, Mercy didn't argue. She'd learned that the only medical facility on the estate was a hut near the cane fields where the contagiously ill could stay till they died or recovered. Celeste said Eric had twice hired English doctors, but both had been such drunkards that they were of no use, and workers had to rely on their own smattering of herb knowledge. Having learned this, Mercy had been trying to think of a way to persuade Eric to let her run a sort of clinic and teach interested people what she knew so the widely scattered cattle and lumber workers wouldn't be far from someone with a certain degree of medical knowledge. Mercy, of course, needed the task for her own sanity, but since the good of other people was involved, she didn't feel guilty about catering a bit to Eric in the hope of achieving her aim. So she stood quietly while Celeste rubbed in the spice-scented balm and Eric watched her with lazy eyes beneath slightly drooping lids.

"The oil's not a hint that you're wrinkling, my dear, but it's my opinion that any body stays more beautiful if it's pampered and cherished. How old are you?"

"Almost twenty-five."

"Such an age!" He grimaced. "Would you guess that in August I'll have twelve years' seniority over you? When's your birthday?"

"This month."

"What day?"

"The twenty-eighth," she said unwillingly.

She didn't want one of Pierre's feasts or gifts from Eric, which could only seem like manacles of gold. But then she remembered that she did want some things that were within his power.

"We must celebrate," he said, catching her hands and kissing them. "I have one thing for you, but perhaps you have a few secret longings?"

Absorbed in this chance, Mercy scarcely remembered she was naked, her flesh warming and giving out the piquant sweetness of her anointings. "There are two things I want very much."

"And you haven't mentioned them before?" Eric frowned. "That almost makes me angry! Tell me now."

Mercy hesitated, not sure which request would be less likely to irritate him. "Turn the quetzals loose, and let me start a hospital," she said in a rush.

His jaw dropped. "The quetzals in my court?" he said at last.

"Quetzals don't belong in cages," she said. "It makes me miserable to think of them."

"So that's why you keep the shutters closed on that side," he mused. "But they're a king's ransom and I love the glimmer of their plumes. Let me think about it." His frown deepened. "What kind of hospital?"

"There must be injuries in the fields and refineries, with cattle and logging. Then there are ordinary ailments, and sometimes women have trouble giving birth. There should be something more than a hut where people die or recover without much help."

"I've tried to bring doctors here, but only drunkards will come, and they're worthless."

"I'm not a doctor, but my father taught me some things, and I learned from a woman at La Quinta who knew about herbs. If you'd let me train a few people and equip a building, it'd pay off in the loss of fewer working days and better health and productivity."

His lip curled. "Not that you give a damn about my profits!"

"But you do."

He let out a gusty breath of annoyance. "I don't want you fooling with dirty field hands!"

"I could see the women and children, except for emergencies, and if you let me find some volunteers, they could take care of the men."

"You wouldn't start spending all your time aping Florence Nightingale?" he demanded. "You'd remember you're here for me?"

"How could I forget?" she asked wryly.

"An infirmary *is* needed," he said, as if convincing himself. "And I suppose it's futile to expect you to read or embroider all the time you're not with me. Give McNulty a list of supplies and in a day or two we'll find a building."

Rising, he nodded dismissal to Celeste, dropped on his knees in front of Mercy, and began to nibble and kiss her stomach and breasts, cupping her to him with his hands. When her legs refused to hold her, he laughed softly and carried her to the bed.

McNulty nodded approval when she gave him a list compiled from experience and her father's books and letters: quinine; morphine; laudanum; calomel; chloroform, which she knew Queen Victoria had taken to ease the birth of one of her children back in 1853; scalpels; probes; needles; scissors; suturing silk; bone saws; tweezers; cloth for bandages; several iron cots with mattresses and sheets; a variety of basins, pails, bowls, and cups.

"I've long been after Mr. Kensington to bring in a nurse, since those rascally doctors were of no use, and set up a place where the workers could have some care, at least." He looked more dubiously at a second list, longer

239

than the first, naming plants, herbs, and roots that Chepa had used with good effects. "You think this stuff does any good, ma'am?"

"If it came to choice, I'd rather have them than the supplies from the city," Mercy said.

McNulty scratched his fringes of red hair and peered through his glasses. "Well, I'll send some Indians who claim to know plants on a gathering expedition," he agreed. "But some of these things will have to come from England."

"Then the sooner they're ordered, the sooner they'll come," said Mercy.

Slowly, McNulty grinned. "Be more to ye than a pretty face," he admitted. "I'll get a messenger off this very day."

She thanked him and went her way, almost happy for the first time since her abduction. She was doing something useful without accepting Eric's mold; she'd have something outside herself to stay busy with several hours a day. All this gave her a bracing sense of potency; she felt less a victim.

She awoke her birthday morning to soft Spanish singing under the balcony. "On the morning you were born, were born the flowers. . . ."

"I arranged for you to be serenaded." Eric smiled, stretching lazily. "But that doesn't mean you have to leap up!"

Going to the window, he called his thanks and tossed down a handful of coins before returning to her.

There was the usual opulent breakfast, which Mercy never more than sampled, but which was evidently, for Eric, one indispensable heritage from England. There was always ham, tongue, pheasant, and frequently grilled fish, turkey, quail, partridge, or curassow. There was oatmeal, cooked without salt, and viewed by Pierre with considerable disgust, which was what Mercy ate, unless she had an omelet and toast. There were deviled kidneys, a variety of mustards, chutneys, and sauces, and tempting arrays of fresh fruit, pitchers of juice, and silver urns of coffee, hot milk, and tea. Pierre always made croissants, crisp and buttery, and today there were delicate almond pastries.

After breakfast Eric suggested a ride, though he ordinarily worked mornings. They started for the sugar refinery. Dismounting by the store, Eric flourished her into the long building next to it.

"Your infirmary," he said.

The walls were freshly whitewashed, there was a curtained section for privacy, a high wooden table, several iron cots with white sheets, open and locked shelves, and a large washstand. Three older women and two men kissed Eric's hand and would also have kissed Mercy's, but she put them behind her, uncomfortable with that sort of obeisance.

"These people gathered the herbs, roots, and bark you needed," Eric explained. "They know some curing and want to work with you. When the men know enough, they'll go to the loggers, so we need to recruit another man or two for the sugar works. The things you ordered should start arriving gradually in a week or so, but I have quinine and laudanum in the highest locked cabinet, and apparently your helpers found most of the native items you want."

Both elated and awed at the materialization of her wish, Mercy suddenly felt terribly inadequate and wished Chepa or her father was there. But something was better than nothing. She asked the names of the men and women, said how glad she was they would be helping, and promised to come the next day.

"I have two presents for you." Eric smiled as they rode toward the house. "I wonder which to give you first."

"The infirmary is wonderful."

"But hardly a gift for *you*."

They left the horses with a groom. Eric took her around by a different way to enter the courtyard from the rear. She hadn't been there since the day she arrived. Glancing around the flowering sheltered place, she saw the cages were gone, but her swift delight vanished when she saw the quetzals were still imprisoned by a net above the garden. They could fly from tree to tree now, their wings were no longer tightly cramped, but they were denied freedom, their high cloud forests.

"Well?" Eric asked, tilting up her chin. "Isn't this better?"

"Oh . . . better, I suppose."

"Nothing can hurt them here. You can't say they don't have plenty of space."

"But they aren't free!"

"You think that's so important?"

241

"To fly free must be the essence of birds, just as blooming is for flowers."

He shrugged. "Come here, then." He handed her a rope, then told her to pull on it. When she did, the net slid back along the grooves to which it was attached.

The sky was open. Glinting blue and green, the colors of the gods, of earth and sky, the quetzals perched where they were. Eric clapped his hands. One fluttered up to be followed by another and another; till all were flying, passing out of sight beyond the walls and palms.

"Will they find their way home?"

"Probably."

He was watching her so strangely that Mercy asked, "Did you mind it a lot—letting them go?"

"Not as much as I expected to." He kissed her on the mouth slowly, deliberately, claimingly. "I still have my quetzal woman. And here's my other gift."

He took from his pocket an envelope and shook out a long, glittering strand of emeralds and sapphires mounted on a supple golden chain. "You can weave it into your hair," he said, "twine it around your neck, or wear it as a girdle. I thought of a tiara, but this seemed less formal."

"It . . . it's very beautiful."

His eyes narrowed. "And you can wear it against your naked body, love, which is where I wish to see it now." He didn't need to add the rest—that she had accepted his other gifts, the released quetzals, the infirmary. He had been generous. But as they moved inside and he followed her up the stairs, she vowed to resist his indulgence, as she had his brutality, and she swore she would never love him. When, in bed, he festooned her breasts and loins with the sparkling jewels, she closed her eyes and remembered the flash of wings. The quetzals, for no reason they could understand, could go back to their mates and mountains. Someday, perhaps, just as mysteriously, the sky might open for her, too.

Pierre outdid himself with the birthday dinner: capon; *galantine de poulard* with aspic jelly; pheasant; turtle soup; oysters; a decidedly ugly-looking pig's head; mushrooms; candied yams; savory rice; a fantastic trifle in a large-stemmed crystal bowl; with its cake, pudding, jelly, fruit, and whipped cream layers saturated with sherry; Neapolitan cake; jellies in assorted elaborate shapes and flavor combinations; chocolate *gâteau; blanc mange.*

Though Mercy ate sparingly, she had a little too much brandy before Eric took her up to bed, and she woke up the next morning feeling bilious enough to use some of her own brews.

A single croissant and coffee righted her. Then after Eric shut himself up with McNulty, she called for Lucera, and, accompanied by Celeste, as earlier agreed upon with Eric, she went to the infirmary. She had her supplies and books, including the irreplaceable *Badianus* translation. Francisca, a wrinkled woman with graying hair, explained that Maria and Concha were helping at a childbirth and would be along later.

"Women can have their babies here," Mercy said in broken Mayan.

Francisca looked aghast and said there was no need for that; the mother was healthy, the baby in position, and a steambath was ready for her cleansing when she had delivered. That sounded good and natural. Mercy was more than glad to leave childbirth to the midwives as long as there were no complications. Their experience was greater than hers, and a woman was sure to be more relaxed and comfortable in her own home.

It was an interesting morning: a child wheezing with asthma who got relief from the smoke of *toloache;* an old man with no family, with the fever and chills of malaria, was dosed with quinine and put to bed in a hammock, given water in which willow leaves had been steeped, and bathed with the same liquid when he felt he was burning; several babies with festering sores from *garrapata* bites, which Francisca poulticed with crushed pulp from maguey leaves; a man burned badly on his shoulder and arm where he'd fallen against one of the refinery boilers. Mercy used Chepa's remedy on him: lime juice mixed with egg yolk. Sweat stood out on his face at the first application, but in a few minutes he cast Mercy a thankful look and mumbled that it was better, so he was given a few eggs and limes and sent home.

Mercy guessed, of course, that she was getting those with nothing to lose, or else with trifling but nuisance ills, like the infected bites. It would take time and successes to win people's confidence. That was fine. It was going to take *her* time and some degree of success to gain confidence.

Concha and Maria returned from the birth in time for the consultation Mercy and the staff were having. Since all had some cures and experience, it seemed wise to have these discussions to share knowledge and problems and work out the best ways of serving.

It was agreed that one person would sleep at the infirmary to tend overnight patients and respond to emergencies. Morning would be the main treatment period, though the helpers would stay in shifts during the afternoon. Contagious diseases would be tended to by visits to the home, though it would be a good idea to partition off a room in the infirmary for this purpose.

Most procedures were fixed upon by common consent. Mercy wanted this center to continue, whatever happened to her, so right from the start she tried to let these experienced people do the planning. She did insist, though, on washing with soap between seeing patients and frequent changing of the loose white smocks supplied by the sewing women. Since daily baths were a part of Mayan tradition and her helpers appreciated cleanliness, Mercy didn't have to battle for these simple hygienic measures, as she would surely have had to do with almost any group of doctors from Europe or the United States.

Encouraged by the acceptance of the staff and the fact that so far they'd been able to help everyone who'd come, Mercy was just leaving when a frazzled little woman brought in a young man, apparently her son, gripping a hideously swollen arm crusted with blood and oozing pus. He had cut himself several days ago while cutting sugarcane and had held the wound with his hand till he got home to his mother, who had finally stopped the blood flow by tying one cord beneath the wound and another at the bend of the arm about it.

The flow had stopped, but circulation had been cut off and the hand and wrist dangled like those of a corpse, while the bound-off part of the arm stank of putrefaction. Mercy's stomach turned, and none of the helpers came forward. While they shook their heads and murmured, she cut the cords and explained to them and the mother that such bindings might stop the blood from pumping from a cut, but that it also prevented any blood from reaching the affected parts, causing them to become poisoned and to rot.

She rubbed the withered-looking hand and wrist, massaged where the cords had marked, and set the mother to chafing her son's fingers while she opened the suppurating wound. A mass of evil-smelling blood and pus oozed out.

While Mercy pressed gently, Francisca caught the vile discharge on swabs of wild cotton, one luxury that cost nothing. A final jet of yellow, blood-tinged foulness spurted out, and then came a burst of blood that Mercy knew was from an artery because of its darkness and the way it maintained a rhythm.

Mercy gripped the vein and pressed tightly, stopping the stream. Then she got Paco, a younger male assistant, to hold the pressure while she sewed up the cut. Working with difficulty because of the blood and her own squeamishness, she dabbed on a salve of egg yolk, wax, cypress root and *ylin,* put a heavy pad over it, and bandaged this in place with clean strips of cloth.

Telling the old woman to come for help if there was much bleeding, to keep on rubbing the blood-starved hand and wrist, and to bring the young man back the next day for a change of dressings, Mercy sent them away with some of the willow water that had such beneficial effects on headaches and fevers. She tossed her thoroughly disgusting smock into the laundry basket— Eric had assigned the infirmary a laundress and cleaning man—scrubbed her hands, and rode home feeling she could never face food again, but knowing that a man who'd surely have died soon in agony now had at least a chance of living and keeping his arm.

The young man not only lived, but he regained the use of his hand. Don Manuel requested a jar of burn salve to keep near the boilers for immediate use. The old man recovered from his malaria, and he had enjoyed the bustle and company so much that he asked to be the night watchman and aide to the regular person on duty, and he made himself useful as a handyman and herb collector.

Now people began to come whose disorders were beyond Mercy's skill or the wisdom of her helpers, people with growths or complaints of pain in their entrails or convulsive fits. But when no treatment could be thought of, Mercy and her staff listened, gave out pleasant herbal teas that would give temporary relief, and, in cases of extreme pain, gave native pain-killers or morphine and laudanum.

Paco and Juan had gone to the loggers, carrying a chest of medical supplies and instruments, but there were two new male recruits, an older man eager to leave the strenuous labor of the fields, and a young man,

Natividad, who'd lost a hand in the cane crusher and became intrigued with the infirmary when he was brought in for clean amputation of the shredded stump. He had a gift for diagnosis and some degree of unexplainable healing power, for he had cured or relieved the pain of several people no one had been able to help.

Celeste always accompanied Mercy to and from the infirmary, but she got sick at watching any pain or ugliness, so she spent the mornings with her mother, who lived in the village. Celeste seemed puffy-eyed one day and Mercy asked her if something was wrong.

At first Celeste evaded her, but finally she wailed that she wished to marry Thomas.

Mercy gazed at the flower-graceful young woman and couldn't believe any man would resist her. "Doesn't he want to marry you?" Mercy asked.

He wanted to. The trouble was that Celeste was having a baby and it wasn't that of Thomas. He'd be very angry when he found out. Thomas, like the master, was an adherent of the Church of England, and he didn't share the tolerant views some blacks had of premarital sex.

"*Madame* must have a secret," Celeste wept. "Please help me!"

"But Celeste, if you love Thomas, 'why did you get mixed up with another man?"

Dark uptilted eyes studied her somberly. "And why does *madame* sleep with the master? In your sleep I hear another name. I think you love someone different, yes?"

Mercy's heart skipped a beat. She hadn't thought about whether Eric still used estate women, told herself she didn't care, and yet, astoundingly, there was an odd, strong stab of jealousy, a sense of having been betrayed.

"Do you mean the baby is Mr. Kensington's?"

Celeste's drooping head was answer enough. "He doesn't care for me, madame, but the prettiest girls—he always tries to sire a child from them. He says it's the best way to increase the size and strength of estate people."

Mercy had noticed a few ruddy-haired or fair children tumbling about the village, but she had thought them to be the offspring of *ladinos,* mestizos, or even McNulty or Pierre. She felt as if she'd been kicked in the stomach, was furious that she should care. Was it possible that though she still loved Zane, her body was becoming dependent on Eric, as it might after a time of forced use come to crave a drug? Humiliating—not to be allowed! But just now Celeste's trouble took precedence.

"How far along are you?"

Celeste spoke so rapidly that Mercy was sure the desperate girl had counted over and over, hoping there was a mistake.

"It's two weeks since I should have had my time, *madame.*"

Mercy sighed. Another month or six weeks and she'd have confronted Eric, urged him to talk to Thomas and make whatever reparation that would induce his man to overlook what was scarcely Celeste's fault. Mercy was reluctant to give the poinciana to other women since Chepa had warned that it could have harmful effects, but she wasn't able to refuse to Celeste the deliverance she might need at any time herself. So, at the infirmary, she made the potion and sent Celeste to her mother's home to drink it, saying she'd stop by at noon to see how she was.

At noon, Celeste was pale and trembly but relieved of the threat to her marriage. The mother, a silent wraith, with signs of having once possessed her daughter's startling beauty, nodded when Mercy said Celeste might hemorrhage if she rode and had better stay in the village overnight.

Riding home alone, Mercy brooded, sad and oppressed at serving death instead of life, though she still believed the choice was right and one she'd make for herself. A child of Celeste's and Eric's would have to be beautiful, but its face and body and mind would never form now, never exist. How fragile life was, how full of chance and miracle and grief.

She passed the small church and saw that a bier stood just inside the doorway, holding a small body wrapped in a paper garment trimmed with red and gold tinsel. A woman knelt beside it, supported by an older woman. The religious needs of the people were dependent on a worker who'd been a sacristan and knew many rites by heart. The women must be waiting for him to come in from the field and bury the child.

Mercy started to ride on, helpless before such loss, but light gleamed on golden hair, and she stopped, tied Lucera up, and went into the church.

The baby's eyes were closed, but curls clustered around the small face were golden and the skin was much fairer than the lovely young woman's. Mercy knelt and mourned for the tiny life ended here and the one snuffed out back in the village hut. She was sure Eric had fathered this child, but the woman buried it alone, would grieve alone. It was her baby, not an improvement of working stock.

A worm edged out of the baby's nose. "How long till the *maestro* comes?" Mercy asked.

The grandmother hunched a thin shoulder. "At sunset we brought the *angelito* here because there are other children in the house and my daughter needed peace."

"I'll send the *maestro*," Mercy said. She rode back to the village, found Don Gerardo at his meal, and said the *maestro* must come at once and end the women's heartbreaking vigil.

"But Doña Mercy!" protested the mayordomo, nervously smoothing his moustache. "To bring a man from work to mumble a few prayers! He's not a real priest, you know. And these women enjoy their mourning; it gives them an importance."

"Fetch the *maestro* or I'll get him myself!" Mercy ordered. "And don't subtract the time from his wages."

"Wages?" Don Gerardo laughed harshly. "Why, that Indian has such a debt at the store that he couldn't pay it off if he worked double the rest of his life!"

"Then a few hours won't matter," Mercy said. "Are you going for him, Don Gerardo?"

He bowed. "But Doña Mercy! Of course, I am at your orders! I only wished to explain . . . "

"Explain what?" Eric's great body filled the doorway and he ducked to step inside. "So here you are, my sweet! When you were late, I came looking for you." He glanced around, frowning. "Where's Celeste?"

"She's at her mother's. She doesn't feel well so I said she could stay there for the night."

"You know I don't want you unattended."

"Oh, what does that little way from here to the house matter? I would have been there by now, but I saw the dead child in the church and came back to send for the *maestro*."

"You're taking a lot upon yourself."

Mercy drew in a deep breath. "Did you see the child?"

Eric raised a warning hand. "Bring the *maestro*," he told Don Gerardo, who was watching them with considerable interest. As soon as the mayordomo was gone, Eric turned again, his voice purring silkily. "Now, my love, what of the brat?"

"He was very pretty, very blond."

"So? I saw a couple of women bent over a bier, but I didn't go to look."

"No," agreed Mercy, aware of saying a foolhardy thing but too angry to care, blaming him for the load on her conscience, as well as for the child in the church. "I suppose you can't keep track of all your bastards. After all, their mothers can bury them, just as they give them birth!"

Eric loomed over her. She braced for a blow, staring into his eyes, which had dilated in the poorly lit room. "Why, Mercy! Under all that indignation, you're jealous!"

That was too near the truth, depriving her of an effective retort. "Come along," he said, slipping his big hand beneath her arm.

As they passed the church, he reined in and called.

The young woman came out, as if sleepwalking. He put some coins in her hand. She looked up at him and said, "*Señor,* his hair was gold."

17

Eric was so gratified by what he considered her jealousy that he laughed at her barbed comments about being the father of his people and about how amazing it was that a well-born Englishman didn't think more of his bloodline than to scatter it through his fields and industries.

"Why, love, half the county had my grandfather's nose," he said. "Painless way to breed up the stock."

"But what if the girl's in love with someone else?"

"Wonderful! I certainly don't want them in love with me." He swept her into his arms and kissed her till his mouth grew hot and seeking. "But I'm not doing well by the estate girls anymore. I spend myself with you." Holding her face, he frowned. "When are *you* going to conceive? There's plenty of time, but as much and as often as I'm with you, it's a marvel you aren't increasing."

She hadn't yet needed the poinciana. "I think it may be difficult for me," she said. "I was my parents' only child, born after ten years of marriage."

"We'll do better than that," he vowed.

That may have been the day his seed rooted, because her flow, due a week later, didn't begin. Eric noticed this, for he was one of those men who was excited by the odor and swelling of the menses, so unlike Philip, who'd treated her as unclean and repellent at such times. She liked to think that Zane would find her periods neither erotic nor disgusting, would kiss and hold her without pressing on, as Eric did, even when it was painful or she was embarrassed by the stains.

"Isn't it your time?" Eric asked when she was four days late. He smoothed her stomach and slowly kissed it, her loins, and breasts. "Maybe you've kept a little something of mine!"

So Mercy drank the brew and was soon wracked with cramps and an unusually heavy flow, so nauseated that she couldn't eat and missed, for the first time, going to the infirmary.

"This seems rather more than late flowers." Eric used the English euphemism. As he watched her and she didn't look at him, she could sense his concern was changing to suspicion. Taking her hands, he insisted silently that she meet his gaze. When she did, those crystal eyes seemed to reflect her secrets. "You took something." he said positively. "You know a good deal about herbs and potions, don't you, sweet? And you know as well as I that my child would link you to me."

Mercy, more frightened by his contemplative words than she would have been by anger, stared at him, unable to speak. "I can take all your herbs away and keep you out of the infirmary, set a guard on you," he mused. "But that would make you feel oppressed, perhaps to the point of some irreparable foolishness." His words fell on her like cold, shrouding sleet. "I'll have to think of something. As a last resort, I can bar your windows, quite literally lock you up till you're not only heavy with child, but delivered. I know how you hate cages. And it may be romantic of me, but I'd prefer our baby to be carried in contentment, if not in happiness."

Mercy laughed bitterly at that, then shrank as his falcon's gaze hooked into her again. "Take note," he said at last, heavily, "if I ever come to believe you can have no softness for me, never be my love, even I am afraid to think of how I might use you before I throw you away. You may despise it, Mercy, but my need for you is your only safeguard."

He left the room and the solid planks reverberated with his weight.

Shaky from the draft, feeling overpowered, crushed down, Mercy tried to gain some strength and comfort from writing a letter to Zane, a letter he'd never get, but it was a way for her to feel she was talking to him, telling him of her narrowing choices, the slow, steady pressures. She wrote painfully:

Is the revolution over? Are you at La Quinta? Did you believe what Eric made me write? Do you hate me now? Oh, my darling, if you're still alive, let me know it! Somehow, sometime, let me see you again!

Celeste tapped on the door. "*Madame,* luncheon is waiting."

"I'll be right down," Mercy called. But Celeste opened the door and looked sympathetically at Mercy. "It is better now?"

Mercy nodded. "But *he* knows."

They exchanged glances of mutual female comprehension, the ancient understandings going back through thousands of years of male domination. "I'm sorry, *madame.* You know I will do for you anything."

It was good not to be friendless, though both women knew their impotence. "Thank you," Mercy said. "Has Thomas asked permission to marry you?"

Celeste nodded, seeming ashamed to admit her fortune in the face of Mercy's despair. "The master has consented. That means he won't have me again. He never uses married or betrothed women. But we have to wait until a clergyman comes through or until the master lets us travel to one. Thomas is very correct." She spoke with mingled regret and pride. "He wants everything to be proper."

So a proud servant would never know his master had taken his bride, filled her womb. The deception seemed a shame, but the alternative was worse. Mercy wished Celeste happiness and went downstairs.

Eric was preoccupied, overcourteous when he emerged now and then from his thoughts. Mercy was sure he was trying to decide how to control her, and she dreaded the moment when he'd reach a decision. They were having coffee when McNulty appeared in the doorway.

"Mr Kensington, there's a message!"

"Excuse me, my dear," Eric said to Mercy, rose in that lazy fashion that was deceptively swift, and went down the hall with his accountant.

Disturbed, Mercy went out on the terrace and looked down at the river and the pier. Eric was down there with McNulty, talking to several men who were making a good many motions with their hands. After a while Eric said something that made them cringe, turned on his heel, and strode toward the house while McNulty hurried off toward the sugar works.

What was the matter? Mercy was still staring after McNulty when Eric called from the door, "Come with me love This is your chance to learn if that handsome Dionisio will rid me of Canul in return for his freedom."

Catching Mercy's wrist, Eric pulled her along with him to the stable, called for their horses, and in a few minutes they were heading for the village.

As they rode, Eric cursed the Icaiche Mayan leader, Marcos Canul, who'd come down on one of Eric's logging centers and confiscated the cut mahogany, claiming it was cut on Mayan land. Eric had three days in which to "buy" the logs, or Canul would sell them to another Englishman. Canul's sixty or seventy men had rifles Of Eric's men, only the logging overseers were armed, and their men would be more likely to fight alongside the Mayas than against them.

"I thought Canul would try something like this in time," Eric growled. "It's just earlier than I expected. Well, he'll find he picked the wrong *dzul* to rob!"

"But why send Dionisio to kill him?"

"One can blot out Canul with overwhelming force, which I don't have, or by sneaking an assassin into his camp Dionisio, as *batab* of an independent group, could be a useful ally to Canul and would certainly be welcomed if he came on the pretext of joining with the Icaiches. There'd be feasting, drunkenness, and, sooner

252

or later, an easy chance to do Canul in and get away."

"But if Dionisio were suspected, wouldn't the Icaiches raid his people? As I remember, he thought they might, and that was why he bought guns for you."

Eric chuckled. "There'll be plenty of Icaiches glad to see Canul gone, and Dionisio's people would be less menaced if that firebrand were dead, for then they could make stronger ties with the Cruzob and stir up their general of the plaza, old Crescencio Poot, to chastise the Icaiches. It shouldn't be hard. He hates them as traitors to the Mayan cause and drove them out of Chichénha ten years ago, the same year he sacked Tekax."

Stopping in front of Don Gerardo's house, Eric lifted Mercy down and curtly told the mayordomo that his help was required. While Don Gerardo was expressing indignation at Canul, McNulty appeared with Dionisio.

The young *batab* seemed thinner, but he still wore the small gold earring and his face was as proud as ever. "Kiss El Señor's hand!" snapped Don Gerardo, but Eric waved him out of the office. "If you will excuse us, Don Gerardo, kindly wait outside in case you're needed."

With a glance of muffled resentment, the mayordomo went out and closed the door. Eric towered over the Maya, but he couldn't dominate him. It was like seeing a hawk confront a golden eagle. The eagle could kill the hawk, but it wouldn't be easy.

"Canul is a danger to your group," Eric told the *batab* in fluent Mayan that impressed Mercy in spite of herself. "He's taken one of my logging camps. I want him dead."

A faint smile curved Dionisio's lips and Mercy noticed that he had tawny eyes. White blood somewhere, in spite of that classic Mayan profile? "Many people of Belize want Canul dead, but he's still alive in the jungle."

"You could go as if to make an alliance, then find a quiet way to kill him. For that you may have your freedom, the new rifle I will give you, and ammunition."

"I have said it before, *señor*. I cannot do it."

"You're afraid?" Eric jeered.

"I don't care what you think of my courage," shrugged the *batab*. "I bound myself to cut your cane, not to kill in treachery."

Eric gazed at him a long time. "If you don't change your mind, in a few minutes we're going out of here to the whipping post. You'll be whipped till you agree to go or till you die."

"*Señor,* I would rather die at once than to be so disgraced."

"Your preferences don't interest me."

Mercy looked imploringly at the young man and Eric laughed. "Shall I say it for you, darling? You want to advise him to say he'll commit the murder, but to take to his heels once he's where I can't touch him!" He put this in Mayan for Dionisio, who held his head even higher.

"I will not lie to you. I will not kill Canul."

Rising, Eric pinioned Mercy's wrist. He brought her along with him as he flung open the door and called out to Don Gerardo, "Fetch your most skillful whipper!"

"Ah, *señor,* I'm that one," cried the mayordomo, preening his moustache.

McNulty cleared his throat. "Mr. Kensington! Such may be necessary, but I don't agree with it. Let me take the lady along to the house."

"Take yourself off if you like, James, but Doña Mercy stays here."

"Sir . . ."

"James," said Eric in a cream-smooth tone, "you're excused."

McNulty cast Mercy an unhappy look, but he wasn't of the fiber to defy his employer, who could have smashed him to the ground with a single hand. He retreated from the village and was out of sight by the time Dionisio had been tied to the post by his wrists, his shirt torn off, forced to stand on tiptoes.

"Please!" Mercy whispered to Eric. "Please! He won't do what you want. You'll have to kill him, and what good will that do?"

As he scanned her, a smile dawned slowly on Eric's face. "Why, this Indian may prove useful even if he won't go against Canul! Begin, Don Gerardo. Flog him till he promises to obey."

Don Gerardo drew back and raised his arm. The plaited rawhide whip sang, then landed on the brown shoulders with a sound that wrung a cry from Mercy's lips. The lash fell again. Again.

Blood beaded the weals. The man's shoulders began to quiver, though he had not cried out. Mercy was sobbing wildly, trying to get free of Eric and fling herself on the overseer, who was panting now, his eyes gleaming as he swung the whip.

Beside herself, Mercy began to scream. Her helpers stood by the infirmary. She saw, hurrying to their houses, a few women she'd treated. But there was nothing they could do, nothing. Dionisio slumped. His head hung sideways. Blood trickled from his wounds. At a word from the mayordomo, a man tossed a pail of water over the fainting *batab*.

He raised his head.

"Will you go?" called Eric.

No answer. Eric signaled the eager Don Gerardo to proceed. Mercy's throat was raw. She flinched at each descent of the whip, her eyes shut.

The lash halted. Dionisio had lost consciousness again. Eric raised Mercy's chin and made her look at him. "So you hate me? But I treated you like a queen, and you aborted my child. Let us try again, my dear. Shall Don Gerardo finish off that Indian, or would you have him live?"

"Let him live! Don't beat him anymore!"

"You would be grateful?"

"What do you mean?"

"You'd make every effort to hold my seed when it starts to make a child?"

"You know it must be true that it's hard for me to conceive."

"But you'll try. For every month that proves you barren, this fellow shall be whipped again—and you'll watch."

"And I'll hate you!"

"Till you have my child."

Wearily, Mercy said, "Please let them dress his cuts in the infirmary."

Don Gerardo looked disappointed, but at Eric's order two men untied Dionisio and carried him to the infirmary. Mercy cast Francisca and Paco a pleading glance, but they watched her with closed eyes, then followed the beaten man inside.

Mercy felt as beaten in spirit as the *batab* was in body. Eric had his method now, his way of taming her. She would go mad, she would scream herself into insanity, if she had to watch such a thing again. When Eric lifted her into the saddle, she felt like a puppet, a doll held together by pegs or wires, moved by Eric's will.

"I'm going to get that bastard Canul myself!" he vowed as they rode back to the house. "The militia's been disbanded, and he'll have sold my mahogany to that other blighter, God rot his soul, long before I could get the regular army after him."

"Are the logs that important?"

"What's important is that Canul's decided to test me. If he gets away with this one cutting of logs, he'll try to exact 'rent' on all my woodlands, maybe steal some cattle and mules. He's got to be stopped—quickly."

"How?"

"Most of the men can use guns, and they all have machetes. I'll offer a bonus attractive enough to get them to risk their skins. As soon as they can be organized, we'll go around through the jungle and hit the camp. My guess is that they'll be grand and gloriously drunk from the camp supplies, and we could take them easily if they're off guard." He gave Mercy an unpleasant smile. "Are you worried about my safety, or, could it be, upon reflection, that you'd rather be raped by me than some savage?"

Mercy didn't answer. Whatever happened, her situation was desperate. But if Eric would be gone for a few days . . .

As always, when she thought of escape, she remembered the river, the crocodile-infested swamps, and the jungle where, if she encountered any humans, they would probably be white-hating Cruzob. She would be incredibly lucky to survive those dangers and make her way to La Quinta or any friendly haven. But if she stayed here, Eric was determined to make her pregnant. She couldn't thwart him with the poinciana when that meant another beating for Dionisio, nor could she endure the floggings the *batab* would get till she conceived.

It was intolerable. Eric had found the way to break her. Whatever the perils, she must try to escape. As they climbed the steps, Eric took her hands, standing several steps beneath her so that their eyes were level.

"I don't want you to feel nervous or unprotected while I'm gone," he said. "So I'll have one guard at your door and a watch on all the downstairs entrances. You'll be perfectly safe. And now, my love, excuse me. I must get my expedition together."

With a light kiss, he went inside and Mercy stared toward the river. Guards or no guards, she had to get away.

It was easier to resolve than to do. She'd spent that afternoon putting together a pack of her most valuable possessions and things necessary for survival. Celeste now paid in full for Mercy's help. Enlisting the help of her mother and mother's friends, Celeste amassed several weeks' supply of dried meat and the sour cornmeal dough that could either be mixed with water to make a nourishing gruel or eaten as it was. There was honey in an oiled leather bag, matches pilfered from Pierre's kitchen, a hammock, a lightweight poncho for sleeping, an extra pair of sandals, and a waterskin for the northern region, where streams or springs would be hard to find. She also brought from the infirmary Elkanah's books and the *Badianus* translation. And, of course, she wore the black coral necklace.

"But won't Mr. Kensington suspect you?" Mercy asked worriedly.

"But you aren't running off!" Celeste laughed, shaking her head. "No! You died of the black vomit, the cholera, and, of course, had to be buried deep right away. Very sad."

"What a splendid idea!" cried Mercy, dazzled. No one would suffer for helping her. And there'd be no pursuit, for Eric would think her dead.

Celeste nodded. "I talked to Francisca at the infirmary. She'll be called up to nurse you the day after tomorrow. She and I will wrap up in sheets what's supposed to be you. Everyone fears the black vomit; it's very bad. No one will want to look."

Embracing her friend, Mercy began to feel more hopeful. The journey was as perilous as ever, but she was strengthened by the goodwill of the people who were helping her.

"You have a headache tonight, and pretend your stomach is upset," advised Celeste.

The effects of the poinciana and flogging wouldn't make that difficult. When Eric, appearing a little late for dinner, announced that he had eighty men ready to move at dawn, Mercy was glad that his excitement made him less likely to notice hers.

They went to bed early. The march on his enemy seemed to serve as an aphrodisiac on Eric, and he took her repeatedly in spite of her complaints of headache and nausea. "Whatever you took to scour your womb made you ill," he said roughly. "But you'll have three or four days to cosset yourself and be fragile."

She gritted her teeth and told herself this should be the last time she ever slept with him, the last time he would spend in her the charged energy and force of that powerful body.

Clever Celeste! Only if he thought her dead would Mercy be safe. Would Zane be home yet? She hoped so, yet she hated the certainty that if he was, he'd have read that letter and considered her a faint-hearted deserter.

Whatever he thought, though, she could explain. If he were only alive and well! She lay sleepless, even after Eric had finally exhausted himself and slumbered heavily. She feared the journey. Chances were against her getting through to Zane. But at least she'd be trying. She was taking her fate in her hands and plunging, and in that, along with dread, was great exhilaration.

It was still dark when Eric awoke and possessed her a last time, deeply, slowly. "Good-bye, love," he said. "McNulty's in charge while I'm gone. Tell him if you need anything."

"I'd go downstairs with you, but my head . . ."

"Go back to sleep, sweetheart." His hands strayed over her and he kissed her. "I'd rather think of you like this the few nights I'll be stringing my hammock in the jungle." He crossed the room and was gone.

Out beyond the stable, there were voices and commotion, but within fifteen minutes the sounds faded away. Mercy dozed, for it had been agreed that Celeste would tell Pierre she wanted no breakfast. There'd be no luncheon, either, and by dinner time Celeste would begin to act frightened and ask the symptoms for the black vomit. Francisca would be fetched and confirm the terrible suspicion.

After that, no one would want to see Mercy, and she'd leave before dawn. The young Indian whose arm had been putrefying when Mercy saved him would wait for her at a landing out of sight just down the river. He would take her across and put her on the trail going north, the Cruzob supply line.

Compelled to stay in her room that day, Mercy dreamed of Zane, of being back at La Quinta with Chepa, Jolie, Salvador, and Mayel. It helped keep up her courage. Even if she were destined to die on the way or be captured by warriors of the Talking Cross, dwelling on those not-so-remote possibilities wouldn't arm her for the effort.

She asked about Dionisio. He was remarkably strong and resilient, according to Francisca. She had given him some of the healing ointment kept prepared in the infirmary and he was back at work. Mercy hoped that the *batab* would feel released from his work bond after the way Eric had treated him.

Strange, he was the reason she could no longer endure life here, yet she'd probably never know what happened to him. Much as she hated to lose touch with her helpers at the infirmary and Celeste, Mercy took satisfaction in knowing that the medical care she'd begun would continue since it was something Eric knew was to the estate's benefit.

Mercy couldn't bring herself to give up her treasured medical books, but she spent most of that day copying out treatments and directions for mixing medicines. None of the infirmary workers could read, but Celeste could, so it would be useful to leave behind as much information as possible.

Pierre had insisted on sending up some custard and fruit juices. Mercy enjoyed these, though she felt a trifle guilty at the genial cook's concern. However, she couldn't think of any way Eric would blame his staff for her illness, and though Pierre and McNulty might feel sad over her untimely death, neither would mourn.

When Celeste smuggled up healthy portions of food from the servants' table, Mercy invited her to share them. Though she was diffident at first about sitting with her mistress, Celeste was soon talking about how happy she and Thomas were. Though both now lived in dormitories for unmarried servants, he was building them a house. All they needed was a clergyman.

"And if one doesn't come soon," Celeste announced, "Thomas will ask the master to let us go to Belize. That would be grand! A real wedding trip!" She hugged her arms against herself. "I wish Thomas weren't a good shot, wish he hadn't had to go on this raid. But the master is sure to thrash that Canul, isn't he, *madame?*"

"He certainly seemed to think so," Mercy reassured her. There were almost certain to be dead and wounded, but why talk of that?

Mercy had a last luxurious bath and hair-washing that evening, lying with her face turned to the wall when the boys brought in the water. It was too bad that they'd have to worry for a while about catching the black vomit, but their stories would confirm Mercy's illness.

Upon hearing Celeste's worried questions about the signs of the dreaded plague, Pierre had muttered numerous prayers and sent up broth. Mercy disposed of this while relishing rice and chicken with Celeste. Then Francisca was brought in.

Her eyes glistened as she caressed the cures Mercy had written down. "You have been good to us. Go safely to your own place, but think of us sometimes."

Francisca pushed back a straggle of gray hair. "That young *batab*, that Dionisio, he asked who you were. Don Gerardo told him he'd be vulture's meat except for you. Dionisio asked me to thank you." She gave an amused cackle. "He also said you look like the Virgin before she was with child, but I was not, I think, supposed to say that."

Mercy blushed, but she was pleased that the hawk-handsome Maya had noticed her, and not just as a hated *ladina*. Francisca confirmed that Pablo, the young Indian of the artery wound, would meet her in the morning at the agreed-upon spot. Then, before Mercy could prevent it, the old woman kissed her hands, blessed her, and said good-bye.

To ensure a sound night's sleep, Mercy had a soothing cup of tea at bedtime and the potion worked, for Celeste, who'd slung her hammock in the room, had to shake her awake in the predawn darkness.

While Mercy dressed, Celeste put out some fruit with juice and rolls she'd brought from the kitchen the night before, insisted they be consumed to the last drop and crumb, and then showed Mercy a back way out from upstairs, which avoided the guards. Carrying the pack, Celeste guided her along a path that turned off the route to the village, leading to a small pier used by the villagers for fishing.

Pablo greeted Mercy as if it were his regular morning habit to help his master's mistresses escape. He put the pack in the middle of his dugout, a smaller version of the pitpan in which she'd been brought to the House of Quetzals two months before, months that even now seemed unreal, like a half-waking nightmare interspersed with the baroque ostentation of Pierre's concoctions and the sanity-preserving hours at the infirmary.

Mercy embraced Celeste. Then with Pablo's help she got into the boat.

The hand that had once looked useless and dead was now as facile as the other, but before they shoved off he pushed up his sleeve and showed her the scar, still slightly ridged. It was haard to believe the sound, firm brown flesh had once been a mass of poison. If those blood-strangulating cords had stayed in place a few more hours, another half a day . . . The body was subject to so many ills, yet wonderfully self-healing when given a chance. It was a benediction to cross the river by the grace of a man she had saved.

Mercy waved to Celeste, who made an answering gesture and faded into the cypress and willows, festooned with passionflowers and morning glories just becoming visible in the pale light.

The river was shallow here and Pablo poled more than he rowed, but they were soon on the other shore. Taking the pack, he led her for a little way across tangled bare roots and vines, then moved up the bank past a giant tree whose huge palmate leaves had a silvery underside. Pausing, the young man drew aside a mass of vines, disclosing a narrow trail through the dense growth.

"This will take you to the trade route above Bacalar," he said. "You're not likely to meet Cruzob till then. But if you hear anyone, leave the trail and hide. Don't go far, though. You could get fatally lost half a stone's throw from the path."

Mercy thanked him and took the pack, looping it over her shoulders with the wide straps she and Celeste had devised. When she glanced back, Pablo had vanished. Only slightly moving vines showed anyone had been there.

The jungle pressed in on all sides and from the top, which almost touched her head in places, stifling, seeming to grasp at her with clinging, entrapping vines, hidden thorns, and protruding branches.

It would take ten days, at least, probably two weeks, more if she wandered. How would she ever sleep? The hammock would lift her off the ground, but things could drop from above, or crawl along the woven strands. She remembered where the horses had mired in the swamps and shuddered to think she must travel that road, wade up to her knees, or worse, in that black slime.

It was one thing to see crocodiles when mounted and protected by half a dozen rifles and men. She thought she

261

would simply die of fright if she met one of the loathsome beasts while struggling through muck. She had a long knife sheathed at her waist, but she devoutly hoped she wouldn't have to use it on anything but vines.

You can go back, she told herself, *now, before the story of your death gets out, now, while you can still shout to Pablo. But you must decide now. In an hour, Celeste will have lied for you, and to give that away would be unthinkable.*

So was going back. Again, Mercy weighed crocodiles, Cruzob, and the jungle against watching Dionisio being whipped and against bearing Eric's child. She knew that only through the jungle trail did she have a chance for life, a chance to find her love. She begged her father's spirit to be with her, sent her love and hope silently to Zane, and started on.

18

The sandals she wore were comfortable, but she was not used to steady walking. By the time the sun sent luminous shafts spiraling through the various layers of leaves so that the diffused glow reached her, she stopped by a seeping from the rocks to drink, rest, chew some dried meat, and rub into her feet the ointment she'd brought, a concoction of *toloache* and oils of turpentine and artemisia. The artemisia healed blisters and cracks, turpentine was an irritant and cleanser, and *toloache* dulled pain. She was likely to need a lot of it before this trip was over!

Her pack couldn't weigh more than fifteen pounds, but it seemed to double and triple in weight as the afternoon wore on and the humid heat grew oppressive. Mercy had chosen her divided muslin skirt and blouse as the most practical garments, and the change she carried was the poplin divided skirt and another thin blouse. The skirts were long, somewhat full, and terribly in the way, catching on roots, vines, and taking on the hue of mud.

Tripping as a hem caught on a fallen log, Mercy reached for her knife and was going to hack off the encumbering material at the knee when she remembered that the cloth was some protection from chiggers, mosquitoes, and scratches. She compromised, ripping and cutting away the bottom five or six inches. Relieved of several yards of cloth, which she buried in a hollow tree trunk and felt much freer without, Mercy promised herself a rest and food at the next sight of water.

This was a spring slowed to a trickle by the dry season, but sweet to the taste. She made a hollow to accumulate enough to soak her weary feet, mixed water into the sour cornmeal in her hollow gourd cup, and savored the pungent gruel, rather liking the taste, though she smiled to imagine what Pierre would have said.

The sun was slanting low to the west. She reckoned she'd been walking for most of the past eleven hours and was thoroughly tired. Should she stay all the night near this water?

In the short time she had been resting, all kinds of rustling sounds had seemed to multiply. She heard a scuffling above and a crashing sound as something struck the ground a short distance ahead. A scream pushed to her lips, but she swallowed it as she recognized the monster shape as an iguana, which lay stunned for a moment before it raised its thick, dragon-like body and darted into the brush. It must have been after birds or birds' eggs and ventured onto a limb too thin for its weight.

Iguanas were harmless and reputed to have excellent chicken-like meat, but the startling materialization of a four-foot-long lizard convinced Mercy that she'd be stupid to stop any sooner than she had to and be devoured by taut nerves and imagining. There were enough real dangers without fantasizing any. So she rubbed in more salve, changed sandals in the hope that differently angled straps would discourage blisters, and started out again.

The sun dipped lower and lower. She was beginning to think she should have filled the waterskin, because she was going to have to stop soon before real darkness, when she heard the sound of water and found a stream welling from the roots of a huge cedar.

She drank gratefully, then secured her hammock out of sight of the trail and far enough from water so that, she hoped, any creatures that wanted to drink would be neither frightened nor tempted by her.

Jaguars weren't supposed to attack people, but if one got curious and came sniffing around, she'd probably screech and scare it into jumping on her. And spider monkeys could be unpleasant if threatened. She refused to even think about snakes.

Her clothes were sodden with sweat and she felt muddy, as if the dust of travel was glued to her. Undressing, she hung her things to air out over a limb, stood in the stream, and washed all over. She had no towel so she dried by the air, rubbed on some of the resin Chepa recommended to keep off mosquitoes and chiggers, anointed her feet, relieved that she had no blisters or open sores, and decided to sleep in her clean clothes.

In the twilight that thickened swiftly in the forest, she sat in her hammock and slowly chewed spiced dry meat and sipped sour corn gruel. It was highly concentrated food and very satisfying. Spreading her soiled clothes over her pack at the end of the hammock, Mercy covered herself with the light poncho and seemed to fall asleep.

She awoke to stealthy padding and lay frozen as something touched the lowest-hanging part of the hammock, then nudged her hip. Opening her eyes slowly, she could see nothing in the darkness. The nudging came again, reminding her of a rooting pig's snout.

A wild pig? Peccaries could be dangerous if cornered, but if that was what was inspecting her, she could treat it as she would a barnyard pig at home.

"Scat!" she hissed.

The animal fled, taking with it a flurry of other boundings and slitherings. Mercy tried to sleep, but her nerves responded to every rustle. A long trill came from above her, swelling till it seemed to fill the night, then stopped abruptly. Only then did she realize it was a screech owl. She would have given her change of clothes and half her food for Flora's protection—and company.

What time was it? Would it never be day? Her muscles ached, but she longed for it to grow light enough to travel again. She thought of Elkanah, how he used to stay by her bed when she was afraid at night or had a bad dream. "We're all afraid of the dark," he'd said, not making fun of or shaming her. "But it can be a warm, friendly place, too. All depends on what you feel about it."

So she thought of Zane, remembered their nights, and tried to imagine the ones they would have—if she got home, if he came back safe from the war, if he still loved her. She forced those fears away and pretended the curve of the hammock was his arm, that his other hand was stroking her.

When she heard muffled sounds by the spring, she told herself it was only shy, small brocket deer. Gradually she slipped into a sleep that lasted till dawn.

She didn't know how many miles she had come and didn't remember the frequency of water on the route between the House of Quetzals and Bacalar, so she drank deeply and filled the water bag half-full before starting out, rubbed her feet well with ointment, and dressed in her dirty clothes.

Eating dried meat as she walked along, she told herself it was a good thing she had a few days to get used to the woods before she came to the Cruzob trail, where wild things would take second place in her anxieties.

Eric might return this evening or the next day, but surely even he wouldn't insist on exhuming a pestilent corpse, and who'd believe a lone woman, a foreigner, would start out through Cruzob territory?

No, he'd believe her dead; there was no one to blame. And if it meant she couldn't go to Mérida for fear of meeting his Aunt Elena or someone else who knew him, that was a trifle. She must run no risks of his learning that Celeste and others of the estate had helped her get away.

Zane, of course, might want to kill him, but she hoped to dissuade him from that. They'd been separated long enough; there'd been too many dangers. If they were ever reunited, it would be a long time before she'd feel comfortable about his riding to the fields without her. But he'd laugh and kiss her, tell her not to be silly. Only sometimes he'd not leave right away. . . .

She let her thoughts settle on him and a pulse within her quickened to dream of how it would be. One day was gone—one-tenth of the journey if made by horse, she thought, remembering the trip to the House of Quetzals those months ago. And by foot? Was she one-twelfth of the way home, perhaps? Whatever, today brought the goal closer, and the woods didn't seem as alarming as they had yesterday, when Pablo dropped the vine curtain and she'd been suddenly by herself.

It was a time of flowering. Besides the many vines,

there were copal trees with pyramids of flame-red flowers, wild cotton trees with big poppy-like yellow blooms, rosewood thrusting its pink blossoms high into the air, and many others she couldn't name.

About mid-morning she found a spring, washed her feet, drank, and filled her water bag with fresh water. A few hours later, hungry and tired, she found a rock hollow that held a fair amount of water accumulated from a drip in a crevice. She washed her drawers and skirt, spread them on a limb that caught the sun while she bathed, mixed corn gruel from the drip, and, clad in clean underwear from her pack, ate and rested. Her washed garments were still wet when it was time to go on, so she rigged a sort of holder from vines and fastened this to the top of the pack so she could walk while the laundry dried. She wanted to save her clean skirt for arriving at La Quinta, and she decided that for now her drawers and chemise were adequate, as well as much cooler.

Late that afternoon, the narrow trail joined one that ran north and south, and which showed mule tracks. She knew she must have now passed Bacalar, and that this was the Cruzob trade route she sought. Mercy's heart turned over and then beat faster. Though her skirt was still slightly damp, she put it on, then pulled her knife from the sheath to be sure it moved easily. There was nothing else she could do to prepare for the Cruzob, so she turned left and kept herself alert.

Please let there be no Cruzob traveling down to the Hondo or returning. Please let her maneuver past Chan Santa Cruz without detection. It was probably fifty miles to the city of the Talking Cross, and Mercy figured that the next seventy-five miles were the most dangerous, because surely the farther north she got from the city, the less likely she was to encounter scattered Cruzob villages and patrols.

With any luck, five or six more days should get her through the worst part. She was no outdoorsman, but she could move quietly through the woods, and it seemed certain that she'd hear any groups of people before they could hear her. This should give her time to hide off the road. Since it was for trading that the Cruzob went south, they weren't likely to travel alone.

She was beginning to convince herself of all this when she heard voices. Slipping into the trees, dodging vines,

266

and dropping to a crouch, Mercy scurried behind a thick mass of morning glories and bushes and lay close to the ground as the men came nearer. She couldn't see through the growth and prayed that they couldn't, either.

There were at least three voices. Their owners must have been barefoot because she could detect only a faint padding. For some time after the men had passed, Mercy lay with her heart thudding like a scared rabbit's straining her ears.

At last, when she heard and saw nothing, she got cautiously to her knees and worked her way to where she could see the trail. Empty. And she couldn't skulk in the brush all day.

But what if they came back?

She'd hear them, wouldn't she? Forcing her unwilling legs to carry her back to the road, Mercy walked nervously along, glancing over her shoulder every time she thought she heard anything, which was often, and wished she knew better the calls of birds so she could be sure that was really what they were.

One stretch of high grass rippled. Frozen, she stood as if rooted to the trail, then gasped with relief at the curassow's distinctive curly black crest and yellow knob above the bill. Later on there was a crashing through the trees and she saw a large, thin monkey flash through the limbs and vines, eerily, like a small, hairy man with a tail. Mostly, though, the jungle was quiet, though she had a sensation of secret teeming life.

Twilight was settling in. It was time to look for a camping place. Hoping for water, she went on for a while, but she found none. She knew she'd better find a hidden spot for her hammock while she could still see. She could stretch her water through tomorrow, but if she hadn't found any by noon, she might have to follow a stream bed to hunt for a spring or natural cistern.

Constantly turning to fix in her mind the major trees she was passing, Mercy got well out of sight of the trail, found two suitable limbs, and slung her hammock. Perched in it, she chewed meat and corn dough, preferring to drink her water plain till she found it brackish from the skin and mixed in enough corn to flavor it. She rubbed salve into her feet and on some scratches on her arm, then brushed her hair and braided it. Since she couldn't wash, she wouldn't change to her clean skirt. Stowing her pack at one end of the hammock, she pulled the poncho over her head and dropped out of consciousness, as if leaping from a bridge.

If peccaries rooted around her that night, or monkeys chattered questions, or jaguars sniffed, or snakes glided past, she didn't even dream of it, but slept till light pressed insistently against her eyelids.

Yawning, stretching, the feel of the hammock oriented her at once. She gazed cautiously around, listening. When nothing seemed unusual, she mixed gruel, broke camp by the simple action of putting her hammock into her pack, fastened on her sandals, and made her way back to the path.

She must be vigilant, ready to run for cover at any moment, and she must watch for water. Either she was getting used to the woods and more confident of surviving, or fear of the Cruzob left her little worry about natural perils, for she began to see thick brush and trees as her refuge now, the trail a focus of danger that she had to follow.

Not as stiff as yesterday, she felt comparatively free of aches after an hour's travel. Her feet were toughening, too, and she had been tremendously fortunate not to get blisters, for which she credited the ointment and switching sandals.

A brocket deer, dainty and rust colored, sprang across the path. Mercy hoped if something pursued it that the sight and smell of a human would frighten off the hunter. In the sky she saw black vultures circling and caught the sweet-sickish smell of carrion: leavings, probably from some predator's night kill. Mercy shivered and quickened her steps.

When would she find water? There'd been several dry watercourses, one boggy stretch, and a hollowed rock with mineral rims, showing that it held water some of the time. She'd thought herself lucky to travel before the rains began, but if water became a problem and searches for it added to her journey, she'd rather have waded through mud and been soaked so long as she could drink.

The dried, salty meat made her thirsty, so she left it in her pack at noon and sipped gruel, treating herself also to some honey. There were only a few cups' worth of water left in the bag. At the next promising place, she'd better leave the trail and hunt for the liquid, which, like air, was so necessary to life that it was taken for granted till there was none.

It was strange how fears changed and shifted. At first she'd dreaded the jungle, then Cruzob, and now the lack of water. But she'd never wished herself back in Eric's power, and she didn't think she would even if she perished miserably. She'd rather take her chances with the soldiers of the Talking Cross, though, than die from lack of water. With them there was a chance of living, of getting back to Zane.

She sipped carefully and walked on till she came to a wide slough. It might just go on like this, slimy mire, but there could also be a pure source of water. She had to see.

Leaving the track, she found herself sinking into mud concealed by myriad orchids and other plants. She retreated to firmer ground but kept the mire in sight. Before long she saw a few inches of mucky fluid, but she could have used it only as a last resort, for it looked stagnant and vile enough to precipitate the black vomit, malaria, typhus, and all the other jungle plagues.

Sometimes sinking into ooze above her ankles, she brushed aside mosquitoes that swarmed from stale puddles and pushed through entangling, claw-like branches. Dear God, wasn't there a rock with a comparatively clean supply of water, a source to feed this morass? Or was it from some underground seepage?

A snake slithered past her like a liquid dagger. She barely choked back a scream. How far should she go on? She must be over a mile from the road. There was no certainty that this bog would lead to good water if she followed it for another day. Water might be up the path, clean, clear, easily reachable, just a bit farther on.

That was the maddening part—not to know. She could turn back from this quest, with water only a little way ahead, or she could waste the rest of the day and be caught by darkness with only a cup of water. A wrong choice could mean death. And she didn't know. She didn't know.

Panic rose in her. She took a deep breath, then fought it down. She still had some water left. A person could live several days without any. At the worst, she might drag herself as far as Chan Santa Cruz, where there'd be water if they spared her life. She'd go on for about fifteen minutes. Then, unless prospects improved, she'd go back to the trail.

She started on. In a few minutes, as if to reward her decision, she was staring down at a long, narrow pond fed by a lazy seepage from what seemed to be a cave or grotto almost hidden by massive cypress roots. It would take time, but she could fill the bag there and wash herself, though she'd get muddy again on her way back to the trail.

Moving around the bank, Mercy took off her sandals, put them beside her pack, and waded toward the rock with her gourd and bag. A log detached itself from the mud of the bank, and another, and another—logs with eyes, with long, slit mouths, logs that swam toward her.

Crocodiles!

Mercy was trapped between them and the grotto. There was no place to scramble up. They were on all sides, a dozen, twenty. . . . They must have been basking at the banks and edge of the water, so indistinguishable from the mud that only motion could make them take form.

Frantically, she tried to remember what she'd heard about them. They would snap at anything that came their way; they were attracted by motion. She told herself that they were curious rather then hungry or hostile, but if one gave her a questioning nip and her blood flowed . . . she went ice cold with the terror of what would happen next.

One immense creature was close to her now. Mercy stared at it, believing her end had come. She had only her gourd and water bag, and no weapons except her knife. But one of these might divert them for a minute, give her a whisper of a chance.

She swung the bag back and forth, then tossed it toward the middle of the pond. The nearest crocodile snapped at it, others dived in, and the big monster closest to her churned about. She threw the gourd to encourage it and then splashed for the shore, floundering in water up to her waist, then trapped in mud.

She knew the awful things could move on land. She heard a thrashing behind her. Jerking her knife free, she turned, determined to at least fight the horror before its teeth did what they must. She would give it a slash to the throat or belly if she could thrust that far while she still had an arm. . . .

There was a crashing sound. The animal convulsed. A man with a rifle fired again. Mercy clambered up the bank, her garments heavy with mud, as another shot resounded. By then the crocodiles were devouring the dead or wounded ones.

Mercy leaned shuddering against a tree. Whoever that

270

man was, he'd saved her from a frightful death. He was dark-skinned; that was all she'd noticed. But she couldn't see him now. Then she heard the soft sound of naked feet and knew he was coming to her. She couldn't run, couldn't get away.

But she still had her knife.

Stand up! she ordered herself. *Cruzob or mestizo or sunburned ladino, he'll treat you better if you don't act as frightened and helpless as you are.* But it's hard not to look afraid when you've just been chased by crocodiles. It's hard not to look helpless when you're mud-sodden and thirsty and tired. *Try!* Swallowing hard, she stepped away from the tree and tried to smile, though she kept the knife in her hand.

"Thank you," she said in Mayan while the man was still hidden by vines and leaves. She still didn't know the tongue well and groped for phrases. "I'm lost. Help me home. You will be paid well."

"I'm already paid." The reply came in good Spanish as the man came out of the brush.

Mercy stared at him unbelievingly. But there was the golden earring, the hawk face, the tawny eyes.

"Dionisio!"

He smiled. "Ixchel," he said.

"I . . . I don't understand." He'd sent thanks and she'd thought him kindly disposed, but who could blame any Maya for hating whites?

"Ixchel was our goddess of healing. Since I saw you in the infirmary that day, that's what I've called you." His smile deepened and she grew conscious of the way the mud and water plastered her clothes to her. "Ixchel was also the goddess of the moon, love, childbirth, and weaving. She had a famous shrine at Cozumel, but now that's where *ladinos* send their political enemies. You can't care much for that right now. though!" Slinging his rifle across his shoulder, he picked up her pack. "You need a place to bathe. Come."

She fastened her sandals and followed him back to the trail, so grateful not to be in some crocodile's jaws that she scarcely minded the discomfort of the caking mud. He wore a shirt. She knew that beneath it his back must be a mass of scabs.

"How did you get away?" she asked. "How did you find me?"

"I was looking for you." He answered the last question

271

first. "It wasn't hard to follow your sandals off the track." So much for her faith that she could have eluded Cruzob if they found her footprints. "There's a well not far ahead where you can cleanse yourself and rest. I'll tell you then about what's happened at the estate."

The crude stone well had a hollowed log trough beside it for watering pack animals. After giving her a gourd of clean, sweet water, Dionisio filled the trough full and told her to bathe.

She did this, left with no choice but to change into her clean things. Dionisio changed the water twice while she washed and rinsed her clothes. When these were spread over a bush, he mixed corn gruel and produced some tortillas, which made the jerked meat much tastier. When they had finished with a bit of honey and dried coconut, Mercy sighed and cut off the cumbersome, voluminous bottom of her divided skirt. Dionisio tucked the cloth into the woven fiber bag he wore over the shoulder that didn't bear the rifle. He also had a machete and knife.

"Tell me," Mercy said.

She listened, unable to take it in, then tried to make it real by asking questions. "You say that Canul's outposts ambushed Eric's men and most of them were killed? And Eric? Presumed to be among the dead? Ah, Dionisio! And Canul came down to the estate, looted what he could, and set the rest on fire?" Alison's harp, Alison's portrait. What a strange way for them to be destroyed after journeying so far. "Canul didn't kill anyone but Don Gerardo and the overseers?" she said finally.

"No. He said why should he kill Mayas and blacks with whom he had no quarrel, or the fat cook? But the red hair, the man of accounts, he tried to stop the looting and was macheted."

Poor McNulty. He hadn't lived by the sword, but by his ledgers. He'd been out of place on the estate, with no stomach for cruelty but no will to stop it, either. But Celeste? Her adored Thomas?

Dionisio didn't know if Thomas had died in the fight, but he was positive that no women had been killed or raped and that the accountant was the only person to die in the great house. Canul had taken food, the contents of the store, weapons, tools, mules, horses, even some of the black pigs, but he'd left the village standing, suggesting to the people that *they* might take over the refinery, and if they did well, they should pay him yearly tribute for use of the land and removing their master.

"And you're on the way back to your village?" Mercy asked.

He nodded. "When it was clear that Canul wasn't going to slaughter everyone, Francisca knew I'd be leaving. She told me your 'death,' which had caused great mourning in the village, was a ruse, and she asked if I'd try to overtake you and help you get to your home."

"I was certainly never more glad to see anyone in my life!"

He laughed. "I can believe it. If you hadn't thrown your waterskin and gourd, I might not have been in time." He glanced at the sky. "Can you walk farther before we stop for the night?"

Mercy glanced at the well, reluctant to leave it. "I have a water bag," he said. "And I know where water is, providing this dry season hasn't scorched it all up. I don't like to stay long at this well."

"Why?" she asked as she tied her sandals and collected her laundry. Dionisio fastened her clothes to a limb that she could carry over her shoulder while he took her pack, slinging it beside his bag.

"This is where Jacinto Pat was murdered. Pat survived the longest of the three rebel chiefs who began the war, but a jealous man killed him here while he was on his way to Belize for guns."

"Do you think the well's haunted, then?"

"It is for me, because if the leaders had listened to Pat, a peace might have been negotiated that would have saved many lives. But they were jealous and called him a traitor. So Pat died, the war went on, and Yucatán lost half its people, all in a few years."

"Was your village in the war?"

"My uncle was *batab* then and sometimes he fought alongside the Cruzob, but as much as possible my village stayed aloof. We had never been much bothered by *dzuls*, and we simply wanted to be left alone."

Mercy nodded. "That's probably what most people wanted."

"Yes. It was the Huits—'loincloths,' or untamed Indians —who were having their lands taken or being forced into servitude, losing the freedom they were used to, who were the thrust of the rebellion. They now control the southeastern part of Yucatán, bonded together by the Talking Cross."

"And Canul with his Icaiches are enemies of the Cruzob?"

"They're supposed to be, but Canul would rather raid below the Hondo and try to absorb other independent groups like mine. If he could dominate the Macanches, Lochas, and Ixcanhas, he might be strong enough to occupy most of Belize and hold power equal to that of the Cruzob."

"Yet you wouldn't kill him."

"I may kill him in a battle, but that will be clean, not a deceitful trick to serve a *ladino*." He said the word like a curse.

What did he mean to do with her? He hadn't said, though his manner was protective. Mercy screwed up her courage to say, "I'm a *ladina*."

He glanced over his shoulder with a smile. "You're Ixchel."

Was he serious? A prickle of fear edged her spine. She forced herself to speak lightly. "I'm plain Mercy Cameron, Dionisio. Please, will you help me find my way to La Quinta?"

Halting, he turned to regard her with eyes that were the color of dark honey. She'd had a cat once with eyes like that, a cat that had loved to be held in her arms but that would never stay in the house. "I'll take you wherever you wish, Doña Mercy, even to Mérida or Campeche, but first I must stop at Chan Santa Cruz to try and arrange for a closer alliance. Canul won't molest my people if he knows that would bring retaliation from the Cruzob. It was General Crescencio Poot of Chan Santa Cruz who drove the Icaiches out of Chichénha. No one cares to anger him."

"You mean I'll have to go into Chan Santa Cruz? Can't I wait in the forest?"

"Are you so fond, then, of crocodiles?" He laughed. "I'm required to spend a month each year in garrison duty at Chan Santa Cruz. Mine's overdue because of the bond I gave the *dzul*, Kensington, for those rifles. Since I want assurances from the Talking Cross, I had better first render my service." He frowned, scanning her so intently that she blushed. "You're a woman all the *batabs* would like in their hammocks. The best way to protect you is to say you're my captive."

274

"But a month! I'd rather go on by myself!"

"I won't permit that. It's too dangerous."

"You mean I am your captive?"

"No. Truly, Ixchel, I am yours. But I must fulfill my obligations to the Talking Cross for the safety of my people."

"Could you send a messenger to La Quinta, then, to request an escort for me?"

He laughed mirthlessly. "Two difficulties, Doña Mercy: to find a man who would go, and to persuade the Talking Cross to allow outsiders to come for you and depart. I don't think it could be done, not without imperiling those who helped. A month is not so long. And you'll learn things that no other *ladinos* know, except slaves, who'll finish their years at the shrine city."

Mercy bit her tongue to keep from saying that she didn't want to learn about Chan Santa Cruz. "A month seems a very long time to me," she said. "I don't know if the people of the estate knew, but Kensington abducted me."

"It was known. People wondered why he went so far to steal a woman when he had many beautiful ones in his household."

"Then you should understand that I want to go home. Please take me safely past Chan Santa Cruz and let me travel on."

He stopped in a small glade, put down their bags, and fired at a ripple in the tall grass. Something leaped, convulsed, then was still.

"A small wild pig," he said. "Good. We'll camp here and cook it."

"But we just ate!"

"When you taste this meat, you'll get hungry," he promised "And we'll carry the rest to eat tomorrow. Find some big green leaves while I make the fire pit."

It might be better to give him time to think about her request. Though Mercy was determined not to let him ignore her urgency, she first helped him collect rocks for the hole and then went searching for the largest leaves she could find and presently returned with dozens from a nearby tree.

He had a fire burning inside the rock-lined pit and was apparently dressing the animal over at the edge of the grassy stretch. Bringing it back to the fire, he sprinkled it with a mixture of seasonings from his bag, and wrapped it in leaves. When the fire had burned to ashes and the rocks glowed with heat, he raked out some of them, put more leaves in the pit, nested the pig there, and put on the rest of the leaves, a little earth, the hot rocks, then more earth.

"It's like *pibil*," Mercy said, thinking of Chepa and La Quinta with great longing and growing anxiety.

Had she only traded one captor for another? Could Dionisio intend to leave her, another *ladina*, in Chan Santa Cruz? She didn't know what to think, couldn't gauge his feelings toward her, though she couldn't deny the man-woman magnetism that flowed between them.

"*Pibil* requires many more herbs," said Dionisio. "But the method's the same."

Twilight deepened. He hung their hammocks close to each other, as if he guessed that Mercy was beginning to have desperate thoughts of slipping away in the night.

She could stand it no longer. "Dionisio," she said, "stay at the shrine, since that's your duty. But let me go home."

Evidently he'd been thinking, too, for he took a while to answer. She found this reassuring. If he meant to hand her over to the Cruzob, he needn't be velvet-gloved. "The *tatich*, Bonifacio Novelo, loves women. No doubt I could win his favor by sending you to his house. Your sweetness might even charm Crescencio Poot, though he'd probably not feel satisfied until he'd cut your throat. I swear that I will not give you to them, nor leave you when I go. But you shall wait with me this month of my service. I owe you my life. That debt can't be paid by letting you risk death or violation."

"I tell you, I accept my chances, and I prefer to take them!"

"No. I will serve my time—one month. Then I will take you wherever you wish."

Mercy abandoned the argument. He sounded honest. But he might be killed or die or succumb to pressures now unforeseen. She'd travel with him till they were near the shrine and then she'd try to get away in the night.

In the darkness, Dionisio grasped her hands. "By my honor as a *batab*, I will protect you with my head. You will go to this La Quinta, if that's your desire. But you must promise me not to journey by yourself."

"Why should I promise?" she demanded angrily. "I haven't asked you to be responsible! If you're as grateful as you say, you'd let me do what I want to!"

276

His laughter was softly amused. "Did your mother let you play in the fire because you cried to touch it? You will not go alone. So, till I can take you, will you agree to be my guest?"

"What if I won't?"

The long, slender hands grasped hers more tightly. "Then. for your own good, you'll really be my prisoner. Tonight I'd tie you up, and at Chan Santa Cruz, when I couldn't be with you, I'd ask that you be closely watched."

"What gratitude!"

"I grieve at your displeasure," he said, not sounding grieved at all. "But I prefer your anger to your death. You may consider it till it is time to sleep. Then I need an answer."

To be tied, have her steps dogged everywhere, have no privacy! Even her captivity at the House of Quetzals hadn't been that demeaning as far as physical restraints went. "I'm a captive either way," she said cuttingly. "But I'd rather not be trussed up or spied upon. I'll stay your month at the shrine if you'll promise to send me home earlier if a suitable person or escort turns up."

"Why. yes, I'll agree," he said so promptly that she thought perhaps she'd misjudged him, blamed him for being overcautious. "So, now, Ixchel, that's settled. Let's be friends. I know you're eager to get back to your people, but this time with me can be pleasant if you don't set yourself against it." He chuckled and released her hands. "A story to tell your grandchildren! How you escaped through the jungle and were the guest of a *batab* at Chan Santa Cruz!"

Grandchildren! Would she ever have any? Would they be Zane's grandchildren, too?

"You don't like to think of growing old?" Dionisio asked.

"I just wonder if I shall!"

"Be sure of it," he said confidently. "You're having your adventures now. Calm will follow. You will grow very bored! There's a man at this La Quinta?"

"Many of them."

"A man for you?"

"Yes. We are to marry."

It was a moment before the Maya spoke. "That explains your impatience. He is *ladino?*"

"His parents were from Louisiana. His father once

277

saved the life of Crescencio Poot, which seems to be why La Quinta hasn't been raided."

"A strange *ladino*, to save the general of the plaza, the man who ordered the massacre at Tekax and many others!"

"This was back before the war started."

"Ah! Most fortunate for La Quinta. But you, Doña Mercy—it is said you come from Texas, far to the north, where the Mexicans sometimes made Yucatecans fight."

"Yes. Texas was part of Mexico, then a republic, then joined with the United States, then allied with the Confederacy—the southern states against the northern ones."

"It is very dim to our ears. Perhaps I confuse your war with that of Juárez against the French and the emperor. But didn't your Texas lose its fight?"

"Yes," said Mercy, and for a time they talked of that war and the one in Mexico and the present revolution in Yucatán.

"Has your man taken sides?" asked Dionisio.

"He served under Peraza in another revolution that lost," explained Mercy. "And some of his friends had been sent to the penal colony on Cozumel. He felt he had to fight."

"But you did not?" Dionisio sounded as if he were smiling.

"I didn't try to stop him, but I could have wished he'd had a different sense of honor."

"A man can only have his own. Crush it and he's nothing."

Mercy had never thought much about honor herself. She only knew what she would and would not do. It was important to her to live. She'd been Eric's mistress rather than let him kill Jolie or beat women, but when it came to bearing his child or watching this *batab* slowly whipped to a pulp, she'd had to take any chance, however desperate.

"So," pursued Dionisio, "your man may not be at La Quinta. Perhaps at Chan Santa Cruz they may know what's happening. The *tatich* has many spies; in fact, there's a department of them under the orders of the *tata nohoch zul*, Great Father Spy. But what will you do, Doña Mercy, if you learn at La Quinta that your man is dead?"

"Don't say that!"

"It happens."

"I won't think about it!"

"Of course not," he said soothingly. "Our dinner should be ready. I think you'll find it even better than *cochinita pibil.*"

It was delicious. Mercy told him so and ate with relish after almost three days of jerky and corn gruel. Dionisio gave her water in his gourd and more tortillas.

"What is the Talking Cross?" she asked. "Has it always been among the Mayas?"

"You know that each family has a cross, and each village, some more potent than others. When the tide of war turned against the Mayas in 1850 and they were being hunted down, one band settled at a forest wellspring almost hidden between rocky hills, with a mahogany tree at the entrance to the grotto. On this tree was carved a small cross, no longer than my middle finger. This was the Little Holy Cross from which Chan Santa Cruz got its name. The Mayan leader, José Maria Barrera, set up a wooden cross on a hill just east of the wellspring. When the people prayed, the Talking Cross spoke, God's voice. The cross was called by them *la santísima,* which means 'most holy.' "

"Do you believe all that?"

"Some say it was Manuel Nahuat, a man who could make his voice come from other places. The cross doesn't often speak anymore. It usually delivers written messages through a scribe. But in those days it spoke, and the Mayas believed. At its command they attacked Kampocolche in the night and fought desperately till morning. They were defeated."

"But they still believed in the cross?"

"Those struggling to survive as a people will believe what gives them hope. *Ladinos* attacked the shrine in 1851, killed Mañuel Nahuat—the one some say was the voice— and carried off the cross. But Barrera himself had eluded the *ladinos.* He discovered another cross. Instead of a voice, he found a scribe to interpret for *la santísima.* The cross gave the scribe a message for the people, urging them to fight and promising protection. But on the Day of the Holy Cross, May 3, the *ladinos* attacked again. Barrera lacked guns and ammunition, so he took his men out of the shrine city and let the whites find it empty. There weren't enough of them to hold such a remote place and they pulled out quickly, but the Mayas they sought were in a serious plight. It was too late to burn new cornfields, so they had to plant old clearings, which wouldn't produce much. They had to exist on roots, bark, and palm nut milk. And some starved."

Dionisio fell silent, but after a while he went on with how Barrera, knowing it was the end of Mayan freedom unless he could encourage and inspire his beaten, hungry people, had built a thatched church with a sanctuary for the cross, which was guarded day and night. It spoke again, and its voice seemed to come from the air.

"Do you believe that?" Mercy asked.

"*You'll* certainly never get a miracle!" Dionisio growled. "If you must know, and prefer clumsy facts to mystery, there was a pit behind the altar and a wooden cask was used to make the voice of the man hidden there boom out. My father heard it and he believed while he was there, even though he knew better."

"What happened then?"

"The Mayas were beaten, they were starving, and yet they gathered around the cross. The *ladinos* collected every man who could possibly fight and began a clean sweep from the northeast coast to the west, trying to put an end to the rebels once and for all. The *ladinos* marched on Chan Santa Cruz.

"Most of the able-bodied men had gotten away. Fresh graves were near every cluster of huts, and there were dead people in hammocks and children dying of starvation. Soldiers found the pit and barrel in the church, laughed, and mocked this 'God-voice' of the Indians. The *ladinos* decided the best way to stop the cult was to get rid of the mahogany tree by the grotto, the 'Mother of Crosses,' which seemed to spawn new ones when the old ones were captured. This tree was supposed to be able to resist any ax. . . ." Dionisio's voice trailed off in the darkness.

"Did it?" Mercy asked.

"The *ladinos* collected their two hundred famished prisoners and cut it down before them, then asked if it hadn't fallen like any tree. Maybe it had, the Mayas answered, but the cross had a power no *ladino* could touch. Clearly, the rebels were defeated, by starvation more than by arms. The *ladinos* even let their skeleton prisoners go and marched south, taking scattered prisoners, to Bacalar and Chichénha, where they met the flank commanders, who'd had similar luck. The rebels were done, finished. The reserves went home, the regular army went back to camp, and the *ladinos* fired victory salvos from the cannons of San Benito."

"But that wasn't the end," Mercy protested, fascinated, appalled, pitying, and awed.

Dionisio sighed and continued. Yucatán had made peace with the Chichénha Mayas, who were then known as Pacíficos del Sur and who were supposed to help keep down the rebels of Chan Santa Cruz. This treaty was signed at the government house in Belize in September, 1853, but in November Indians seemed to swarm all over the frontier.

Town after town fell, outpost after outpost. The militarist regime in Mérida had provoked a revolt by liberal federalists—this was the fight in which Zane had followed Peraza. The army was called north to put down the revolution, stripping the frontier, and cholera, the black vomit struck. Under these conditions, starved, fanatical Mayas could take the exposed settlements and harry the few troops left on the frontier.

In 1854 the army hadn't marched on Chan Santa Cruz until after the spring harvest, and it had been sniped at and ambushed all the way. When the *ladinos* finally fought their way to the shrine city, they found a new well in the center of the village and several log troughs. They drank, and before long began the horrible vomiting that led to death while Mayas taunted from the jungle, inviting the attackers to drink deeply of the sweet, healthy waters of Chan Santa Cruz. The new well had been treated with the clothing of cholera victims.

At the end of the week fewer than a hundred soldiers had been able to fight. The commander got the sick and wounded on litters, but he lacked enough men to carry them, let alone fight off the Mayas, who killed everyone except a few who managed to escape into the bush.

Fighting had gone on all summer and fall, with the army pursuing as the Mayas faded into the jungle to harass and attack. *Ladino* political warring had given the Mayas a chance to capture crucial weapons and supplies. In 1855 the army lost about half its men in action while hundreds more died of cholera.

"So the Mérida government decided the War of the Castes was over," finished Dionisio. "Since they couldn't defeat these mad followers of the cross, it was decided to ignore them and concentrate on protecting the frontier. After eight years of war, starving because they couldn't

281

plant and harvest properly, the Mayas planted and rain swelled the corn ears, and no *ladino* master or official claimed any part of it. No, and not the *ladino* church. Wouldn't you say, Doña Mercy, that the Indians had earned their land and their harvest?"

"Yes. And I thank you for telling me. I don't like staying in the shrine city for a month, but I'll never doubt now that it's holy."

Through the faith and courage of the people, not through the cross.

Dionisio guided her to the hammocks. "Sleep well," he told her. "Don't be afraid. I must serve my time, but my life is wrapped around yours—a shield, till you're where you wish to go."

Once she swallowed her disappointment, she knew it was best to wait the month and journey under his escort. Thanking him, she said good night and got into the hammock.

As she shifted into a comfortable position, she felt more peaceful than she had since Eric had abducted her.

Dionisio was close. He knew the jungle; he could protect her. How good to know that, and to sleep.

19

Each corner of the shrine city was marked by a cross housed in a thatched shelter, and no mule, horse, or other animal was allowed within the boundaries. The *balam na,* or church, ruled the east side of the plaza, buttressed with walkways designed for defense running the length of the structure on either side. There was an unfinished tower at each end, and bells stolen from Bacalar hung in the southwestern one. Arcaded wings fanned out on both sides; these were barracks and schools. Behind these was a compound for slaves, primarily women, who did most of the work in the barracks.

The life of Chan Santa Cruz began in the church before

dawn when the *maestro cantor* said the little Mass, with the commander of the guard and some of his men kneeling in the chapel. There was a second Mass at eight, and rosary in the evening. Sometimes the *tatich* celebrated Mass, but he often held private worship in his own chapel before a cross gleaming with gold and jewels.

The *tatich*, or *tata nohoch*, Great Father, lived in a palace across the plaza from the church, a building one hundred feet long with arcades on both sides. To the left of this was the residence of the general of the plaza. More barracks, a council house, a jail, and other flat-roofed stone buildings surrounded the flat, rocky plaza, with its sapodilla, or chicle, tree.

"Most wrongdoing is taken care of at the village's whipping post or stocks," Dionisio told Mercy. "But serious crimes—witchcraft, murder, having dealings with *ladinos*—are punished near that tree. The criminal is hacked to death by a number of men with machetes so that he's killed by the whole society."

After that she never looked at the tree without an inward shrinking.

As many villages had grown up around Chan Santa Cruz as the water supply allowed, but the city itself remained primarily a ceremonial center. Every Cruzob male over sixteen was obligated to spend a month each year on guard duty there, causing a steady turnover in population, while even the general of the plaza often preferred to live in his home village and to come to Chan Santa Cruz only when needed. The *tatich* and his three officials who served the cross were the only year-round residents.

Besides the Secretary of the Cross, who took down its messages, there was an Interpreter of the Cross. It was probably he who hid in the pit behind the altar.

A stone shrine, open to the west, had been built near a little *cenote* grotto, and special celebrations were still held there. Mercy often went to a rocky vantage point above the valley, where, hidden by flowering vines and trees, she could watch the rocky hollow with its inner waters, which people said always stayed at the same level.

Most of the time, though, Dionisio was with her. Guard duty at the shrine, though an important way of preserving faith and binding together men from different villages, wasn't strenuous. In the time between morning Mass and rosary, except when they were sentries, the men usually idled in the barracks and talked as soldiers always have of past battles and adventures, of their homes, and of women they'd had or hoped to have.

Dionisio, as *batab* of an allied group serving without his company, was allowed to occupy one of the thatched huts located at an intersection of two of the wide streets on a block enclosed by stone walls and fruit trees. The city was laid out *ladino*-style in streets that crossed at right angles, and five small rocky hills within the boundaries had been fortified.

Walls of rubble enclosed the city and sentries were always on watch. Outside were lime kilns where limestone was shattered by heat and made into mortar, as had been done from the days of great Mayan building. Some of the male slaves worked there or hauled stone for new construction around the plaza. Others cut wood or cleared the forest for new cornfields.

Most of the captives were of the poorer class, though Dionisio said that some women of the aristocracy were among the barracks servants. "The pampered, proud ones usually die soon," he said. "Educated men often have easy work, like giving instruction in reading, writing, Spanish, and music, and that band playing at morning Mass is *ladino*. It was captured seven years ago when Governor Acereto sent a huge expedition against Chan Santa Cruz. Crescencio Poot let the enemy occupy the city while he gathered troops and then attacked in overwhelming force. The army lost fifteen hundred men, all its artillery and ammunition, several thousand rifles, mules, supplies—and the entire band, along with its instruments. They've taught many young Cruzob how to beat drums and blow bugles."

"But doesn't the government—anyone—care about the slaves?"

Dionisio shrugged. "Mérida has more pressing worries, even when it's not under siege, as it is right now. Sometimes a well-to-do family will hunt for and ransom a member, but most of these people will live here till they die."

"How terrible!"

His face tightening, Dionisio said coldly, "Is it more terrible than Mayas being slaves?"

"But some of these are Mayas!" Mercy argued.

"Yes. They are *hidalgos,* as Mayas were called who fought for *ladinos* against the rebels, or Pacificos from Chichénha, who had also agreed to make peace with the

284

ladinos. And there was slavery, wasn't there, in your Texas? Black men like those in Belize?"

There was no answer to that. After a moment, Dionisio relented. "You can be glad for one thing, Doña Mercy. Very young captives are brought up as Cruzob, and any child is born free. At least there'll be no generations of slavery."

Then in that, the Cruzob were superior to whites, but Mercy felt sad, almost guilty, when she saw the women carrying water or cooking over the fires, hurrying to obey their masters. She could so easily have been one of them, but in a short time she'd be leaving, while they spent their weeks and months and years serving warriors who might have killed their families and burned their homes.

Dionisio let Mercy fetch water from the *cenote* to support the fiction that she was his prisoner, but the fruits of her efforts at tortilla-making were so lopsided and tough that he begged her to let him bring them fresh from the barracks. He brought in game and fowl and traded an excess for honey and eggs. Their stews and pit-roasted meats were tasty, and Dionisio cooked as much as Mercy did.

In spite of the grim circumstances, it was almost like playing house. The cool white-mortared hut had no furniture except for a couple of log stools and a cooking stone. During the day, the hammocks were slung out of the way. Mercy washed their clothes a little distance from the *cenote* where there was a natural rock basin, a good place to beat and rub soil from their garments.

If Dionisio hadn't been with her most of the time, she'd have been lonely. The wives of the officers and officials stared at her with curiosity and some jealousy, doubtless thinking her far too indulged for a slave.

One day at the wellspring she saw a child wheeze and strangle with asthma and told the mother that copal fumes would help. She offered to show her if some copal could be found. Since this was the child of *a maestro cantor,* who had a supply of the incense, Mercy was able to quickly demonstrate the treatment. After that, she was sometimes approached about one ailment or another and helped when she could.

Often the *maestros cantores* were taught the skills of *H-men* along with their religious functions, and they knew some cures, but though Mercy talked to several of the priests, she thought Chepa knew more medicine than all of them together.

"I've told them you're Ixchel," Dionisio teased one day when they were walking. "They're beginning to believe it." He sobered. "Don't be too good a doctor or they might want to keep you here."

"Could they do that?" Mercy asked in quick alarm.

"The cross can order anything."

"But you promised . . . "

His golden eyes went over her with that strange meditativeness that made her wonder what he really thought and felt. "I'll keep my promise. But if the cross ordered you to stay and I helped you escape, I'd be hacked to death in the plaza if I were caught. Just a warning, Ixchel—don't be too merciful."

"But I can't *not* help when I can!"

Watching her, he sighed and smiled. "No. That's how you make yourself."

"What?"

"You make your real face, your real heart, from what you do, from your intent. You are for healing. It's your nature." His smile deepened and there was great tenderness in it, as if he knew and accepted something difficult. "But freedom is your nature. When it was known the quetzals were released from Señor Kensington's courtyard as your wish, some called you the Quetzal Lady."

"The workers knew about that?"

"Oh, much came from house servants with families in the village: the Frenchman's stove of many ovens; the peculiar food; when Señor Kensington had women beaten to arouse himself; when he had a young boy. It was believed that after you came he dropped those amusements."

And amused himself with me. Mercy shrugged. "That's over. He must be dead. I want to forget it."

Mostly she could. Only now and then did she dream of his weight, his inexorable hands, and his devouring mouth, just as she sometimes dreamed the terror of the crocodile coming toward her. But now she always roused to hear Dionisio's quiet breathing from the hammock only a few feet away. Once when she must have been moaning, she awoke to find him caressing her, murmuring reassurance as one does to a child in nightmare. He was a *batab*, a fighter, and she had seen him whipped into unconsciousness rather than be Eric's assassin. He was clearly respected and valued by these hard-bitten,

286

battled-proved Cruzob. Yet there was a gentleness in him, a sensitive response to the world around them that he seemed to wish to share with Mercy.

"Forget the estate," he told her now. "But remember the people who were helped by your medicine. Remember the flight of quetzals." His voice changed. She knew he was reciting poetry or holy words, as he sometimes did.

"On an emerald pyramid the quetzal bird is singing.
Within he sings, within he cries, alone the quetzal bird."

"Beautiful," she said as they turned from the cleared land into forest. "Did the poet have a name?"

"Poets, singers—they had no names, no more than the artists who carved the temples. Poetry comes from the gods; surely the man is only a voice." Dionisio laughed softly. "We believe that flowers and poetry are the ways gods speak to men."

"Gods?" Mercy frowned. "But you're Christian, Dionisio!"

"Yes. But when I plant corn, I still make offerings. The corn gods, called *yuntzilob,* take care of my cornfield and village. The great God can't worry about such things. His concern is the soul." Dionisio chuckled. "Most of the time, I care more about my corn than my soul. Those who plant in your country, don't they beseech the spirits?"

"Protestants have only one God for everything, and He's asked to give good crops. I think that in Europe there were celebrations, especially at harvest time. But now, a ceremony called Thanksgiving, celebrated by a big meal late in the fall, is about all we have left."

"Maybe your God didn't want to share offerings with the *yuntzilob,*" decided the Maya. "Your people should be careful. When your God is busy with wars and governments, He may forget the fields."

There was seldom a drought in east Texas, but freezes and blights struck often. Mercy could imagine that to a farmer farther west, it would be comforting to believe that his wheat or corn was guarded by beneficent spirits hovering just above him

"Do the *yuntzilob* bring rain, too?"

"No, it is the rain gods, the *chaacs,* that bring rain. There are several kinds of them. The four most important stand at the four directions of the earth, the eastern one being the strongest. Some *chaacs* bring the soft, steady rains, others cause lightning, there are 'flooding-sky' *chaacs*, and even sweeper *chaacs*, which clean up the heavens after the rains."

They were passing a field cleared from the forest where a man was planting, digging holes with a pointed stick, and dropping in several grains, which he covered with all the brooding care of a mother putting her child to bed.

"When he picked that land, he set up that cross and brought gourds of gruel, which he offered to the *yuntzilob*, which were then supposed to send away the snakes and dispose of the trees being cut down. When it was time to burn, he offered more gruel and prayed to Jesucristo for the spiraling wind that helps the flame burn as it should. This wind is the soul of sinners who must pay for their wrongdoings by blowing fire through cornfields." He stared at her in wonder. "And men in your land do none of this?"

"No. They pray if there's drought or disease, but they don't make offerings ahead of time—unless you count what some give to their churches."

Dionisio frowned so at this that Mercy tried to explain that in the United States corn was only one of many crops, that there were grains such as wheat, rye, and oats, plus potatoes, many vegetables, and fruits; cattle, pigs, poultry, eggs, and dairy products were also depended on. Dionisio shook his head at such outlandish habits.

"Corn is our main food. It makes our bodies now as surely as the gods made our ancestors from maize after other substances failed."

He told her then how the Tzotzil Mayas cut a child's umbilical cord over an ear of corn. This bloody grain was then planted in a special little field where it was carefully tended, since its growth foretold the child's. All the family ate this blood crop in a special meal.

"The Tzotzils have another belief you would like," he said with that warm, protective smile that made her feel touched by sun-gentled wind. "They think unweaned babies who die are wrapped in a soft mantle and placed in a great tree with many breasts, which the children rest upon and suckle. A good heaven for babies, yes?"

"Oh, yes!"

A screech came from the edge of the field. "He's the guardian of the cornfield." Dionisio pointed out a small hawk in a tree. "He scares blackbirds away from the corn.

He belongs to the *yuntzilob* and should never be hurt, nor should the white-winged or white-breasted doves, or red-billed pigeons, or the x-kol bird, which sings for the corn and keeps it contented, and another that stretches the corn plants, or the bird that whistles to call up the rain."

It was beginning to seem to Mercy that growing corn was the true Mayan religion, one that went back to the beginnings. If people anywhere got most of their food from one source, that source would almost be a god. "We call corn the jade of divine grace, and sometimes the Grace of God," said Dionisio, reading her thoughts. "And we believe it's a sin to waste it and that drought can be caused if people trade it for liquor."

"Who's planting your corn while you're away? And who acts as *batab?*"

"When I bound myself for rifles, my lieutenant assumed my duties, and, of course, he has helpers and the council of elders. My wife and child died two years ago, so there is only my mouth to feed, and my brother will plant enough for that."

He paused when he mentioned his wife.

"I'm sorry you lost your family," Mercy said.

"My wife was like a flower. Like a flower, she withered, quickly, with fever, a few days after the child was born."

There was nothing to say to that, but Mercy knew now why he treasured the baby heaven of soft mantles and the warm-breasted tree. It was a time of flowering, and as they skirted a village and started back, he picked for her some of the large rose-red cups of the frangipani, then urged her to smell their almost dizzying fragrance. "It's good for wounds," he said, "and it's always been known as the flower of passion, of desire."

She felt his gaze burning her and could not look at him. She loved Zane! Why could Dionisio make her feel like a bloom longing to open, like a field parched for rain?

It was weak, shameful, not to be allowed.

But natural. His care and protection and wanting you to know about his people have planted something in you, something that's growing. Now will you say that he's your brother? she scorned. You know better. When he touches you, flame spreads. You want him. This is a thing of bodies.

But she knew it was more than that.

*　　*　　*

During the following days, her tension increased, though she couldn't see any change in Dionisio. He was like the sun, from which sometimes she hid or other times sought, there and constant.

Was it possible to love two men? She tried to summon Zane, remember their loving, his eyes and mouth. But that seemed a world ago, two worlds, really: Eric's estate and Chan Santa Cruz. She loved Zane. But he was far away, like a memory of summer, while Dionisio had saved her life and was shielding her now.

In the white world she would never have known him like this. Here he was her interpreter, the revealer of his kingdom. He was more to her than a man—he was the revealer of secrets, some terrible, some beautiful, of his world.

The rains had not yet come, though the corn was planted, and one day they encountered a tortoise sunning near a rocky cave. It had tears in its eyes, and Dionisio said it wept for men who needed rain and that its tears would help bring it.

"The tortoise belongs to the *chaacs*," the young *batab* said. "So do other creatures that live with them in *cenotes* and caves: frogs, bats, and toads. They shouldn't be killed."

Perhaps the tortoise's tears moved the *chaacs*, for the rains began that day, violent at first, then steady and persistent. Morning was bright, but afternoon brought furious storms. Water began to collect in rock hollows and wherever it couldn't sink into the ground. Dionisio was at rosary when one of the slave women, scarcely more than a girl, ran up to the hut and tinkled the bells above the door.

"My baby, he's drowned!" she cried in Spanish. "He wandered off while I was making tortillas and I found him in a ditch! Can you help him?"

Mercy put the little boy across her lap and let water drain from his mouth, pressing on his sides. His face was bluish. Too late? Was it too late? He gave no sign of life.

A method that had worked once for Elkanah shot through her desperate thoughts. He thought it was how the prophet Elijah brought the widow's son back to life.

"I'll try!" she told the frantic woman. "Pray!"

Placing the boy on his back, she crouched over him and opened her mouth on his, sucking out as powerfully as she could, then breathing in. Out-in, out-in, she sent the air.

Out-in, out-in . . . Their bodies were glued together with ditch water and sweat. Was that a faint motion? Was there anything? No. The child was still.

Dead. Of course he was dead. Dead when he was brought to her. But she couldn't get up and face the mother, so she kept breathing in and out, trying to start the child's lungs, trying to begin that rhythm, so wonderful, that people took for granted until it stopped.

There was nothing but the small prone body, nothing but this willing it to breathe. As if from a distant place, Mercy heard the mother praying, and she heard Elkanah's words: *You must not stop. Keep breathing. Breathe for the child.*

And then the body moved, the boy choked, then struggled. Mercy took her mouth from his as he spewed water and the contents of his stomach. Mercy held his head as the mother knelt, gathering him to her.

"What is happening?" called Dionisio from the door.

The woman lifted her child, who clutched her tightly and began to cry. But he was breathing. "My son was dead!" said the mother. It was to Mercy like an echo of Elkanah's voice telling the Old Testament story. "My son was dead, but he is alive again!"

She had sunk to her knees, trying to kiss Mercy's hands, but Mercy had made her sit down and gave both mother and son gourd cups of the honey-sweetened herb brew she and Dionisio enjoyed each evening when he returned from services.

"The child wasn't dead," she explained slowly, asking Dionisio to make sure the woman understood, because she certainly didn't want it spread around that she could revive corpses. "I gave him air till he could breathe himself—a practice my father taught me."

"It was a long time," the mother protested. "My Juanito didn't move. He *was* dead!"

"No. The spark of life was in him. Luckily, I could fan it back into a glow."

Rocking the boy, the mother pressed her lips stubbornly together.

"Listen," said Dionisio sternly, "it would be poor thanks to this lady to make her sound like a witch or miracle worker. What if the *tatich* was jealous? What if she were asked to do something beyond her powers?

Would you see her die for witchcraft under machetes in the plaza?"

"Madonna save us, no!" whispered the woman, her eyes widening. "I . . . I hadn't thought, Lord! But others saw. Others said I was wasting my time, that he was dead."

"Then tell them he wasn't," Dionisio ordered curtly. "Say the lady knows, from her own country, a way of sometimes restoring one who has *almost* drowned."

"Yes, Lord," promised the woman. Her dark eyes came to Mercy, thanking her more deeply than words. "I'll tell them that. I'll even say he stirred while I was carrying him."

Putting down the gourds, with thanks, she went to the door, shifting the boy to her hip. He had stopped fretting now and regarded Mercy with black Indian eyes, though his skin was fair. He was a very handsome child who would grow up free; at least his mother had that for comfort. "Go with God, *señora*. I will pray for you each day of my life."

She left. Mercy poured tea for Dionisio, but he was plainly troubled. "Was the boy dead?" he finally asked.

Mercy stared. "I thought so. But he couldn't have been. Once my father did the same kind of breathing for over an hour and revived a man. Another time it didn't work."

"The story will spread." Dionisio frowned. "You'll be expected to do the impossible, blamed when you can't, and if I ask to leave my service two weeks early, everyone will be sure I am bewitched."

Their eyes met, locked.

"Perhaps I am," he said.

"What?"

"Enchanted. It is my *castigo*."

"Punishment?"

"To desire what I cannot have—because I tried to have it in a small way for a small time. I thought that would cure me, purge the madness."

She watched him in distress and a sort of fear. As long as the force between them wasn't in words, as long as it wasn't admitted, it didn't have to be confronted. He seemed driven now to voice it, keeping a distance from her, though his gaze held her.

"Do you understand, Ixchel? I could have taken you to that hacienda and returned here for my service.

292

It would have been much extra travel and time, but what could that matter when I might still have been working in Señor Kensington's fields? I could have delivered you to your people and have come again to my own."

"Dionisio . . . "

"I told myself it would be good for one of the *dzuls* to live with us, learn our ways, and have that vision to show others. Later, when we walked and you laughed or your eyes grew as large as a child's at something I said or showed you, I thought . . . forget what I thought!"

"Surely you're too worried about this. The slaves may gossip, but outside of their compound probably no one will hear of it."

He gave a short, harsh laugh. "We are a people of miracles. Our existence, this city, is a miracle. The story will sprout wings and fly straight to the *tatich*."

Crossing the room, he didn't touch her but stood so near that she was aware of the heat of his body. "We must wait and hope that my standing as an independent ally will allow us to go at the appointed time. But if the leaders wish to keep you as a healer or kill you as a witch, I'll get you away or die."

"Perhaps you could go to La Quinta and get them to offer ransom. Even if my fiancé isn't there, his mayordomo would do that—I think."

"And what might happen to you while I was gone, even if the *tatich* accepted ransom?" Dionisio stood tensely, balanced as if receiving a load that took all his brain and strength to manage. "No, I won't leave without you, and if you stay, I'll always be with you in this place, for I shall die here."

She couldn't reproach him for bringing her to the city, any more than she could regret saving Juanito. "You'll always be with me wherever I am," she told him. "When I see cornfields, birds of the *yuntzilob*, the tortoise weeping, smell frangipani, or feel the sun, I will remember you."

It was strange and formal, a kind of swearing. "It's not that you're graceful," he said, "or that you're lovely in all your parts or had compassion for me. You are for my spirit. And you are to me Ixchel, of healing, Ixchel, of the moon, Ixchel, of loving."

She put her hands in his. He drew in his breath. Then they went out of the hut, past sentries, out of the city, and into the woods, where they found a bed of wild thyme. The moon shone on them and the plants were damp from earlier rain, but she felt consumed in sun.

She felt no guilt, no unfaithfulness to Zane, and after some puzzled searching of her feelings, she didn't try to. This bond with Dionisio was deep-rooted in something other than themselves, elemental affinities joining together in spite of the otherness that must divide them. They were together for this time, in this place, with possible death before them and, absolutely, separation. Zane was her love, her life, her home country. Dionisio was another world.

Two days after she had revived the child, Juanito, Dionisio was on sentry duty and she was washing clothes when she sensed someone watching. Glancing around, she stiffened. Beyond the *cenote* stood a squat, broad-shouldered man with graying hair whom Dionisio had pointed out as the *tata nohoch zul*, Great Father Spy. She went on with her rubbing and rinsing, hoping he'd go away, but he just stood there.

At last, when further delay would have been obvious, she wrung out the garments, put them in a hemp carrier, and was nearing the plaza when the man stepped in front of her.

"I thought you'd make those clothes into rags," he said in excellent Spanish. His skin was light and she thought he was mestizo, as many of the Cruzob leaders were, including the present *tatich*. Pitiless eyes bored into her. "It is odd that one with your gifts should be such a zealous washerwoman."

"It is my work, *señor*."

He frowned. "But you do not work much. It's no secret that the *batab* of Macanche is the prisoner of his prisoner."

"*Señor*," she said desperately, "I don't understand."

"You are a *dzul*, but not Spanish." He frowned. "Are you from over the great water, like that fool Maximilian and his woman, who passed through Yucatán, dancing in Mérida and Campeche, giving medals and smiles and promises? The booted ones of Mérida followed her like puppies, eager to fight for a foreign empire when they wouldn't defend their own frontier!" He spat on the stony ground. "Well, they have their reward—trapped in Mérida! General Traconis sustained siege in Tihosuco for fifty days, and he may hold out longer in the fortress of

San Benito, but there'll be no relief. Maximilian has surrendered. His empire has fallen. And I pray that Juárez,
who is also Indian, will not spare his life."

"It's over?"

"Yes. But I ask the questions. Woman, are you one of
Maximilian's foreigners?"

Mercy thought of Carlota, hoped the young empress'
insanity would let her escape to happier days. "I'm not
European," she said to the chief spy. "I'm from the
United States, from Texas."

"Ah! Texas! You rebelled against Mexico!"

"Before I was born."

"Yes! Santa Ana made many Yucatecans, many Indians, go fight in those wars with Texas and the United
States. And I recall that boats from the Texas Navy were
paid to protect Yucatán from Mexico." He chuckled. "It's
good, very good, to watch *dzuls* fight! Would that they
might devour one another and vomit the filth into hell!"

Mercy's arm ached from holding the wet clothes. She
switched the hemp carrier to her other hand. "May I go,
señor?"

An unpleasant smile played on his thin lips. "I'll accompany you, slave, while you put your laundry out to
dry. Then you'll accompany me. You are greatly honored. The *tatich* wishes to speak with you."

Mercy's heart turned to heavy, freezing ice. They had
picked a time when Dionisio was out of the way. Even
if he knew, how could he oppose them? He would die
for her, she was certain, but what good was that?

Be calm, she told herself, *calm. Don't show your fear.
It may be only curiosity. You're not an enemy; you've
done nothing wrong.*

"I am honored," she told the spy. "It'll be interesting
to speak with the *tatich*." She gambled, thinking it best
to show any strength she had before the Cruzob hierarchy
committed themselves to any action they couldn't retreat
from without losing face. "Perhaps if General of the
Plaza Crescencio Poot is in the city, he would like to send
a message to my fiancé."

Startled, the spy stared fixedly at her. "What has the
general to do with him?"

"I'm to marry Zane Falconer, of La Quinta Dirección," Mercy said. "Long ago his father saved the general's life."

"I've heard of that. Most interesting! The general isn't

here, but when he returns I will ask him if he wishes to speak with you."

"Thank you." Mercy started for the hut, aware that she'd thrown the spy off balance and hoping that the information would possibly help her without causing trouble.

No one had fought longer or more ferociously for the cross than Poot. She couldn't imperil him, but in the moment of speaking, she hadn't had time to reflect on all the possibilities. Dread made her break into perspiration at the chance that jarring the leaders' memory about La Quinta might make them decide that while Poot had owed a debt to Zane's father, it didn't extend to the son.

Her fingers were clumsy and trembled as she spread the clothes on several bushes and turned to the *tata nohoch zul.*

"Arrange your hair," he ordered critically. "For the fiancée of a rich man, you wear shabby rags. Have you nothing better?"

She shook her head, angry, yet somewhat amused that she was evidently supposed to preen for this interrogation. He glanced around the bare hut and looked even more disgusted, since there was no place where anything could be hidden.

He picked up and examined her books, squinted at her father's letters, and scowled at the *Badianus* excerpts. "These are in Texas language?"

"English. Our language is like that of the English in Belize."

"Say some," he directed. "Speak this English."

Dumbfounded, she said the first thing that came into her head. "I'm Mercy Cameron, from Texas, and though England is across the water, English is the language I speak."

"It is not!" said the man combatively. "I've been much in Belize and understand many words, though I don't speak it. Your language *may* be a debased dialect. It isn't English."

Mercy couldn't keep from laughing, though the situation was far from humorous. "I'm sure the English people would agree with you! But, you see, the eastern part of our country was settled mostly by people who were English. I would suppose that Spanish-speaking people here sound different from those in Castile."

He studied her suspiciously and peered again at the books. "What are these about?"

"They tell about cures and medicines. My father was a doctor."

"An *H-men?*"

"No. He only tried to make people well. He couldn't see the future or make spells."

"Could he raise the dead?"

The question was as sudden as a blow. "He couldn't," said Mercy, "and I don't think anyone else can."

After a long, piercing stare, the chief spy dropped the books and letters. "Come," he said. "The *tatich* is waiting."

20

Bonifacio Novelo, one of the few survivors from the early times of the War of the Castes, was priest-king of his people, supreme military and spiritual commander of the Cruzob. He was reclining in a hammock within the arcade of his palace, savoring a sliced mango, and though he didn't rise at Mercy's appearance, his smile was affable.

"Be seated, *señora*," he invited. "Will you have hot chocolate? Coffee?"

"No, thank you." Mercy didn't want to be served by one of the slaves, either white or native, and the thought crossed her mind that slavery in the South would have ended at once if all the dominant race had undergone a stretch of bondage.

The *tatich* was heavy-fleshed, perhaps sixty, wearing cotton trousers embellished with lace from the knee down, embossed sandals, a brightly striped shirt, and a sash. Around his neck hung an enormous gold cross on a chain of massive links. He had been known twenty years ago as the "assassin of Valladolid." The blood of hundreds of helpless women, children, and aged victims was upon him, and yet the expression on his handsome weathered face was frank and genial.

"Then you must taste my fruit," he said. Leaning forward, he pressed a mellow slice against her lips so that she had no polite choice except to eat it.

The *tata nohoch zul* spoke in such rapid Mayan that Mercy comprehended only that he was summarizing her answers to his questions. The *tatich* nodded thoughtfully and gave her a smile of great charm.

"You learned your skills from your father?"

"Yes, and from a Mayan woman at La Quinta. She taught me much about herbs."

"The child you breathed life into—where did you learn that?"

"From my father. But the child wasn't dead, *señor*."

"Some say he was."

"I was afraid so, too, but I started his breathing by forcing air in and out of his lungs—like a bellows—and it worked."

Did he believe her? Mercy's palms were clammy, but she made herself sit in a relaxed fashion, as if this were a social call It was impossible to guess from the *tatich's* bland face what he thought.

"If you were to marry the owner of La Quinta, how did you become a captive of the *batab* of Macanche, who's been in Belize?"

Mercy gave the essentials of her abduction by Eric, but she omitted having known Dionisio on the estate, simply saying that she had run off and, freed by the Icaiche raid, he'd come upon her and made her come with him.

"But you, of course, wish to return to your fiancé?"

"Of course." Mercy didn't know what more to say without creating problems for Dionisio.

The *tatich* asked her questions about Texas and about how she came to Yucatán, then roared with laughter when he pried out of her the admission that her husband had lost her to Zane at cards. "For one who looks so young and innocent, you've had adventures!" he said. "And you may have more. Many women have wished to marry the *batab* since his wife died, but it's said he looked at no one till he turned up with you." The *tatich* frowned. "How do you know your fiancé is alive?"

"I hope it very much."

The huge mestizo shrugged. "It is a pity the *ladinos* don't finish each other off. If they hadn't warred so

298

much, always struggling for power, Campeche against Mérida, one general against another, they could have wiped us out. But now we're too strong."

He and the chief spy harked back to former battles, comrades, and foes, both dead and alive. "Cecilio Chi— now, there was a strategist!" sighed the *tatich*. "He'd fought in Yucatán's war against Mexico and he knew how to take a city. When we came down on Valladolid late in 1847, he first burned the outlying haciendas, took the cattle, cotton, honey, coffee, and money and sent them to be traded for weapons in Belize. Next he burned the villages and crushed small outposts, but he never tried to fight a large attack; he just melted into the trees till he had the *ladinos* scattered along narrow trails where a rush with machetes would wipe them out! A real general, Cecilio!"

"Dead for a woman!" said the chief spy with a scornful glance at Mercy. "But at least his whoring wife didn't outlive him long!"

Talk turned to the present and Mercy learned that Santa Ana, being deported by Juárez, had been taken off a United States steamship near Sisal and ordered shot by Colonel Peraza. Zane's commander! Apparently Peraza's advisors (could that include Zane?) had warned him that since the old dictator had been taken from the protection of the U.S. flag, his execution could cause international problems, so Santa Ana's life had been spared.

"I'd take a machete to that one," said the *tata nohoch zul*. "He gave his favorites the proceeds from selling Mayan slaves to Cuba."

"He will die in his bed," predicted the *tatich* and looked accusingly at Mercy. "You of Texas should have killed him when you had the chance."

"That might have saved Mexico and Yucatán a lot of trouble," Mercy agreed.

So the fighting was still going on at Mérida. Zane would be there unless he was dead or wounded. Though she mourned his continuing danger, she rejoiced that he probably hadn't seen her letter or been told about her apparent departure for the United States. With luck, if she got out of Chan Santa Cruz, she might be at La Quinta when he came home!

This was such a heady, dizzying thought that she didn't realize the interview was at an end. The spy touched her bare arm with his cold machete blade and jerked his head toward the plaza.

"Good-bye," said the *tatich* paternally, reaching for another mango and swinging himself gently. "It has been interesting to speak of your country, yes, and interesting to meet such a valuable woman."

Confused, Mercy protested. *"Señor,* I'm not rich. I have nothing."

"Too modest!" he teased, shaking a finger. "You seem to be worth a great deal to at least three men though it's likely the Icaiche killed your Englishman. So do we ask ransom from your fiancé? Do we tell your *batab* the cost of keeping you is a stronger alliance, utter commitment? Or would the prestige of the cross be enhanced by having a healer at the shrine city?"

"I'm not that experienced, *señor!"* Mercy cried, appalled. "Many of your *H-men* can do as much or more."

The *tatich* smiled. "None of them has restored a child to life. Yes, you might be the most valuable of all to attract rich offerings to the shrine. I will think about it."

He raised his plump hand in dismissal.

"But, *señor . . .* " Mercy began.

The *tata nohoch zul* gripped her arm and moved her from the arcade. "You've been honored to see the *tatich.* He will consider your best use for the cross." A smile made those straight lips more cruel than ever. "Whatever your future, woman, it should be interesting."

He'd enjoy her pleading, which would gain nothing, and stood braced with his legs apart, arms folded, barring her from the *tatich,* who had killed so many seen so many of his own die, that any person must be to him little more than a pawn.

She reached the shade of her street, but even as she turned into the hut, she felt the spy watching her, and even within the walls, she felt that he could see her.

"He's not *tata nohoch zul* for nothing," reminded Dionisio when she told him of this uncanny fear after his first outrage at her interrogation had been controlled. "He is a careful man, and"—the *batab* finished somberly—"he will be watching you . . . and me."

"All this because I helped a little boy!"

"It's necessary to your *tamen,* your harmony, to heal when you can." He drew her against him, stroking her hair and shoulders, thinking aloud. "For protection from the Icaiches, my council of elders has been favoring

300

closer bonds with the Cruzob. Anything I negotiate must be approved by them, of course, but perhaps the best thing is for me to go at once to the *tatich* and offer him a company for guard duty one month of the year and our full support in battle against whatever enemy."

"You mustn't involve your people for my sake."

He stiffened in offense. "I'm a *batab*. If the good of my people required it, I would machete you myself. That's my *tamen*. But a stronger alliance will be, I think, to the benefit of Macanche. I can offer it in good conscience. The *tatich* knows it must be approved by the council."

"Do you think he'll accept?"

Dionisio spread his hands. "Such a binding would be more valuable than any ransom paid in money, especially if the Icaiches grow strong enough to challenge the Cruzob for their old lands. And it's possible that once the Juaristas consolidate their power, Mexico might help Mérida try to crush Chan Santa Cruz."

"Then the alliance should be tempting, certainly."

"Yes. But a healer at the shrine might be even more useful. Besides an increased flow of offerings, the mystery and power of the cross would be enhanced, knitting the empire more closely together, cutting the chance of vassal *batabs* building their own strength to the detriment of Chan Santa Cruz. The cross united and heartened a defeated fugitive people. But fresh miracles give new life to old ones, true?"

Mercy saw the logic of that. "Dionisio, what do you think he'll decide?"

"He won't decide till he's had time to think over and test the appeal of a mystical shrine healer. He'll gain this by telling me that he can't seriously consider an alliance till it's confirmed by the council, which means that I'll have to travel to my village and back."

"I can't go with you?"

"Unless the alliance is accepted, they'll never let you out of Chan Santa Cruz. You won't be able to step from the hut without the *tata nohoch zul* hearing of it almost at once."

"What if the *tatich* decides your people will make the alliance sooner or later, anyway, and he wants to keep me here?"

"I swore to take you to your own place. It may take a while, but you'll go free, Ixchel, if it takes my life."

His eyes caressed her from across the room. Before

301

she could move to him, he turned and strode toward the plaza.

Dionisio's acumen was proved. The *tatich* did exactly as he'd predicted, withholding a decision until Dionisio could present an official offer approved by the council of elders.

"And he's delaying all he can," Dionisio said bitterly. "I asked to go at once to Macanche and serve the rest of my guard time when I returned, but he wouldn't permit it."

"I'm glad you're not going just yet," Mercy said with a small shudder. "Maybe by the time you leave I'll have gotten used to being spied on, but right now I'm afraid!"

He took her cold hands, warming them in his. "No need to fear their hurting you. You're precious as jade, as treasured as quetzal plumes!"

"But what if I'm asked to treat someone I can't help?"

"The *tatich* will announce that your medicine was impotent because the cross knew the patient was a sinner or doomed to terrible trials if he lived." Dionisio chuckled. "Don't worry. It's to the *tatich*'s best interests to stress your successes and bury your failures—quietly."

"But I hate for people to think I can do more than I really can! Suppose they carried a dead baby in from some far-off village or someone died making the journey who might have lived otherwise? What if . . . "

Shaking his head, Dionisio hushed her lips with his fingers. "Your father was a wise, good man. Did none of his patients die?"

"Of course, but . . . he was a *real* doctor!"

"Oh." Dionisio's brow puckered. "You mean he'd accept and do his best for people who he knew were going to die? He could endure their deaths because, perhaps, he made these easier, and there were other people he could help?"

Mercy bit her lip. "I don't think I'd be a good doctor. Maybe I never can accept that there'll be those I can't do anything for. The reason I worked with Juanito so long was that I couldn't bear to get up and face his mother."

"A good thing in his case." Dionisio held her and she wondered why, though he was only a few years older than she, he often seemed so wise, possessed of a fatalistic understanding that made her feel childish and spoiled. "Don't be troubled, my heart. Until he decides what to

302

do, the *tatich* won't make an effort to spread tales of your powers. You won't suddenly be surrounded by the ailing. Let me give you a thought. It's from our prophet, Chilam Balam. It helped me heal from Señor Kensington's whipping, and also when my wife and our child died." Dionisio's voice softened. " *'His word was a measure of grace, and he broke and pierced the backbone of the mountains. . . . Who? Father, Thou knowest: He who is tender in heaven. . . .'* "

She received his gift, this talisman that couldn't be stolen. *Tender in heaven.* The words were like him. They lay down in his hammock, sweetly close. He talked to her in Mayan, as he often did, telling her stories—children's stories of gods, animals, and mortals. For that night, he could have been an older brother, cheering her in the darkness.

Early in June Dionisio's service was completed and he set out for Macanche with his rifle, machete, bag of corn-meal, and water gourd. "I'll return as quickly as I can," he said. "But councils enjoy long arguments and persuadings. Be patient."

He held her, his arms warm and strong and cherishing. She walked with him to the western way out of the village and watched till he turned at the edge of the forest and raised a hand in farewell before he vanished. Her throat burned and she fought back tears.

He'd be back. There was an excellent chance that the *tatich* would consider the alliance more useful than a *dzul* healer, that Dionisio would be able to take her straightaway to La Quinta.

And then?

Then he'd go to his own village. In a year or two he'd marry and have children, just as she hoped to have babies with Zane, at least one with hair and eyes like his. But she'd never forget Dionisio, his forest, his people, and all that he'd taught her.

If Zane could accept—and she wasn't sure he could—that she'd been used repeatedly by Eric Kensington, he should be able to accept the good and natural thing between her and the *batab*, though she hoped Zane would never question her till she had to lie or try to explain. Zane was her lover, her man. But she loved Dionisio as she did the sun and flowers and birds, knowing they weren't hers.

As she turned from the western boundary, the *tata nohoch zul* stood in her way, his stout, hard belly protruding under his bright sash, his eyes narrow as he smiled.

"You're sad at your master's leaving? He's young and lusty, yes? But save your tears for later. The *tatich* would speak with you now."

She fought down the urge to cry out to Dionisio. Braced for almost anything, she followed the chief spy to the long arcaded palace. The supreme leader again occupied his hammock, enjoying fruit, crusty bread with honey, and aromatic coffee. He wore lace-trimmed white trousers still, but this time his shirt also was white, richly embroidered.

He motioned for her to take a stool near the hammock. "The bread is fresh-baked," he said. "And you like coffee, don't you?"

The golden-brown loaf did smell tantalizing but it must have been made by one of the women in the slave compound. Mercy declined it and the coffee, also.

"The *batab*'s departure has left you too sad to eat?" chided the *tatich*, devouring alternate bites of honeycomb and mango. "Strange, when you are affianced to another man." His eyelids drooped and a slow, sensual smile curved his lips. "Possibly you cling to whatever man is closest."

There was no mistaking the suggestion in the deep, pleasant voice. Mercy went cold. If he wanted her, she was completely in his power. The Cruzob priesthood wasn't celibate. Under the *ladino* clergy, villagers had preferred a priest to have one woman so that he'd leave the others alone. There were no moral checks on the Great Father. Mercy stared beyond him, at the execution tree in the plaza, summoning her courage, trying to still her careening thoughts.

He was physically repulsive to her, but she dreaded even more the smell of death and power about him, lives and pain absorbed and fattening him like the food he took. It made no sense, perhaps, after Eric, but she knew she really would rather die than belong to this man. She would rather run off and take her chances in the jungle, or try to kill him, though that would mean being hacked to bits by machetes.

"The *batab* was kind to me," she said firmly. "He told me much about the Mayas. We were friends in the soul."

The *tatich* laughed. "But souls inhabit bodies. Will

304

you say you never pleasured each other amidst the wild thyme?"

Involuntarily, Mercy glanced at the spy. So he'd been watching even then. She turned proudly to the mestizo. "I'll say that what's between the *batab* and me was for us, for our spirits, and it doesn't concern the man I wish to marry."

"He'll be a most unusual male if he agrees," said the *tatich* dryly. He let honeycomb melt in his mouth as he lay back and studied her, then swallowed and gave a small dismissing shrug. "But if the cross allows its vassal, Dionisio, to keep you, I shall use my influence to get him to offer you for ransom to your *dzul.* It's all right for Cruzob to keep white slaves, but it's not good that they should love them." His broad face twisted with disgust. "This thing of souls! You would blight his, destroy him!"

"No!"

"Yes. It is as our prophet wrote: *'The* dzuls *trampled the flowers, and they sucked to death the flowers of others so that their own might live. They killed the flower of* Quetzalcoatl.' " The sonorous tone boomed on accusingly. " *'The* dzuls *only came to castrate our sun! And the children of their children remain among us and we receive only their bitterness.' "*

The *tatich* brooded, his dark eyes fixed on Mercy, though he appeared to be seeing something else. "You're honey to the *batab* now, and he is the sun to open your bloom. But when your honey's gone and your flower is withered, the bitterness left would unman him. I need whole men. Yes, I will try to persuade the *batab* to sell you to the *dzul*—if I accept the alliance. Now, tell me of your country. How are the leaders chosen? And is it possible, as I have heard, that heretics live beside Catholics? Will the black slaves have their own country now that they're free? And what of the Indians? I've heard of the Comanches, very fierce, and the Apaches, too. Some of the Mexican troops that were sent to fight here had also served on those northern frontiers."

He had a keen, wide-ranging intelligence. Having apparently decided not to concern himself with Mercy's body, he feasted on her mind, drawing from her information she'd never analyzed or considered before in depth. Once she believed the sexual danger past, Mercy found herself stimulated and engrossed. She even accepted coffee when the military band was playing sprightly polkas interspersed with religious music at the eight o'clock service. The *tatich* said that nowadays he often let a *maestro cantor* celebrate the mass, and that he himself worshipped in his private chapel.

"I don't fight now, either," he chuckled with a sigh. "Too old, too weary. I've earned my rest, *señora*." He extended his muscular, heavy hand toward the plaza and swept it to indicate the shrine city. "When I think of when God first spoke to us in the little valley yonder! We were starving, beaten, whipped. *Ladinos* cut down the tree by the *cenote,* the Mother of Crosses, they defiled our chapel, and looked on us as carrion! We couldn't plant corn. So many of us died. But the cross saved us, *señora.* Counting allies, I command an army of eleven thousand, and I have a treasury of two hundred thousand pesos and much rare jewelry and plunder. The *ladinos* were so routed when they attacked here in 1860 that I don't think they'll ever again have the stomach for it."

The *tata nohoch zul,* standing through all their conversation, growled rapidly in Mayan. The *tatich* responded, laughing, then said to Mercy, "He thinks we should take advantage of the *ladino* war, let them bleed each other well, as they now do at Mérida, and then fall upon the victors while they're drunk and happy." He swayed the hammock gently. "Ten years ago I would have been rallying men. It would be a great chance, perhaps our last chance, to fulfill the dreams we had at first, driving out all the *ladinos,* leaving them not even Campeche and Mérida. But I've fought so many battles, *señora.* Unless the cross commands it, I won't march."

And the cross can't command it unless you do, Mercy thought. With all her heart, she was glad that the *tatich* was disinclined to risk what the Cruzob held in a challenge to the whites.

The spy spoke again and she recognized the name of Crescencio Poot and the gist of the comment, that the general might have a thirst for conquest even if the *tatich* didn't.

"The general of the plaza is under my orders," snapped Novelo. "I can send him to the whipping post or the stocks, just as I can do to anyone—from soldier to general!"

The spy bowed his head. "Indeed, Father, that is your power."

Mollified, the *tatich* resumed his questions. It was noon

306

when he gave Mercy leave to go, telling her to visit him again in the morning. Grateful that the spy ignored her, Mercy went to her hut, ate corn gruel, and tried to rest, but the loneliness was oppressive. Zane at Mérida, Dionisio on the way to Macanche—both seemed terribly far away, while the chief spy was close.

Getting out of the hammock and fastening her sandals, Mercy decided to see if she would be allowed to leave the city and walk in the woods. She could collect frangipani flowers for a healing ointment, and the flowers and bark of the magnolia were supposed to be useful for a failing heart. She needed to steep some willow leaves in case someone came to her with a fever or headache, and she hoped to find a red morning glory, which, according to the *Badianus* copy, was a good purgative.

With a hemp bag to hold her finds, Mercy passed a sentry who ordered her to stop and asked where she was going. She explained in halting Mayan that she wished to gather plants. While the sentry hesitated, a plump young man who resembled a Buddha strolled from the nearest street and told the guard he would accompany Mercy.

At first, being trailed by a man she was sure was one of the *tata nohoch zul*'s agents made her nervous, but once they reached the woods, he kept mostly out of sight. The fantastic truth was that she soon forgot him in her pleasure at finding some thistles reputedly useful for fever and an exceedingly beautiful magnolia from which she gathered blossoms and bark.

She wandered on and found herself by the cornfield where Dionisio had shown her the birds of the *yuntzilob*. In just these weeks, the corn had broken from the earth and its tender green stalks stirred very gently in the slight breeze. Passing the village as before, she encountered a tortoise among some rocks, but it wasn't crying now.

"Did your tears bring the rains?" she asked it softly.

It moved on, ignoring her, but, glancing up, she saw the skies were overcast, and she quickened her pace, reaching her hut just as the showers started. The unobtrusive young Buddha had melted away. She hoped if she was to be shadowed, he or someone equally invisible would do it, not the *tata nohoch zul*, who turned her blood to ice.

She spread out her discoveries to dry, and then there was nothing to do—nothing, and it was a long time till night. She sat in the light by the door and read her father's worn letters for the hundredth time. Even though she knew the words by heart, they encouraged her. Constantly, in what he did more than what he said, his message was that one must keep trying, help with the load of the world as much as one could, and find some grace and laughter in the struggle.

The rain had stopped. She put away the letters and decided to go to the slave compound and see if anyone was sick or if she could help with the work. She was no good at making tortillas, but she could carry water or mash the soaked corn into paste.

She skirted the plaza and the great mortared pile of the church, giving it a curious glance. She'd never been inside, but Dionisio had told her *la santísima*, the Talking Cross, was kept in a wooden chest, though there were other crosses on the altar. A sentry guarded the sanctuary day and night. She prayed that the cross would stay mute and never command the holy war that the head spy had plainly wanted.

As she started to enter the group of buildings behind the church, the Buddha came out of the shadows of the barracks. "You may not mix with the other slaves," he said in soft, apologetic Spanish.

"I wanted to see if anyone is sick."

"If they are, they'll come to you."

He watched while she went back across the plaza, trying not to show her dejection. She fetched water from the *cenote*, lingering to at least see other women come and go. The mother of Juanito smiled at her shyly but filled her buckets and hurried away at a harsh word from a sentry. Mercy went slowly back to the hut, which, without Dionisio, seemed bare, alien.

Putting down the bucket, Mercy sank into the hammock and wept. She hated Chan Santa Cruz—its walls and sentries and *tatich* and spy! Dionisio would be gone at least ten days. How would she ever stand it? And then, when he did return, what if the *tatich* refused the alliance?

What if? What if?

Maddened by tormenting questions, Mercy pressed her hands to the sides of her forehead, as if she could force them from her mind. This wouldn't do. She must pull herself together.

If the Macanche council approved, *if* the *tatich* let Dionisio keep her, it wouldn't be long till she'd be at La Quinta. The siege of Mérida couldn't go on much longer with the empire fallen. Zane would come home. The months with Eric would seem a dimming nightmare; this strange, bittersweet time with Dionisio would be a dream. After all that had happened, all she had endured, surely she could get through this little time.

Rising, she found a basket of tortillas and tamales on the cookstone. Arranged by Dionisio? Sent by the *tatich?* From Juanito's mother? Mercy didn't know, but it was nice to have something besides corn gruel and mangoes. She carried the basket outside and ate slowly in the deepening twilight, enjoying the delicate flavor of the tamales, which were wrapped in banana leaves and stuffed with flavored squash and other vegetables she didn't recognize. Savoring them to the last morsel, she sat on a crude bench, listening to the village sounds, thinking of Dionisio and hoping him safe wherever he'd slung his hammock. Then, turning her thoughts to La Quinta, she visualized Jolie, Salvador, Mayel, Chepa, and the way it'd be when Zane came home.

Clinging to this image, she went inside, washed in the dark, brushed her hair, and was soon in her hammock. She thought of the growing corn and how Dionisio would smile to see it. *Father, Thou knowest: He who is tender in heaven. . . .* She could almost hear his voice. Settling deeper into the hammock, she pretended he was telling her stories until she fell asleep.

The days took on a pattern. She spent several hours each morning with the *tatich* telling him all she could about her country and the world beyond. He was especially interested in England because of Belize, but he found it incredible that a woman ruled such a far-flung empire till Mercy pointed out to him that Belize had been colonized by the English during the reign of one of its greatest sovereigns, Elizabeth, who had encouraged her captains to attack Spanish ships.

"Can your president be a woman?" the *tatich* asked.

Mercy gasped. Such a thought had never occurred to her. "Women can't even vote," she said resentfully, for she *had* thought about this.

Novelo laughed. "Voting's not so much, *señora*. Indians were given the vote here in Yucatán while at the same time they could be forced into debt-bondage and made the same as slaves. But you say former male slaves can vote now in the United States. That makes them better citizens than women?"

"I suppose it does. But women don't vote in England, either, although they consider one capable of ruling."

When the *tatich* dismissed her, Mercy did her few chores, rested during the worst heat, and then, if it wasn't raining, went collecting herbs and plants, always trailed by the Buddha. In the evening, Juanito's mother brought tortillas and whatever else was being cooked. She was afraid to stay and chat, but she said that Dionisio had asked her to bring the food and had arranged it with the guards.

Usually, Juanito was with her. He was, she confided, the child of a handsome major who had promised to ransom her when he got enough money or trade goods saved. He lived in a village to the east, but it was almost time again for his month's duty at the shrine. Maybe this year he'd have her price.

"You'd rather marry him than go back to your people?" Mercy asked.

The woman nodded. "He's good to me. And I've been here so long, *señora!* My family were all killed in the raid when I was taken. I would rather stay with Juanito's father."

"Then I hope he has the money this year," Mercy said and thanked the woman, who smiled and hurried back to the compound.

So she had a major. That was next to a general in the Cruzob Army. Dionisio had explained that they had no colonels, skipping from general to major, captain, lieutenant, sergeant, corporal, and soldier. Except for the head spy and general of the plaza, all officers led companies and were elected on New Year's Day by the men of the company, each company being of a village after the old militia plan.

The *tatich* had decreed that no officer could command men of another company, but a few of the more powerful ones did, and since justice was administered at company or village level unless the crime was serious enough for the *tatich,* some of these commanders dominated a number of villages with their fighting men. That was one reason why the yearly month of guard duty at Chan Santa Cruz was so important, binding each able-bodied adult male to the shrine, faith, and authority of Chan Santa Cruz.

Would the Cruzob ever try to overwhelm the *ladinos* again? Or would they be content to draw in more allies, perhaps absorb the Icaiches, and actually rule all of Yucatán except for a thin cresent of the northwest—the centers of Campeche, Mérida, and Valladolid? Would La Quinta remain safe or would Poot decide his debt didn't extend to his savior's son?

Even a general as tough, ruthless, and wily as he couldn't live forever. But it was almost inevitable that when the central Mexican government gained enough strength, it would crush the rebel state, or at least severely limit its territory. The economic arguments for henequén, sugarcane, and lumber would grow stronger as the need for these products increased. The Cruzob, dependent on corn and constantly busy with clearing and burning new fields to replace infertile ones, couldn't hold out forever against an unremitting, well-armed, massive force that came prepared to occupy Cruzob strongholds and stay in the jungle as long as necessary instead of being called back to Mérida or Campeche to fight with other *ladinos*.

Bonifacio Novelo, himself partly of the *ladino* world, seemed to know this, for he sometimes discussed the advantages of the Cruzob attaching themselves to the British empire and acquiring that protection while still maintaining effective self-rule.

"That queen is far away," he said with a twinkle one morning a week after Dionisio had gone. "She's never visited Belize, and I don't think she would come to us. It's like a mother with many children, no? She can't watch them all."

Mercy's face must have shown her skepticism, for he pressed for her opinion. "I don't think the British would want to have trouble with Mexico or the United States," she said.

The *tatich* frowned. "The United States? What have they to do with us?"

As simply as possible, Mercy explained the Monroe Doctrine. If any country in what the United States considered its sphere of influence was threatened, then the U.S. would intervene. Mexico, she pointed out, was within this sphere of influence. She reminded him that it had been U.S. pressure on France that had played a decisive role in compelling Napoleon III to withdraw troops from Maximilian's support, and that it had been the U.S. supply of arms to Juárez that had kept his men in the field when they'd otherwise have succumbed to the well-trained and equipped imperial armies.

"If the United States hadn't ended the Civil War in time to threaten France and help Juárez, there's little doubt that the emperor would be solidly in power by now instead of a prisoner."

Novelo chewed on that. "In this case, yes, I think I'm glad your country aided the Indian Juárez. Why should more *dzuls* come to Mexico? But I don't like it that your country seems to believe it has the right to keep the *dzuls* away from us and interfere in alliances that might be good. I speak daily with God. He hasn't told me that the United States is ordained as our guardian."

"You must remember that my part of the country just fought a long and terrible war because it felt the federal government was taking improper power. We lost and are being treated like conquered traitors."

"Ah, the conquered are always traitors!" The *tatich* laughed. "But I understand what you say. Right is what the strongest says it is." He brooded a while, devouring guava candy. "Isn't the British empire stronger than the United States? Surely it could win a war."

"It didn't win the last one," Mercy reminded him. "And it depends a lot on which country would have to transport troops and supplies. I think Great Britain has enough colonies and territory to worry about without making agreements that would lead to war with the United States."

The *tatich* sighed, as if relinquishing a brilliant vision. "I'd be happy for the English to fight your country, but I fear they'd make us their battleground, and when it was over we'd have lost, either way." He scratched his chest and lifted himself out of the hammock with a flutter of lace-trimmed trousers and surprising grace for so heavy a man. "I must receive the general of the plaza, who's returning from the north with an interesting proposal. He sent a runner so that we could prepare. You may watch if you please."

"You will watch," said the *tata nohoch zul* as the *tatich* vanished into his private section of the palace. "The *tatich* will later require your judgment of what is offered. Woman and *dzul* though you are, your acquaintance with the foreign world and ways may serve the Talking Cross. Stay with me."

Mercy had come to almost like the *tatich*, but the *tata nohoch zul* continued to fill her with dread. Uneasily, she followed him as he detoured around the plaza, evidently wishing to see the approaching party before the official meeting.

Cruzob soldiers were massing in the plaza and the thirty-man band began to play vigorously. Down the street from the outskirts of the village came a woman, moving with regal grace, surrounded by a military escort, carrying something red in her arms. Beside her strode a stocky Maya who reminded Mercy of a scarred tree, but she only glanced at him a second before, startled, her gaze shot back to the woman.

That proud head, slanting yellow eyes, full, flower mouth, that bell-like laughter trilling as she spoke to the eagle-visaged chief! How could it be? Yet, undeniably, terrifyingly, it was.

Xia!

21

As the procession moved toward the plaza, saluted at each cross street by a sentry presenting arms, Mercy stood as if dazed. The fierce-looking soldier must be Crescencio Poot. What offer could Xia make that would occasion this state visit and great ceremony? It must go beyond seeking an alliance with Chan Santa Cruz. Mercy had a frightening conviction that Xia's plan was dangerous to Zane, or at least to La Quinta.

And what if Xia saw her! Mercy's stomach knotted and it was hard to breathe. When Xia learned the woman she'd betrayed into Eric's grasp had escaped him, she'd probably make sure that Mercy never returned to La Quinta.

With Dionisio gone, Mercy's only protection was her importance to the *tatich*. She had to hope that would be enough.

"Come, woman," snarled the spy, giving her a push after the escort.

"I . . . I'm sick. Please excuse me."

He gave her wrist a painful jerk. "Not so anxious after all to meet Crescencio Poot? Hurry up! The *tatich* wishes you to observe. You'll do so if I have to drag or carry you!"

There was no help for it. Her only hope was to avoid detection. She was wearing a scarf over her hair. As she unwillingly kept pace with the spy, she untied the cloth and draped it as concealingly as possible around her head and shoulders. If she kept her eyes cast down and her face shielded, perhaps she could escape Xia's attention.

Reaching the plaza with her guard, Xia was being presented to the *tatich* by the general. She sank on her knees with smooth fluidity, kissing the Cruzob leader's hand.

"A miracle has come among my people," she told him in a clear, ringing voice. "I bring a sign and a message, Great Father, for *la santísima*, the Talking Cross." Unwrapping red silk from the object in her arms, she lifted high a branch with pale green compound leaves. "The Heart of Heaven has sent new strength and vigor to his Mayan children! He has sent us Pacal, priest-king at the flowering time of the Mayas." She handed the copal branch to the *tatich*. "When Pacal appeared among us, this dead branch burst into leaf. I bring it as a sign from God and from Pacal, whose messenger I am."

"I will hear your message in my house," said the *tatich*. "If it's worthy, the cross will give us an answer."

He turned to his palace, followed by Xia and the general of the plaza. Mercy hoped she'd be allowed to slip away, but the chief spy waved her toward the palace.

Pacal? What did it mean? What did Xia want? Out of the tumult of questions racing through Mercy's mind, one stayed constant, a looming dread. Could she avoid Xia's recognition? If Xia saw her, then what?

The *tatich* received Xia in his reception chamber, which was filled with officers, the Interpreter of the Cross, the Organ of the Divine Word, and the *maestro cantor*. Mercy stood near the back of the room, trying to obscure herself behind soldiers and the spy, who kept a vigilant eye on her while listening intently to the exchange of Mayan. Since the *tatich* and the woman spoke solemnly and slowly, Mercy caught most of the words, listening with growing fear.

Pacal had walked out of the forest, Xia said, and the copal branch, dead these seven years since it was found on the cross, a transmutation of the dead body of her

314

son-sacrifice, had come at the instant into full leaf, and the incense on the altar began to smoke and perfume the air. Pacal had been sent by the ancient ones, but he was ready to revere the Talking Cross and join with the Cruzob in a great holy war that would force the *ladinos* into the sea, breaking their power forever.

The *tatich*, who had for years helped maintain the mechanisms and trappings enhancing the cross's mystery and rule, wasn't visibly impressed with Xia's miracles, but he questioned her much as the owner of a theater would interview a magician or stage act, trying to calculate drawing power and effect.

At last, rubbing his plump chin, he asked abruptly, "Why should the cross aid this Pacal? What does he offer that we don't have?"

"A fresh miracle, Great Father." Xia bowed her head respectfully. "In the weeks he's been among us, he's visited and won the support of a number of villages along the frontier that don't presently serve the cross. At least a thousand men will follow him. And, Great Father, he will lead in battle himself, an inspiration to the soldiers."

Was the *tatich's* cold stare a rebuke for Xia's subtle reminder that he no longer led excursions and attacks? He summoned forward Crescencio Poot, and he examined him with careful, deliberate questions that were answered with the same dispassionate caution.

Had the general of the plaza talked with this Pacal? Was he an impostor?

Pacal was magnificent, fit to be a king. As the *tatich* knew, it was sometimes more important to have the appearance than the fact. There was no doubt that Pacal had captured the enthusiasm of the frontier Mayas.

Was he capable of leading them?

Most capable. And lead them he undoubtedly would, with or without the Cruzob.

The *tatich* stared at the aging but formidable soldier who, with him, ruled the Cruzob. "Does this mean, old friend, that you, general of the plaza, would be willing to fight beside Pacal?"

"Yes!" Poot's answer rang out like clashing machetes. "Whether he really is the returned king of Palenque, I don't know or care. He can make even Pacíficos eager to fight. You know already, Great Father, that I believe we should take advantage of the *ladino* revolution to re-

315

claim the whole country. If we waste this opportunity, can the cross forgive us?"

Pondering, the *tatich* suddenly ordered all the soldiers out except for Poot. "Now," he said, "we can consider this matter without fear of false impressions getting out. General, you need not guard your words. Tell us in detail your observations of this Pacal."

Poot did so, clearly finding in Pacal a hope for achieving the long-awaited Mayan dream of freedom from the *dzuls*, with Mayan country wholly back in Mayan hands, united by the Talking Cross.

Next the *tatich* cross-questioned Xia. After probing her at length about Pacal, he rapped out suddenly, "Your child was crucified for power. Through his death, you won the place you enjoy. What will you not do to dominate men's minds?"

Xia's eyes glowed. She controlled herself with obvious effort. "My brother sacrificed my son, as commanded by God, to give the Mayas a savior. It pleased God to replace my son with a copal branch that has worked many cures and is much revered. As a mother, I mourn my child. As a Maya and servant of the Heart of Heaven, I'd offer him again if it would hearten our men to overcome the foreigners!"

"If a dead copal branch can be replaced with a leafed one, such a branch can also be substituted for a boy's body." The *tatich*'s dark eyes bored into the priestess. "Did you hide your son away in some village? Does he still live?"

Mercy cast a side glance at the spy. Could his men have uncovered the truth about Salvador? Or was the *tatich* attacking to learn all he could?

"I didn't change my son's body," returned Xia. "I saw my child on the cross and swooned and prayed and wept. When I roused, the branch hung there." She added softly, "It was a sign from God. Whatever else, it was that."

Novelo motioned her to one side and called the *tata nohoch zul* forward. It was soon clear that his spies had learned nothing to discredit either Xia or Pacal.

The *tatich* seemed lost in meditation. At last, sighing, he said, "Where is this Pacal?"

"He fasts and prays at a sacred grotto an hour's journey from here," said Poot.

"Send for him."

The general knelt, was blessed, and left the chamber.

The *tatich* commanded that Xia be given a room in his palace, and he called in a guard to escort her to it. She passed within a few feet of Mercy, who shrank as much as possible behind the chief spy, averting her half-covered face, holding her breath as Xia moved past her without a glance.

"Now, *señora*," called the *tatich*, "I will hear your thoughts."

Her weakened knees slowly regaining the ability to carry her, Mercy obeyed his gesture and sat on the stool he indicated. "I hardly know my thoughts, *señor*. I have only questions." Thinking fast, she decided, why not be open with him? What had she to lose? "That's the woman who betrayed me to the Englishman," she said, "the one I already told you about. Of course, *I* don't trust her. Where did she find this Pacal? Who is he, really?"

"You don't even consider that he could be the king resurrected?"

"No more than you, *señor*."

A slight smile edged his lips at that. "Leaving that aside, *if* the Mayas rally, *if* they overwhelm the *ladinos*, what do you think would happen? Would the outside world leave us in peace?"

"I'm no prophet, *señor*. Ask your *H-men* or the Talking Cross."

"I ask *you*!"

Mercy shrugged. "I would guess that Mexico couldn't blink at a rebellion or the loss of Yucatán's products. The only way you could hold them off would be through an alliance with some major power."

"Like England?"

"Yes. But if you make such a pact, the United States would see it as a European intrusion. As you yourself said, *señor*, Yucatán might become a battlefield for two foreign powers."

The weary eyes lanced into her. "You're to marry a wealthy *dzul*. You say what you think will help him."

"I say what I think, as you ordered, *señor*."

"Why did the priestess lure you for the Englishman?"

"She greatly desired my fiancé."

"You hate her?"

Mercy thought back to Eric's assaults, to the times she'd suffered in his hands, but even more to how those she loved at La Quinta must have despised her for pre-

317

sumably running away to the States. "What's hate?" she said at last. "Xia is to me a deadly viper."

"You don't want her to know you got away from Belize. That's why you draped that absurd scarf over your head." When Mercy didn't answer, the *tatich* surveyed her under down-dropping eyelids. "I thought to use you for a miracle to strengthen Chan Santa Cruz, but now we have a leafy copal branch and nothing less than Pacal! If he impresses me as much as he has our general of the plaza, there'll be no need for you at the shrine. The *batab* can have you." The *tatich* chuckled softly. "Strange, wouldn't it be, if the *batab* sold you to your *dzul* in time for you to be our prisoner again?"

He made a sign of dismissal. The chief spy followed Mercy out, saying harshly in her ear, "You will not wander in the woods today or until I give you leave. The *tatich* may want you."

Mercy didn't answer. He knew, damn him, that she had to obey. As she made her way along the edge of the plaza, where soldiers still talked excitedly and peered toward the palace, she hoped desperately that this Pacal would annoy or disappoint the *tatich;* otherwise, it seemed all too likely that the cross would speak, decreeing war.

Was there any way to warn La Quinta? Any chance that Poot would somehow arrange to spare one *ladino* hacienda? In all-out war, that seemed impossible, though the general's gratitude might stretch to sparing Zane's life if it rested in his hands.

And Xia? Why did she plot the destruction of the man she loved? Could it be this Pacal was now her lover, that she no longer wanted Zane?

If only Dionisio were back! He might be able to sway the *tatich*. And at least Mercy wouldn't have felt so sinkingly, horribly alone with her worst enemy likely to see her. Had it been wise to tell the *tatich* that Xia was her foe? He may have known, anyway. With his network of spies, his bits and pieces of information must be like a magpie's trove, full of glittering bits, some useless, some to be patched together for valuable clues.

Unless Pacal's group traveled at night, which it almost surely wouldn't, it couldn't reach Chan Santa Cruz before tomorrow.

It would be an excruciating wait.

* * *

Her sleep was full of nightmares. A dead Mayan king pursued her with a copal branch writhing with serpents' heads while Xia smiled at the *tatich,* who kept his back to her. Dionisio fell into a swamp, then sank out of sight till his outstretched hand was swallowed up. Zane came home to a La Quinta burned and overgrown by the jungle, while she screamed soundlessly from the tower, which flamed around her.

Unrefreshed, both desiring and fearing the dawn, Mercy was up at the first light. Avoiding the palace area, she went to the *cenote* and did her laundry, spread it to dry around the bushes by the hut, and wished she had more work, something to keep her busy. After a breakfast of coffee and a leftover tortilla with honey, she brushed her hair, braided it, and, deciding the *tatich* wouldn't want to see her that day, settled down with her father's letters. How she wished she had some of Zane's!

Why didn't that war end so he could come home and see to things? While revolutionists were trying to take Mérida, a Mayan attack could demolish both sides, and if the man she loved hadn't been in the line of fire, she could almost have hoped the Mayas would win.

But not quite—not to butcher Doña Elena or the helpless, or slaughter thousands who'd been born and reared in Yucatán and knew no other home. If war was agreed upon, Mercy knew she'd have to try to find some way to send a warning before the frontier started going up in flame.

The head spy's voice broke into her thoughts. "Why haven't you come to the *tatich,* woman?"

Mercy got up from the log stool. "I didn't think he'd want to see me today."

"It's not for you to think," returned the spy sourly. "Come immediately!"

Grabbing her scarf, Mercy arranged it as protectively as possible around her face while she accompanied this most detested of her captors. She'd hoped the *tatich* would be in his private rooms, where Xia would be less likely to appear, but Novelo was at his usual ease in the hammock on the arcade.

"Tell me all you know of this Xia," he said at once. He consumed several mangoes with lime juice while Mercy told him what Zane had told her, except for the substitution of the copal branch for Salvador and what had become of the boy. She was determined to reveal nothing that spies couldn't easily learn.

"You've said the priestess had a lust for your *dzul*," the *tatich* mused. "She's very lovely. Do you think him so virtuous as to refuse her?"

Mercy flushed. "He . . . admired her."

"They were lovers?"

"How would I know? I have no *tata nohoch zul.*"

The *tatich* laughed but persisted. "Women know such things."

"You must remember that we became engaged only a few days before Señor Falconer left. Till then I was his employee—bond-servant, really. It was not my place to pry into his personal affairs."

"How decorous!" scoffed the mestizo. "You almost persuade me, though I know women in love are governed by nothing—certainly not by etiquette!"

"Nevertheless." Mercy spread her hands.

The *tatich* flashed ivory teeth. "You will watch when this Pacal arrives. Who knows, he might be some ambitious soul lured off your *dzul*'s hacienda! What I must know is: Is he Xia's tool, or is she his, or are they evenly matched?"

"I can't judge," Mercy protested. "I met Xia only once. That last time, in the dark, scarcely counts."

The *tatich* smiled and mimicked Mercy's gesture of widespread hands. "Nevertheless."

It was doubtless part of his strategy of learning all he could about everybody that led the *tatich* to command Mercy's presence at Pacal's reception. And if Xia recognized Mercy, her reaction would give the *tatich*, that wily manipulator, further insight into her aims and character.

Getting out the cloth she'd cut from the bottom of one leg of her second divided skirt in order to walk more freely, Mercy opened the wide hem and fringed the material. It made a respectable shawl, much better for concealment than her small scarf. This took a long time, which seemed longer because, as her fingers unraveled threads, her mind tugged vainly at the snarled tangle entwining her life and love with Xia, the Cruzob, and this mysterious Pacal.

She was sipping corn gruel when the Buddha-like young spy came to the door, tinkled the bells, and said she was wanted in the *tatich*'s reception room. Pacal was approaching.

Again there were sentries at the cross streets, the band playing incongruous polkas, and soldiers massing in the plaza. Her escort took Mercy through the crowd to the palace. The *tatich*'s throne-like chair was empty, but his religious assistants were there and there were enough officers and guards for Mercy to hide behind.

The *tatich* came in, followed by the *tata nohoch zul*, who took a truculent stance behind the chair of state. Voices and shouts swelled outside, rising above the music.

"Pacal! Pacal!" "Death to the *dzuls!*" "On to Mérida!" And running through it all was the chant: "Pacal!" "Pacal!"

Mercy thought the *tatich*'s mouth hardened at the tribute. He couldn't like this popularity of another leader, though to survive as he had, Novelo knew to a hair's fineness how to use enthusiasms and men. He could temporarily grant prominence to Pacal, but he would see that the would-be hero vanished or was discredited when his purpose was served.

"Pacal!" "Pacal!"

The cries grew to a roar, filling the plaza, pressing into the *tatich*'s audience room. Rumor had swiftly permeated the barracks, or Xia's followers had excelled in conversions. This eagerness to believe, to applaud a new crusade, must prove to the *tatich* that his people had reached a level of security and well-being that could become stagnation if they weren't challenged, drawn out of their personal lives by a new miracle.

The *tatich*'s task would be to exploit this hunger to the strengthening and glory of the Talking Cross. That was why he'd played with the idea of using Mercy as a shrine healer.

Nurturing and directing the Pacal cult would be dangerous, but much was at stake—complete Mayan sovereignty in Yucatán. The general of the plaza was for it, and, though the *tatich* was nominally commander of the army, he'd probably hesitate to wager his prestige against Crescencio Poot's. No, the *tatich*'s personal wish might be for calm and peace, but if the prevailing mood of the companies and officers was for war, the Talking Cross could always give orders through another *tatich* while Novelo's peace might deepen quickly into that of eternity.

The general of the plaza stepped into the long room.

321

The man behind him paused in the archway, filling it. A sighing murmur ran through the chamber.

Pacal was a giant. To enter, he had to bend his towering feather headdress, and the quetzal plumes shimmered and moved. He wore a beaked eagle mask, a kilt of feathers and a jaguar skin draped his broad shoulders. His skin was painted green and crimson. Barbarically splendid, decked in feathers and hides, his size alone would have made him awesome.

His size . . .

Mercy choked back a cry. Eric!

Of course it was, behind the paint and costume! He hadn't died in the raid. But what was he doing here? Why would he lead a Cruzob assault on the north?

Shrinking behind the Buddha-spy and an officer, she prayed Eric wouldn't see her, notice the face shadowed by the fringed cloth, but he stared at her for a heartbeat and she knew she was discovered. The tawny eyes swooping pitilessly from the eagle mask seemed to consume her. She had to steady herself with a hand against the wall as he turned and advanced on the *tatich,* followed by Xia, whose white cotton dress shimmered with embroidery.

"The old faith bows to the true one," he said in carrying tones, kneeling to kiss the *tatich*'s hand, but standing haughtily erect when he resumed his normal stance. The thundering sound of blood in her ears forced Mercy to concentrate in order to hear. "Your brave struggle against the *ladinos* has stirred your ancestors, awakened the old powers. I'm their emissary, chosen to aid in restoring the greatness of the Mayan domain."

"How do I know this is true?"

"Watch me lead a few battles."

The *tatich* laughed. "I have a bull that has a deep chest and a fierce bellow. I haven't given it command of my armies."

Xia stepped forward, saluting the *tatich*'s hand. "Great Father, Pacal has eight companies of men ready at his word. If your bull could commit to you that many warriors, I think you'd give it a chance to command." Laughter swept the room, easing the strained tension.

"Eight companies?" The *tatich* frowned.

"I've seen them, Father," said Crescencio Poot. "They're drilling in their villages when they're not busy with the corn."

322

"And what of the corn?" growled the *tatich*. "What will happen if the men are off fighting at harvest time?"

"Aren't there old and young able to harvest, though not able to fight?" asked the general. "Besides, there are *ladino* stores and granaries. We could lose a harvest if we won the country and all its harvests forever."

The *tatich* stared at this gigantic possible ally, possible foe. "We will talk more," he said. "Then I must take your messages to the Talking Cross and wait for the wisdom of *la santísima*." At a signal, everyone except Poot, the chief spy, Xia, and Pacal started to leave.

Her thoughts a despairing tumult, Mercy made herself small beside the ample Buddha and tried to drift out with the crowd. She must try to get away and alert the frontier and La Quinta. But how, guarded as she was? And Eric had recognized her! If only Dionisio would come! He might know some way to rouse the Mayan from this bloody dream before it brought fire and death to thousands, Cruzob as well as *ladinos*.

And Eric. What would he do about her? She couldn't believe he'd let her remain long in her hut. But it was Xia who suddenly stepped before her, blocking the way to the door, snatching away the shawl.

"You!" The priestess' eyes blazed with hatred, then dilated. She flicked her tongue across her lips and smiled. "This time we'll teach you to stay where you belong!" Grasping Mercy's wrist, she swung her toward the *tatich*. "This *dzul* slave! What price is on her?"

"She's a healer," said the *tatich*. Pacal hadn't moved, though the eagle mask made him seem to lean avidly forward. "And she's the captive of an allied *batab*."

"Then I'll buy her from him!"

"Not presently. The *batab* is on a journey."

"So easy, then, for a slave to die or run off," suggested Xia with a smile as coaxingly sweet as if she begged for candy.

"Not this one. She's brought a dead child to life. She's valuable to the shrine."

"With Pacal you don't need an herb doctor who was lucky once."

The *tatich* slapped his thigh resoundingly. "I decide what's needed! Let the captive go."

Xia had the sense to duck her head submissively, but she gave Mercy's arm a cruel dig with her pointed fingernails before she released it.

"Señora!" the *tatich* called to Mercy. "Wait in the arcade!"

The head spy came to watch her from the door and the Buddha arranged himself patiently in one of the archways. There was nothing for Mercy to do but take her usual seat by the empty hammock. And wait.

The Buddha seemed to doze, but every time Mercy moved, his eyes opened wide, fixed on her. Once she went to stand in an archway. The *tata nohoch zul* followed to stand so close that she could smell his breath. She quickly went back to the stool.

What was happening inside? The *tatich* had heard his soldiers hailing this new leader, had to believe what the general told him about eight companies ready to answer a call against the *ladinos*. The *tatich* must be deciding whether to go against the mood of the moment or how best to shape it to his own ends. And he was wily enough to know that a Cruzob leader who wouldn't fight would very soon be past any need to.

Mercy felt too overwhelmed to think about her own fate. Both Eric and Xia had recognized her. About the only hope she could have was that Eric hated her now and wouldn't want her for himself. Whereas previously Mercy had prayed Dionisio would come, now she was afraid he'd endanger himself to protect her.

It seemed forever, but at last the *tatich* came out of his chamber, Pacal looming behind him. Xia wore a pleased smile, and the general of the plaza had a confident spring in his step.

"Tonight," the *tatich* told them, "we will listen for the Talking Cross. *La santísima* will decide."

Pacal and Xia kissed the *tatich*'s hand and went to their own rooms in the palace, though Pacal stood for a long moment watching Mercy through the eagle's mask. Novelo loosened his sash and sank thankfully into his hammock, reaching for a mango as he glanced at Mercy.

"Old friend," he said to the general, who was gazing north, as if picturing future conquests, "this captive was to marry Zane Falconer, son of a foreigner who, so I understand, saved your life long ago."

Poot turned to examine Mercy. It was hard to believe that a man could cause so many deaths over so many years and still look like a grizzled planter of corn. "That was long ago," he said. "In the ordinary counting of days,

324

I'd spare the son for the father's sake, but in the kingdom Pacal will bring, there'll be no place for *dzuls*."

He strode off to his own residence across the plaza. Mercy hadn't expected much from him, but this was worse than nothing. She'd been deliberating as to whether or not to reveal Pacal's true identity. Poot's attitude made it clear she had nothing to lose.

"*Señor!*" she cried out to the *tatich*, her tone surprising him so much that for a moment he stopped chewing. "That man who claims to be Pacal is really an Englishman, Eric Kensington, the man who abducted me!"

"You're sure?"

Mercy grimaced. "I know his body! And his eyes!"

"So Marcos Canul didn't kill him," muttered the *tatich*. "You understand him, *señora*. Why would he fight with Cruzob against *dzuls?*"

"He's sold guns to the Cruzob for years," said Mercy. "The whites aren't English, so he doesn't feel that he's betraying his own kind. I doubt that he'd care if he did. He knew Xia before. When he lost so much, he must have thought she could help him recoup."

The *tatich* listened, his brow slightly knit. "If this is her idea, it's a good one. There'll be much loot if the cross takes Mérida and Campeche."

"If! You're going to let Kensington deceive your people?"

"What is he but a symbol?" The *tatich* shrugged. "If he inspires the people, it doesn't matter if he's stuffed with cornhusks. But it's useful to know what he is. I thank you for revealing the secret."

Mercy got to her feet. "I wonder what would happen if I shouted it in the plaza."

"Try it," said the *tatich*, smiling. "You'd be hacked to death in seconds unless I interceded. My men want to believe Pacal, and so they will. You may go to your hut, *señora*." As Mercy started to leave, he added, "Tonight the Talking Cross will speak. You must hear it."

"I'm not Cruzob."

"But you will come." He signaled lazily. The Buddha spy moved after her. Mercy thought she heard, from a long way off, Xia laughing.

It was the longest day Mercy had ever known. She'd been afraid that Eric might visit her, but either he had no such wish or he judged it inadvisable. She still clung

325

to the hope that if she could expose Eric to the common soldiers, they'd abandon the crusade. The *tatich, tata nohoch zul,* general of the plaza, and others of the ruling hierachy might know Eric was not Pacal, even that he was white. For them, used to wielding power through the Talking Cross, Pacal's value lay in others' belief, not their own. Real faith, to them, would be a drawback.

Somehow she must unmask Pacal in public when there was a chance of getting the soldiers to listen to her long enough to at least plant doubt. If she died immediately afterward, she could know she'd done her best to keep Yucatán from erupting in racial slaughter.

But how would she get that moment of attention before machetes ended her words? She was resigned to losing her life; she only hoped to sell it high.

She went to the *cenote,* trailed by her guard. She listened to the excited buzzing among the slave women as they chattered about the resurrected giant priest-king. They all seemed as credulous as the soldiers. Mercy had to clamp her teeth shut to keep from shouting out Pacal's true identity. Even if she convinced these women, they had no influence. Anything they said would be taken as an effort to shield their people from Pacal's victory.

No, Mercy told herself, *wait for the right time, the right place—maybe tonight when the cross speaks. . . .*

After carrying water home, she bathed and washed her hair and stepped outside in back of the hut to dry it in the sun. But soon she went inside, inhibited from tossing and fluffing her hair by the ever-present young Buddha. Juanito's mother brought venison for dinner, along with special tamales. A feast was being given for the visitors and the plaza was rapidly filling with men, women, and children from nearby villages who had come in to hear the commands of the Talking Cross.

Juanito's mother had a child by a major who'd certainly be mobilized if war came. It couldn't hurt to leave a message in case she, Mercy, failed in exposing Eric. So, as the woman's eyes widened, Mercy told her who Pacal really was and asked her to tell her major when she saw him.

"He's using the Mayas to do more than regain his power and wealth," Mercy warned. "It's possible that he'd try to make himself ruler of Yucatán. He doesn't care a bit for Cruzob rights, or anyone else's. To him, Creole, mestizo, and Indian are all un-English, hence, inferior—to be used and dominated."

"You're sure of all this, *señora?*" The woman swallowed. "I . . . I don't want to get my man in trouble. If he opposed what the *tatich* approves, he could be executed very fast. I've seen it happen."

"Your major would have to find a good chance to prove Pacal's an Englishman," Mercy said. "But if he did this, it might save both Cruzob and *ladinos* tremendous suffering." She put a comforting arm around the frightened young woman. "I'll unmask Pacal if I can. In case I fail, I wanted someone else to know."

"I owe more than my life to you, *señora;* I owe Juanito's. If necessary, I'll tell my major." She caught Mercy's hand. "What will happen to you if you're not believed?"

"What will probably happen, anyhow." Mercy shrugged. "The priestess hates me. Unless the Englishman wants me, I'm sure she'll find a way to kill me."

"If only your *batab* were here!"

"I'm afraid he'd only lose his life. But when he does come, tell him. He was a bond-servant on Kensington's estate, and he knows him well."

Mercy froze. It could be fatal for Dionisio, unprepared, to meet Eric, who was bound to learn how Mercy had been brought to Chan Santa Cruz. Even if Eric didn't crave Dionisio's life for his closeness to Mercy, he'd remove him as a person who might guess the truth about the face behind that eagle mask.

"I must ask you another favor," Mercy pleaded. "Warn the *batab* about the Englishman before they can meet. Otherwise, Eric might kill him before Dionisio grasped what was going on."

Now it was the woman's turn to comfort Mercy with an embrace. "Don't worry about that, at least, *señora.* I'll get word to your *batab.* But please, don't risk yourself till you have to!"

Unwilling to distress the young woman further, Mercy didn't say that she was already risked. Xia knew her; so did Eric. Instead, she thanked the woman and sent her away.

Considerably relieved that Pacal's secret would be known where it might destroy his scheming, Mercy slowly ate the spiced meat and delicately flavored tamales. She could hear the band in the plaza and the soft, distant rumble of singing voices, swelling as night descended and more and more villagers streamed into the shrine city.

When would the Talking Cross speak?

From dreading a summons, Mercy began to wish for it as minutes dragged into hours and the night wore on. *Let it happen!* her tortured mind told her as she paced from door to door and stepped outside always to see the dim figure of the Buddha spy watching from where he could see both entrances. *Whatever will be, let it be! Just so it comes quickly while I'm still in command of myself!*

At last, wearied, thinking perhaps plans had changed, she lay down in the hammock and dozed fitfully. She dreamed Pacal was tearing her apart with his eagle beak when a voice reached through her terror.

"*Señora!*" It was the Buddha spy. "You will come now to the church. At midnight the cross will speak."

Icily awake in a second, Mercy put on her sandals, tidied her hair, and slipped the shawl around her, though it could no longer act as a disguise. It made her feel a little less exposed, though.

Would she be coming back? Was her life to end in this Cruzob city, severed by causes she'd never heard of a year ago? Would Zane ever know what had happened to her? And what would become of him and of everyone at La Quinta, on the frontier, and in Yucatán?

She touched his black coral necklace, tried to find strength in their love, and followed her guard.

Torches burned here and there along the plaza, flickering light and shadow on the Mayas thronging the plaza. Passing through the praying, singing crowd, Mercy was brought through an completely darkened church, also massed with worshippers, made to stand in a clear space that she supposed must be near the altar.

Was this the time? Should she shout out that Pacal was a fraud? How far would she get, and would anyone believe, before she was hushed? Mercy was keying herself up to seize the first pause in the chanting when a soft hand gripped her shoulder and a fine dust was thrown into her face. It entered her lungs in a gasp, and when she tried to cry out a hand closed her mouth.

More dust filled her nostrils. Suddenly she was floating, light and free. Nothing mattered, especially not whatever she'd wanted to say. The only truth, the only reality, was this pure high drifting. In a moment she'd be part of it, merged completely, entirely at rest. The blackness was bright, dazzling, colors she'd never seen, colors to hear and smell, the taste of the rainbow filled her mouth, penetrated, became her.

She scarcely knew when the singing stopped, but she felt the silence, reverberating with a sound like thunder rumbling from a long way off.

There was a trilling, piercing whistle, silence that made the darkness a thick, living, palpable thing, and then a voice spoke from the middle of the air.

"I welcome my son Pacal, who kneels to me, as is fitting. He worships me. His heart is no longer heathen. But the old powers are still strong, so I send them a present, a gift to obtain their blessing as you, my children, march on the *dzuls.* I command that the white captive known as Mercy be thrown into the *cenote,* where the Lord Pacal awaited my invitation, and where the *yuntzilob* told him they required this woman."

This woman? One layer of her mind knew what was happening. It didn't matter. But because there was something, deep, almost forgotten, that didn't matter, she tried to speak. Her mouth wouldn't open. Her tongue couldn't move.

There was more dust in her face. The colors exploded, and she sank into them.

22

The colors were still before her eyes when she opened them, and they throbbed in and out of her brain. Her mouth was dry. She was a husk, a paper-thin shell, with only the colors real. But there was a voice, calling a name. Her name?

Sighing, Mercy looked through the spinning, dancing colors to a face, smiling, evil. "Stand up. Those rags won't do for a gift to the gods, though neither, certainly, are they getting a virgin!"

Xia's silken tones brought Mercy back to herself, to

what was happening, though haziness fogged her mind. She could remember the aromatic dust in her nostrils, the shrill voice of the Talking Cross, and vibrating, sensuous colors.

Nothing more. Nothing till now. She lay in a hammock, watching Xia, whose slanting eyebrows rose higher. "Don't sham. *Yoyotli*'s effects don't last this long."

"That's what you threw in my face?"

Xia nodded. "Its use is what has always made sacrificial victims so complacent, why they seldom struggle against the knife." Her laughter tinkled. "I thought you *might* struggle, shout what you knew about Pacal, so I decided to make sure there were no unruly outbursts. Now, stand up and be dressed, or I'll drug you again."

The *yoyotli* could make her go without caring to her death. Resolved to stay aware, snatch at any opportunity, Mercy got out of the hammock. They were in a large room, bare except for hammocks and a few chests. There were guards at the door, through which Mercy glimpsed an arcade and supposed they were in the *tatich*'s palace.

She felt slightly betrayed that Novelo, with whom she had spent many hours and whose liking she could sense, would drown her at Xia's behest, but he wouldn't be *tatich* if he shied at a little murder. He couldn't be faulted, as a leader, for choosing Pacal's bold miracle of holy war to Mercy's quiet one of healing.

Two women, at Xia's orders, disrobed Mercy and anointed her with sweet-scented oil. "We have no fitting garments for a bride of the gods," said Xia. "But this girdle of serpent skins will cover your loins, and the *tatich* has let me pick out jewelry from his plundered treasures. It's a shame to waste it on a corpse, but we must make a good show; otherwise, the people might wonder why the powers wanted *you*."

Through the window Mercy watched the hinting of dawn as Xia decked her with necklaces of jade, abalone, coral, and shell. A feather-and-bead collar stopped just above Mercy's nipples, which Xia stained crimson, ignoring Mercy's protests.

"We must give people something to look at! By all gods, it's difficult—you're scrawny as a reed!" Her nails dug in savagely. "How Zane could want you is a riddle! Perhaps you are a witch!"

"Why are you helping Eric Kensington? Don't you care

that such a revolt will be put down? Do you want La Quinta destroyed?"

Xia's smile sweetened even more. "La Quinta will be part of my reward. Zane, if he lives, can be my mayordomo if he serves me well—in all ways."

"Don't you care at all that you'll cause the deaths of thousands of your own people?"

Xia lifted and dropped one slim shoulder. "Those people took my only child from me so they could have their savior! I wept and cried and pleaded, but he went on the cross, anyway! My little boy! When I thought he was dying, it was as if the human heart left my breast and one of jade was left there. I learned then that all that counts is power."

"So you'll condemn many mothers to weeping? Sacrifice men by the hundreds?"

"I will be priestess of Pacal, the most important woman in Yucatán. Then I can have my son with me without fearing for his life or my own!"

"But," said Mercy slowly, "will he want to be with you?"

Xia was small, but a blow with the full force of her body behind it made Mercy stagger. "He'll be a *cacique* greater than Jacinto Pat or anyone since the Spaniards! Even if Mérida and Campeche don't fall, we'll hold all the country outside."

"Till armies come from Mexico."

"We've defeated them before. We will again."

"This time they won't be called to the mainland to fight for or against an emperor, the United States, or Texas. Those wars are over. After what's happened to Maximilian, it'll be a long time before any European power interferes with the Mexican government, which will now have a chance to put its house in order—and part of its house is Yucatán."

"A part that keeps detaching itself," reminded Xia, "even without the Mayas."

"It'll be different now. Since independence, Mexico's been fighting other powers. But now its borders are settled with the United States, Europe's backed off, and the next years are bound to see a knitting together of the country and subjection of rebellious parts."

"I don't believe you!"

"Don't."

Xia's full lips curved. "It's a pity you won't know if

331

your croakings come true. I'm surprised that Kensington agreed to your death, but apparently this escapade with the handsome *batab* quenched even his itch for you. He didn't want to attend the ceremony, however. You're to enter the *cenote* when the first ray of sun strikes it."

Xia shone with power and her full lips curved. "Don't you remember water, Mercy?"

"Why?"

"The body remembers the way it died," Xia said dreamily. "It thrills and dances in the presence of the element that caused it to disintegrate before. I remember fire. My flesh tingles, wants to spin into particles. I shall die in fire. But you, Mercy, doesn't your body sense its doom? Come now."

Maybe there'd be a chance at the moment before sacrifice, when all eyes were on her, to shout out the truth about Pacal, tear off his mask and headdress. It would be hard for the wildest fanatic to believe such a fair-haired man was Mayan. Mercy took a deep breath and moved for the door.

As she passed Xia, the priestess' hand came up. Fine powder burned Mercy's eyes and nostrils. *Yoyotli!* She tried to cough it out, but a second casting filled her spasming lungs.

And she was . . . floating.

Leaves were edged with diamonds and gold, flowers expanded and contracted, and brilliant petals reshaped themselves to dance like living things. They *were* alive. The stamens pulsed, showering sun dust, and stems swayed languorously. Grass was jade and emerald, the red bark of the *indio desnudo* tree glowed in points of rosy flame, even rocks dissolved, laughing, into millions of spinning, whirling particles, freed to mingle with heaven-blue of morning glories, ruby chalices of frangipani, dragon heads of orchids, trailing plumes of air plants.

Mercy flowed with the colors, entered and was with them, now a purle iridescent feather of a jay, now a yellow bloom of the cotton tree, or tendril of a vine. She felt sorry for the people, hundreds of them, following the body that was her temporary covering. These women, children, and soldiers couldn't see the colors. They were too heavy to float.

Curiously, Mercy examined the people nearest her.

332

The woman's head became that of a beautiful undulating snake patterned with jewels. The fat man in the lead was really an immense bull frog, and the men with him were toads and lizards, ridiculously garmented in men's attire. The eagle-masked man wasn't there, and she wondered how he would have looked with his feathers charged with the light and splendor now touching everything. Here and there a child flamed, or a baby burst into flower. A woman incandesced, and then a young warrior.

The shallow cave before them reflected water sparkles on its glistening walls from a luminous oval pool that lay partly within, partly outside the cave. Rainbows shimmered above, around and deep inside the quicksilver surface.

So beautiful.

But there was something . . . something! The memory trying to pierce through the gossamer webs hazing her mind couldn't do more than make itself felt as a vague disquieting, a wondering. It had seemed so important. Before she saw the colors. Before she could float.

The toad men fastened a carved rock to her legs, a rock that didn't fly into fragments and dance, a rock that was heavy, dragging at her legs in the instant before she was lifted. The serpent woman cried out words, her adder's tongue darting back and forth, and the toad men let go of Mercy's arms.

The water exploded with sun as she fell into it.

Again, her head ached as she awoke. She retched, nauseated, but only water ran from her mouth. At first she could see only black laced with flame in myriad arabesques that spun away to infinity when she tried to watch them, but gradually a pair of glowing eyes dominated the patterns and a face took shape.

She retched again, bringing up bile and water. "So that's what the sight of me does to you." Eric's coldly amused voice chipped at her eardrums, though he held her head and wiped her mouth with a clean cloth.

When the paroxysm ceased, he began to dry her body, chafing her hands and wrists and feet till her shivering grew less violent. She was lying on blankets in a cavern lit by a lantern that cast fantastic monster shadows from the icicle-like growths hanging from the top and growing from the bottom, in some places almost fitting together like irregular teeth in an immense misshapen jaw.

That's where she felt she was—locked behind the teeth of a dark prison deep inside a hidden place, unbelievably in Eric's power, yet, unbelievably, alive. Beyond that she was too nauseated from *yoyotli* and near-drowning to think.

He took off the clinging snakeskin girdle, smoothing her thighs, spreading his broad hand over her belly in a claiming gesture. Covering her with a blanket, he took off the necklaces, collar, and bracelets.

"Quite a dowry to the gods," he chuckled, "though Xia chose it for show more than for value, of course."

"Does . . . does she know?" Mercy's tongue felt huge and she moved it and her lips with difficulty.

"That you're alive?" Eric shook his head. "That's *my* secret."

"And I suppose I have you to thank for being sacrificed!"

"The grotto *cenote* was my idea, yes. I knew about this hidden cave with a lower passage connecting it to the water. One of the general's men had told me about it; it's where I rested while he and Xia went on to the *tatich*. Xia was for burning you, but I persuaded her this way was more traditional and would have greater impact. All I had to do was wait in the passage till I saw you in the *cenote*." He laughed softly, his face a golden mask in the yellow light. "We're well matched, my love, both of us resurrected from seeming death. I'm sure you never expected to see me again. When I finally got back to the ruins of the House of Quetzals, Celeste told me, with very convincing tears, that you were dead from the black vomit." He placed a finger across Mercy's lip. "Don't tax yourself to conjure up an excuse for her. I won't strangle the bitch since she and Thomas are married by now, and I left him in charge of getting the estate back in operating condition. With the house burned and you lost, I wanted only one thing, revenge on Marcos Canul, and knowing that Xia was ambitious, I thought she might help. I went to her, and you can see the stakes we're playing for now."

"You could pay off your grudge at Canul without setting fire to the whole country!"

"But this is so much more interesting."

Pillage and death and fire and blood? Just when the

people on both sides and in the middle of the War of the Castes were beginning to prosper, when there was a tacitly agreed-upon boundary, peace with pride for the Cruzob? Mercy swallowed the appeals. They'd mean nothing to him.

"You must know that Mexico can't tolerate a complete takeover by the Mayas. The only way it could work would be for the *tatich* to make an alliance with some European power. And then the United States would interfere. Better than any of the Cruzob, you know all this!"

He shrugged. "Yes, but Juárez would make many concessions before using troops and money in another costly war. He's Zapotec himself and won't mourn deeply for the rich creoles of Mérida and Campeche who so readily joined the empire and supported a foreigner against him."

The idea of the Cruzob negotiating formally with Mexico, paying lip service to the central government while existing as a separate entity, hadn't occurred to Mercy. It *was* possible. Yucatán, because of its isolation, was regarded by its citizens and those of Mexico as almost another country.

If the Cruzob could take *ladino* strongholds *now*, present Juárez's newly forming government with an accomplished fact and a face-saving and economically useful alliance, Juárez could hardly be blamed for accepting what would take another tremendous effort from his war-weary people to change.

"A bold stroke?" demanded Eric.

"Worthy of a butcher!"

His eyebrows raised mockingly. "Why, my love! I expected you to support the oppressed Mayas, as you were so fond of doing at my estate!"

"If the *tatich* or general of the plaza or even Xia had planned it, I could understand their feelings. But you're in it for your own benefit. You'll be making war on your friends in Mérida, your own aunt!"

"Not by blood. I'll do my best to see that she's protected. And I'm sure that any *ladinos* who don't pose a threat to Cruzob rule will be allowed to leave the country."

"If they survive the fighting."

"There's that, of course."

"I can't believe you!"

His eyes changed. "You will."

Roughly, he dried her hair, draped a dry blanket around her, and held a gourd of corn gruel to her lips. For a moment, Mercy wanted to push it away, but she stopped herself. She drank. As long as she lived there was a chance she could expose him to the Mayas or warn La Quinta. She must stay as strong as she could. If his plan worked, if Zane died, if it seemed she'd be Eric's prisoner forever, she'd do anything to escape that.

If she got the chance, would she kill him? The thought entered her mind with no accompanying revulsion. The horror he calmly planned to loose on Yucatán must be stopped in any possible way.

She'd kill him if she could.

He smiled, slipping his hand inside the blanket, fondling her breast. She tensed, then began to shake uncontrollably. "Still cold?" he asked. "Or so eager?" His fingers stroked her nipples and searched hungrily along her loins and thighs. She knew resistance was futile, but this deliberate toying drove her frantic.

She jabbed at his eyes with her thumbs and brought her knee up sharply, but he only laughed and pressed her down with his weight. "Like a frightened virgin? I know you better than that, my sweet. Fight all you want. It forces your body to me in a maddeningly seductive way. Is that what you want to do—tempt me?"

"I hate you!"

He held her spread beneath him, raised to stare into her eyes. "You still love the noble Falconer?"

"Yes!"

He smoothed her contemplatively with his hands before they tightened on her flanks with ferocity that made her gasp. "Then what are these stories about you and that *batab* who brought you to Chan Santa Cruz?"

"He was taking me to La Quinta as soon as he served his month at the shrine."

"You believed that?"

"Yes! He was grateful to me for keeping you from beating him to death!"

"And you were grateful to him? How grateful?"

"It's none of your concern!"

"But it is. We had to argue a long time with the *tatich* to persuade him to give you to the water. He thinks Dionisio would even kill him over this, so, of course, the *batab* must never get that chance. He'll be accused of treason as soon as he returns and macheted in the plaza."

336

Numb at this new horror, Mercy felt lifeless, a mere husk, scarcely knowing when Eric's questing grew more urgent. She roused at the pain of entry, screamed as he thrust, but his mouth shut off her cry. He took her in a brutal, punishing way till she lay half-fainting.

"Did that *batab* have you?" He panted, slackening a moment, staring down at her as he rocked back and forth, apparently enjoying her pain.

She stared at him wordlessly. He withdrew, then plunged so deep she closed her teeth against a moan. "Did he have you?" Eric asked again, poised above her.

Mercy closed her eyes, dismissing him, trying to capture again those colors, that floating, when not even death had mattered. She hadn't realized Eric had been quiet a long time before he spoke against her ear.

"The *batab* will die. So will Falconer. That will mean that I'm the only living man to have you, the only one who'll ever possess you again. I have you now. That's all that matters. I have you now and you'll never get away!"

As if the claim released something in him, he gripped her and pumped swiftly to his release, then lay collapsed beside her with one great arm pinioning her.

Shifting her gaze around the cave as much as she could without moving or arousing him, Mercy looked for a weapon. Some hemp sacks leaned against a stalagmite that looked like a guttering, half-burned taper. On another rock were gourds and a pail. Eric must have a knife and rifle, but she couldn't see them.

A faint hope stirred in her. He'd have to appear at Chan Santa Cruz. Unless he tied her up, which wouldn't be too practical if he had to be gone for hours at a time, she'd certainly try to escape through the *cenote*. She could swim enough for that.

And then? If she went to the city, her "resurrection" should gain her a few minutes, a chance to bring Pacal's authenticity into question. That didn't matter to the cynical leaders, but it would, vitally, to ordinary Cruzob. But what if she were silenced before she could speak? Going to the shrine meant almost certain death. She was willing to die to avert a race war, but she didn't want, in vain, to give up air, sky, sunlight, and her love.

Try to get to La Quinta or some place from which an alarm could be spread and then return to Chan Santa Cruz with enough of an escort to guarantee attention while she proclaimed the truth about Pacal? That had the overwhelming advantage of alerting the whites of their danger no matter what success she had with unmasking Eric.

The fearful part was that Dionisio should certainly return several days before she could reach La Quinta and come back here. If he came, unwarned, into the city, he would surely die.

It was an agonizing choice. And before she could even make it, she had to get out of this cavern. Eric's arm weighed heavier each second. He was crushing the breath from her, the life. But when she tried to slip out from under it, his arm tightened and he drew her closer and said, almost as if he knew what she'd been thinking, "You'll never get away."

After what seemed to be hours, but which couldn't have been more than half of one, he yawned, shook himself awake, looked at her, and laughed exultantly.

"I can do this all I want," he whispered, caressing her, tasting her breasts with nuzzling teeth. "When I thought you were dead, like Alison, I thought I'd go crazy. But you're alive. I have you. And when you have my baby, you'll forget the dead men, just as you forgot Philip."

"I hated Philip!" she blazed. "But not as much as I hate you!"

"You *will* love me." He turned her face to him so cruelly that she thought her jaw would break from his gripping fingers. "If I have to, I'll kill everyone on this earth whom you care for. It's your nature, like Alison's, to love. If I'm all you have, you'll love me."

"No!" She could barely force sounds between her constricted lips as his grasp forced her mouth against her teeth, but she gazed into his eyes and felt as if her blood had turned to molten, fiery steel. "I'll hate you more than I ever loved everyone put together!"

"Then such a hate will be the strongest thing in your life," he said with terrible softness. "I'll still be your center."

Pinning her arms above her head, he took her like a storm.

I'll get away, she thought, sending her mind away from the tearing lunges into her swollen softness. I'll get away . . . or kill you . . . or myself. But this won't go on. I'll get away.

When he had finished, he heaved himself up with a harsh laugh. "That wasn't supposed to happen. I've got to

338

turn up at Chan Santa Cruz and meet with the *tatich* and general. I'll be back as soon as I can. There's food in the sacks." Completely naked, a magnificent being out of a Viking saga, he paused where the chamber narrowed to a small passage. "You won't be able to follow me out. I'll close the way with a boulder you can't budge. And the other way becomes a labyrinth of underground rivers and bottomless pits twining together."

Her resolution must have showed on her face. He stopped abruptly, swore, and strode back. "But you'd try the maze, wouldn't you?"

Reaching into one of the sacks, he brought out a length of rope, quickly tied her hands and feet, and propped a water gourd near her and another of gruel so that she could maneuver them. "This should make you glad to see me," he growled. "It's too bad you can't know when you're well off without such lessons!"

This time he didn't look back as he bent to enter the corridor. In a few minutes she heard the grating of stone on stone. Then there was nothing, no sound at all.

She tested the ropes, found them tight, and fought down the dread of being helpless in such a place. She must think carefully. There was a ground-level exit, since Eric had brought food, blankets, and a lantern here, but that entrance was probably sealed off with the rock, along with the way to the wellspring.

It was probably true that the other passage from the chamber turned into the deadly confusion Eric had painted, but she'd at least try to find a way out—if she could get out of those ropes! Hopefully, she remembered the stories she'd heard about underground passages connecting many parts of Yucatán: the old woman of Uxmal who guarded a subterranean route to Mérida; Dionisio's story of the passage from Tulum under the ocean. This cave might end in solid limestone, but one of the corridors *might* come out in another cave or wellspring.

Anyway, there was no choice. She had to do anything that might let her spread the warning about the plot shaping at Chan Santa Cruz—and she had to do it quickly!

Pushing herself erect, she found that her feet were too tightly bound to take even the tiniest shuffle forward. She sat on the rock floor and hitched herself toward the supply sacks on her buttocks, feet, and hands. There might be a knife for food.

Her wrists and ankles were chafed raw when she

reached the ledge and peered into the bags, tilting them over so she could examine the contents: a shawl and cotton Indian dress, sandals, more candles for the lantern, fruit, sour corn dough, tortillas, dried meat, and honey.

No knife or machete. His own clothing and personal trove must be in some other part of this cavern, perhaps near the outer entrance, where he must have left his Pacal mask and garments.

Disappointed, though it had been a forlorn hope that Eric would leave a sharp blade near her, Mercy frowned at the lantern and wondered if she could endure the searing if she could get her wrists above the flame. It would be tricky, even forgetting the pain, to get her hands where the flame could reach the rope. She held that for a last resort and scanned her prison.

The stalagmites and stalactites?

Those near her had no jagged, sharp surfaces, but over by one of the walls her sharp gaze fell on a stone shelf where a jutting growth had broken off, leaving an edge that looked thin.

Resuming her awkward method of moving, Mercy reached the wall and struggled upright. The broken rock, like a shark's teeth, stood at an angle. Mercy brought up her hands and began to saw at the ropes, ignoring the scraping cuts on her hands and arms.

The rope was new and tough, and it bit into the other side of her wrists, but the strands *were* severing. Mercy's heart pounded and she pulled her hands back and forth as fast as she could. Eric would surely be gone for hours, but if she made too many false turns it might take her days to find a route out. And he might find her!

Every minute was precious. Exhausted, she had to stop several times to catch her breath before doggedly resuming the tedious, painful labor. But at last she could pull apart the last few strands and let the bloodstained hemp fall to the ground.

A memento for Eric. She took grim joy in thinking of his rage when he saw what had happened, that his bonds hadn't held her. Of course, if he was right, if there really was no other way out than that passage blocked off by the boulder, he'd catch her or she'd perish in one of the pits or rivers, but she meant to try anything to escape.

Sitting down, she worked at the knots on her ankles. They were most securely tied. Her fingers tugged at them uselessly. She stood up again, decided it was impossible to use the protrusion to cut the ropes, but gave a cry of delight as she saw a broken-off spear of the stalactite lying in the shadows. Crawling around to it on hands and knees, she made comparatively short work of the rope, rubbed her ankles to restore proper circulation, and slipped into the dress and sandals. Wrapping food and all the candles into the shawl, she tied that around her waist along with a water gourd, hastily sorted out the black coral necklace from the mass of jewelry, fastened it around her neck, picked up the lantern, and plunged through the mineral-encrusted arch.

The corridor narrowed gradually till she was doubled over, though the width was ample. Then that decreased, dwindling to a small hole. She hesitated.

What lay beyond? A river, a pit? Bending lower, she thrust the lantern ahead of her. It yellowed the rounding walls that stretched as far as she could see before darkness swathed the passage. She shifted her supplies around to fit beneath her stomach, pushed the lantern in front, and crawled into the tunnel. The only way Eric could enter would be by wiggling along in a prone position.

This comforting thought helped her get through the occasional wetness and slime she encountered. The air was thick, heavy. Her lungs strained for more oxygen; her knees grew sore from the rock, though it was smooth. After what seemed an interminable time, the passage began to widen.

Gratefully standing erect, Mercy flexed her knees and shoulders and hands, lit a new candle from the one nearly used up, and saved the stump. If she had to wander for days in this total stifling blackness, she'd be glad for any way to extend the light a few more minutes. With this horrid possibility in mind, she watched for any wood that might have been washed into the cavern by water or wind, but there was nothing from the outer world.

She emerged in a great chamber, much larger than the other, a fantasy of pinnacles and weird hanging masses of white tinged with pale green and gold.

And here, in the splendor, terror began, for there were at least five openings off the vast arena. Which to choose? Did some lead out, others to cul-de-sacs or danger? All were of roughly equal size. In the hope that some flicker of light, draft of air, or other sign might help her decide, Mercy went to each orifice and peered inside and stood alert for a freshness of air, any distant light.

Nothing, except the last tunnel, where her gaze met solid rock. She had to go inside only a few paces to make sure that this was only a small cave. Little time was lost there. Putting down the lantern while she sipped from the gourd, Mercy pondered, keeping a tight leash on the panic that hovered as close as the humid air.

Never had taking the right direction been so important; never had she felt so strongly the anxiety, the pressure, of being in the center with the power to move any way but having to do it blindly, not knowing what waited ahead. But only in moving, choosing, was there any hope at all—for her, those she loved, and countless others.

Sighing, she picked up the lantern and took the passage opposite the one she'd followed, hoping that a principal vein ran through the honeycomb and would come out somewhere on the surface. The size of the corridor seemed to justify her theory, but soon there was a side corridor that seemed, upon brief examination, to be as big as the other.

With a shrug, she continued on, deciding to stick to this hall unless it became impassable or another branch looked infinitely more promising. Thus armored against indecision, she passed a dozen openings, checking each one for light, sound, or the promise of richer air. She had been walking so long that she began to fear that the passage wove itself in convolutions and might even feed back into the way that led to the prison cave.

The candle burned low, spluttering the wick's protest at sinking into melted wax. With a thrill of alarm, Mercy lit another candle and again salvaged the stump.

There were five candles left, perhaps fifteen hours, after this one's dying. If she wasn't out by then—*you'll just go on slowly, feeling your way.* And when the food runs out? The water?

Do your best. Last as long as you can. It's at least better than waiting for Eric and Xia to launch a holocaust. And don't think about it till you have to. You might find water. With that, a person can live a long time without food. You're incredibly lucky to have food and light.

Steadied, Mercy moved along as quickly as she could while watching the sides of the cavern, which converged to a small space leading upward, the bottom littered with rock. She hoped she wouldn't have to crawl here. The height stayed sufficient, but the walls were sometimes so close together that she had to thrust her supplies ahead of her and worm her body after, flinching at the clammy stone encasing her almost to immobility. Still, though sometimes she had to hold her breath and push, she always squeezed through.

One good thing: even if Eric somehow tracked her this far, he could never manage this defile, and she wouldn't have been physically much threatened by anyone who could, unless they were armed. Unless the maze circled back to an accessible area, she was safe from him.

The upward shaft expanded into a low, wide glimmering of contorted mineral formations. The air was so dense that she felt she could scarcely breathe. Perspiration and dampness beaded her face and neck, forming as soon as she wiped herself off, till she finally tore off the bottom of the dress and tied it around her forehead to keep moisture from running into her eyes.

The ceiling sloped down at the far end, vanishing into darkness. Was that a soft murmuring? Stooping to avoid stalactites, weaving through turrets and miniature mountains, she made her way to the opening.

With each step the sound increased, the continuous sibilation of water. Would the tunnel end at one of the vast underground rivers, or would there be some way to cross or move alongside it?

Bending low, Mercy gazed at water rippling with gold flickers from the lantern. It seemed to flow from beneath the cavern where she stood. She guessed that it was the same flow that fed the *cenote* where she'd been sacrificed, running under the rock to emerge at various levels.

Would it finally break out under open sky?

There was no bridge across, and the opposite wall rose sheer above the water. There weren't, in sight, any ledges or ways to go on without following the river.

So, either get in that water, swim or float with it, or go back and try another one of the several passages from that largest amphitheater.

All rivers weren't deep! With sudden hope, Mercy took off her sandals, pulled off her dress, and lowered herself gingerly into the cold stream . . . down, down, stretching with her toes as she sank to her chin.

No footing. For a distance, at least, she'd have to swim. The current wasn't swift, but it would be impossible, for far, to hold the lantern above it while she maneuvered downstream. She'd have to leave the shawl, which would become heavily sodden, and carry only food that the water wouldn't ruin.

If the river flowed into rock where she couldn't follow, if it swept into a chasm, again presenting her with dark passages to choose between, when perhaps she'd have no light and little food, there'd be no turning back. Her fate was whatever lay ahead.

But to go all the hours back, return to a region where by now Eric might have followed, then pursue another corridor that might end at impenetrable rock or even this same river . . .

The water should flow out someplace—maybe after waterfalls and gorges, maybe after narrowings only water could rush through. Mercy prayed to be right and chose it.

She drank sparingly and emptied the gourd, which she could fill again if she left the river, and ate the sour dough and a tortilla, regretfully leaving the rest on a ledge. It seemed unlikely that anyone would ever see it, but if they did, they might think it an offering to the spirits of this place.

Savoring honey from a gourd, Mercy left most of it and one mango. She tied her sandals, dry meat, water gourd, a mango, several guavas, and the candles into her dress, which she tied securely around her waist. If she had to discard the lantern, the candles would be useless, but she couldn't risk being without them if the river brought her to another cavernous passage.

She thought of her father and drew strength from a sense of his knowing and caring about her peril; she thought of Zane and longed with real physical pain to see him at least once more. She smiled and blessed Dionisio, wished for him life and all good things good. Then, holding the lantern above the secret river, she slipped into it and began to swim.

23

Her arm soon ached from the strain of keeping the lantern dry. She kept dipping her feet down in the hope of finding footing, but there was none. The river might be up to her nose or unfathomably deep. It didn't matter. If she couldn't touch bottom, rest her arm, the water might as well be the ocean.

She had no idea of which way the river was carrying her, whether she'd emerge farther from or closer to La Quinta. Her dream of finding her way there or to some settlement seemed wilder by the moment. The lantern skimmed the water. She raised it again, but her numbed arm soon gave way. Changing it to the other hand, she swam on, moved more by the current than her cumbered efforts, and changed the lantern again.

The tunnel stayed smooth and rounded on either side, with no protrusions or visible rocks, except for the incrustations on the ceiling. These were curving, polished, as if the river rose high enough at times to keep them worn away.

The water was cold. Mercy chilled even more at the thought of being trapped in a subterranean flood, battered against the stony passage, drowned if the river rose to the ceiling. To die here, in darkness, where she'd never be found, far from the light and sweet air . . . Mercy shifted the lantern, then stiffened as she heard sputtering she could no longer ignore.

How could she change candles? There was no place to support herself while she got out a new candle and removed the old one. Good God! Why hadn't she thought of that and kept another candle easily reachable for lighting? There was no way she could stay afloat without paddling with one hand.

Groaning, she took the single chance—that the lantern would float long enough for her to fumble out a taper and light it before the lantern submerged. It was made of tin with punctured patterns and an open top.

Mercy let the lantern settle gently on the water, reached in the same instant for her supplies, swimming with one arm. Her fingers closed on soggy meat, a guava, then found hard wax. But the lantern was starting to list. Mercy grabbed for it.

Too late. Mercy sobbed. The light gone? It couldn't be! As frightening as the labyrinth had been, she'd been able to see, make judgments.

She was blinded. She might float till she starved in this murky blackness, or drowned from exhaustion and chill. Why hadn't she gone back, preserved the precious light?

Gasping, weeping with despair and dread, Mercy kept afloat by instinct till the feeling of overwhelming horror had passed. She couldn't see; neither could blind people, but many were amazingly self-sufficient. It was learning to operate by different guides, subtleties one usually ignored.

There was the chance she might be carried past some corridor, but, apart from that, did it really matter? If she were about to go over a precipice, the water would probably take her in spite of her struggles. Since there was almost nothing she could do about dangers, being able to see them wasn't of much actual advantage.

No. But the night was terror. The dark pressed damply against her, smothering, hideous. *Zane! Zane!* She called his name mentally till the fog of panic cleared from her mind.

It was light somewhere. There was day and air and her love. Now that she wasn't handicapped by the lantern, she could swim much faster. What she'd feared had happened; it couldn't happen again, it couldn't get any darker.

Swim. Float when you're tired, but not too long. Swim. Rivers all go somewhere. She seemed to hear Dionisio's warm voice. *The backbone of the mountain . . . Who was born in that place? Who? Father; Thou knowest. . . .*

Let me be born again, out of the river and rock and darkness. Let me come out. Oh, He who is tender in heaven, let me not die in this place.

Swim.

After what seemed to be hours, she felt as if she'd never been anywhere else, that memories of a bright world with flowers and birds and people were fevered dreams. Sometimes she floated on her back, but soon she grew cold and swam again.

She drank when she was thirsty and dug some of the meat from the pocket around her waist, sucking new strength from the salty, flavorsome taste. She could be moving about twice as fast as on land, the current aiding her strokes.

But was it in the right direction? And even if it was, would the stream emerge before she died? The river might flow right under La Quinta, but that wouldn't help unless it surfaced.

How long had she been in the river? Judging from the number of candles used, she'd been in the corridors for about five hours before taking to the water. Eric had certainly returned by now, but even if he got through the first crawl-way, he couldn't force through the narrow upward aperture that led to the final chamber before the river. She didn't see what he could do, unless he happened to know of an exit or where the river would flow out.

She ate a guava, willing herself to concentrate utterly on the texture and sweetness, gain a respite from where she was, but when she swallowed the last bit, the oppressive, moist darkness seemed even thicker. She was very, very tired. Slipping over, the water slapping softly around her ears and chin, she let it carry her.

Would she stay on the surface if she went to sleep? How long could she endure?

A sound penetrated her exhaustion, a rushing turbulence that charged the suddenly urgent river. There was a distant sound of crashing. Righting herself as the tumult rose, she glimpsed a dim glow ahead, then was swept toward it.

She didn't fight the inexorable grip of the current. Falls must lie ahead. How high they were, whether they crashed on the rocks below, whether she'd survive—all were futile questions. There was no way out of the stream, no way back.

And there was light ahead!

It would be ironic if she reached it a battered corpse. But if she had to die, she was glad her body might drift out at last into the good air and warm sun. She had tried. She had done her best.

The crashing became a roar.

Father, Thou knowest. . . .

* * *

347

Sound and force, an irresistible streaming, thundering chaos pounding, dissolving, absorbing, scattering body and mind. She was the water, she was the fall, her consciousness ceased. Then she was floating, her feet dragged to the bottom, her numbed bones and flesh and muscle began to reunite and fit together with blood and breath. Her brain belonged to her again.

And up ahead was a brilliance that hurt, a glory of luminous sky brighter than any jewel, more wonderful than any heaven. For the rest of her life, Mercy would be a worshipper of light.

Coughing out water, she swam weakly for the entrance. The dress and its contents had been wrested from her waist in the waterfall. It didn't matter. None of that did —not the darkness and fear, not the cave and the river. She had come out of them, out of death, and surely her love waited, surely there'd be a way to avert the Cruzob attack or at least warn of it. There'd been a way through the maze. There had to be a way, now, through anything.

The water was so shallow that she tried to stand and wade. Her legs wouldn't hold her. So long supported by the water, her body felt grossly heavy, ponderous. Floundering to where there was only a foot or so of water, she sat rubbing her legs and ankles, coaxing energy back into them, becoming again a creature of land.

When she staggered up again, she managed to walk, falteringly to begin, but with increasing certainty as the feeling of unbearable weight gradually worked out of her. The cavern grew sunnier by the moment.

Once, once only, she glanced back and shivered at the glint of tumbling water spilling down from mysterious blackness.

She could see trees now, craggy limestone. The entrance was only large enough for a tall man, but it opened into the world. Mercy had control enough to listen carefully and peer out before she followed what was now a gentle stream into a bowl-like *cenote*. She was able to stay above it on a limestone ridge, then rejoiced as she saw a path leading through the forest. This was a water supply for some village. If only it weren't Cruzob!

She realized that even her sweatband had been lost. Except for the coral necklace, she'd come out of the cave as naked as when she was born. As she followed the path, she collected leafy vines and soon had enough twined around her to afford at least some cover. Then she saw a

348

stone figure ahead, majestic amid ruins, and she gasped.

Hurrying forward, she touched the jaguar, unable to believe, then began to laugh hysterically. This was the jaguar Salvador and Jolie had showed her. She was just outside the village, only minutes from La Quinta! Weak with relief and joy, she leaned on the altar till her head cleared and then began to run.

She slipped through the space between the mayordomo's house and the great one. It was noon, the time of rest during the summer heat, and no one was at the well or in the center compound.

Would Zane be here? Was the war over? She wanted to shout, know everything at once, tell everything in a breath, wanted most of all to be in Zane's arms. But there were steps to run up, the arcade to cross—and Zane was in the doorway of his office, staring in disbelief, then springing forward. Those arms she dreamed of enclosed her, his mouth took hers, and he swept her up and held her against his heart.

"My love," he said, choking. "Oh, love . . . "

She began to tell him her story.

Within an hour she had eaten, dressed, and helped Zane make a plan which, though desperate, might save Dionisio and even destroy the scheme for Cruzob conquest. While Chopa anointed her cuts and swellings, administering refreshing brews and muttering that Mercy needed bed and care for a week, while Jolie clung to her hand, watching with fascinated eyes someone who'd been thought to be in the United States, while she was actually a prisoner in Belize and Chan Santa Cruz, Mercy explained why she thought that her appearance at the shrine city might serve to shatter the plot.

Everyone knew she was sacrificed. When she exposed their Pacal as a white man who'd used this trick to get her for himself, it would discredit Xia for being allied with him. The *tatich* had never been keen on the crusade, fearing to forfeit what the Cruzobs had attained with much agony. Since the appeal and enthusiasm rested largely on Pacal's challenge to arms, his downfall might well dash the ordinary Cruzob's zest for battle.

The *tatich* and general of the plaza would have to repudiate the plotters to retain their leadership and somehow cover the Talking Cross's gullibility.

Zane had immediately sent messengers to Peto, Tekax, and Valladolid with instructions to be on the alert, though not the offensive. He'd sent Vicente to Mérida with a complete explanation to Peraza, who had conquered and held that city since a treaty was signed on June 15, two weeks ago. Zane had been back at La Quinta only a few days and had still been stunned with wounded disbelief by Mercy's letter when he saw her running up the steps of the veranda.

Since time was so important, they decided to leave at once. Because of the massed troops at the shrine, it seemed useless to take armed men. They had to gamble on Mercy's "resurrection" to win them the chance to proclaim publicly the deceit of Eric and Xia.

Mayel had been listening, her eyes shining with joy as she helped take care of Mercy. Now she said with soft firmness, "Let me come with you. Jacinto Canek, my martyred forebear, would want me to speak against this bad white man. I can swear that all Doña Mercy says is true, tell how he came here with her husband, trying to get her. I can speak for Canek!"

She pulsed with fervor and beauty. Thinking of the danger, Mercy started to refuse. Then she thought of Dionisio, who needed a wife. And whatever the Cruzob did to Mercy and Zane—for even if they were believed, they might be murdered or enslaved—it wasn't likely that a lovely young girl of Canek's blood would meet with anything but cherishing and acceptance.

Mercy was bruised and weary as Zane lifted her into Lucera's saddle. An hour could make the difference for Dionisio if the *batab* had returned, and Eric's fury at her escape might impel him to urge immediate mustering of outlying Cruzob and allies.

"Be careful!" Jolie begged, tears in her eyes as she hugged Flora to her, standing with Salvador and Chepa as the three riders started out of the stableyard.

"We will," promised Zane. Macedonio was already organizing a defense in case it was needed.

"Go with God!" called Salvador.

Mercy was very glad he didn't know that Xia was his mother.

It was over eighty miles by road to Chan Santa Cruz. Mercy's underground route, aided by the speed of the river, had vastly reduced the distance and time, but because of the falls, it could only be followed from the other side—not that Mercy would have undergone it again if there was any alternative.

Since Mercy was exhausted and they'd have to spend several days on the road, Zane halted them while it was still light and made Mercy rest in a hammock while he and Mayel took care of the horses and prepared dinner. After they had eaten, Mayel tactfully retired and Zane carried Mercy to a bank of thyme where he spread out a sheet and gathered her into his arms, caressing and kissing her, touching her face, laughing with tender delight.

"When I read that letter . . . oh, my darling! I couldn't believe it, yet there it was!" His tone hardened. "If the Mayas don't get him, I'll make sure Kensington never bothers you again!"

There was so much to tell, so much to ask, but Mercy was so fatigued that she kept drifting off to sleep. After the cold, dark river, it was bliss simply to lie in Zane's arms and hear his voice. But his hands trembled on her breasts, she sensed the ardor behind the controlled gentleness of his kisses, and she knew what his restraint was costing him.

"Zane . . ."

He laughed shakily, then kissed her fingers one by one. "No, love, not while you're like this. I never want our times to be anything but wonderful for us both."

"It . . . it's not because of Eric?"

His hands tightened on her for a moment. "I'll kill him if I have a chance for what he did to you—but that's over, sweetheart. Just you get rested so my conscience won't smite me for showing how I want you, and you'll have no doubts! Now, kiss me nicely and I'll carry you to your hammock."

As they rode the next day, he told her more of the siege and fall of Mérida. Colonel Traconis, who'd been feted in the plaza when Mercy arrived in Yucatán for his holding out at Tihosuco for fifty days, had fought off Peraza's army for fifty-five. Contesting the capital house to house and street by street, Traconis had hoped that somehow the Imperial forces could retreat to Yucatán and use that as the nucleus of a brilliant Central American empire.

Cannon fire blew up buildings, snipers fired from the

roofs, and news came of the emperor's capture of Querétaro.

The empire had fallen, the people were famished, and ammunition was gone. Peraza, a gallant soldier who'd been on the losing side often enough to sympathize with men in that position, guaranteed there'd be no executions or confiscation of property and offered safe passage out of Yucatán to Imperial leaders.

Meanwhile, General Garcia, who'd vanquished Campeche, was shooting his Imperialist prisoners, and he wanted Peraza to follow his example. When Peraza declined, Garcia sent a squadron to intercept the fleeing Imperial commissioner off Sisal. Peraza warned Garcia that he'd defend his prisoners, and so the Imperialists had sailed variously for New York and Havana about the time news came that Maximilian had been shot between two of his loyal officers on the Hill of Bells, the Cerro de las Campanas, outside Querétaro, on June 19.

"He never belonged here," Zane said. "But he died well. Up to the very end he had chances to escape, but he refused to go without his officers. His dying wish was that his blood be the last shed, and he met the volley with a shout of *'Viva Mexico!'*"

"Poor Carlota!"

"Poor Mexicans. Because of Napoleon the Third's ambition and Maximilian's credulity and Hapsburg stubbornness, so many humble peasants died, ravaged by both sides." Zane shrugged. "Maximilian's death was the finest thing about his life. He won some glory and respect by it, which he wouldn't have had if he'd fled, beaten, to Europe to hang around the rest of his life as a superfluous member of the Austrian court. Anyway, thank God, it's over. Mexico's wounds can start healing, and so can those of Yucatán—provided we can head off this new war."

He wanted to know then more about conditions in Belize, the Icaiche raids, and the position of the unallied Mayas. "So Crescencio Poot is ready to forget, for large enough stakes, the debt he owed my father." He frowned. "If the Cruzob had attacked Peraza a month ago, caught us between them and the imperialists, and then taken Mérida at their leisure, it might have worked. But they've missed the time. Peraza's governor now and in control, and morale's high. Garcia would be only too delighted to march up from Campeche and indulge his thirst for slaughter. For the Mayas' own sake, I hope we can

352

squelch the rising. They'd lose most of their warriors, and, pushed to it, Peraza might decide to counter-invade their territory and crush them forever."

Mercy thought of the great mass of the *balam na,* the crosses at the Four Directions, and the grotto in the valley where the Talking Cross first heartened a desperate, starving remnant. "They've earned Chan Santa Cruz," she said. "And I think the general of the plaza will listen to what you say about having lost the strategic moment. I'm sure Dionisio would counsel for peace."

Riding ahead, Zane glanced back, a strange questioning in his gray eyes. "You seem to admire this *batab.*"

"I do." Mercy spoke evenly, though her heart missed a beat. "Those crocodiles would have had me if it hadn't been for him, and even without that I'd probably have been picked up by the Cruzob long before I could have reached La Quinta."

"I'm in his debt for that."

"No. I kept him from being whipped to death. I'm sure Dionisio feels, as I do, that we've paid our debt to each other and owe each other only friendship and goodwill."

Zane's jaw hardened. "He's young? Strong?"

"Of course."

"Then he must hope for more than that."

Faced with the issue she'd hoped to avoid, Mercy was almost glad it had been raised, that it wouldn't lurk between them as tacit deceit. Well enough for her to argue it made no difference to how she felt about Zane, that it would never have happened if Dionisio hadn't kept her in Chan Santa Cruz. It *had* happened. If Zane thought it mattered, it did. She'd no right to make that decision for him.

Mercy swallowed, straightened her shoulders. "Zane." She had to make her voice louder, brace against the swift darkening of his eyes, the shock worse than anger. "Dionisio had more."

Seared by Zane's gaze, Mercy bit back a flow of explantations and pleadings, though she cried wordlessly, *Oh, my love, understand! It has nothing to do with you; it was his gentleness, his sharing with me his world.*

Zane turned his back, sent Kisin faster along the trail. "We'll talk of this tonight."

During the rest of that unending afternoon, when he spoke to her it was in a courteously detached manner, but neither had much heart for conversation. Mercy imagined the train of his thoughts. *Philip, her husband. Eric, who carried her off. Now this Dionisio, when she was supposed to be in love with me, when I'd asked her to be my wife, though she was my bond-slave and I could have had her anytime, the way others did. . . .*

They made it a long day, hoping to reach Chan Santa Cruz by noon tomorrow. After Mayel had shyly wished them good night, Zane and Mercy walked far enough away not to disturb her. Mercy felt as if she were bleeding inwardly, for, though when she tripped Zane quickly steadied her, he removed his hand at once—as if she were unclean, as if he couldn't bear to touch her.

"Now," he said, pausing by a large tree, "tell me about it. Did he drug you, the way Xia did? Get you drunk?"

On his words, on sunlight, on frangipani flowers.

"No."

"I suppose he'd be too noble!"

"Yes. He wanted me, but he wouldn't use tricks."

Zane's laugh was bitter and short. "It would seem he didn't need to! Did he ask you to marry him?"

"There was no question of that, of anything after he brought me to La Quinta. He . . . he knew I loved *you.*"

Long fingers bit into her shoulders. "And you thought it was perfectly all right to share his hammock and then marry me?" She couldn't answer. He shook her fiercely. "Well?"

"I'm sorry that I've hurt you. I'm sorry if it makes you think I loved you any less."

"Aren't you sorry you let him have you?"

Mercy listened to the center of herself, tried painfully for honesty, because whatever came of it, she and Zane must accept or reject the truth about each other. "I'm not sorry." She spoke without defiance. "He gave me his world, his sweetness. Because we shared, I'm wiser, and I think I'm better."

"My God! The next thing you'll say is that I should be grateful to him!"

He didn't understand: the birds of the *yuntzilob,* the mantled tree of dead babies, the young corn. But, then, how could he? She wouldn't have, either, unless she'd lived as a Maya, cut off from her own culture and people, while loved and instructed by someone who wanted her to know.

"All I can say is that he didn't take anything that was yours, and his loving left me more than I was."

354

"He took your body. Wasn't that your betrothed's?"

The old question, going far, far back: to Philip's debasing use of her, his wagering of her at cards; to Eric's treatment of her as a possession; to Zane's wish to shut her in the tower. Strangely, only Dionisio had imposed no bonds. Though he'd constrained her to spend one month with him, beyond that he'd demanded nothing, and he had been willing to deliver her to Zane. Anger tinged Mercy's distress. She drew herself up proudly.

"My body's my own."

"Then you may keep it, madam!" Zane released her so abruptly that she almost fell. "Come, we have to make an early start in the morning."

Feeling turned to ice, Mercy went back to camp and groped into her hammock. He didn't want her now! The happy dreams she'd had of their life together would never come true. Miserably, she decided that if they survived this mission, she'd ask him to let her go back to the States, where she could find work as a housekeeper or perhaps a nurse and gradually repay him her passage and whatever price he set on her bond. It would be impossible to live at La Quinta.

She was settling into restless sleep when arms closed around her and a hard mouth closed savagely on hers, stifling her cry, which ebbed, anyway, as soon as she knew it was Zane. He carried her a distance, stumbling in the dark, laid her on the grass and took her without wooing so that it hurt, and she gnawed her lip to keep from moaning, as much from contrasting this with the ecstasy they'd had before as from the brutality.

"Why should I lie there aching when you're such a willing partner?" he asked cruelly. "It seems you're cut out to be some man's body servant. Why not mine?"

"Zane! You . . . you can't mean . . ."

"To keep you for my pleasure? Why not?" His laughter was discordant, as if something was broken and jangling in his depths. "You can live in the tower till I weary of you. Then we might see if your *batab* would trade some stands of mahogany for you."

She slapped him, struggling to rise, but he gripped her between his knees. "Your body is mine," he said. "I own you as I do my horse. And be sure that from now on I'll ride you with a tight rein and curb bit."

"I won't live that way!"

355

"Why not?" he scoffed. "You've done it readily enough. Under all that softness, Mercy, you're tough!"

"I endured Eric because I had a hope of getting back to you. I hated him and that preserved my soul. But to be used by you like a whore, to be nothing but a body—no! I can't bear it!"

"You should have thought of that before you gave yourself to the *batab*."

She sensed that if she wept, pleaded, soothed his male pride, said she was sorry, swore eternal faithfulness, Zane would relent. But the need for truth between them that had made her confess in the first place wouldn't let her. If Zane couldn't love her as she was, let him not love her at all, and if he didn't—she would never tamely submit to living in the tower.

"In the same time and place, I'd be Dionisio's again," she said, "just as I'd choose to see if the river led to the sky."

"Are you reminding me that your warning may have saved La Quinta and the frontier?"

"No. I'm saying that I've done what was according to my nature. From that I'll never change; for that I'll never ask your pardon."

"You put yourself beyond the rules that govern other people?"

"In the months you were with Peraza, in the days after Mérida fell, was there no woman? Have you been celibate all this time?"

"Rubbish! For men it's different."

"Yes. They make the rules, roving like tomcats while gluing foul labels on women who love more than one man."

"By God, a man would have to gag you to get a comfortable bedmate!" Ungently, he brought her to her feet. "Get to your hammock!"

Stiff and sore from his vengeful lust, Mercy followed him and found her hammock. Oddly, now that he'd insulted and forced himself on her, she felt better, much less guilty. After the way he'd acted, she'd grant him not a shred of moral superiority. She could fight him now.

It was small pleasure he'd have of her if he locked her in the tower. And she wouldn't, as she despairingly thought earlier, throw herself from the window or kill herself some other way. She'd live—and get away. If Zane wasn't able to love her in truth, she'd live husbandless! There were other ways to love; there were children to teach, people to heal.

Zane could break her heart, but he couldn't break her life. Yet she had to bury her face in her arms to smother her mourning.

They were on their way before sunrise, Mayel, sweet and helpful, Zane as haggard as Mercy felt. Their quarrel was small beside what would be decided that day in Chan Santa Cruz, but it affected both of them at a time when they had monumental tasks before them: to discredit Xia and Eric and win over the Mayan leaders. How many disasters, Mercy asked herself, had been intensified or allowed to happen because of lovers' arguments, someone's headache, or indigestion?

It was noon when Mayel called out, pointing to the towers of the *balam na*. At almost the same moment, four men stepped into the road, rifles over their shoulders, machetes in their hands.

"We seek the *tatich* and the general of the plaza," said Zane in Mayan. But the guards were staring past him—at Mercy.

"The woman who was given to the spirits!" one cried.

They shrank back. "The *batab* of Macanche called her Ixchel," muttered one. "It must be so! Weights were tied to her feet and she sank to the bottom of the *cenote!* But she lives!"

"I bring a message," Mercy said, hoping they wouldn't think it strange that Zane, a white, spoke better Mayan than one of their ancient goddesses. "I must speak with the *tatich* before he offends the Heart of Heaven."

More escorts than guards now, two Cruzob led the way, trotting ahead of Kisin, and two followed. Zane cast Mercy a wondering glance edged with respect. "You think like them, though I have more command of the language."

Which could get you nothing but a bullet or machete if they hadn't believed me risen from the dead!

Mercy shrugged. "I learned in Chan Santa Cruz."

From Dionisio. The thought hovered between them as their escorts spoke excitedly to the sentinel on duty at the boundary crossing.

The man gaped at her. "The *batab* who had this woman—this goddess—is to be executed! It may already be done!"

357

"Run to the plaza!" Zane cried as Mercy sat paralyzed with dread. "The *batab* is protected by this lady! There will be terrible vengeance if one blade touches him!"

"We can't ride past the boundary," Mercy warned Zane. "Animals are forbidden."

"Then let's run!" Zane swung her down and Mayel followed.

Their escort sprinted through the streets of the slave compound, past the church, and into the plaza. Mercy's head spun, both at Dionisio's peril and Zane's response. Dionisio stood in the center of the plaza by the huge sapodilla tree, ringed about by a score of men with raised machetes. At a little distance stood Xia, the *tatich*, his assistants, the general of the plaza, the *tata nohoch zul,* and half a dozen other officers. Towering above them was an eagle-masked, brilliantly mantled giant.

The shouting guards, the arrival of the aliens, froze the ritual. The *tatich* peered toward Mercy, then barked a command that sent the poised executioners melting back, leaving Dionisio unmenaced as Mercy ran toward Pacal.

"This is no Maya!" she called in a voice that echoed against the great bulk of the *balam na.* "He's a man of lusts! For power, wealth! He'll use your lives for his ambition, just as he used your faith to get him a woman he wanted!" She stopped, gasping to catch her breath, in a fever to say it all before she could be silenced. Putting an arm around Mayel, she plunged on. "This girl is of the blood of Jacinto Canek, a true leader. She can tell you that this *man* who calls himself Pacal is English, that he has long desired me! I am *not* Ixchel, you Cruzob! I am *not* risen from the dead! I've only escaped from this false Pacal, who brought me out of the *cenote* into a cavern and thought to keep me there while he led you into a doomed war! Tear off his mask! He has a white face, a white heart, and can only be death to you!"

"I am Pacal," said Eric in a resonant voice. "This woman is mad, crazed by whatever way she escaped sacrifice. My mask is sacred. Whoever touches it dies."

"I'll touch it, Kensington!" Zane asked the nearest man for a machete. "But first I must tell the *tatich* and the general of the plaza that I am Zane Falconer, of La Quinta Dirección, freshly home from Mérida. The war is over! Campeche and the capital are in secure hands, and the frontier is being alerted of this evil schemer's

358

plan, made with the help of this false priestess Xia. Her son never died! I took him from the cross, then put that copal branch in its place! She knew this, but all these years she's been revered because of the 'miracle.' The only wonder about her is her viciousness!"

As Zane faced the leaders, Eric sprang forward, pulling a knife from its jeweled scabbard. Zane leaped to one side. Before Eric could swing around, Dionisio felled him with a sweep of a machete that struck the head off the magnificent shoulders. As the trunk collapsed, spouting a fountain of blood, the head struck the sapodilla and the eagle mask flew off. Eric's eyes were open, fixed amazedly on the sky in the seconds before the *tatich* gave an order.

The men who'd been ready to kill Dionisio hacked to bits the head and body of the white man who had tried to be a god, and with those bits, after another word from the *tatich* and one choked scream, mingled parts of what had been a beautiful woman. Mercy hid her face, sickened, shuddering. Xia's body had lied to her; she was not destined to dance with, dissolve in, flame.

"Come," said the *tatich*. "You, *señora*, you, Señor Falconer; you, descendant of Canek; and you, *batab* of Macanche. I must hear all your words."

An hour later, reaching for a guava as he swung in his hammock, the *tatich* said reflectively, "The Talking Cross will speak tonight. It will tell God's Cruzob children that this was a way to snare impostors who would otherwise have worked later mischief, and that God desires us to plant and harvest our cornfields in peace."

General Poot growled something. The *tatich* smiled. "If you worry about lax discipline and need practice for your troops, there are always the Icaiches. And we will defend our frontier, too." He gazed steadily at Zane. "You'll tell this to your friend Peraza?"

"I'll tell him."

"Good." The *tatich* looked next at Mayel. "So, maiden, you descend from Canek?"

"Yes, Great Father." She spoke shyly but with pride.

"It's not fitting for you to be a servant, even to friendly *ladinos*."

"She's free," said Mercy. "There are no slaves at La Quinta."

The *tatich* looked at Mayel. "You should marry free

and raise Canek children who owe no grace or favor to the *ladinos*. Doña Mercy, will you give me guardianship of this girl?"

"If she wishes it."

Distressed, Mayel stood mutely between Mercy and Novelo, who suddenly chuckled and reached forward to pat her hand. "My child, daughter of Canek, do you see the *batab*, Dionisio?"

Slowly, she looked at him and flushed, casting down the dark fringes of her eyelashes. "I see him, Great Father."

"And he pleases you," observed the *tatich* with great satisfaction. He signaled to Dionisio. "*Batab* of Macanche, the treason charges died with those false ones. We are pleased to accept you as an ally and confirm you in your lordship over your captive, Doña Mercy. But we would also ask that you take as a wife this flower of Canek's line."

Dionisio looked at Mercy, his gaze warm on her, yet sad. "Good-bye, Ixchel," he said in Mayan, and then in Spanish, "Be happy, Doña Mercy. You have saved my life again, and much more, also. If ever you or your betrothed need my help, it is yours." Turning to Mayel, he smiled and took her hand. "If she agrees, I will be honored to wed this maiden."

Mayel peered at Mercy, who took her in her arms and kissed her. "Your life will be good with him, Mayel. Bless you. Bless you both!"

"It's my place to do the blessing," said the *tatich* gruffly. "Now, *señor, señora,* you'll be our guests for a few days?"

Zane inclined his head. "If you'll excuse us, Great Father, we have a wedding of our own to attend to." As Mercy caught her breath in shock, he said to Dionisio, "You saved my life. Thank you."

Dionisio smiled, his gaze just touching Mercy. "We have all saved each other. God guard you—and your lady."

"I command you to eat and drink," rumbled the *tatich*. "Then you may go. And Doña Mercy, may I say that though you've been excellent company and told me many interesting things, I hope to never see you again? You cause too many problems!"

After they reclaimed their horses from the sentry, who

explained that the bundle tied on the back of one saddle held Mercy's books and other things, and had ridden a little way into the forest, Mercy could restrain herself no longer. "Did . . . did you mean what you said to the *tatich?*"

"About what?"

"A . . . a wedding."

He turned in his saddle, and his face was that of her love's again, young and tender, smiling. "That depends on you. Will you be my wife?"

"But you said . . . " she mumbled, dazed, but slowly started to hope.

Zane slid down from Kisin, strode back to her, and lifted her down. "Listen! For a month, for a moon, you were Ixchel for Dionisio. But you descended into hell; you came back to me, not as a goddess, but as my woman. He saved my life; he gave you to me. Even Eric was right about one thing—you are a quetzal woman, very rare. I'd have to be a bigger fool than I am not to know my luck!"

She reached up for his kiss, joyous in his arms. She would live at the center of his life, not in the tower. And as he tied up the horses and carried her off the road, she hoped their first child would have eyes like his, but that it would also look a little like Elkanah.

Source Notes

I drew on many sources for this book, but the most valuable printed ones were: *Mayan History and Religion*, by J. Eric S. Thompson, University of Oklahoma Press, Norman, Oklahoma, 1970; *The Rise and Fall of Mayan Civilization*, by J. Eric S. Thompson, University of Oklahoma Press, Norman, Oklahoma, second edition, 1966; *The Book of Chilam Balam of Chumayel*, translated and edited by R. L. Roys, C. I. W. Pub. 438, Washington, D.C., 1933; *The Indian Background of Colonial Yucatán*, by R. L. Roys, University of Oklahoma Press, Norman, Oklahoma, 1972; *The Maya: Diego de Landa's Account of the Affairs of Yucatán*, translated and edited by A. R. Pagden, Philip O'Hara, Chicago, Illinois, 1975; *A Treasury of Mexican Folkways*, by Frances Toor, Crown, New York, 1947; *Medicine in Mexico*, by Gordon Schendel, University of Texas Press, Austin, Texas, 1968; *Land and Society in Colonial Mexico*, by François Chevalier, translated by Alvin Eustis, University of California Press, Berkeley and Los Angeles, California, 1972; *Decorative Design in Mexican Homes*, by Verna and Warren Shipway, Architectural Book Publishing Co., New York, 1970; *Mexico, Land of Volcanoes*, by Joseph Schlarman, Bruce, Milwaukee, Wisconsin, 1951; *A Flower Lover's Guide to Mexico*, by Phil Clark, Minutiae Mexicana, Mexico City, Mexico, 1973; *A Guide to Mexican Poetry*, by Irene Nicholson, Minutiae Mexicana, Mexico City, Mexico, 1972; *La Literatura de los Mayas*, by Demetrio Sodi M., editorial by Joaquin Mortiz, Guaymas, Mexico, 1970; *Ensayos Henequeneros*, by Renan Irigoyen, Cordemex, Mérida, Yucatán, Mexico, 1975; *Early Texas Homes*, by Dorothy Bracken and Maurine Redway, Southern Methodist University Press, Dallas, Texas, 1956; *The Common Soldier in the Civil War*, by Bell Irvin Wiley,

Grosset and Dunlap, by arrangement with Bobbs-Merrill on 1943 and 1951 copyrights; *Escape from Reconstruction*, by W. C. Nunn, Potishman Foundation, Fort Worth, Texas, 1956.

The interested reader will find much information and pleasure in *The Caste War of Yucatán*, by Nelson Reed, Stanford University Press, California, 1973; the four travel books of John L. Stevens with engravings by Frederick Catherwood: the two-volume *Incidents of Travel in Central America, Chiapas, and Yucatán*, 1969 Dover reprint of 1841 Harper & Brothers edition; and the two-volume *Incidents of Travel in Yucatán*, 1963 Dover reprint of Harpers' 1843 edition. I also found many helpful articles in my files of *Mexico This Month*, edited by Anita Brenner.

Chronology

1519–46	Conquest of Yucatán by Spaniards under the Montejos, whose ancestral house still faces the plaza in Mérida
1520	Conquest of Mexico by Cortez
Early 1600s	English settlements along Honduras coast, part of rivalry with Spain
1697	Conquest of the Itzá, last free Mayas
1761	Jacinto Canek revolts at Quisteil, is executed in Mérida
1810	September 16, Hidalgo declares Mexico's independence from Spain
1821	Mexico's independence acknowledged by last Spanish viceroy
1836	April 21, Santa Ana's Mexican forces defeated at San Jacinto by Texans furious to revenge the Alamo; Texas becomes a republic
1838	Iman's revolt against Mexican rule of Yucatán, his fateful arming of the Mayas, hiring of Texas Navy to patrol Yucatán's water boundaries in 1841 after adoption of extremely liberal constitution in Yucatán
1840	Yucatecan separation from Mexico

365

1843	Reunification of Yucatán with Mexico
1845	Second separation of Yucatán from Mexico; Texas annexed by United States
1846–48	Mexican-American War; Campeche revolts (when menaced by United States naval forces) in order to stay neutral
1847	January, massacre at Valladolid; Mayas see their strength
	July 30, Mayas attack Tepich; start of War of the Castes
1848	Sieges and battles; fall of Valladolid; sovereignty over Yucatán offered to Spain, Great Britain, and the United States if they would help subdue the Mayas; Tekax, Ticul, Izamal, and Bacalar fall to Mayas in June, Mérida under heavy siege, saved when Mayas go home to plant corn; *ladinos* counterattack and recover much lost territory; Mayas driven into forests by December and Cecilio Chi, one of three original Mayan conspirators, is murdered
1849	Slave trade in captured Mayas begun, but stopped by Mexican government; Jacinto Pat, another of original three conspirators, the only one willing to negotiate with *ladinos,* is murdered at a jungle well on the way to Belize; English officials meet in Belize with Mayas
1850	First appearance of the Talking Cross as rebels cluster at Chan Santa Cruz
1851	Shrine of Cross raided twice and sacred tree felled but cult continues to grow
1854	Shrine invaded twice by *ladinos;* last *entrada* struck by cholera from deliberately infected well

1855	*Ladino* bases in Cruzob area are given up, one garrison massacred; Santa Ana falls from power in Mexico; War of the Castes considered "officially" over, though Cruzob, in effect, have their own small kingdom and *ladinos* retain only a crescent along the coast
1857	Revolts in Campeche give Cruzob cover for massacre and loot of Tekax; Chichénha Mayas defeated by Cruzob, retreat to Icaiche and are nominally peaceful, though they later make a good thing of raiding into British-owned Belize instead of fighting the Cruzob, as they are expected to.
1858	Campeche and Yucatán separate; Cruzob take Bacalar, slaughter inhabitants and make it a garrison to protect trade route to Belize, where they can obtain guns and ammunition from the British
1859	Juárez becomes President of Mexico. Country in debt to England, France, and Spain
1860–65	United States in Civil War and unable to repel foreign presence in Mexico
1861–67	French intervention in Mexico; an aristocratic faction of Mexicans offers Maximilian, an archduke of the Hapsburgs, the rule of Mexico, and he accepts, with guarantees of support from Napoleon III, Emperor of France
1863–64	Yucatán and Campeche fighting each other, Campeche blockaded by French Navy; French (imperial) forces dominate Yucatán; imperial commissioner sent to govern from Mérida
1864	June, Maximilian and his empress, Carlota, reach Mexico City. They evidently hoped to be benevolent rulers, but most Mexicans

wanted self-rule, and Benito Juárez, the lawful president, was determined to drive out the usurpers.

1865   April 9, General Lee surrenders; Civil War over
April 14, President Lincoln assassinated
September 15, Maximilian invites Confederate refugees to colonize in Mexico, an exodus begins, including many former governors and military men; several colonies begun, including Carlota, near Vera Cruz. Some Confederates hoped to fight for Maximilian, secure his throne, and then influence him to make war against the United States and regain the South.
November, Carlota visits Yucatán, is much admired, and wins friends for the empire among aristocracy.

1866   February, Secretary of State Seward (U.S.) demands withdrawal of French troops from Mexico.
April. Napoleon III announces a gradual withdrawal.
July, Carlota leaves Mexico to plead for help from Napoleon and remind him of his promises.
August, heavy Mayan raiding; by midmonth Tihosuco cut off, under siege till September 23, when Mayas abandon attack
October, Maximilian learns by cables that Carlota, unbalanced by worry and refusals of help from both the pope and Napoleon, has become mentally ill; decides to abdicate
November, victory parades for Tihosuco soldiers in Mérida, though the frontier is moving back to Peto; MERCY AND PHILIP ARRIVE IN MÉRIDA
Maximilian is persuaded to return to Mexico City and continue struggle, though Napoleon has completely abandoned him and French troops are leaving as rapidly as possible.

368

Secretary Seward writes that U.S. forces will aid Juárez, short of actual invasion.

1867   Increasing Liberal (Juarista) victories as French withdraw; in January, in Yucatán, Peraza jonis rebels against imperial government (ZANE JOINS HIM AND MERCY IS ABDUCTED BY ERIC); Confederate colonists leave Mexico, except for a scattered few

Fifty-day siege of Mérida by Peraza, who wins and signs treaty June 15. Icaiches invade Belize.

May 15, Maximilian defeated and empire falls

June 19, Maximilian shot at Querétaro

But it was not until 1901, during the presidency of Porfirio Díaz, that General Bravo conquered Chan Santa Cruz. However, the Cruzob region became the Territory of Quintana Roo, separate from Yucatán.

Actual People

Jacinto Canek—descendant of the Itzá who led revolt at Quisteil

Marcos Canul—leader of the Icaiche Mayas who raided into Belize. A *pro forma* official of Campeche, he was supposed to fight the Cruzob

Carlota—empress of Mexico during French intervention; went insane; died in her native Belgium fifty years after her husband was executed

Cecilio Chi—Mayan *batab,* one of original starters of the War of the Castes; favored killing all whites

José Ilarregui—imperial commissioner in Yucatán 1864–67; allowed to leave Mérida by Peraza after city fell

Benito Juárez—President of Mexico at time of intervention; insisted on Maximilian's execution in spite of foreign pleas for mercy; he and Lincoln greatly esteemed each other; probably Mexico's most revered leader

Maximilian—Austrian archduke, brother of Franz Joseph, who was Emperor of Austria and head of the Hapsburgs; shot at the Hill of Bells between two of his loyal Mexican generals

Manuel Nahuat—probably threw his voice to make the Talking Cross speak; killed in 1851

Bonifacio Novelo—"The assassin of Valladolid," one of

the original conspirators, a mestizo; *tatich* at the time of this novel

Jacinto Pat—an original conspirator who wished to replace *ladino* government but was willing to allow whites to remain in the country; negotiations with *ladinos* angered rival chiefs and he was murdered in 1849

Crescencio Poot—general of the plaza at time of this novel; a man of blood and massacres

Cepeda Peraza—an idealist who fought repeatedly for liberal values and Yucatecan independence; took Mérida from imperialists and was governor of Yucatán till his death in 1870

Daniel Traconis—commander of the fifty-day holdout of Tihosuco against the Mayas in 1866, and in charge of Imperial forces in Mérida during the fifty-five-day siege of that city by Peraza in 1867.

Glossary

administrador—manager of hacienda. Wealthy Yucatecans seldom lived on their plantations, preferring the cities.

aguada—water hole

aguardiente—strong drink, most often rum

Balamob (Mayan)—Mayan deities who guard cornfields and village crosses

balam na (Mayan)—God's House, particularly the one built at Chan Santa Cruz

batab (Mayan)—chief

cacique—chief

camino real—main or royal road (which wasn't saying much)

cargador—member of a religious brotherhood who was in charge of putting on a patron saint's fiesta

ceiba—sacred tree of the Mayas, the kapok

cenote—a cave well or hole in limestone, northern Yucatán's main source of water

chaac (Mayan)—rain god. There were also lesser *chaacs*.

chan (Mayan)—small

Chan Kiuic—valley where Talking Cross first appeared, slightly west of Chan Santa Cruz

Chan Santa Cruz—Little Holy Cross; shrine and center of Cruzob empire; now known as Felipe Carrillo Puerto, after Yucatán president who translated constitution into Mayan

Chilam Balam (Mayan)—Prophet of God; alleged author of holy books

choza—thatched hut, basically the same now as in classical Mayan times

copal—tree whose resin was used for incense, also to treat asthma

Cruzob (Mayan)—rebel Mayas united by the Talking Cross

cuatro narices or **barba amarillo**—fer-de-lance, poisonous snake

degüello—bugle call for "no quarter," known as the "throat-cutting," and played, among other places, at the Alamo, in Texas

dzul (Mayan)—white man, foreigner

epazote—wormweed, used as a purgative

garrapatas—chiggers; small larval mites that suck blood and cause irritation

hacendado—owner of a hacienda or large plantation

henequén—type of agave from which rope and twine were made

H-men (Mayan)—sort of priest herb doctor who retained some bits of ancient Mayan knowledge and advised when to plant, etc.

huipil (Mayan)—woman's garment, often embroidered

Huits (Mayan)—"Those who wear loincloths"; Mayas who hadn't been brought under Spanish influence at time of War of the Castes

Itzá—strong group of Mayas and last to be conquered. Tradition said one of them would successfully vanquish the whites.

Ixchel (Mayan)—goddess of healing, the moon, and childbirth

Kisin (Mayan)—earthquake god (equivalent of the devil)

Kuilob Kaaxob (Mayan)—guardians of the wild forests

ladino—Yucatecan of white or mixed descent who owed allegiance to white culture rather than Mayan. Some mestizos or mixed bloods were *ladinos,* while some of the most important Cruzob leaders were mestizo.

maestro cantor—lay leader of religious rites, often filling in for priests. One great strength of the Cruzob was in creating their own religious hierarchy and being independent of *ladino* priests.

mayordomo—overseer; **mayordomo secundo**—overseer of second rank

Mazehual (Mayan)—ordinary Maya

mestizo—of Spanish and Indian descent

milpa—cornfield

nohoch (Mayan)—great; **tata nohoch** or **tatich**—Great Father; **tata nohoch zul**—Great Father Spy

Pacal—priest-king during heyday of Maya. His tomb, at Palenque. is very splendid.

pibil (Mayan)—way of roasting meat, highly spiced,

wrapped in leaves and buried in pit. **Cochinita pibil** (little pig pibil) was and is a popular dish, but other meat was also cooked thus.

plaza—square at the center of town. Larger towns might have several, and then the main one was the Plaza Mayor. It was a place for markets, celebrations, and executions.

pozole—corn gruel and beans

ramon—breadfruit tree. People ate its fruit, and its leaves were valued for grazing by horses and cattle.

La Santísima—Most Holy, the Talking Cross

sapodilla—chicle tree

tamen (Mayan)—harmony between man and heaven

tata polin (Mayan)—interpreter of the Talking Cross

tata chikiuc (Mayan)—general of the plaza, supreme military commander of Cruzob, though he was under command of the *tatich*

toloache—jimsonweed; a narcotic pain-killer

tunkul (Mayan)—long wooden drum used by Mayas

yuntzilob (Mayan)—spirit protecting fields

yoyotli—plant whose powder was tossed in face of sacrificial victims to narcotize them

yoloxochitl—Mexican magnolia, used for heart ailments

zic (Mayan)—cold pit-roasted meat dish